MW01088779

TO STAND
DEFIANT

BOOK EIGHT OF THE CASTLE FEDERATION
BOOK TWO OF THE DAKOTAN CONFEDERACY

TO STAND
DEFIANT

BOOK EIGHT OF THE CASTLE FEDERATION
BOOK TWO OF THE DAKOTAN CONFEDERACY

GLYNN STEWART

FAOLAN'S PEN
PUBLISHING
faolanspen.com

All rights reserved. For information about permission to reproduce selections from this book, contact the publisher at info@faolanspen.com or Faolan's Pen Publishing Inc., 22 King St. S, Suite 300, Waterloo, Ontario N2J 1N8, Canada.

This edition published in 2022 by:

Faolan's Pen Publishing Inc.

22 King St. S, Suite 300

Waterloo, Ontario

N2J 1N8 Canada

ISBN-13: 978-1-989674-29-1 (print)

A record of this book is available from Library and Archives Canada.

Printed in the United States of America

1 2 3 4 5 6 7 8 9 10

First edition

First printing: October 2022

Illustration by Viko Menezes

Faolan's Pen Publishing logo is a registered trademark of Faolan's Pen Publishing Inc.

Read more books from Glynn Stewart at faolanspen.com

1

"YOU CAN'T BE SERIOUS."

With everything that had changed over the last three weeks, it was a tiny thing for James Tecumseh to find a step too far, but the insignia laid on his desk was perfectly familiar—and that made it the problem.

The jewelry box held four gold stars, each of them a match for one of the three he already wore. Except that he'd only been a *Vice* Admiral for a few months—and these were the four stars of a full admiral.

"The new Cabinet was unanimous," Quetzalli Chapulin told him. The new Interim President of the Dakotan Interstellar Confederacy— formerly the First Chief of Dakota itself—was a pale and delicately built Nahuatl woman whose build showed no sign of her sixteen years as a Marine officer.

"Unanimous," James echoed, still staring at the rank insignia. There were only three people in Chapulin's office, and he knew the other two women well by now. *Very* well, in the case of the new Interim First Chief of Dakota, Abey Todacheeney.

His girlfriend had enjoyed the noncommittal title of *secretary* when he'd first met Dakota's leadership, but by the time James had talked the planetary representatives of two sectors of the Terran Commonwealth into secession...well, it hadn't been a *surprise* when the currently black-haired woman had been elevated to Interim First Chief.

"We *need* to show the people of our new Confederacy that we have an equal military force to the Commonwealth we have abandoned," she told him gently. "That means we need a Fleet Admiral in command of the new Confederacy Navy.

"And there is *no one else* we can put in that role. Even if we wanted to."

"Which we don't," Chapulin concluded. "You led us into this whole mess, Admiral, and you're not getting out of it this easily. Put on the damn stars."

"There's more changes to the uniform than just the stars," James warned drily. "I'll have to warn Chief Leeuwenhoek to get started on those. God alone knows when she'll have time to swap them out, though."

Chief Steward Sallie Leeuwenhoek was James Tecumseh's personal steward and general minder and keeper. Since she had previously conspired with Todacheeney on such things as completely redecorating James's quarters and office while he wasn't around, he suspected she already knew—and his girlfriend's slight grin told him he was bang on.

"She already knows, doesn't she?" he asked.

"I messaged her the moment I handed you the box," Abey told him. "We weren't going to let you turn this down. As our President said, you led us into this mess."

"I know a fight I can't win," he conceded. "Though that wasn't what I came down here to discuss with you two."

"We know," Chapulin confirmed. "Politics, as always."

A silent command from the President's neural interface brought the office's holoprojectors online, the blinds on her windows automatically closing. The room had been the office of Dakota's First Chief—it hadn't moved over to Todacheeney with that job, as the new Confederacy needed a space for its head of state.

That meant that it was on the top floor of one of the taller buildings of Táála'í'tsin, Dakota's planetary capital and the DIC's temporary interstellar capital.

Twelve key star systems lit up on the display, in a clear wedge of territory covering space from the Arroyo System, the closest Dakota Sector system to Sol, to the Persephone System, the farthest Meridian Sector system from Sol.

"We have heard back from all of the Dakota Sector systems," Chapulin told him. "We have at least interim approval from Shogun, Gothic, Desdemona, and Krete."

"What about Arroyo?" James asked, looking at the sixth system of the sector.

"While Patience Abiodun had the authority to do a lot of things, her governor feels that *seceding from the Commonwealth* was an overstep on her part," Todacheeney said grimly. Head of state for Dakota or not, she was still fully linked in with the new Confederacy's politics and government.

"Governor Hoxha will come around. I have no concerns," Chapulin noted. "She's putting it to a vote of the planetary assembly, which will take some time to arrange. Minister Abiodun assures me that vote will go our way, but Hoxha wants that authority—given that she's the most vulnerable of our systems…"

"I understand her position," James conceded. "We're going to have to look hard at how we secure Arroyo going forward. Without q-coms, I need central fleets, but I also need warning."

The Terran Commonwealth's interstellar communication network was gone, destroyed by the people they'd tried to conquer in the Alliance of Free Stars. That had thrown a hundred–plus inhabited worlds into chaos, allowing their enemies in the Stellar League—on the opposite side of the Commonwealth from the Alliance—to try to conquer border systems.

And had set into motion the chain of events that had led to Fleet Admiral Walkingstick becoming Imperator of the Commonwealth— and ordering James Tecumseh to turn the Dakota Sector into the arsenal of the Commonwealth, regardless of the price for the systems of that Sector.

Every lesson James Tecumseh and the other Commonwealth Admirals had ever learned about strategy, operations and tactics had been predicated on the assumption that they would have FTL communications the Alliance had wrecked. Worse, their enemies—like the Stellar League—still *had* those coms.

"The other systems are holding votes of some kind, yes?" he asked delicately, which got him amused looks from both women.

"You know Dakota did," Todacheeney told him. "A planetary referendum with eighty-seven percent in favor, if you forgot."

"None of the others have had *time*. We have encouraged them all to hold referendums," Chapulin noted. "The approvals so far are interim but sufficient for us to move forward as a nation for the moment."

James nodded with a sigh.

"Sorry, starting to get…twitchy about everything."

Freedom. Justice. Democracy. Unity. These were the principles and core values of the Terran Commonwealth. Except that the Commonwealth had always put unity above the other three, leading to the whole campaign of Unification…and some other, even-less-pleasant things.

"This nation will be born and built on democracy," the Interim President told him. "Or we are throwing away the opportunity you gave us, James."

"Gothic should be holding their referendum today," Abey noted. "We won't hear the results for a week or so, but the last polling we saw was suggesting an even-more-thorough blowout than here.

"All the planetary governments seem to need to do is put your little speech on the airways on constant play."

James grimaced at that. He was a soldier, not a politician, but his appeal to the Dakota Sector Governance Conference had come from the heart…and it had worked.

"So, everything is proceeding as planned?" he asked.

"On our side, yes," Chapulin confirmed. "Yours?"

"We're finished the repairs to *Saint Bartholomew*." The battleship had carried the Imperator's chosen representative to Dakota—and when James had decided to defy the Imperator's orders, he'd had his Marines storm the ship.

"She's being brought back online under Captain Ferreiro." Arjun Ferreiro had been James's chief of staff when he'd been the *second*-in-command of Sector Fleet Dakota. He'd been at loose ends since then, as James had inherited the Sector Fleet staff along with the fleet.

"Though"—James looked down at the insignia and tapped it—"may I assume that this comes with blanket authority to promote as I see fit?"

"*You* are the uniformed head of the Dakota Confederacy Navy," Chapulin told him firmly. "Once we have a full constitution and legislature, I'd like to run flag ranks through them—but for now, the Cabinet would like to be consulted on flag-rank promotions.

"But with that condition, you may promote as you wish."

"I need a personnel bureau," James realized aloud. "But for now, I'll stick to making Ferreiro a Commodore so there's no argument whether he's senior enough for a battleship, and mull over stars for my staff."

Saint Bartholomew was his largest battleship, too—and if she'd been a second *Volcano*-class carrier, the *Saints*' fighter-carrying counterpart, James would have picked a more-senior officer to command her. But even *Saints* didn't rate *that* highly on his list. Battleships were backups.

Carriers fought wars.

"There are a lot of changes to come as your ships move from being TCN to DCN," Todacheeney reminded. "Obviously, the civilian side of the Confederacy admin will support as we can, but we have our own tasks ahead of us."

"We're all going to be very, very busy," James agreed. His implant pinged, notifying him that a new ship had arrived in-system. No, two ships flying in company.

That was unusual—and so was the fact that their vector suggested they were from the Brillig Sector. There'd been limited contact with the sector to their galactic north—decided by the orientation of old Earth, a hundred light-years away—which at least explained why the ships weren't on any schedule.

"James?" Chapulin asked.

"New arrivals," he told the two politicians. "From Brillig, though my people haven't nailed down the exact system yet."

"That's a good sign, if we're seeing trade come in from outside our sectors now."

"It should be, yes," James agreed, but he was rolling the information around in his mind.

"You seem concerned," Abey said softly.

"It's nothing…I think. But I also think I'm going to cut this meeting short with my apologies," he told them. "Something doesn't sit right… and if there is anything even *remotely* out of the ordinary, I should be on my flagship."

"Of course," Chapulin agreed instantly. "We can pick up the rest of what we were talking about this evening on a holocall.

"We trust your judgment, *Fleet Admiral* Tecumseh."

2

Dakota System
18:30 January 30, 2738 ESMDT

Wing Colonel Anthony Yamamoto was the scion of a long line of sailors, spacers and pilots, stretching back through Scotland to Japan and the architect of the attack on Pearl Harbor—via around fifty generations and at least three famous soldiers of one stripe or another.

He was also the man tasked with assembling the starfighters of a dozen scattered local defense forces and three battered fleets into the newborn Dakotan Confederacy Starfighter Corps.

With five carriers and as many strike cruisers, plus the defensive formations, Anthony was responsible for somewhere in the region of three thousand starfighters, nine thousand starfighter crew, and about a hundred thousand people all told.

And the dark-skinned Japanese-Scotsman knew *perfectly well* he had no business being in a Katana starfighter flying an in-system patrol between Dakota and the Second Dakota Belt. He had more datawork floating around the back of his implant and the networks attached to his office on *Krakatoa* than he could shake a stick at.

But he was also a *pilot*, and he did some of his best thinking with his brain interfaced with a starfighter. So, his command ship, a twenty-meter-long egg shape massing fifty-five hundred tons, led another Katana in a sweeping eight-hour patrol.

The lack of FTL communications increased the value of a senior officer being farther out, and he needed to share his people's tasks and see how they performed…but he knew all of that was excuses. Or he would have told the Admiral what he was doing.

"You see those ships?" he murmured to his crew, highlighting the two freighters. "Gut check?"

Anthony had seen images of Isoroku Yamamoto and knew he was the spitting image of his distant ancestor. That meant he leaned *hard* into the Scottish burr he'd grown up with, partially to confuse people but mostly to intentionally break their assumptions.

"Vector is definitely from the Brillig Sector," his new flight engineer told him. Lieutenant Lindiwe Navarro had replaced another officer who had decided it was appropriate to make a pass at their pilot and commanding officer. To smooth over some of consequences of that change, Anthony had picked up an entirely new flight crew, with Lieutenant Kattalin Gunther now managing the fighter's weapons.

The Hispanic Navarro was from Gothic in the Dakota Sector and was almost as dark in her way as Anthony was in his. Gunther, on the other hand, was from central Germany on Earth and was as blonde and pale and heavyset as the CAG and the engineer were dark and slim.

"Can you narrow it down?" Anthony asked. "The Brillig Sector has seven inhabited star systems, and Sector Fleet Brillig was headquartered at Brillig itself. If they're coming from *Brillig*, I'm relatively comfortable with them.

"But we've heard nothing from the entire sector since we lost communications. So, I'm a bit concerned to see *two* ships show up."

The problem with replacing his flight crew was that he had to teach the new duo what he needed—and since the justifications for First Fleet's Commander, Air Group who was *also* the head of the DCSC to get into a starfighter would be few and far between, he wasn't going to get many chances.

"Gunther, keep an eye on their current vector," he ordered.

"Course is toward Dakota orbit at fifty gravities," the gunner replied instantly.

That was Tier One acceleration, the first of several efficiency plateaus in the interaction between antimatter thrusters, inertial compensators and mass manipulators. At fifty gravities, the big freighters were spending a tiny fraction of the fuel their true mass would require for their acceleration.

His fighter wing was currently accelerating at two hundred and fifty gravities, Tier Two acceleration. Still far more efficient than uncompensated engines, it was maybe one percent as efficient as Tier One.

Only starfighters were rated for Tier Three thrust, around five hundred gravities, and only missiles and sensor drones for Tier Four's thousand.

There was no way the freighters could escape the warships in the system without going back to FTL. Anthony was running vectors in his implants as he waited for Navarro to narrow down the origin of their new guests. Of the fifteen two-fighter wings patrolling the inner system, he could vector eight to intercept the strangers.

"CIC back on *Krakatoa* will probably be able to nail it down more closely," Navarro finally said, "but I think they're coming from the Blyton System."

"*Krakatoa* has a thirty-minute turnaround for information from these guys," Anthony pointed out. "We're only two light-minutes away. That puts the burden on us, Lieutenant.

"What does your database have on Blyton?"

"Single habitable world, six planets, no belt, seven hundred million people," the engineer reeled off. She'd anticipated that request, which was a good sign.

"How many freighters chartered from there?" Gunther asked. "If it's not a sector capital, two coming directly from there seems odd."

"Exactly," Anthony agreed. His orders began filtering out through the long-range communications network. So far, he wanted his people to be subtle—but he was redirecting the entire active patrol force toward the freighters and ordering another three squadrons' worth of starfighters launched from *Krakatoa*.

The *Volcano*-class ship wasn't the only ship in orbit with starfighters, but she was Anthony's base ship. Also the *only* pure carrier and the one most readily able to put thirty more Katanas into space.

Something about the freighters was making the hair on the back of his neck twitch.

"Commonwealth records show six freighters home-chartered in the system," Navarro said slowly. "But neither of that pair are among them."

Anthony's crew were on board with his suspicions now, and the conscious conversation was starting to fall by the wayside as they ran through the data together. *Paradise by Twilight* and *Lakewater* were transmitting their beacons, and the information on the beacons matched the scans so far.

Both were spherical *Troubadour*-class ships, roughly forty million cubic meters and with a cargo capacity of around twelve million metric tons. Something about the *Troubadour* class rang a bell in Anthony's mind, but if there was backup information, it wasn't in his implants or the starfighter's database.

Even the massively dense data storage media of the twenty-eighth century didn't allow *everything* to be stored in a Katana's computers. And the designers had expected to have q-coms linking the fighter to the carrier's databases.

"We'll move up on them slowly enough," Anthony decided aloud. "Gunther, set up to transmit. With First Fleet in orbit, they really have no ability to cause trouble...but this stinks."

"They've cut their acceleration."

Anthony saw the change even as Gunther was giving her report. The two freighters had been accelerating toward Dakota on a standard course for a zero-velocity arrival in orbit. They'd now cut their thrust to zero and were drifting toward the planet slowly.

They were still ten-plus light-minutes from the planet and only two from Anthony's fighter.

"Update from *Krakatoa*," Navarro told him. "First Fleet Actual is returning aboard. Actual has ordered the fleet to amber alert and the deployment of the ready fighters."

Anthony smirked. His crew would feel his amusement, even if they couldn't see his expression—and he was unsurprised that he and Tecumseh were having the same reaction to the strangers.

After over a hundred days of silence, a ship from the Brillig Sector was to be expected—but two ships, flying together, from a secondary system that *wasn't* the closest to the Dakota Sector?

The body language of the ships' maneuvers added to his suspicion, though he knew the Admiral wouldn't have seen that yet. Civilian ships should have been unbothered or even *pleased* to see nine warships in orbit of the sector capital.

Instead, these ships were acting hesitant. Nervous. Like they hadn't been expecting that at all.

"Kattalin, what's the closest processing node in the Second Belt?" he asked softly.

Gunther looked over at him, questioning, but she was checking as she did.

"There's a refinery node, Blackhawk Processing Five, three degrees clockwise of the freighters," she told him. "Total distance...fourteen light-minutes."

"Gravity wells?"

"They're still well clear of both the Second Belt and Dakota itself," Gunther replied. "They can go FTL anytime."

The Alcubierre-Stetson space warp drive required certain safe distances from natural gravity sources to be safely used—or *extremely* careful calculations. Asteroid belts had a misshapen well around them that was far shallower than a planet's effect. If the strangers were to make a run to the belt under A-S drive, they could be there in a few minutes.

They couldn't do the same to Dakota, not without far better sensors, computers and navigators than most civilian ships would have.

Anthony studied the geometry for a few more seconds, then leaned into his mental interface with the starfighter. At full control, he *was* the multi-thousand-ton spacecraft, and changing her course was a matter of a single thought.

"Patrol-Six and Patrol-Seven will continue their intercept course for the freighters," he ordered softly. "All other patrol wings divert to Blackhawk Five at maximum thrust."

"Sir?"

"Either they're entirely innocent, in which case Major Maldonado will gently calm their nerves and send them on to Dakota—or they've just realized the full extent of First Fleet and are looking for a target of opportunity.

"They're close enough to have the sensor data on Blackhawk Five to make an A-S microjump...and there's enough refined material there to make a smash-and-grab almost worth it."

He smiled thinly.

"They're pirates, Lieutenants, and they thought we were going to be just as much of a mess as I'm guessing the Brillig Sector has become.

"We're going to need to disabuse them of that notion."

———

Anthony would definitely have preferred to have guessed wrong. It would have made him look a bit foolish when his orders put thirty starfighters at Blackhawk Processing Five two hours later, but he could live with that.

But within minutes of swinging his own two spacecraft toward the distant refinery, gravity signatures flared around the two Brillig ships and they vanished into the inviolate sanctuary of an Alcubierre warp bubble.

"Patrol-Six and Patrol-Seven will divert to Blackhawk Five," Anthony ordered calmly. None of his fighters were close to the refinery —but Six and Seven were among the farthest. They were seven light-minutes away and he *hadn't* initially diverted them.

Anthony's wing was just under five light-minutes away, with an

ETA of two hours. Nine more patrols would reach the station inside that window, which left one very critical question.

"Gunther, do we have a vector on their jump?" he asked.

"Angle is toward Blackhawk Five," she confirmed. "We're too far out for charge metrics on their destination, but I don't see why they'd take that vector unless they were doing what you said."

He grimaced as he brought up the info on the processing station. Dakota had been a sector capital for the Terran Commonwealth, deep inside her borders in every direction. There hadn't really *been* a threat to the system, which meant that a random processing node in the asteroid belt had zero defenses of its own.

"Let me know the moment we have eyes on them," he ordered. "And get a call back to *Krakatoa*: I want the fleet analysis team to put the data collection from all of our units and stations together.

"They *should* have enough to tell me what we're running into."

If First Fleet's analysts could confirm that he was looking at pirate ships, likely by the presence of some kind of unexpected weaponry, Anthony would feel a lot better about firing first.

"Contact; ships have reemerged on the direct line to Blackhawk Five," Gunther told him. "Range was sixteen million kilometers five minutes ago. They are accelerating at…one hundred twenty gravities."

"Found a few more gees somewhere, I see," Navarro grumbled. "We can catch them."

"ETA for them is two hours. ETA for us is two hours," Anthony agreed. "Assuming zero-zero, anyway. They'll want to send in shuttles as well."

If the pirates thought they could handle the Dakotan fighters heading their way, they could secure the processing facility and fill the two freighters with refined ore. It wouldn't be a spectacular haul, but it would be one that only required them to handle twenty starfighters.

Whereas, if they wanted anything from Dakota, they needed to go through First Fleet and nine capital ships.

Anthony just wished there was a way he could get some capital-ship support of his own. The ready fighters would be several more hours behind the patrols. If they couldn't take the pirates with the patrol ships, a lot of people were going to be in serious trouble.

3

"ANALYSIS IS DOING the best they can, but if there's any clear sign of weapons or starfighters aboard the freighters, we haven't picked it out yet."

The tiny holographic figure of James Tecumseh stood straight-spined on Anthony's control panel, dark eyes concerned as he presumably looked at the grand tactical display.

"I figured," Anthony replied. "They were planning on sneaking up on us. They just weren't expecting the Fleet, so they're bailing for a target of opportunity."

He and the Admiral would be talking past each other, with a ten-minute-plus loop on the conversation. He wasn't surprised when Tecumseh continued speaking after a moment.

"You are authorized to do whatever you judge necessary, Wing Colonel. And when this is *over*, we will discuss whether the commanding officer of the Dakota Confederacy's Starfighter Corps should be flying regular system patrols at all."

"There are a lot of reasons why I should be, yes," Anthony promised. "And one of them is to make sure we have someone with the authority to make the call."

"The Cabinet has requested that we at least attempt to communicate before we start shooting," Tecumseh told him. "I have faith in your judgment, Wing Colonel. Mostly. We will speak again when this is over."

Tecumseh vanished from the console, though Anthony knew the Admiral would still get his responses.

"It's reassuring to be told to do what I was already going to do," he said drily. "What's our range down to?"

They'd just made turnover, beginning their deceleration toward Blackhawk Five. His fighter was moving at just over five percent of the speed of light after an hour of accelerating, but he'd need to shed almost all of that velocity if he was going to rendezvous with the refining station and the other eighteen starfighters heading there.

The Brillig ships weren't *quite* on a direct line between him and the cluster of space stations, but they were close enough that he was actually coming up *behind* them.

"Range is twenty-four million kilometers. Round trip for communications is two minutes, forty seconds."

"Good enough." A few mental commands opened up the starfighter's communications systems again, targeting the main transmitter at the two freighters.

"Unidentified freighters, this is Wing Colonel Anthony Yamamoto," he introduced himself brightly, intentionally thickening his brogue. "We seem to be getting off on the wrong foot here. Your approach to Dakota and sudden flight, plus your unannounced and unapproved approach to Blackhawk Processing Five, are leaving me with the worst assumptions about your intentions.

"In the interest of avoiding potential conflict, I'm sending you a new course vectoring away from the processing station. You will follow that course and prepare to be boarded by Dakotan Marines. If you do not, I will have no choice but to take extreme actions to defend this system."

He'd put the course together while he was speaking. It was basically a ninety-degree angle from their current vector at their full shown acceleration. They'd still be moving "forward," but they'd be building a velocity away from Blackhawk Five.

As they waited for a response, Anthony updated the courses for his other patrols. He and his wing would reach missile range of the freighters seven minutes before they arrived at Blackhawk Five. Without a great deal of adjusting, the other nine patrol wings could coordinate their timing to reach missile range at the same time.

Starfighter missiles were shorter-ranged than bomber torpedoes and capital-ship missiles—but his twenty ships would put eighty missiles into space three times. Depending on what the pirates had brought to the game, that should be more than enough.

But *should* and *depending* were words Anthony didn't like in his battle plans, especially when he only had two squadrons in play.

"Initial transmission lag is past, sir," Gunther told him. "No response."

"Unfortunately expected. Start prepping your missile sequences, Lieutenant," he ordered her. "Lieutenant Navarro, prep your decoys and electronic-warfare protocols."

His flight crew set to work and Anthony focused on flying the starfighter. There was still time for this to end without violence, but he no longer had any reason to think this was an innocent mistake.

———

"Contact! New contacts!"

"Finally," Anthony hissed, surveying the screens as icons spread out from the rogue freighters. "I mark fifty."

"I have the same," Gunther confirmed. "Ten are proceeding toward Blackhawk Five. Four are heading out toward each of our patrol wings."

"Idents?"

"No beacons. Running analysis against the warbook, but I'm *really* missing q-com links to the mothership," Gunther admitted.

Anthony nodded, but he was also watching the performance envelope...which told him a lot of the answers.

"They're pre-thirty-six-refit Scimitars," he told the gunner. "Four hundred fifty gravities, but they're definitely flying Commonwealth engines and those are Commonwealth freighters."

Gunther paused for a long second, a small eternity with them neurally interfaced, then chuckled.

"Warbook agrees, sir," she told him. "System is calling it eighty percent likelihood."

"Good news, then, is that we have them badly outclassed," Anthony continued. "*Bad* news is that they have us outnumbered two-to-one and we need to save our missiles for the freighters themselves to stop them jumping to FTL."

He would admit, at least in his own head, that he'd been expecting more fighters. The pirates had only stuffed twenty-five of the spacecraft on each of their freighters—they didn't have any of the proper refueling and storage systems of a carrier, but if there was one thing freighters had, it was *space*.

"Orders, sir?"

"All fighters are clear to engage at will, but they are to use no more than one salvo of missiles."

Anthony knew he was handicapping his people. The Scimitars carried as many missile launchers as his Katanas *and* had an extra missile per launcher to boot. His wing would reach missile range of the pirates well before any of his ships could range on the freighters.

And while his fighters vastly outranged the older ships in a positron-lance duel, they would have to survive the missile fire to get there. The Scimitars were older and the new ships had better electronic warfare and sensors—but that wasn't going to get any of his ships between the enemy starfighters and Blackhawk Five.

Geometry and physics were harsh mistresses—and Anthony Yamamoto had given his orders. The fighter duel was down to his people...and all he could do for Blackhawk Five was hope that the pirates weren't feeling nihilistic.

Ten fighters weren't planning on capturing the facility. Securing it for shuttles to land, yes, but they wouldn't have the hands to take control of it.

But they could very easily *destroy* it—and Blackhawk Processing Five had sixty-three thousand human beings aboard.

———

Anthony's wing was the third that would reach range of the pirate fighters, not the first. That gave him almost thirty seconds to judge the competence of his opponents. Not enough time to form a full evaluation—the flight time of the Javelin VI starfighter missiles in both his and the pirate's magazines was two and a half minutes, after all—but enough to get a feel for the people on the other side.

His opinion wasn't complimentary.

"Launching late, uncoordinated salvos," he noted aloud. "They launched five seconds late, and it took another five seconds for four fighters to put sixteen missiles in the air."

Five seconds, in a war between computers and humans interfaced into those computers, was an eternity. It was the difference between the defensive lasers trying to take down sixteen missiles with two salvos and trying to take them down with *four*.

"Launching *our* missiles," Gunther reported. "Range is two point one million kilometers. Lance range in two minutes."

Anthony was the pilot. His focus was on flying the ship, avoiding any incoming fire he could and leaving running the missiles and defenses to his gunner and engineer. If it came to lance range, he'd control *that* weapon—it ran the full length of the Katana and was aimed by maneuvering the starfighter.

He was *also* the force commander, but the limitations of lightspeed coms meant all he could immediately command was the single fighter on his wing.

They'd put eight missiles into space, and he had to *wait* seven entire seconds before he saw his enemy's response.

"Well."

This quartet knew their business better than the two flight groups that had already run into his patrol wings. Sixteen missiles ripple-fired the moment they were in range, launched at the minimum safe interval and getting all of them into space in under a second.

"Not uncoordinated salvos," Gunther said calmly. "Lasers up."

"Decoy deployed, ECM and EW systems live. Let's make them dance," Navarro agreed.

The Katana only carried two decoys. One might be enough. One would have to be enough, at least against the first salvo—because the pirate fighters launched their second salvo thirty seconds after the first, and Anthony *couldn't* match it.

Not without leaving the freighters untouched as they arrived at Blackhawk Five.

"Are we synced with Alpha-Two-Bravo?" he asked.

"Fully," Gunther confirmed. "Sequencing the laser sweeps now. We've got this, sir."

Verbal communication dropped as the missiles closed into the range of the defenses.

These pilots were good, and Anthony could feel it in the way the enemy missiles were flying and maneuvering. The range was long enough to minimize direct control, but the pirates had staggered the engines enough to merge the missiles into a single wave.

The other pirate wings engaged so far weren't as good, and it was making his people's lives a lot easier—but it seemed that Anthony Yamamoto and his companions had been sent the enemy's best.

Their sync with Alpha-Two-Bravo—Major Zayna Sundström, the executive officer of the second squadron of the first fighter group aboard *Krakatoa*—allowed him to track the paths of the lasers fired by both fighters, and he took the starfighter through a spiraling semi-random dance, one that Sundström mirrored with her own chaotic flight.

The lasers were carrying the main work of taking down the missiles, but there were moments when the positron lance lined up with a target, and both Anthony and Sundström knew to take the shots. Flashes of antimatter filled the space around the missile salvo, both from the starfighter's main guns and the destruction of missiles.

The chaotic pattern of radiation that followed as antimatter missiles detonated didn't *help* their targeting, but the missiles were leaving most of it behind as they surged toward Anthony's fighter.

A wordless report from Navarro flashed through the network, confirming that four of the missiles were heading for the decoy. Gunther took a moment longer than Anthony would have *preferred* to adapt his targeting—but was fast enough that the last missile died five thousand kilometers short of the starfighter wing.

"Decoy down. Deploying second decoy."

"Targets destroyed," Gunther responded to Navarro's report. "Scimitar electronics weren't up to the task."

Anthony double-checked the report and smiled coldly. Sixteen missiles against two Katanas were bad odds for his people—the decoy pulling a quarter of the salvo off-target had saved them and that was almost pure luck.

Eight missiles against two Scimitars were better odds for the Scimitars...but not by much, given the older fighters' inferior electronics. The pirate pilots had been *decent*, but they hadn't been *good*. Veterans, most likely, but ones that hadn't seen combat.

"Keep your eyes sharp," he told his people. "Rest of their missiles are still incoming."

He'd seen more than one fighter destroyed because the crew had unintentionally dropped the threat rating on uncontrolled missiles—but even the relatively small Javelin VIs in a starfighter's launchers were driven by special-purpose synthetic intelligences capable of finishing their missions, and there were still two salvos of missiles heading toward them.

"Engaging now," Gunther replied a few seconds later, the lasers once more spitting out energy.

The gunner wasn't quite up to the standard Anthony Yamamoto would like in his personal crew, but she was getting there. They'd survive this, and that meant the two freighters were screwed.

The pirates might have managed to fit *some* weapons and deflectors on the starships, but they weren't going to stand up to twenty modern starfighters.

Anthony was hoping that the inexperience most of the pirate ships were showing would keep his people alive, but the *real* concern he still had was the starfighters heading for Blackhawk Five.

Right up until the moment all ten of them *disappeared*.

"Gunther...what did I just miss?" he asked slowly.

"Scanning and analyzing," the gunner replied, her datafeed mirroring to his interface as they continued to hurtle toward the pirate freighters. "Um. I do believe we all assumed that Blackhawk Five was just going to sit there and be captured.

"The crew disagreed. Those fighters just collided with a field of refinery slag."

Anthony stared at the sensor data for a few more seconds and then began to chuckle.

"Two things a refinery station complex has, I suppose, are mass and mass drivers," he conceded. "I'm guessing the slag is usually returned to orbit in the asteroid belt to maintain mass levels?"

"I think so, yes," his gunner confirmed. "The mass drivers aren't nearly up to the standard of military mass cannon, but they also fire a *lot* more mass."

Military mass cannon had used the same mass manipulators warships used to increase their engine efficiency to fire projectiles very, very quickly. They'd been obsolete for the entirety of Anthony's career, but he was aware of the concept.

The pirates, it seemed, either *weren't* or hadn't thought about the fact that refinery stations possessed larger and slower versions of the same fundamental system. And it apparently didn't require much work to take a system designed to put half-million-ton chunks of rock that *had* been iron ore back into the asteroid belt and turn it into a giant shotgun.

"Make sure we have the vector of that debris cloud nailed down," Anthony ordered, still chuckling as he spoke. "I wouldn't want it to hit anyone we *like*."

His amusement faded rapidly as he checked in on the rest of his patrol wings. The pirate fighters had definitely *lost* the dozen small skirmishes they'd courted, but clearing Dakota's skies had cost him six of his own ships.

Hopefully, some of the eighteen crew aboard those Katanas had managed to eject. The automatic systems were *supposed* to handle that, but he'd never trusted their reliability.

"Let's bring up that transmitter again," he murmured. "Our new friends have very much run themselves out of options and, well, those ships are worth a *hell* of a lot if we can take them intact."

Even a freighter with an Alcubierre-Stetson drive had a price tag most easily measured in percentage points of system GDP, after all.

4

Dakota System
08:30 January 31, 2738 ESMDT

"THEY DECIDED to see sense after losing all of their fighters and realizing they couldn't engage their drives that close to the Belt," James reported to Dakota's new Cabinet.

Not that long before, the twelve politicians on the other end of the virtual conference had been the delegates to the interim governance conference for the Dakota Sector, an attempt to establish a temporary regional government still loyal to Terra and the Commonwealth.

Now, one member of each planet's elected government had found themselves forming the core of a regional government. In the medium term, a new Confederate Interstellar Congress was planned—but the Confederacy had existed for twenty-two days.

Enough analysts, bureaucrats and politicians had been concentrated on Dakota for the governance conference that a draft constitution was almost ready. Still, the twelve members of the Interim Cabinet —usually plus Abey Todacheeney, standing in for Dakota, as Chapulin needed to be President and not her planet's voice—were the effective authority over twelve systems and approximately twenty billion human beings.

"What happens to the ships now?" Chandler Leon, the Minister for Desdemona, asked. A slimly built man with pale skin and bright red hair, Leon's family ran most of Desdemona's shipping.

"For the moment, the Marines are still securing control of them," James replied. "My suggestion is that they be brought into Confederacy service directly, to serve as both peacetime government transports and couriers, and wartime military logistics ships."

"Right now, that means logistics ships," Sanada Chō pointed out. The absolutely massive Minister for Shogun was the acknowledged deputy president—a powerful presence both literally and figuratively, given that he'd once been Shogun's planetary champion sumo wrestler.

"Most likely," James conceded. "Our ships are designed to operate with minimal or no secondary logistics support, but without FTL communications, I am hesitant to pin my ships down for the amount of time necessary for replenishment fabrication."

He'd made an exception for replacement starfighters, which had kept First Fleet pinned down in Dakota for the last three weeks. If he'd needed to sortie, he'd have done so—but until a few days earlier, he'd have been short on both fighters and missiles.

"Being able to lean on Dakota's industry to manufacture replacement fighters and missiles and carry those with us aboard noncombatant vessels improves our flexibility," he told them. "We are still in a very awkward phase, Ministers. As we saw yesterday, we don't know enough of what's going on in the sectors around us.

"Meridian has joined us. The Commonwealth has betrayed us. But we know nothing of the fates of the Brillig, Rossiya and Amandine Sectors. We have limited information on the Cossack and Angola Sectors.

"We had all assumed that our main threats were the League and the Commonwealth," he continued. "And I think that remains true, but we —*I* appear to have underestimated the extent of our 'lesser threats.'"

The virtual conference was silent for a few seconds.

"Does this change your recommendations for our strategy and operations?" Chapulin finally asked.

James suspected that if she was truly concerned, she would have pinned him down in private before the meeting. The interim President knew she had permanent access to his coms, after all.

Their friendship and professional relationship had helped get the whole Confederacy to this point, after all.

"In the immediate term, no," he told them. "In truth, there's very little we can do in the immediate term beyond what has been planned. Our limitations on communications and hull numbers remain.

"Our military priorities will be heavily shaped by our political priorities," he noted. "If, for example, one of the twelve systems represented in this call decides *not* to join the Confederacy, we will need to assess our positions relative to their defense and see if we can work out how to protect them against the League with minimal risk to ourselves."

Because there was no way in void or earth that James Tecumseh was going to leave anyone to the mercy of the mercenary-admiral-turned-dictator who ran the Stellar League. Kaleb Periklos had forged the loose alliance of system-states that made up the League into something resembling a nation at the point of a battlefleet—and while James could see where the Dictator was coming from, he couldn't approve.

And he wouldn't permit the systems he had promised to protect to be annexed into that empire.

"We do not believe that is a major concern," Chaza'el Papadimitriou told him drily. The Minister for Persephone spoke for the system with the longest communication loop from Dakota—but he *also* spoke for a system that had been occupied by the Stellar League until James had relieved them.

"I agree," James said. "But that is a political calculation, and I need to prepare for the possibilities that we do not expect to occur.

"Either way, our immediate military priority is *industrial*. We have begun the construction of permanent starfighter- and missile-production facilities both here in Dakota orbit and at Base Łá'ts'áadah."

Base Łá'ts'áadah had been a covert Commonwealth shipyard. Now, the ships under construction there would guard the Confederacy *against* the Commonwealth.

Eventually. He'd have a repaired and refitted *Hercules*-class in June, *Ajax*, but the earliest he was expecting any *new* warships was Christmas. In *theory*, there should have been three more by the following March, but they were using key parts supplied for those ships to build the first one.

Dakota would be able to provide replacement parts. *Eventually*. But the Class One mass manipulators that were essential for FTL drives were complex, fragile, and on the verge of impossible to build.

A full set of four was two-thirds of the cost of a freighter—and *still* forty percent of the cost of an FTL warship, even with the additional costs for weapons and electromagnetic deflectors.

Starfighters existed because no one could afford to lose starships.

"What about the other star systems?" Chō asked.

"I am hesitant to ask too much," James admitted. "It was the demand that we force this sector to become the Commonwealth's arsenal that led to our secession, after all."

"There is a difference, Admiral Tecumseh, between the imposition of a distant state, backed by the unquestioned threat of force and the denial of our rights and self-governance…and voluntary contributions to our common defense," the Shogun Minister told him calmly. "Speaking for myself and my government, we would be *horrified* to see Dakota bear the entirety of the financial and industrial burden of said defense."

"Dakota has more spaceborne industry than any other system in the Confederacy," Patience Abiodun, Minister for Arroyo, pointed out. "But while it is difficult to admit, Arroyo is likely the *poorest* system in our twelve…and we are entirely capable of producing fighters and missiles if we are provided the necessary schematics.

"First Fleet and Meridian Fleet provide for the security of the Confederacy against major attack by the League or the Commonwealth," she continued. "But against pirate attacks like this, a battle fleet seems to be overkill."

"Our sectors are not used to this kind of conflict," Chapulin warned. "We do not have the preparations and defenses more...traditionally unstable regions possess."

"There are systems and tools for that mission," James told them. "Currently, all of our systems except Persephone have at least a small number of guard corvettes and some orbital defenses, improvised or otherwise. Persephone has two of our carriers in orbit to replace the defenses the League destroyed."

James wasn't happy to give up those ships, but Persephone needed *something*—and he wasn't going to pretend that *Paramount*-class carriers were going to change much anywhere. They were old and obsolete... but he had three of them and only two more modern carriers.

"The plan to begin mass production of starfighters and missiles in any system that is willing to host and fund the factories will allow us to deploy those fighters and missiles for the defense of those systems," he told them. "The only addition I would make at this point is to increase our production of Class Two mass manipulators and begin a crash design program for a guardship.

"We have some hundred or so high guard corvettes across the Confederacy, but those vessels do not have missile launchers and are intended entirely for police and antidebris work. Few Commonwealth systems have deployed true guardships."

The TCN had certainly *fought* enough guardships over the years that James had a solid idea of what the sublight vessels needed. Most importantly, though, the Class Two mass manipulators that underlay even a starship's sublight maneuvering were exponentially cheaper and easier to make than Class Ones.

"I am not prepared to scatter the DCN in penny packets across our systems," he warned. "Our total strength is only seventeen capital ships, already split into three deployments.

"Against a major Commonwealth or League deployment, we may well not have enough warning to concentrate our forces sufficiently to stand against them."

The members of the Cabinet were all in the same room, allowing a layer of nonverbal communication that James couldn't follow. Some of it was electronic between neural implants...and some of it was just people who'd learned to know each other very well sitting in the same place.

"We'll find the money," Chapulin told him. "I am not an expert in space combat, but it seems that a squadron of guardships backed by a few squadrons of starfighters should suffice against this kind of danger?"

"Not an expert" was doing some serious lifting in Chapulin's case, James knew. A former Commonwealth Marine Colonel with thirty years of experience, the interim President was only "not an expert" in space combat compared to, say, James Tecumseh himself.

"I agree, which is why I suggested it," he told them. "My preference is to concentrate the DCN into a maximum of two fleets. Mostly, right now, that requires bringing *Champion* and *Goldwyn* from Persephone to rejoin Meridian Fleet—but *that* requires assembling a sublight defense force for the system."

James was surprised to realize that Papadimitriou hadn't even twitched, let alone objected, when he'd suggested stripping Persephone of defenders. Whatever else the Minister for Persephone was thinking, he apparently trusted James.

And the level of trust the entire Cabinet had for him was terrifying. They'd already seen one Commonwealth Admiral attempt to make himself dictator of a new empire in the Meridian Sector. James had chosen a different course—but the influence and trust the civilian leadership were prepared to give him were occasionally worrying.

"From the perspective of growing our overall economy, I see using centralized funds to build Class Two manipulator factories and guardship yards in every star system as a useful approach from several directions," Abey noted. "Any counter to the inevitable economic disruption of our split from Terra is a good thing.

"We don't even have an agreed-upon interstellar *currency* yet."

Most planets, in James's experience, had at least a semi-formal local currency. But it was the Terran Commonwealth dollar that had been the medium of interstellar trade for every world in the new Confederacy—and, for the moment, the dollar *remained* that currency by necessity.

Which meant that, for a while yet, taxes and government investment would be paid in the dollars of a state that they were grimly certain was going to become their enemy.

————

After the Cabinet had broken up, the ministers leaving to the seemingly infinite tasks of establishing a new state and government, James found himself still in the virtual conference with the two Dakotan women.

"Was there something else?" he asked. "I enjoy speaking with both of you, but we are all extraordinarily busy people."

"We had another project we wanted to discuss with you yesterday, before we were rudely interrupted by those pirates," Abey told him with a smile. "And that's laying aside my *personal* complaint about the interruption."

Chapulin melodramatically covered her eyes, and James couldn't keep from chuckling. He'd been supposed to spend the night planet-side, which meant staying over with his girlfriend.

She understood that duty came first—the same was true for her, though her time as First Chief was *supposed* to be limited. As the Interim First Chief, she wasn't expected to put together the full cere-monial headdress that Chapulin had worn for the role, but that was the *only* part of the job she wasn't handling.

"I will endeavor to get back to the surface soon," he promised her. "Though I'm due to take another trip out to Łá'ts'áadah. Commodore Krejči and Ms. Gardinier have promised me good news, but without q-coms none of us really regard our communications as secure."

Commodore Izem Krejči was the commander of the shipyard at Virginia-Eleven, but Ekundayo Gardinier was the operations manager for the Centauri Dynamics team that was building the ships. So far, the Dakota branch of the multistellar company had continued operating on behalf of the new government, even though James suspected that Gardinier was going to face difficulties over that eventually.

He *also* suspected, however, that the Cabinet already had a plan for that.

"Any assistance or funding the shipyards need is among our

highest priorities," Chapulin told him. "Outside of *Ajax*, those capital ships are the only new warships we're going to see for a while yet."

"Unfortunately," James confirmed. His hand spasmed unexpectedly, and he looked down at the artificial limb and grimaced.

"James?" Abey asked softly.

Both his girlfriend and his new civilian boss knew that James had three artificial limbs. He'd lost the organic ones when a deep-penetration operation against the Alliance of Free Stars had gone badly wrong. The necessity of the situation had required him to have emergency cybernetics installed immediately, which had prevented proper regeneration.

His current limbs looked normal enough to most inspections, though there was some ugly scarring at the attachment points. One of the prices of that near-real appearance and function, though, was a stringent maintenance schedule.

One James had *not* been keeping up with.

"Hand is acting up," he said mildly. "It's fine."

"Admiral Tecumseh, are you failing to maintain your cybernetics properly?" the President asked sharply.

Of *course* the ex-Marine was familiar with cybernetic limbs. James sighed.

"Basically," he admitted. "There hasn't been time for the standard check-ins. Which, of course, means I now need a *longer* checkup."

"Will an order from your *President* be enough, Admiral, or do I need to have your girlfriend talk to your steward?" Chapulin asked drily.

James side-eyed Abey, who gave him one of the most beatific smiles he'd ever seen from the Dakotan woman.

"You would too, wouldn't you?" he asked, his accusatory tone only half-joking. He was well aware of the degree to which a chief steward managed their Admiral. If Abey told Sallie Leeuwenhoek to make certain one newly promoted four-star Admiral made it to the sickbay for cybernetics maintenance...the noncommissioned officer would make *damn* certain their Admiral made it to sickbay.

"I'll set up the appointment," he promised. If he was having involuntary motions, the argument that *everything is fine, I don't need a checkup* didn't even hold water with *him.*

"Good. Then let's get to the point of what we're ambushing you on," Chapulin told him. "Uniforms."

"Uniforms?"

"The Dakotan Confederacy Navy is *not* the Terran Commonwealth Navy," Abey pointed out. "We want to make that clear—and also to show our support of the DCN personnel by providing new uniforms that are more distinctive than simply removing the sash from TCN uniforms."

James's hand almost automatically touched his shoulder, where he'd worn a red sash as part of his uniform for his entire career. That sash, along with the matching red lapels on his jacket, had marked him as a member of the Navy as opposed to the Marines or the Starfighter Corps—who'd worn green and purple, respectively.

The lapels remained, but he'd ordered all of his people to ditch the sash to mark the changeover from the Commonwealth to the Confederacy. Something about the thought of ditching the entire uniform didn't feel right, but he gestured for Abey to continue.

"We had three possibilities done up," she told him, gesturing three holographic figures into the air.

James studied them in silence. All three figures wore a standard full-body shipsuit as the base layer, though the colors varied, but had quite different exterior layers.

The first had the shipsuit itself in a beige color with a stylization of the waistline storage compartments that made the garment appear like a short tunic worn over pants. Over that was worn a brown leather jacket with decorative tooling around the waist and a Navy Captain's stripes embroidered onto the sleeve cuffs.

The three gold bars of the main rank insignia had moved from the shoulder boards to a patch on the left chest, above the heart, which were joined by a new dolphin emblem. The same dolphin was repeated on a gold buckle closing a dark red belt around the shipsuit.

It was a darker red than the TCN's version, but James could see the link—especially as two additional belts hovered next to the image, one in emerald green with a canine emblem and one in navy blue with an eagle emblem.

The uniform was *very* different from the TCN uniform James already wore, but that was true of the other two as well.

The next uniform was at least using the same black shipsuit as his existing uniform, but where the current uniform used a short black jacket derived from the old United States Navy and included a dress shirt over the shipsuit, this one had a one-piece double-breasted red jacket, sealed on the right side with an insignia board.

Like the first uniform, the jacket had the sleeve stripes of a Captain. The three gold bars were spaced evenly up the board that sealed the uniform, and the same dolphin insignia was placed over the left breast.

The jacket was piped in the same dark red as the first uniform, and two additional graphics showed Marine and Starfighter corps uniforms in green and blue with the dog and eagle.

The last uniform also used the black shipsuit, with a shorter blue jacket with a brown leather swatch, lined in Navy red, on the left breast that held the dolphin insignia he was expecting. The cuff lines and shoulder boards were identical to a TCN uniform, though the cut and style of the jacket overall were quite different—and it sealed at the neck, removing the need for the white undershirt of TCN dress wear.

"We had some of our best designers take a stab at the concepts," Abey told him. "We wanted to keep a military feel, obviously, while also drawing a clean line between your people's TCN service and their time with our new nation."

James nodded slowly, running his gaze across the three holographic images and trying to muster his thoughts.

"You seem concerned, Admiral," Chapulin finally said into the silence of his thoughts.

He exhaled a sigh and looked the President in the eye.

"I understand what your intention is," he told her. "But I will tell you right now that if we roll out an entirely new uniform, we will insult the officers and crew under my command. We would be telling them to be *ashamed* of their service to the Commonwealth."

There were reasons, perhaps, that they *should* be ashamed—but it was the oaths and honor the Commonwealth had given them all that had led to the mass mutiny.

"In the long run, perhaps we do want to switch to an entirely new uniform. But for the moment..." He shook his head. "We must respect who we were. We must respect who our soldiers were."

"I...hoped that this would be a sign of our respect and support for them," Chapulin told him slowly. "I, for one..." She sighed. "I *am* ashamed of the uniform I wore, Admiral, and at least some of the things I did wearing it."

"There is blood on those uniforms," he agreed. "But for all of that, they are *our* uniforms. Still, we do need to make a change and mark our new allegiances. More than just abandoning the sashes."

He reached out and touched the dolphin on the red uniform's rank badge.

"What are these?" he asked.

"New imagery for the different branches," Abey said instantly. "Dolphins for the Navy. Eagles for the Starfighter Corps. Coyotes for the Marine Corps."

He hadn't recognized the canine on the Marine Corps badge before, but he grinned now that he did. *He* knew the role of Coyote in a lot of North American stories—and the dangerous trickster god was an excellent emblem for what his Marines would have to be if the Confederacy was to survive.

"My suggestion, though I think you will need those 'best designers' to take a stab at it, is to work within the confines of our existing uniforms," he told them. "Recolor the lapels to these new hues. Redesign the shoulder boards to include both the new colors and the new branch designators.

"Issue new unit and branch insignia with the new emblems. We keep our uniforms, keep our unit and ship names, but we change small things and add icons that speak of Dakota and the Confederacy to us.

"We don't want to abandon what we were—we need to embrace what we have become."

Both of the local women looked thoughtful, and then Chapulin nodded firmly.

"You are correct, Admiral, of course," she told him. "I'll talk to those designers and our textiles people. We'll confirm the new jackets and insignia with you again before we mass-produce them, but I think we should have all of your people reequipped within a week or so."

"I take it you have factories standing by, waiting for the final designs?" James asked with a chuckle.

"Oh, yes," Abey confirmed. "We want to show our support for your people, James. We recognize the sacrifices they have made to stand at our side. We will not let that be forgotten."

5

EVEN TAKING a detour and using an A-S jump to cut the trip down, the journey from Dakota, the system's second planet, to the shipyards orbiting the eleventh moon of the fourth planet took most of a day. It was a long trip, one that James Tecumseh wouldn't have made in ordinary times with FTL communications.

Today, it was necessary. He felt more than a bit silly taking an entire carrier out from Dakota orbit, but there were no *small* Alcubierre-Stetson ships. *Krakatoa* was overkill for a taxi, but the big ship also needed some tender loving care that was most easily provided in Base Łá'ts'áadah.

The eight shipyards orbiting Dakota herself had been built to handle building civilian starships at the relatively sedate pace of about four years per ship. Five of those yards were still building freighters, though resources were being deployed to accelerate the completion of those ships. A sixth had been dedicated to repairing and refitting the crippled battlecruiser *Ajax*—a modern ship, but one the League had beaten to pieces taking out the Commonwealth's Clockward Fleet.

The last two yards had released their newest products and were undergoing massive refits that would allow them to build modern eighty-million-cubic-meter warships. While that work was ongoing, the yards couldn't take *Krakatoa* in hand, and what refit capacity was available outside the main yards was busy with the damage to her smaller sisters.

Base Łá'ts'áadah—*Base Eleven* in English, sharing a name with the moon it orbited—hadn't been intended as an active fleet repair and refit facility. The massive slips on James's display were brilliantly lit and surrounded by active support platforms and four *Zion*-class battle platforms—but they were far enough away from Virginia/Dakota-IV's main industry and population centers to provide secrecy.

And the same industrial nodes that could build a battleship or carrier from scratch could provide the annual refit and workover *Krakatoa* was due for.

James had to hope that *Krakatoa*'s "annual physical" went better for the carrier than his own appointment with Dr. Vijaya Stankiewicz, *Krakatoa*'s senior physician had gone. Stankiewicz was a very good doctor who knew their way around cybernetic limbs, but James had not only been overdue for his annual checkup, he'd also not quite blown off several of the *previous* initial checkups while he'd been on Earth.

He'd been under a cloud of suspicion then, after a mission that had seen a Commonwealth warship taken by pirates. He'd temporarily allied with a Castle Federation task group to take the vessel down and defeat the pirate warlord who'd seized it—it had been the right call, but it hadn't gone down well with his superiors.

But two years without proper updates and care had left his cybernetics in a worse state than he'd expected. The three limbs had *worked* and he'd expected them to *keep* working...an expectation that Stankiewicz had disabused him of.

High-grade cybernetics like his would last forever with proper maintenance and a good long while without it...but after over a year, he was apparently lucky hand spasms were all he was getting. Dr.

Stankiewicz had done the tune-ups, maintenance and software updates. Everything was perfectly fine now—except for an enduring feeling of the artificial limbs being *bruised*.

"We have permission to bring *Krakatoa* in to refit dock one," Commodore Young Volkov's voice said in his implants. *Krakatoa's* Captain was next up on James's list to hang a Rear Admiral's stars on, as soon as he found a role to promote her into.

"Carry on, Captain," he instructed. "I have an appointment with the base's command staff, but I'll most likely be leaving Łá'ts'áadah before *Krakatoa*."

"We shouldn't need that much work, sir," she argued.

"No, but I need to be at Dakota," James admitted. "I needed this meeting and we were sending you out here anyway, but I'll be hopping a ride back on one of the in-system transports."

———

Leaving his office, James concealed his mixed amusement and exasperation at the pair of sentinels outside his door. One of them was traditional, though he'd managed to mostly avoid having a permanent Marine babysitter up until the mutiny itself.

Now, though, his Marines had calmly informed him that he *would* be guarded at all times. And backing them up was the *other* woman outside his door. Deceptively dressed in civilian clothing, Shannon Reynolds was almost certainly *deadlier* than the armed Marine Corporal who was officially James's bodyguard.

The slim blonde woman had been a Commonwealth Internal Security Service agent—the one, in fact, tasked with assassinating James Tecumseh if he stepped out of line.

He wasn't entirely sure how he and Anthony Yamamoto had replaced the Commonwealth government as the arguably psychopathic woman's substitute conscience and moral compasses, but she'd backed his play when another ex-CISS agent had been sent to give him Walkingstick's orders.

And she'd promptly designated herself his bodyguard afterward. Anyone who wished one James Tecumseh ill would have to get through all of the security measures of his flagship, then through the extra measures *Krakatoa's* Marines had wrapped around their Admiral, and *then* past the single deadliest viper-in-human-form James had ever met.

"I need to know which transport you're taking back to Dakota," she told him bluntly as she fell in beside him. Corporal Sanderson trailed behind him, the taller and more visibly armored brunette soldier clearly more amused than offended by any of this.

"Nobody in Base Łá'ts'áadah should be a threat," he pointed out. "And that includes the people we've picked to fly the in-system transports."

Those ships were a new addition, since Łá'ts'áadah could no longer draw resources from out-system. The yards had been placed in Dakota because the system *could* provide everything needed to build warships, but Project Hustle had obfuscated the deliveries as much as possible.

The DCN didn't have the time or resources to do the same, so sublight transports rigged for the same Tier Two acceleration as warships now made regular runs to and from the industrial base.

"Everyone here would have been one hundred percent trustworthy *while you were Commonwealth*," Reynolds snapped. "The situation has changed. Some people that were reliable then are now Commonwealth loyalists and hostile to *you*."

James wished he could argue with her...but she was right.

"I don't know which ship yet," he admitted. "It will depend on when I'm finished with my meetings and whether anything else comes up. *Once* I know when I'm leaving, I will leave selection of the transport up to you. You and the Marines can secure her however you feel necessary."

Reynolds sniffed.

"That'll do, I suppose. Some of the Marines are approaching useful."

Corporal Sanderson, James observed, took that observation in stride. That was impressive on its own, given James's experience with Marines.

If nothing else, it meant that Reynolds had convinced the Marines around her of her lethality. James had mixed opinions on the woman in general—if nothing else, he hoped not to *need* an assassin, even if she'd been occasionally useful.

But she was also putting the Marine platoon assigned to manage James's security through a hyper-compressed version of CISS's VIP protection training.

"You know that once Revie's people are up to your standard, I'm going to give two-thirds of them to the President and make you train another platoon, right?" he warned.

"I am perfectly prepared to train security for the President so long as we do so in the field and the people they give me to protect *you* meet a minimum standard of competence," Reynolds told him.

"I trust that Lieutenant Revie's people met that standard?" he asked.

She sniffed again.

"The Marines know not to send *dullards* to a detail under CISS authority." She paused thoughtfully. "Though...do I even *have* authority?"

James had to laugh. Reynolds had just...taken over his security three weeks earlier, after dealing with the ex-CISS Assembly Lictor that Walkingstick had sent to Dakota as his representative. With the secession of the Confederacy, she had effectively resigned from the CISS.

"You are my bodyguard," he told her. "And if that isn't enough for someone, we'll fix their mistake."

"Oh, that won't be a problem," Reynolds said brightly. "I just suddenly had to wonder...who's *paying* me?"

"If absolutely necessary, *me*," James promised.

Reynolds was both extraordinarily useful and also, he recognized, extraordinarily *damaged*. He felt responsible for the younger woman in more than one way—and he'd be *damned* if he let her following him into treason come back to bite her.

6

Dakota System
13:45 February 1, 2738 ESMDT

EKUNDAYO GARDINIER'S office overlooked the main operations space of Base Łá'ts'áadah, a massive military-style command center squeezed into what would normally have been a set of apartments aboard the *Zion* battle platform.

The one-way window behind her desk allowed James to look out at the status displays for the six assembly slips and the warships building there. Two battlecruisers, two carriers and two battleships, each of them almost twenty million cubic meters larger than *Krakatoa* and *Saint Bartholomew*, the two largest ships in the DCN.

"Any security issues?"

Shannon Reynolds wasn't even officially *part* of the meeting, but she'd followed James into the office, and he was still looking at the status displays when she spoke.

"Less than I'd feared when we learned what was going on,"

Commodore Izem Krejči told her. If anything, the Black commanding officer of the Base's security forces looked even *more* muscular than he had when James had first met him.

He figured he could guess how the Commodore reacted to stress.

"How bad?" James asked his subordinate, still looking out at the operations center.

"I offered all of the personnel, military and civilian, the opportunity to be paid out and transported to the civilian infrastructure closer in to Virginia," Krejči told him. "Only lost about two hundred of the spacers and fifty of the civilians. About half what I expected, which set my paranoia a-ringing."

"Few of the civilian workers are loyal to something as abstract and distant as Centauri Dynamics, let alone the Commonwealth," the white-haired woman behind the desk observed. She was leaning the back of her chair against the desk as she watched James.

"Loyalty is more personal for my people. They are loyal to their shift managers, their teammates, *maybe* their department heads and, at the furthest extreme, me," Gardinier concluded. "Many are locals, anyway. Most of the ones who took the Commodore's offer were from Earth or Alpha Centauri directly. I lost a third of my senior management team in one moment, but I prefer that to dealing with people who are going to argue with me without good reason."

"The Commodore's paranoia sounds justified to me," Reynolds said. "There were problems?"

"Inevitable," Krejči admitted. "Nothing serious so far. A few attempts to store secured information in ways that could be smuggled out. Some intentional slow work."

"Only *one* thing serious," Gardinier corrected. "Let us not play games, Izem."

"Commodore?" James asked softly.

"One of our IT people tried to wipe the Project Hustle database," Krejči admitted. "Except she was too junior to have the right access and not quite good enough to hack herself access, and bounced off our security. Her coworkers reported her.

"Since she hadn't managed to do any actual damage, we paid off her owed wages and dumped her on the refinery platforms without severance and a black mark on her file, which means she won't work IT again in this star system," the Navy officer concluded.

"There is much to be said for making an example of the first one you catch," Reynolds suggested.

"And that is exactly what the Commodore has done," James murmured. "The example being that we will punish people who act against us—but that we also do not overreact."

"It may be seen as weak," she warned.

"Then let them make that mistake."

James knew perfectly well how to use tone to *end* a conversation, and the assassin-turned-bodyguard promptly shut up. He turned back from the ships to look at the pair running the covert shipyard.

"I wish we had sufficient communications back for better coordination between you and the yards at Dakota," he admitted. "We won't be laying the first keels there for another six weeks, though. The slips were only sized for sixty-five million cubic meters."

He could build more *Krakatoa*s, for example, and could repair *Ajax*, but given the costs of the Class One mass manipulators that underlay a starship of *any* size, there was only one economically and militarily justifiable size of interstellar warship: the absolute largest that existing technology could support.

The Commonwealth had learned that lesson the hard way, and his fleet included several examples, still, of attempts to economize on hull size. But the *Assassin*-class battlecruisers and *Ocean*-class strike cruisers had still been over eighty percent of the price of their larger contemporaries, the *Resolute*s and *Lexington*s—and almost *seventy* percent of the cost of the follow-up *Hercules*-class battlecruisers over twice their size.

The mass manipulators that underlay the A-S drive were simply too large a component of the cost for any kind of *easy* economizing to be worth it.

"We've kept in contact with the local builders and are watching our timelines," Gardinier assured him. "Class One manipulators are the biggest bottleneck everyone is facing. They're building new spinners right now, but…"

"It takes eight months to spin the exotic-matter coil for a Class One," James finished for her. "So, what *are* your timelines looking like?"

"Well, first off, we renumbered all the hulls," she told him with a grin. "BC-Three-Seventy-Two, for example, is now BC-Zero-Zero-One of the Dakotan Confederacy Navy. Same across the board. So, we're looking at BC-One, BC-Two, BB-One, BB-Two, SCV-One and SCV-Two. With appropriate zeros."

James had never seen a Commonwealth cruiser or battleship with a hull number under two hundred. *Carriers* were a new-enough concept, in their modern iteration, that he'd seen nineties-sequence carriers, but the Commonwealth had maintained an active fleet of five hundred Alcubierre-Stetson drive warships.

There were a lot fewer of them now, after the Commonwealth's losses against both the Stellar League and the Alliance of Free Stars, but hull numbers were based on the total number of the type built.

And for all of the size and scale of interstellar warships, the Commonwealth had built *hundreds* of them.

"Those numbers are going to take a while to sound remotely right," James observed aloud. "I don't suppose lower numbers mean we're getting the ships sooner?"

"Unfortunately, the paint for the hull number doesn't cost much," she told him. "But I do have some good news...that, as usual, comes counterweighted by bad news."

James had been expecting that, so he simply gestured for the woman to continue.

"We have six Class One mass manipulators in storage at Base Łá't-s'áadah," she told him. "One for each ship, for initial testing. We're in a similar state for heavy and medium positron lances. I have the initial guns for each ship.

"As we discussed before, we can put all of that together and make sure BC-Zero-Zero-One commissions. She's the furthest along, thanks to her slip crew being astonishingly efficient."

"You said Christmas before," James reminded her. "With the rest being March, except for the one that will be *next* Christmas due to an accident."

"Good news: because I now know when I'm getting my next batch of heavy positron lances and Class One mass manipulators, I can pull crews from the other ships for work on BC-Zero-Zero-One that can be done in parallel.

"That will move her up into early November, possibly even October. You'll have an eighty-million-cubic-meter starship as much as two months earlier than planned."

"That is good news," he murmured. "And I'm assuming everything else is going to be much, much later?"

"Exactly. We've gone around with the local exotic-matter plants, and we're robbing Peter to pay Paul—or, in this case, to get me two Class One manipulators in October. I'm *not* going to be seeing a lot of heavy positron lances until closer to April, which is around when I've been promised that we'll *start* getting regular Class One manipulator deliveries.

"So, SCV-Zero-Zero-One is going to get those two manipulators and the spare two from my stocks after BC-One. Redirecting crews to her as the battlecruiser finishes up *should* mean that she's only delayed a month from her target date."

"So, April," James concluded. "With her positron lances coming in late."

"I figure, worst-case scenario, she's a *carrier* and we can refit lances in later if absolutely needed," Gardinier said. "Come April, though, I've been promised a steady supply of four Class One mass manipulators every four months. Assuming that the Confederacy can pay for that."

"We'll make it happen," he promised. "And that's just Dakota's spinners, I'm guessing? We may be able to lean on supply sources in other star systems. They might not be up to building twelve manipulators a year, but most star systems are building at least *one* a year."

Arroyo, who even Patience Abiodun grumpily conceded was the Confederacy's poor sister, manufactured a Class One manipulator every year and launched a freighter every four. "Poor" was relative, after all, and Arroyo put many systems outside the Commonwealth to shame.

Former Commonwealth, James supposed.

"So, if the ships were supposed to be ready to go in March, we basically get a ship every four months after that?" he asked.

"You'll get a carrier in April 'thirty-nine," she promised. "Maybe May. Second carrier will be October. Then, yeah, every four months after that. If you can get us Class Ones faster, we can move that up. All of these *were* supposed to be done next year."

"We will move mountains—or, at the very least, money and exotic matter," James told her. "I need these ships sooner rather than later."

Which also meant that he needed Krejčí to protect them, but his glance at the DCN officer told him the Commodore was *well* aware of that.

"It will be years before the new hulls we're laying down are this close to completion," he continued. "I, unfortunately, have to expect that the ships here are the only new warships I expect to see for the next three years.

"We can work, to a degree, with the schedule you've given—but any resources that can be provided that you need, let us know. The Confederacy has twelve major star systems, even if our coms suck. We will make things happen."

If nothing else, he knew that Meridian, the other former sector capital, also had yards capable of building warships. Like Dakota, they would be updating and expanding those yards—and would shortly lay down new keels.

The Confederacy's people understood that they were no longer covered by the shield of the Commonwealth. The price required for that protection had grown too expensive—and that meant they would have to protect themselves.

———

James was halfway through the station, heading to meet the in-system transport selected to take him back to Dakota, when Reynolds stopped.

"Agent?" he asked, glancing past her at the Marines surrounding them.

"New bit of intel," she told him. "Just downloaded from a friend here. Nothing solid, but I was half-considering switching transports at the last minute anyway. Follow me."

For a moment, James considered overruling her. There was a limit to *his* paranoia, and he needed to be *seen* to trust his people—difficult when his Marines had insisted on dispatching a fireteam to guard him and he was accompanied most places by a woman everyone knew was an ex-CISS agent.

"Lead on, Reynolds," he said instead. "I don't like it, but you're right. We can't afford any risks."

"We may not be sure who is writing my paychecks, but I am *very* certain what my job is, Admiral," she told him as the Marines shifted course without a word. "I am going to keep you alive. Without you, the Confederacy will fall.

"Without you, neither the Commonwealth nor its successor states will live up to their ideals again."

"I..." James swallowed hard as he realized just how deadly serious the assassin was being. "The Confederacy will survive without me. I don't know what impact I can have outside of it."

"You underestimate both yourself and the value of a symbol. The Commonwealth *needs* a successor state that is everything the Commonwealth was *supposed* to be," she concluded. "If you die, the Confederacy will falter. It will likely fail, despite the many others who will attempt to take up your tasks.

"If the Confederacy falters, it will not stand as the shining example to lead the Commonwealth's stars and people in the direction they were supposed to go.

"So, *you*, Admiral, are a linchpin on which the future of the ideals I was supposed to serve now hangs."

She shrugged.

"I may not think in the same lines as others, Admiral, but I see that path clearly."

He shook his head.

"We need to get you a hobby," he told her.

"I have two," she replied brightly. "Training your Marines and getting laid."

James found himself pinching the bridge of his nose as they reached the airlock to their shuttle. He had a pretty decent idea of the swathe Reynolds had cut through *Krakatoa*'s crew, even when she'd been hidden aboard the ship under a false identity.

She was spectacularly useful. She was also a spectacular *headache*.

7

JAMES HAD years of practice in waking up exactly when he wanted to, by a combination of habit and alarms programmed into his neural interface. He was more tired than usual that morning—he'd made it back to Dakota and landed in Táálaʼíʼtsin just before midnight, and Abey hadn't let him *sleep* immediately.

He was not, however, used to being woken by a twenty-plus-kilogram furry missile. Said missile landed on his legs, scurried up his torso and started trying to lick his face.

"Um, hello?" he said plaintively, reaching up to grab hold of the dog as it started beating his stomach with a heavily muscled tail.

"Sherlock, down!" Abey ordered, the interim ruler of an entire planet laughing helplessly as her dog introduced himself to James as wetly as possible.

"Please?" James asked. As the lights came on in Abey's bedroom, it became clear that the animal was a mixed-breed creature with a great deal of German Shepherd in him—and, from the pace of the tail that was threatening to bruise important parts of James's anatomy, a great deal of love.

Abey managed to detach Sherlock from James's chest, urging the dog down to the bottom of the bed where he finally laid down, gazing soulfully up at the two humans with his tail still wagging.

"Sorry, I meant to introduce you last night," she finally told James, still half-giggling at him.

"He's new, I take it?"

"Tradition says that the First Chief adopts a shelter dog within a week or so of taking the job," she told him. "Traditionally, the most mixed-breed mongrel Tááła'í'tsin's shelters can find—though I suspect the main selection criteria is personality!

"They're supposed to help keep us calm and stable as we take on the responsibility of guiding a planet." She shrugged, causing her tank top to slip off her shoulder and expose a fascinating amount of skin. "I think it's as much to set an example that people should be adopting and to remind us that the planet's population are as much mongrels as the dogs we're taking care of."

James chuckled and reached down to pet Sherlock, earning another enthusiastic bout of tail-wagging.

"And they help provide security?" he asked. "Assuming that your intruder is afraid of being beaten to death with a tail, I suppose."

"They don't pick high-maintenance dogs to give the First Chiefs." She shook her head with a smile. "I wasn't sure if being *interim* Chief would come with that expectation, but I think the shelters just took it as an excuse to have a high-profile adoption and remind everyone they exist."

"Not a bad plan," James agreed, grinning down at Sherlock and hoping Abey didn't catch it. For all of his lover's protestations that she was an *interim* First Chief, he suspected she was going to find herself saddled with the job full-time unless she tried a *lot* harder to avoid it.

And part of why he loved Abey Todacheeney was knowing perfectly well that she'd never avoid any responsibility people tried to give her. They had that in common, he supposed.

That was why the whole relationship worked, given the stresses involved in seceding from humanity's largest star nation.

———

The *official* reason James was in Tááła'í'tsin was to meet with the Cabinet and update them on the construction progress of their future fleet units.

Having given that update, he found himself standing at the head of the table, surveying the politicians. He knew all of them at this point—he'd had a chance to get to know the original Dakotan representatives before he'd gone off to save Meridian from the Stellar League and a rogue Commonwealth officer, and he'd brought the Meridian Sector representatives back to Dakota on his own ship.

They were nervous and afraid. He didn't blame them for that—but his job was to project confidence to them all.

"So, we are looking at a minimum of nine months before any expansion of the DCN," Chapulin reminded them all aloud. "We can accelerate the later ships by mobilizing the resources of the rest of the Commonwealth, but we will also want to lay down new hulls…well, in as many places as we can justify."

"That's here, Meridian, Shogun, and Delta Zulu," Patience Abiodun said bluntly. "Nowhere else can manage to produce enough exotic-matter coils to support warship construction on top of their own civilian needs.

"Our other systems can produce fighters and missiles and Class Two mass manipulators to enable that construction, but if we were to try to build a warship yard in my own Arroyo…" She shook her head. "Arroyo would benefit from that, but the cost to the Confederacy would be disproportionate."

James wouldn't have been as blunt about it—but Abiodun could be blunter about her system's needs and realities than anyone else could.

"Dakota is six weeks from having yards ready to hold modern warship hulls," he told the Cabinet. "While my last information from Meridian is almost two weeks out of date, Admiral Modesitt and the Meridian planetary government were working on a similar timeline. If

Shogun and Delta Zulu have empty civilian yards and begin conversion immediately upon receipt of instructions from us, we're looking at ten, maybe twelve weeks.

"That said, an eighty-million-cubic-meter starship is going to take any of those converted yards at least three years to build. The Project Hustle yards at Virginia are estimating that their next round of ships will take twenty-eight months."

The new yards would start all construction of their first round of ships before Gardinier's people delivered BC-001—but Gardinier and her people would probably deliver whatever filled that cruiser's slip before the converted civilian yards finished anything.

"We have a period of vulnerability," he warned. "Until that next generation of warships completes, we are limited to what we have—and, frankly, a significant percentage of our current Navy is obsolete. They were third-line units for the TCN."

"And the Imperator has the first-line units," Sanada Chō said grimly.

"More the second-line units, honestly," James told them. "The vast majority of the Commonwealth's modern sixty-million-cubic-meter ships are gone. The yards that were *building* them are gone.

"But the point stands. We have seventeen warships spread across twelve star systems and three deployments. The Imperator has at least a hundred ships, mostly concentrated in Sol—and, including the remaining vessels of the Rimward Fleet, the most veteran and battle-tested formation the Commonwealth Navy possessed.

"But Walkingstick is facing the same constraints as we are," he noted. "Assuming he has held on to at least one set of Project Hustle yards, he's probably looking at the same timeline for his first round of warships as we are.

"On the other hand, he controls the core systems of the Commonwealth, and, even battered by the destruction of the Alliance's deep strike, their industrial might is *immense*."

"How do we fight that?" Leon asked.

James turned to the Desdemonan and shrugged.

"If at all possible, *we don't*," he said. "If it becomes necessary, we will need to concentrate the entirety of the DCN here at Dakota and attempt to defeat Commonwealth forces in detail.

"Our best option if we cannot avoid a fight is to delay any conflict until we have started to roll out ships from Base Łá'ts'áadah and the Imperator doesn't have new ships. That would be a very short window of opportunity but one in which we could potentially inflict sufficient reverses to force a peace."

"And if the League attacks at the same time?" Papadimitriou asked slowly.

"That was a risk we chose to take," James told them bluntly. "We chose to stand defiant between two powers, each of which would make us their slaves. Our lack of communications impedes us, but it also impedes the Commonwealth.

"We are in a dangerous position, one that requires dividing our forces even as either threat could call for the entirety of our capabilities."

"And we do not even know how the Imperator will react when he learns of our secession," Leon murmured. "Or if he has."

"There has, to our knowledge, been no traffic toward Sol since the Admiral seized *Saint Bartholomew*," Todacheeney noted. "While that doesn't rule out the potential of agents with functional q-coms or of the news traveling from other systems.

"At this moment, we do not believe that Terra has been informed of our actions."

That felt...wrong, to James, but he'd willingly surrendered the ability to make that decision himself.

"There is an argument to be made," he noted, "for transparency and honesty in our international dealings. We may be walking our own path, but I feel that it will serve our future reputation better if we make a clean break with Terra."

"From a military perspective, is it not better to string them along?" Abiodun asked. "The less they know, the less likely they are to retaliate, no?"

"The longer it takes for them to know about the secession of the Confederacy, the more likely the Star Chamber and the Imperator are to regard it as black treachery, beyond even treason," James warned.

"The decision is not mine. I merely question if we want to begin our future as an independent nation by lying to the nation we are leaving."

"A formal declaration of independence has value from a political and diplomatic position," Chapulin conceded. "Given the communication delays and the need to talk to all of our member systems, we can justify some hesitation.

"But the Admiral has, as always, hit the key point. Do we want to be the nation born in lies and deception—or do we want to uphold the ideals we want to espouse in *all* of our dealings, external as well as internal?"

"We fear the Commonwealth," Leon admitted. "Is a formal declaration not a challenge, a gauntlet thrown that they must answer?"

Everyone was looking at James. He smiled thinly.

"Yes," he told them. "But if they learn of our actions through a third party, it will be used against us for decades. More immediately, however, it will make it far easier for Walkingstick to sell his allies and spacers on a counterstrike.

"Right now, I have no window, no ability to predict when or if the Commonwealth will attack," he continued. "If we send a diplomatic mission with a declaration of independence, tradition and interstellar law dictate they be allowed to return to us.

"That will give us critical information on both the status and the intent of the Commonwealth. It will allow us to assess the danger posed by Imperator Walkingstick and whether or not there is any chance for peace.

"We do not want to fight the Commonwealth. Formally declaring our independence won't avert a fight if it is coming—but it puts much of the timing under our control rather than up to the vagaries of fate."

"It is a risk," Chō observed. "It seems to me that *control* of the timing is worth something, though—as is transparency and creating the reputation of our nation that we wish to hold."

"It's the reputation part that I think may be the most important," Chapulin finally said, her gaze sweeping across the room and holding James's for a few solid seconds.

"We are in rebellion because we could not concede to the demands of Terra," she continued. "We chose to uphold democracy and justice at the cost of unity. We cannot claim the moral high ground if we leave our former nation in the dark.

"The seizure of the two ships the pirates were using also provides us, for the first time since we made our decision, with A-S drive vessels that are not already contracted for cargo carriage or desperately needed for our internal communications.

"I suggest that we send one of those ships to Terra with a diplomatic contingent carrying our formal notice of secession and defiance. But that is a gesture I am unwilling to make on my own authority."

Her gaze swept the room again.

"It will be some time before we assemble the legislature this Confederacy needs. Until we do, this cabinet and the delegates gathered around this table represent the elected planetary governments of our member systems. Your leaders gave you sufficient authority to commit your systems to this endeavor—and if we are to declare our defiance and deliver it to the Imperator himself, I would have all of your support."

"It is what is just," Sanada Chō said instantly. "The people of Shogun would not have us obfuscate. We deny Terra. We should do so in the light of day."

"Agreed." Abiodun's agreement was important. Arroyo was the closest system to Sol and hence the most vulnerable.

Others joined in the chorus until only Chandler Leon remained silent, the Minister for Desdemona looking at something no one else could see. His system, James knew, was the *second* most vulnerable after Arroyo.

He couldn't blame the Minister for being hesitant. And yet...

"Minister Leon," he said softly. "The time for hesitation was when I laid a Marshal's mace in front of you all and summoned you to defiance. Now is the time for certainty and unity in our own defense and mission."

Leon sighed and shook his head.

"No, Admiral Tecumseh, there was *never* a time for hesitation," he replied. "But it happens anyway, because these are momentous times and momentous decisions. I agree with you all. We should inform the

Star Chamber of our choices and recall our delegates to the Interstellar Congress of the Terran Commonwealth.

"I suggest, in fact, that we recall those delegates and senators to here in Dakota and ask them to act as an interim legislature to support this cabinet as we draft a constitution and prepare for elections."

James was almost stunned into silence. That was *brilliant*.

From the expressions around him, none of the Cabinet Ministers had gone down the train of thought from declaration of independence through to the need to recall the senators and delegates to the Star Chamber, to the fact that those politicians *were* elected representatives of their worlds and could serve as such for the Confederacy.

At least temporarily. If they were willing. James wasn't certain that the people who had served their worlds in the Star Chamber would be entirely willing to defy Terra to *quite* that extent, but they would see.

"That is an excellent idea," Chapulin agreed. "If everyone else agrees, I think we can release the Admiral to his work while we draft the document to be presented to the Star Chamber, and the instructions to be given to our planets' delegates in said chamber."

8

Dakota System
10:00 February 4, 2738 ESMDT

WITH *KRAKATOA* in the capable hands of Base Łá'ts'áadah for at least another day, James didn't have access to his normal office with its Dakotan-made Shawnee decorations. There was a slowly assembling military administration on the planet, tasked with converting Commonwealth military justice codes and so forth to standards for the new Dakotan forces.

Thanks to the assistance of Inmaculada Haines, the woman who'd been the Commonwealth's head of infrastructure for the Dakota Sector, they'd taken over the offices—and, in many cases, the personnel—of several Commonwealth bureaus, and James had found himself *informed* that he had a planetside office.

Somehow, he had been unsurprised to find the office was a top-floor corner unit in the relatively ordinary-looking skyscraper. Táála'í'tsin—*One Tree* in English—was a low-slung city overall, built up around a massive Dakotan greatwood tree a hundred and fifty meters across at the base and over a kilometer high.

Parks and green space and art were woven through the city in a way James had rarely seen before. Even the Commonwealth bureau offices—now *Confederacy* bureau offices—were shorter and less obtrusive than their sisters on other worlds. The building that now housed the fledgling bureaucracy of the Dakotan Confederacy Navy, Starfighter Corps and Marine Corps was only forty stories high.

And while it had been built to the standard steel-and-glass structure of skyscrapers the Commonwealth across, Dakota had left its mark on the building in a web of carefully managed and maintained local vines and moss that covered the entire north and east sides in greenery.

The plant life left the office he'd been given shaded slightly in green from the sunlight shining through it, which added an intriguing layer of depth to the holographic tactical plot in the middle of the room—a temporary installation assembled from *Krakatoa*'s spare parts—and the Shawnee ktapif oowe woven artwork hanging on the inner walls.

James suspected that the Dakotan government's determination to make him feel at home *and* remind him of his ties to one of the many Old Nations that formed the planet's core population was currently supporting the entire fingerweaving industry on the planet all on its own.

He didn't—*couldn't*—object. The reminder of his past and culture was one thing, with a worth all its own, but the sign of respect and affection from his new home was *huge*.

It helped that he *liked* the art style, of course.

James's main focus, though, was on the big holographic tactical plot. It showed him the position of every ship in the system, interstellar or sublight—lightspeed-delayed, of course.

One of those icons, now tagged with the codes marking it as a diplomatic vessel of the Dakotan Confederacy, was the freighter *Paradise by Twilight*. The pirates hadn't even done any refits to the ship to make her more effective as an impromptu carrier. The *Troubadour*-class ship had required a brisk cleaning by a storm of robots and volunteers, and then she'd been able to function as a regular freighter again.

They weren't using her as a freighter today, and she didn't carry any cargo beyond her crew, fuel, and a small detachment of diplomats. With her hold empty, she didn't even mass that much—and yet the documents and instructions she carried gave her a weight that no amount of metal or cargo could ever match.

"Godspeed, my friends," he whispered as the ship vanished from his display. *Paradise* had actually jumped to FTL about four minutes earlier, but he was getting used to that reality. His information on *Krakatoa* was *hours* old, for example.

He was supposed to have his flagship back soon, but he *supposed* the comfortable corner office was an acceptable substitute for the Admiral's quarters aboard the supercarrier—and he certainly wasn't going to complain about his accommodations!

Turning away from the holographic plot, he crossed to his desk and opened the box waiting for him there. He'd approved the contents already, and several dozen *thousand* of them had been produced and were being distributed across the star system, but it was still an odd moment for him to look down at the new uniform jacket.

The cut of the jacket was the same as the one he'd left on the chair. So was the shade of black for the main fabric. The lapels, though, were a much darker red—nearly maroon, as opposed to the scarlet of the ex-Commonwealth uniform.

Each lapel also had a silver dolphin embroidered onto it. The same dolphin was repeated in a silver pin on each of the shoulder boards, along with the four gold stars of his new rank. The boards were the same maroon as the lapels, instead of the plain black of the Commonwealth jacket, and he shivered as he touched them.

It was both very clearly an evolution of the Commonwealth uniform and very clearly something entirely different. He'd have to transfer the rows of ribbons and other markers from his old uniform, but the core pieces had been made for him.

Despite everything, he had a moment of mental resistance to putting on the new jacket. As if, somehow, putting on the new uniform was the true final transition from being a Terran officer to being a *Dakotan* officer.

He did it anyway, shuffling it into place and letting the weight of the transition sink in. It took him a few seconds after that to realize there was something else in the box, and he pushed aside the tissue paper to reveal two transparent blocks, each about twenty centimeters by five by five.

The moment James realized what was *in* the two blocks, he started laughing, staring helplessly at the two halves of the Marshal's mace that Walkingstick had sent him. Sliced in half with a laser and sealed into the crystalline cases, they'd been forever rendered powerless.

Once a genelocked tool that could open any computer in the Commonwealth, the Marshal's mace was now nothing more than a pair of paperweights.

9

Dakota System
14:00 February 7, 2738 ESMDT

THE DOWNSIDE of spending *Krakatoa's* refit period on the planetary surface was that it made it a lot easier for the Confederacy's new government to impose on James for politics. He recognized that was part of his job and was willing to play along, but the additional friction of needing to fly him down from orbit had been useful in limiting how many luncheons and dinners he had to attend.

Spending most of his time in Táałá'í'tsin made him far too available, so he'd given up and left his schedule in the hands of Abey Todacheeney's staff, Chief Steward Leeuwenhoek and Reynolds.

Reynolds was, of course, accompanying him to all of his events—which meant her confusion when they stepped into a conference hall was a *bad* sign.

"Agent?" he asked softly.

"This was supposed to be a luncheon with the Dakota Shippers' Association," the assassin told him swiftly, her gaze sweeping the room and her hand slipping inside her jacket. "There were supposed to be sixty people here."

The room was empty. There weren't even enough *seats* for sixty people. Just a single table, set out for a formal lunch, in the middle of the room.

"Marines," James murmured. He didn't need to say more. The four-trooper fireteam *had* been waiting outside, but his single-word command brought them through the door in less than ten seconds.

By the time the Marines had joined them, he was the only person who *wasn't* holding a weapon.

"We should leave," Reynolds told him.

"Potentially," he agreed. "And yet…someone has gone to a great deal of effort to get me here, and they *aren't* shooting yet. With me."

He stepped forward, his escort moving with him instinctively as he entered the room more fully.

"You have about ten seconds to explain what's going on here," he said loudly. "Or I will let my companions tear this building apart on the assumption there is a threat that needs to be dealt with. Speak *quickly*."

Only silence answered him for at least five seconds, and then the door to his left sprang open and a lightly disheveled middle-aged man in a conservative suit half-ran in.

"Apologies, apologies," the stranger panted out. "After everything we did to arrange this, I got stuck in *traffic*."

Four rifles and a pistol James didn't want to look too closely at were trained on the stranger, who straightened and looked down at the weapons with a pained expression.

"Explain *very* quickly," James instructed sharply.

"I am Gamil Petersen," the man introduced himself, now nervously running his hand through salt-and-pepper hair. "I am afraid I may have bribed the Shippers' Association to book this luncheon, but I did make sure that there was catering!"

"I'm not seeing a reason *not* to shoot you dead where you stand," Reynolds said bluntly. "Only the Admiral's curiosity is keeping you alive."

Petersen blinked, pausing as if it had only just sunk in how terrible an idea it was to bribe and lie his way into a meeting with the uniformed commander-in-chief of a newborn nation's military.

"I am no threat to anyone," he finally said. "I am unarmed and there is no one in the building except the catering staff working away in the kitchen. You are more than welcome to confirm both of those things."

"Marines," Reynolds snapped. "Sweep the building."

There was no formal org chart for James's bodyguards. It was unnecessary—the Marines had their own hierarchy, and Shannon Reynolds was in charge. Everybody knew that.

Three of the Marines scattered to begin the sweep, while Reynolds herself holstered her gun and pulled out a scanner wand as she approached the stranger.

"Twitch and Corporal Ashanti will shoot you for me," she told Petersen sweetly.

"I am completely harmless, ma'am," he told her. "I am here for a lunch appointment and to make a business proposition, nothing more."

"I'm not generally the target for business propositions and, as you may have gathered, neither I nor my people appreciated being deceived," James said coldly.

"He's clear," Reynolds reported, sounding almost disappointed. "No chemical signatures or dense- enough power sources for weapons."

"As I said," Petersen said cheerfully. "And my proposition is most definitively for you, Admiral. My...sponsors, let us call them, insist on doing business directly. We are in the business of discretion as much as anything else."

"And what 'anything else' are you in the business of?" James asked. By this point, he believed the man when he said he wasn't a threat, but he was still inclined to let Reynolds drop him in a cell for a few months as an example.

Transparent government was all well and good, but no one should be lying their way into meetings with the new government or military.

"Weapons, Admiral," Petersen said. Nodding to Reynolds as if she *wasn't* about to turn into a human-shaped tornado of knives and bullets at a moment's notice, he stepped over to the table and took a seat. "I work for an organization that engages in arms smuggling along the border of the Commonwealth and the Stellar League.

"Traditionally, of course, our main stock-in-trade has been funneling Commonwealth-manufactured arms and starfighters to the Stellar League and the assorted single system-states around them," he continued. "But in the current situation, my sponsors see distinct possibilities in trade into the Commonwealth and with successor states like the Dakotan Confederacy.

"Please, Admiral, once your Marines have cleared the kitchen, they will be bringing food for everyone, your escorts included. Have a seat."

"All right," James allowed, stepping up to the table and considering the other man. "You have my attention, I suppose."

Which he would *not* have guessed a few minutes earlier. There were very few things that would get him to forgive the games Petersen had played to get him into this room. But…

"I now have access to the industrial might of twelve former Commonwealth worlds," he pointed out to the other man. "What exactly do you think you can interest me in?"

"Fighters, missiles, torpedoes, bombers… These are things you are building or will be building shortly," Petersen agreed. "But there are things that take time to build the facilities for. It will take months, perhaps years, for your production of these things to reach the level you need.

"My sponsors are prepared to…help fill that shortfall."

There were only two things, really, that James could see him needing to purchase from interstellar arms dealers: Class One mass manipulators—which he didn't expect they'd be able to source—and the quantum-entangled particle blocks that underlay modern FTL communications.

"You said you had a proposition. Stop *dancing* and give it to me," James growled. He still hadn't sat down.

A door opened before Petersen could reply, and one of the Marines returned. She was accompanied by a young man in a black tuxedo, carrying a tray of plates that he delivered to the table with careful aplomb.

As the arms dealer had suggested, there was a plate for all of James's bodyguards. None of them were going to touch the food. Even *James* wasn't planning on touching the food, though the pasta dishes looked and smelled excellent.

For his part, Petersen smiled and took a forkful of lasagna before continuing.

"I am here to provide the...catalog and invoice, let us say, along with the free samples," he said with a chuckle between bites. "Payment, I imagine, will be most convenient for everyone in Commonwealth dollars, but I presume you have access to significant quantities of those.

"Please, though, let us be civil," he continued. "Sit, eat!"

Reynolds ran her scanner wand over the food with a stony expression, then looked at James and nodded slightly. The food was safe, at least.

James didn't care. He leaned on the back of the chair and studied the other man.

"You have a strange way of doing business, Mr. Petersen," he observed.

"This business is relationships and civility, Admiral. It is a question of who can be trusted, both as a supplier and a customer, to both keep secrets and not to abuse the trust we extend."

"If you had not lied your way into this meeting, Mr. Petersen, I might be prepared to extend more trust myself," James noted. "But you started off on rather the wrong foot to be lecturing me on relationships and civility.

"I am sufficiently interested in your proposition to not have you arrested or shot, but I suggest that you get to business."

James knew perfectly well—and he suspected Petersen did too—that the arms dealer had never been in danger of getting shot unless he'd been a threat. Few people, in his experience, valued life as much as those who were tasked to take it.

He would never have ordered the man's death. If Petersen had become a threat, Reynolds would have dealt with him instantly, but so long as Petersen remained harmless, he was only in danger of spending a long time in a cell.

Though James would have to *find* a solid cell, he supposed. Dakota focused on restitution and rehabilitation for their criminal justice system.

"As you wish, I suppose," Petersen told him. "The primary deal will need to be closed in the Meridian. My employer, who will go by Trickster for this engagement, will insist on meeting you, Admiral Tecumseh, in person there.

"In exchange for ten billion Commonwealth dollars, we will provide you with twenty-five thousand q-com blocks operating on a neutral switchboard network, plus one thousand q-com enabled sensor probes on the same network."

"That is a lot of money," James pointed out slowly. Not an insurmountable amount—it was about half a percent of the cost of a starship—but it was about the cost of an *entire carrier group* of starfighters and bombers.

"And when, exactly, do you expect to have your own q-com switchboard online, Admiral Tecumseh?"

James kept his face a mask, though that was definitely a point. There had been *one* q-com switchboard in the Meridian and Dakota Sectors, in the Delta Zulu System. A civilian-operated secondary facility, its lack of government involvement hadn't spared it from the wrath of the Commonwealth's enemies.

The Alliance had at least let the civilians *evacuate* before they'd blown the space station to dust bunnies. Delta Zulu had probably seen the fewest actual deaths of those battles.

"We both know the price is worth it," Petersen continued. "But to reassure you of our capabilities and good faith, three cargo containers have been delivered to the primary Tááła'í'tsin spaceport, storage hangar seventeen.

"They each contain eight basic q-com arrays sufficient for a low-resolution video call. They are yours, a sample."

Twenty-four q-coms would...vastly improve the Confederacy's communication network. It would let James link all twelve systems together and provide communications between key warships.

The bandwidth they were talking about was minimal. Each of those arrays would contain about a dozen entangled blocks, making the whole assembly barely one percent of what Petersen's people were selling.

"You have my attention," he conceded. "But I cannot risk taking myself to Meridian. I presume that this Trickster will be content with a call through said q-com blocks to close the deal?"

"Unfortunately, Trickster insists on closing all major deals in person," Petersen warned. "It is, in fact, a concession on their part that they are prepared to meet you on ground you control like the Meridian System."

The smuggler raised his fork with the last bit of his lasagna on it before James could argue.

"I am afraid, however, that meeting him in Meridian will not be an imposition for you. You will need to be there anyway."

"And why is that?" James asked. He couldn't think of any reason he'd be heading to Meridian soon.

"The other business we are in is intelligence, Admiral Tecumseh, and we hope to build a sufficient relationship with your new Confederacy to make a long-term arrangement between us," Petersen said. He swallowed the last of his pasta, laid his fork aside and reached into his suit jacket.

He froze with his fingers in the jacket. Reynolds' gun had almost magically materialized at his temple, the metal pressing hard into Petersen's flesh.

"It is a holoprojector, ma'am," he assured you. "You scanned me for weapons yourself. I am harmless, I assure you."

"Let him go, Reynolds," James ordered. "You have my attention, Mr. Petersen...but as you have seen, you *also* have Agent Reynolds' attention."

Petersen smiled brightly as Reynolds removed her gun. She was still well inside the man's personal space, but he seemed to be fine with that as he laid a palm-sized holoprojector on the table.

"As with the q-coms at the spaceport, this is on the order of a free sample," he told James. "But this is the New Edmonton System as of five hours ago."

Because, of course, the organized crime cartel that Petersen reported to *did* have q-coms. They had live information from the Stellar League—but as soon as the man had said *what* system the data was from, James could guess what he was being shown.

New Edmonton had been the back-and-forth battlespace of the war between the League and the Commonwealth. It had been the initial target of the reprisal campaign that had *started* the war—a response to the use of League fighters in a deep-strike raid on a Commonwealth research facility—and had seen at least three-quarters of the fighting.

And now, according to the hologram hanging above the untouched plates, it was host to a gathering of the Stellar League Navy at least sixteen warships strong.

"Dictator Periklos has brought his core fleet to New Edmonton, Admiral," Petersen said quietly. "He has decided that the humiliation you inflicted on his brother-in-law in the Persephone System cannot be allowed to stand if he wishes to maintain his control of the League.

"He does not wish to punish his new wife's brother too severely, but he risks fracturing the respect and fear that allows his hold on the League if he lets that defeat stand unopposed. So, he is gathering a force to take the Meridian Sector, Admiral, and if you wish to honor the promises you have made, you will need to travel to the Meridian System for reasons beyond meeting my employer."

10

Dakota System
05:30 February 8, 2738 ESMDT

ANTHONY YAMAMOTO KNEW what his role aboard *Krakatoa* was during the regular "rest stop" refits like this. It was mostly to do the paperwork around the fighter group and make sure his pilots were keeping up with their own duties and training.

A starfighter basically went through the process that *Krakatoa* was currently undergoing every week, if not every time they left the hangar. The refit-and-repair systems on the flight deck had been checked out at the start of the refit, with a few replacement parts installed, and then they'd been left to the Starfighter Corps Chiefs.

All of that meant that the supercarrier's flight deck was surprisingly quiet early in the ship's day as the Wing Colonel walked along the neatly arrayed rows of starfighters and starbombers. The *Volcano*-class ships had been designed to carry two hundred starfighters, but the arrival of the Longbow bombers had forced five of the twenty squadrons to convert.

Anthony didn't complain. The bombers' longer-ranged torpedoes didn't have the range of capital-ship missiles, but they *did* have the same electronic brains, making them terrifyingly efficient weapons— and they had more range than starfighter missiles.

He suspected that, given enough time, the starfighter missile itself would eventually become obsolete and the fighter and bomber would merge again into a new combatant with both a positron lance and a torpedo armament.

For now, though, his carrier groups needed to manage two types of fighters and two types of ammunition. His own preference was for the Katana, but a fighter strike against a capital ship in old-style starfighters was always a painful proposition.

An *effective* one, one that had turned the first war between the Commonwealth and the Alliance of Free Stars against the Terrans, but never without losses.

Quiet for a hangar deck was a relative thing, and Anthony stepped aside as a working party of techs started a test run of a weapons cart— one, thankfully, currently missing its antimatter-laden cargo.

"Sir!"

Turning away from the test run, Anthony looked up at the two men emerging from Primary Flight Control. Colonel Helvius Ó Cochláin had been the recipient of one of the dozens of promotions that had emerged from the transition to the Dakotan Confederacy, turning Anthony's red-haired senior subordinate into *Krakatoa's* replacement Commander, Air Group—an awkward role, when the *Fleet* Commander, Air Group was aboard the same carrier.

And that was before considering that First Fleet's CAG was *also* the Commanding Officer, Dakotan Confederacy Starfighter Corps. Anthony *needed* a commander for *Krakatoa's* group, even if it caused friction to have two senior officers on the carrier.

And the other man with Ó Cochláin could be trusted to make sure Anthony didn't micromanage *too* much. Command Master Chief Petty Officer Thales Brahms had found himself saddled with the distinction of being the fledgling DCSC's senior noncom—and *then* Anthony had hung as many stripes on the man as he could manage.

He had complete faith in Brahms to yank both him and Ó Cochláin up short if they were in any way undermining the effectiveness of *Krakatoa*'s strike group—and in Brahms to provide the voice of reason for the entire fledgling DCSC.

"What's going on?" Anthony asked the two men.

"Check the external sensor feed, sir," Brahms replied. "*Mediterranean* just emerged from FTL at minimum standard safe distance. She didn't push the limits hard, but she's only two light-minutes out and closing at full thrust."

Anthony linked to *Krakatoa* through his interface, pulling the feed into his own implants before the other man had finished speaking. To be a starfighter pilot required the ninety-ninth percentile of "bandwidth," the broadly defined ability to use a neural implant.

At the level of a starfighter pilot, a lot of data intake wasn't even conscious. He'd link to a system and just *know* what he was looking for.

In the case of a sensor feed, it was a bit complicated, but he didn't need a visual overlay to see what was going on. The *Ocean*-class strike cruiser had emerged far closer to Virginia than was generally considered safe when arriving at a gas giant, and that told Anthony all he really needed to know.

"Flight-deck status?" he barked at Brahms. "Anything that would hold *Krakatoa* up from immediate deployment?"

"We've got a few things opened up I wouldn't want to go into combat with," the noncom told him instantly. "Enough to hold us back from a full-deck strike. We'd get everybody up, but it would take longer than usual."

"*Fix that*," Anthony ordered. "Whatever it takes. The deck needs to be fully operational by the time *Mediterranean* tells us what's going on."

"Two hours to zero-zero," Ó Cochláin observed. "Plenty of time."

"Don't count on that," the Wing Colonel replied. "Expect worst-case scenario. I want this deck prepped for a full strike ASAP."

Ó Cochláin looked concerned for a moment, then swallowed. "And what *is* worst case in your mind, sir?" he asked.

"That we're about to make an emergency A-S microjump into Dakota orbit and engage Walkingstick's entire battle fleet."

———

"It's a recall order, of course," Commodore Young Volkov told her senior officers and the fleet CAG twenty minutes later.

The dark-skinned Korean-Russian Centauri native had pulled her XO, Patricia Jack, Colonel Ó Cochláin and Anthony himself into the breakout room attached to her office.

"The Admiral didn't include any details of why *Krakatoa* is needed," she continued. "We are ordered to close up everything that can be closed up over the next six hours. Then we are to proceed, in company with *Mediterranean*, back to Dakota orbit to resume our role as the Old Man's flagship."

"Well, at least the Commonwealth isn't *here*," Anthony said. "I was half-expecting to have to make a suicide run against Home Fleet."

"Not today, Wing Colonel," Volkov said with a soft chuckle. "Though that may still be on the list, depending on just why we're cutting our repairs short."

"Is it that bad?" he asked, glancing over at Captain Jack.

The irony of courtesy titles meant that Commodore Volkov was properly addressed as *Captain* aboard her ship—where Captain Jack was usually addressed as *Commodore*. The Confederacy Navy had kept the Commonwealth's rank structure, with the existing flaws.

They might change that eventually, but they needed time.

"No," Jack told him. "We've got a lot of pieces of our girl opened up to check over and clean out, but the only damage is already fixed. We can seal her up and have her online in those six hours. We won't get to everything I'd like to have checked and cleaned, but we've done a solid first pass."

"Good," Volkov said. "Because there's an interesting addition to these orders that I think you'll find…illuminating." She smiled. "Once we've made physical rendezvous with *Mediterranean* and Captain Werner's people have delivered a package for us, Wing Colonel Yamamoto and I have a scheduled videoconference with the Admiral."

That was impossible...unless...

"The Old Man got us some q-coms," Anthony realized aloud.

"That's not specified anywhere in our messages, but that's the only possibility I see," *Krakatoa's* Captain confirmed. "Currently expected to have the package aboard at oh eight hundred hours; our meeting is scheduled for oh eight thirty."

"Good thing none of us were asleep at oh six hundred ship's time," Ó Cochláin said. "Would have been a shock to wake up to."

In Anthony's experience, very few people made it past O-5 without *some* degree of professional insomnia. Plus, the advantage of being in space was that "day" was very dependent on your shift. Circadian rhythms were easy to manipulate when the only light was entirely controlled *and* all of the crew had computers in their brains.

"Go find yourselves some coffee," Volkov ordered. "Assuming we don't have an *impossible* order, I'll need you all at your best in a couple of hours.

"Sort out any component of the recall you need to handle, then meet back here at oh eight thirty hours."

―――――

The first thing Anthony realized when the virtual conference started was that the new q-coms *sucked*. Normally, he'd have expected to have a hologram of Admiral Tecumseh that could easily have been the man himself if not for legally mandated translucency.

Today, the holoprojector in Commodore Volkov's breakout room was being used in its oft-forgotten two-dimensional projection mode, putting a flat video feed on the wall of the meeting room.

It wasn't even particularly high-quality video—but it was the first long-distance live conversation feed Anthony had seen in months.

"Well, this is both new and very old," James Tecumseh told them. "But it's definitely a pleasure to be talking to people and not worrying about time delay!"

"How many of these do we have?" Volkov asked.

"Not enough, by any stretch, and you can see the limitations of the relatively small number of entangled blocks we have," he noted. "Also, while we are encrypting our communications on these communicators heavily, we cannot trust the security of these coms as much as we could if we controlled the switchboard.

"All of the coms we have received are running on the communications network for the Regalia System," Tecumseh continued. "We have enough coms for the flagships, the individual Confederacy systems and Base Łá'ts'áadah. *Mediterranean* has the parts aboard for Base Łá'ts'áadah as well, but she should have delivered them by now.

"We will also have ships setting off to all of the Dakota Sector systems to deliver communicators. That may take a few days, but we've got enough traffic inside the Sector to cover that. Within two weeks, we'll have FTL communications with most of the Confederacy."

"That'll be a hell of a relief," Anthony said. "And it'll help with reaction forces, too."

"What about the Meridian Sector?" Volkov asked. "My understanding was that we still had less inter-sector traffic than we might like."

"We'll be carrying the communicators for the Meridian Sector with us," Tecumseh told her. "We're deploying the fleet Clockward. We have new intelligence from the League."

The Admiral's image shrank into a corner of the video feed as a tactical data display replaced him.

"The same source that provided us with the communicators also gave us a look at their sensor data from the New Edmonton System as of yesterday morning," he explained as icons highlighted on the screen.

"While our source tells me that Dictator Periklos himself is in command of these ships, we have no way of verifying that." Tecumseh shook his head grimly. "To be fair, we have no way of verifying the sensor data to prove that there is a League fleet in New Edmonton, but it would fit with the psych profile we have of Periklos.

"I am meeting with the Cabinet after this to get their approval, but I want all of First Fleet in orbit of Dakota as soon as possible. From there, my intention is to move our entire force to Meridian and rendezvous with Admiral Modesitt and Meridian Fleet. If possible, we'll arrange for the Persephone detachment to rendezvous with us."

"In New Edmonton," Anthony concluded. It wasn't a question—they *couldn't* keep the fleet concentrated in one place, not with the Commonwealth on one side and the League on the other.

"Exactly. Hence the need for Cabinet approval, as I plan to engage Periklos's forces and neutralize the immediate League threat…one way or another. That could very easily turn our existing conflict with the League into an all-out war in the long run."

"And the Commonwealth?" Volkov asked.

"We have two threats in play, Commodore," Tecumseh replied. "Both could very easily justify the deployment of our entire navy in a single operational area, but we need to handle *both* of them. Finding that balance is key and something that our senior officers are going to be struggling with.

"For now, we *know* that Periklos has concentrated his fleet at New Edmonton and is most likely planning on moving against us. So, we move there and hope the Commonwealth gives us time."

"What if this is a Commonwealth operation?" Anthony asked as a terrifying thought struck him. "The Imperator could be using false intelligence to lure us out of position, allowing them to move against Dakota while our entire fleet is in the Meridian Sector."

"It is a possibility," Tecumseh conceded. "But the Commonwealth is just as short on quantum-entangled communicators as we are. I do not believe that they are likely to put up several dozen q-coms as bait for a trap—and we have validated all of the communicators as working.

"I am *hoping* to confirm the intelligence once we arrive in Meridian and before deploying into League space…but there are other factors that may come into play in Meridian to confirm the value of the source, if nothing else.

"For now, I'm keeping those factors under wraps. Once you've returned to Dakota, I will come aboard, and we will be leaving for Meridian almost immediately.

"Assuming, of course, that the Cabinet approves a first strike against the Stellar League."

That, Anthony realized, was almost guaranteed. Tecumseh might not have chosen to become the warlord in charge of the Confederacy, but the civilian government he was serving knew who the true father of the Confederacy was.

If James Tecumseh told the Cabinet they needed to take out Periklos's fleet, they weren't going to tell him he couldn't do it.

11

THE LAST THING James was expecting to see when he linked into the video call was an extreme close-up of a dog's tongue.

"Sherlock, down!" Abey ordered, but she was laughing at the dog as she did so. "I'm sorry, James, he decided to try to eat the pickup for some reason."

From James's perspective, it looked more like *licking* than *eating*—probably for the best—but the dog backed down as Abey gently pulled on his collar. Sherlock *then* noticed the image of James on the screen and tried to lick *that*.

"Sherlock!" Abey repeated, barely keeping from disintegrating into laughter as the dog finally pulled away from her desk. She spent a moment ruffling Sherlock's ears, and then the dog finally *somewhat* relaxed, settling onto the floor with his tail drumming.

"Sorry about that," she told him. "He *likes* you."

"I think that's a good sign?" James replied. Sherlock's antics were a cheerful reminder of what he was fighting for, one that brought a smile to his face. He could only half make out where the dog had settled down, but the adoring look Sherlock was giving Abey was still clear.

James definitely understood the urge to stare adoringly at Abey Todacheeney.

"If the dog likes you, yeah, that's probably good," she told him. "I have other reasons to think you're worth keeping, though. Even if you are about to charge off to the other side of the country."

"You knew what I was when you decided to seduce me," he pointed out. "Even then, I think you'd decided I wasn't going to be a warlord."

One of the things he'd discovered later was that Abey had at least partially pursued him with the intent of using their relationship to control him if he *did* decide to make himself overlord of the Dakota Sector. She'd stuck around after he'd made it clear that wasn't happening, though.

"I knew that long before I dragged you to bed," she told him. "I trusted you then. I trusted you when you asked to speak to the governance conference. I have yet to be wrong putting my faith, trust or love in you. Is that likely to change?"

"I hope not," he said. "I'm not charging off to Meridian without the Cabinet's approval, you know that."

"And *you* know that the Cabinet is almost certainly going to give you that approval. You have earned *our* trust, not just *my* trust. I haven't gone wrong trusting you yet, and I don't think the Confederacy is going to.

"Though *I* find myself wishing you'd spent more time on the surface while you were here!"

"I fear, Abey, that is going to be a recurring problem," he warned. "We are stuck between two powers that would very much like to consume us. I can't protect the Confederacy from your apartment."

"No, I know. And I can't serve Dakota as First Chief from your suite on *Krakatoa*." She shrugged and looked over at the dog. "So, we do what we must."

"And we do what we can." He checked the time. "Looks like we're out of time for the side conversation," he murmured. "I'm switching into the main conference."

————

Roughly two-thirds of the meetings of the Dakotan Cabinet were virtual. James was on the surface but buried in the datawork of getting First Fleet moving again, which made the virtual conference absolutely essential this time.

Switching from a video call to a full virtual conference resulted in his office vanishing into the illusion of the full cabinet meeting, thirteen politicians seated around a virtual table that duplicated the real one in the former Commonwealth Dakota Infrastructure Center.

They'd have a new name for the building eventually, James assumed, but it hadn't been high on anyone's priority list.

"Admiral," Chapulin greeted him. "You asked for this meeting, and we all know roughly what it's about."

"I did," he confirmed. "Some of what we are discussing is going to need to be classified at the highest levels. Not even your staffs should be briefed on the details of where we learned this intelligence."

That got him the full attention of the politicians on the call. He'd rarely asked them to keep secrets—and most of those had been around Base Łá'ts'áadah and the shipbuilding program.

"I think we can all agree to that, yes?" the interim President told him, glancing around the Ministers. No one raised an objection, so she gestured for James to continue.

"By now, you all know we have received a small number of low-quality quantum communicators that we are distributing," James said. "You also have been briefed on the information we have on the forward deployment of the Stellar League Navy to the New Edmonton System."

He waited to see if anyone had a comment on that. Only silence answered him, so he smiled and continued.

"I was contacted by a member of an arms-smuggling ring," he told the Cabinet. "One that has, apparently, traditionally operated by providing Commonwealth and League fighters and weapons to anyone who can afford to pay.

"They have offered to sell us a significant quantity of q-com entangled blocks, including q-com-enabled sensor probes. The latter are absolutely essential for fighting anything resembling a modern war.

"The cost is...high," he admitted. "I still have access to certain Commonwealth assets and accounts that I intend to use to cover it, but that will be the *last* resources of the Dakota Sector Fleet. All further costs of the DCN will need to be directly funded by the Confederacy."

Plans had already been made for that transition, or he would have hesitated to pay Trickster's price.

"They have asked that I meet their primary agent in the Meridian System to complete the transaction," he told the Cabinet. "They *also* provided the intelligence on the New Edmonton System."

That recording now appeared in the middle of the virtual conference.

"With the replenishment of our fighter strength from Dakota's volunteers and factories, plus the addition of *Saint Bartholomew* to my order of battle, I believe that the DCN *does* have the force necessary to engage and neutralize the fleet that Periklos has moved to our border."

He spread his hands.

"But that engagement will be a risk," he warned. "I will need to concentrate all seventeen of our ships in one place, carrying extra fighters and other munitions aboard *Lakewater* to make certain that the Meridian Fleet is fully operational."

And the availability of the ex-pirate freighter would make his life a *lot* easier.

"That will leave both sectors of the Confederacy uncovered while I launch our strike—*and* that strike needs to be a preemptive one, allowing us no opportunity to negotiate with Periklos before engaging in open conflict with the Stellar League."

"We are already at war with the League," Chō said grimly. "We may no longer be part of the Commonwealth, but Periklos conquered Persephone and *shot* a tenth of their Parliament."

James's gaze was unavoidably drawn to Chaza'el Papadimitriou—who *was* a Member of Parliament for Persephone and had *been there* when Star Admiral Borgogni had literally decimated the planetary parliament.

"Persephone would be...concerned if the Confederacy assumed we were at peace with the League without some formal commitment to that effect," Papadimitriou said slowly. "With the League's actions on our world, *we* certainly regard ourselves as at war."

"And the rest of the Confederacy stands with Persephone on that," Patience Abiodun confirmed. Arroyo might be closest to Sol, but that meant they were farthest from the League.

Abiodun's support for Persephone was important—but James also knew what her next question would be.

"There is no question that we must secure our Clockward border against the League," she continued. "But we also just sent a declaration of independence to Sol, one that will be seen as a challenge to the authority of the Star Chamber.

"Do we risk rushing to challenge one enemy only to be hit from behind by the other?"

James raised a hand to forestall any comment from the rest of the Cabinet.

"Minister Abiodun raises a critical concern," he told them. "And has her finger on the key fundamental weakness of our situation. We have seventeen capital ships. Those are all the capital ships we are going to have for a long time.

"Both the Commonwealth and the League are easily capable of matching our fleet in hulls and cubage—the Commonwealth more so than the League, despite all of the new limitations of our former nation.

"But. The *League* has q-coms. The Commonwealth does not—and will continue to assume *we* do not until proven wrong. Distributing our current q-coms will provide us with a barebones-but-*present* communication-and-warning system, allowing us to move the fleet to the most likely risk zones."

A map of the Confederacy and the surrounding stars replaced the image of the New Edmonton System and the known fleet.

"It will take approximately twelve days for First Fleet to reach Meridian," he reminded them. "There, we will need to coordinate with

Admiral Modesitt and make contact with the arms smuggler to arrange delivery.

"From there, nine days to New Edmonton. *Hopefully*, we will be able to make contact with the ships we left in Persephone and have them rendezvous with us at New Edmonton, but that isn't guaranteed."

He'd *want* those ships for that fight, but time was a factor. Their two hundred starfighters might be critical—but not having a fleet in the Dakota Sector could easily be *more* critical.

"Once the situation with Periklos is...resolved, we will immediately make our course back here. We will, at that point, have at least minimal q-coms with every system in the Confederacy. We can be warned of any threat and deploy based on that information.

"The full round trip from here to Meridian to New Edmonton and back will take approximately thirty-six to forty days, depending on how long we're in each system," he concluded. "The round trip from here to Sol is forty days. Our courier freighter left four days ago.

"Even if Walkingstick reacted *immediately*, we have those thirty-six days. And, truthfully, I do not expect the Imperator to immediately respond with violence."

Logistics, if nothing else, would limit the Imperator's response. The datawork keeping James trapped in his planetside office was proof of how difficult it was to get even a relatively *ready* fleet to move on short notice.

Plus, they *were* sending diplomats and negotiators. He had to believe—had to *hope*—that his old commander would at least *listen* to the delegation. There were conversations to be had, potential treaty offers to be made.

He hoped that they could come to a peaceful separation. He *expected* a war—but he didn't expect Walkingstick to have a fleet in motion within hours of *Paradise by Twilight*'s arrival.

"If only we had waited long enough to have a q-com for *Paradise*," Chapulin said. "But we are limited by the realities of what we have already done.

"The timing *should* be safe. We cannot predict if the Imperator will move before our message arrives, but we also cannot leave our frontier with the League undefended while they prepare an invasion fleet.

"I believe we have no choice but to confirm the Admiral's plan and authorize him to do whatever is necessary to defeat the League."

"Agreed," Chō said instantly. "We must, if at all possible, *end* the League threat so that we can focus on the Imperator and the rump Commonwealth."

That took James a moment to process, until his implant threw up the Rump Parliament of Cromwell's England as an example. The *rump* was, well, a rather crude way to refer to the remnant of the Commonwealth. And *crude* worked just fine for James.

"We are exposing ourselves," Abiodun warned. "But...I see no alternative. Not without far more ships than we can conjure from thin air."

"Once we have FTL communications across the Confederacy, concentrating the DCN into a single nodal force makes the most sense," James told them. "Especially if we can get the guardships we have previously discussed into production and have a decent chance of the member systems being able to hold off an aggressor for several days."

"That is our next step," Chapulin agreed. "Do I need to put this to vote? Do we have any objections to the Admiral's deployment plan?"

James—and the President—took the silence as approval.

12

LIKE KRAKATOA, *Saint Bartholomew* was a powerful modern warship, over sixty million cubic meters in volume and a full kilometer in length. With thirty missile launchers and twenty-four megaton-and-a-half-per-second heavy positron lances, she was probably one of the most powerful direct-fire combatants in the galaxy.

For all her power and the necessity of using her, she was a dark reminder to James Tecumseh as he left the shuttle. *Bartholomew* had arrived in Dakota carrying the Lictor Michael Hardison. Where the Lictors had traditionally been the security officers of the Star Chamber, Walkingstick had fallen back on the old Roman usage of them as personal messengers and representatives.

The ex-CISS Hardison had been the man to deliver Walkingstick's orders to turn the Dakota sector into a tributary structure, with its entire economy and population dedicated solely to the production of new warships for the Terran Commonwealth. And given the skillset of

CISS agents like his new bodyguard, Hardison had almost certainly been authorized, if not necessarily ordered, to kill James if he disagreed.

Instead, Shannon Reynolds had killed Hardison, and Marines from *Krakatoa* had stormed *Saint Bartholomew*. James had chosen the Marine force carefully—only officers and troopers from his flagship—to avoid straining too many loyalties.

Given the number of complaints he'd received from other Marines since about *not* including them in the assault, he apparently hadn't needed to worry.

But while *Bartholomew* was back in operation with a crew mostly drawn from First Fleet's other ships, backed up by volunteers from the system defense forces and Dakota's civilian shipping, taking possession of her hadn't been *clean*.

Standing on the bare metal of her shuttlebay deck, he returned Commodore Arjun Ferreiro's salute crisply, but his gaze was drawn inexorably to the discoloration on the bulkheads behind him. The new crew had scrubbed away blood and debris, but the color change from plasma fire never went away.

"Welcome aboard, Admiral," Ferreiro told him. The tanned Mediterranean officer looked exhausted. "It's been a busy few weeks, sir, but I promise you that *Saint Bartholomew* is fully online and operational."

"Any surprises in her systems?" James asked, gesturing for the Commodore to fall in beside him. He and his staff wouldn't be on *Bartholomew* for long—they were rendezvousing with *Krakatoa* in six hours when the carrier came out of her jump from Base Łá'ts'áadah, and James and his people would return to the carrier.

But there was no purpose in having *Krakatoa* make the six-hour transit in from the edge of the gravity limit to Dakota, or for having the carrier take the risk of emerging closer in. The rest of First Fleet, plus their new logistics support ship, were also heading out of the system, after all.

"A few ugly ones, yeah," the battleship's new CO conceded. "Thanks to Commodore Bevan, we got them all secured away."

"Rear Admiral Bevan," James corrected with a smile. "I threw a pile of stars at my staff and told them to sort it out."

A couple of them had technically jumped two grades to make Rear Admiral, and James did *not* care. His staff were now all two-star admirals, and given the likely needs of the Confederacy going forward, he doubted he'd be keeping them all on his staff for long.

Rear Admiral Ove Bevan, for example, was now the effective head of Naval Intelligence for the Confederacy. Among his tasks had been analyzing the dump of data and security codes from the Marshal's mace sent to James to make certain that their ships were secured against somebody *else* with those codes.

They had, after all, stripped the data from the thing before they'd cut it in half and made matching paperweights.

"We figured it was easier to just make everyone the same rank," Rear Admiral Madona Voclain added, falling in on the other side of James as the Admiral strode toward what his neural implant told him was a conference room set aside for his staff to rest.

"Except Yamamoto, of course."

James concealed a smirk. He didn't expect the Scots-Japanese man to be anticipating the triple-star insignia of a *Vice* Admiral that was accompanying First Fleet's staff to *Krakatoa*.

Yamamoto and Jessie Modesitt were going to be James's right and left hands as he tried to keep the Confederacy safe—and if *he* was going to be a full Admiral, then he was going to make them Vice Admirals so they could keep up.

"We have time to go over some of the details and concepts while we're in Captain Ferreiro's waiting room," James told his staff. "You're welcome to join us, Arjun. I may not be using *Bartholomew* as a flagship, but she's still the second-most-powerful combat unit of the DCN."

And even if James Tecumseh agreed with the logic that had seen the Castle Federation decide not to even *build* a generation of eighty-million-cubic-meter battleships, well...four of his warships were battleships and he was damn well going to *use* them.

———

"There are eight q-com arrays in the shuttles," Rear Admiral Sumiko Mac Cléirich told the rest of the staff as they settled into the meeting room. The table that likely usually filled the space had been removed, replaced with a set of comfortable chairs.

They were waiting more than working today, after all, though James was watching First Fleet set off through his implant.

"One for each system in the Meridian Sector, one for Meridian Fleet, and one spare," he reminded the rest. "For the moment, we're going to rig the spare up on *Saint Bartholomew*. Having our most powerful units all on the q-com link makes sense."

"I'll have my people take a look once Admiral Mac Cléirich releases it to us," Ferreiro promised. "I look forward to having *some* communications again."

"We're hoping to get more in Meridian, but the details of that remain classified," James told the Commodore. "There's a lot of moving parts, but the ops plan is relatively straightforward.

"We go to Meridian and pick up Admiral Modesitt and Meridian Fleet. With q-coms in place, I'm more willing to keep the DCN concentrated as a single fleet. We'll still be missing *Champion* and *Goldwyn*, though I plan on sending a message to them along with Persephone's q-com array.

"That said, the timing isn't right, and Persephone needs those ships and their ex-League starfighters to be safe."

Star Admiral Borgogni had fled the Persephone System without even bothering to pick up the starfighters he'd deployed. The crews had volunteered to join the system defense force, operating off the two *Paramount*-class carriers James had left behind.

They'd now be members of the Dakota Confederacy Starfighter Corps. They'd been trustworthy so far, but James was a bit relieved *not* to be taking them into an offensive action against the League itself.

"Our information on the current status of the League fleet is, of course, trash," James warned his people. "We will emerge into New Edmonton behind McMurray and use the gas giant as a shield against their sensors while we attempt to update our data."

That was a trick he'd learned from the Castle Federation's Kyle

Roberts in the war—when the so-called Stellar Fox had used it *against* him.

"My understanding is that the League fleet is going to have a material advantage in hulls and firepower over us," he admitted. "Taking them by surprise is our only possibility of winning this battle.

"I don't like it, but the Cabinet has authorized it, and I don't see an alternative."

"Surprise is a legitimate tactic, sir," Voclain reminded him. "Periklos wouldn't hesitate to ambush *us*, given the chance."

"That isn't the problem," James said mildly. "The problem is that I don't want to fight the League at all. Even if we crush them from ambush, a lot of people are going to die and we're going to lose ships, crews and starfighters we can't afford. Not with the Imperator breathing down our necks from the other side. If we could talk to Periklos, I'd like to think we could come to an agreement.

"But I can't *talk* to the League's Dictator without giving up the only thing that gives us a chance of winning against him."

James shook his head.

"So, we knife them in the back while they're not looking and hope enough of us come back to protect the Confederacy from the Commonwealth," he concluded. "But I won't pretend I like it. There are too many risks."

And if he gambled wrong, he'd lose the entire Confederacy.

13

ANTHONY WATCHED the shuttles make their way onto *Krakatoa's* flight deck in an orderly fashion. He knew which one *officially* held the Admiral and Tecumseh's staff, but he knew Shannon Reynolds would have changed that at the last minute.

He was unsurprised when the shuttle that was *supposed* to hold Admiral Tecumseh began to offload containers of the new uniforms. *Krakatoa* would be the last ship of First Fleet to make the full transition, though the Engineering department had fabricated the new force designators within hours of hearing about them.

For the moment, Anthony, like the rest of the carrier's crew, wore the Engineering-fabricated version of an eagle pin on his existing purple lapels. He would swap to the new jacket with its dark indigo lapel and eagles by morning, if the ship's stewards were half as good as he figured they were.

But his main role was to meet the commanding officer of the Dakotan Confederacy Navy, standing alongside *Krakatoa*'s Captain.

The two of them were the entirety of the welcoming committee. The rest of the people on the flight deck in the middle of ship's night were dealing with the cargo shuttles and reorganizing the new personnel inevitably coming aboard.

"Wasn't Tecumseh supposed to be on the fourth shuttle?" Volkov asked.

"You've met his new bodyguard," Anthony pointed out. "You know her. Are you surprised?"

"I don't know her as well as you," the Commodore said drily, "but I get your point."

Anthony concealed a smirk. He had no interest in relationships. His brain just wasn't wired that way and Reynolds was wired similarly. That had been convenient and enjoyable, especially as his new exalted rank raised questions over whether it was appropriate for him to sleep his way through the Navy and Marine officers aboard *Krakatoa* the way he'd used to.

Reynolds had no such restrictions, but the whole *point* was that they had no claim on each other beyond friendship and convenience.

"Ninth shuttle," he guessed. "Five bucks."

The Admiral's staff had been supposed to be on the fourth shuttle, and two more had landed since.

"Eleven," Volkov said after a moment. "And no, Flight Control doesn't know which one has him either. I checked."

"So did I," Anthony conceded. Two more shuttles off-loaded with no sign of the DCN's commander—but the ninth shuttle *also* lacked the Admiral.

It was the tenth shuttle that finally discharged Marines in clamshell body armor with a coyote emblazoned on the front, followed by a petite blonde woman who *everyone* knew was probably more dangerous than the Marines.

The tall and dark-skinned Shawnee man who followed Shannon Reynolds off the shuttle wasn't as *personally* deadly as the Marines or the assassin. Anthony wasn't sure he'd be so foolish as to say that James Tecumseh wasn't *dangerous*, though.

"Split the difference, guess neither of us wins," Volkov told him.

"Shame, five bucks buys a nice latte in the Base Łá'ts'áadah commissary," the pilot replied. "But I guess we won't have access to that anytime soon."

"Unlikely," Volkov agreed, then saluted crisply at the Admiral and his tail of bestarred staffers.

Anthony followed suit. There weren't many people starfighter pilots saluted carefully to—but Tecumseh had earned that in the eyes of Anthony's people...and that meant *Anthony* would give the Admiral a proper salute, no matter what.

"Commodore, Wing Colonel," Tecumseh greeted them. "I understand the new uniforms only came aboard with us, and yet you seem... decorated already."

"Don't go into Marine Country without earplugs," Volkov warned. "They found a bunch of videos of old Earth coyotes and are practicing *yipping.*"

"I..." The Admiral paused. "Am I correct in guessing that the *instigators* of this have met Federation Marines? If you've heard those bastards *howl* once..."

"I have not," the Captain admitted.

"I have," Tecumseh replied. "And even though they were on *my* side that day, it's not a memory I'll soon forget."

"The yipping will probably become just as memorable, given time," Anthony promised. "I know my people are thinking about open broadcasts of recordings, too."

"I see we are determined to lean as far into Dakota's Old Nation roots as we possibly can. Promise me no one is going to try to steal horses?"

That had been a Crow tradition, according to Anthony's research—because, yes, his people *had* been digging into the traditions of their new home and the Admiral's people—though other tribes shared it. It was one of the four acts to become a war chief: touch an enemy without killing them, take an enemy's weapon, lead a successful war party, and steal an enemy's horse.

"I think we might stick to stealing starships," Anthony replied. "Which I have to note, sir, *you* have done."

In fact, by Anthony's count, if he was generous with the definitions of "horse" and "weapon," then *touch an enemy without killing them* was the only aspect Tecumseh hadn't achieved. Though...the Admiral had probably shaken Rutherford's hand when they *hadn't* known the rogue Commonwealth Admiral was an enemy.

"Behave, *Admiral*," Tecumseh told him drily.

The title didn't register for several seconds, but Reynolds had clearly been briefed on the Admiral's plan. Anthony didn't even *see* the woman move around behind him until his uniform jacket was suddenly sliding off his shoulders to be replaced by an entirely new garment.

He was expecting the new indigo lapels, much darker than the purple of the Commonwealth Starfighter Corps. He'd been expecting the indigo shoulder boards, with the inner half dedicated to the eagle of the new Dakotan Starfighter Corps.

But the sleeve stripes were wrong and the shoulder boards held the three stars of a Vice Admiral—a rank the TCSC had never even *had*. To reach Vice Admiral in Commonwealth service, he'd have been transferred to the Navy and run through intensive college training on ship deployments—because the only time a starfighter corps officer made O-9 was by becoming a carrier-group commander.

And while the TCSC might have owned the flight decks and would often deploy a fleet CAG, the Commonwealth Navy had been *very* clear on who owned the carriers themselves.

"This...this..." He trailed off and shook his head. "This better not come with a desk, sir."

"Not today, Vice Admiral Yamamoto," Tecumseh told him. "The Cabinet and I agreed that it was inappropriate for the commanding officer of our entire starfighter corps to be a mere Wing Colonel. Admiral Modesitt will join you as the Confederacy's second Vice Admiral when we arrive in Meridian, but you've been doing the work of running the Corps without the proper rank for too long.

"Congratulations."

"Thank you, sir." Anthony swallowed, considering the scope of the responsibility the stars came with. He knew he'd already been doing the job, but part of his brain had assumed it was on an "until we find someone better" basis.

But with three stars on his shoulders, that concept shriveled and died.

"We have work to do," Tecumseh told him. "But you already knew that."

The Admiral turned to Volkov.

"I'm afraid I don't have more stars for you yet, Commodore," he told her softly. "If I promoted everyone who'd earned it, we'd have a thousand admirals and no starship captains."

"I am content to remain your flag captain, sir, for the moment at least," Volkov said with a chuckle. "From what I can tell, any stars you give me would *have* to come with a desk—and I'm going to hang on to *Krakatoa*'s bridge until you drag me out of her with crowbars!"

———

One of the advantages of the supercarrier, from Anthony's perspective as fleet CAG, was that the ship had been built to be a flagship for fleets that were heavily, if not predominantly, carrier-focused. The Commonwealth hadn't moved to quite the "every ship has starfighters" doctrine of their former enemies in the Castle Federation, but there were enough of the parasite spacecraft to require central control.

The doctrine behind the *Volcano*-class carriers hadn't gone so far as to provide the fleet CAG with a separate flag deck of their own, but the main flag deck was equipped with a dedicated flight-control center section that the starfighter officers could easily turn into an operating zone for the fleet CAG.

Anthony still felt that his place was in a fighter or, if absolutely necessary, a bomber. But he couldn't justify that outside of the direst of circumstances, beyond just enough hours to stay qualified and keep him sane.

As First Fleet formed up for the jump to FTL, all of the fighters had been recalled anyway. He joined the Admiral on the flag deck, intentionally ignoring his own people's surprised look at his new rank, and sank his mind into the tactical net.

"All fighters have been recalled," he informed Tecumseh a moment later. "First Fleet fighters are prepared for jump."

"First Fleet ships are reporting in," Sumiko Mac Cléirich reported calmly, with no sign that the fleet staff officers had taken their stations mere minutes before after six hours aboard another ship and half an hour in a shuttlecraft.

"We have confirmed q-com links with *Saint Bartholomew*, Dakota and Base Łá'ts'áadah via the Regalia network," she continued. "End-to-end encryption is online with the new protocols. I still recommend direct radio contact for most classified communiques."

"As much as possible," Admiral Tecumseh told her. "But we have to be realistic."

"Of course, sir."

"All ships are green," Madona Voclain reported, the chief of staff just as calm as the coms officer. "Gravity levels are low; all ships are ready to activate Stetson stabilization fields."

"Course is set for Meridian?" Tecumseh asked.

"Confirmed and locked on all ships," Voclain confirmed.

"You have the call, Rear Admiral," First Fleet's commander ordered.

Anthony, for his part, was taking advantage of the final opportunity to get an update on his squadrons on the other ships. *Krakatoa* might have two hundred of his five hundred and thirty spacecraft, but that still left thirty-three squadrons of starfighters and starbombers on the other ships of First Fleet.

He missed the Stetson stabilization fields going up, but *no one* was blind enough to miss the effect of the Class One mass manipulators activating. Only the Stetson fields stopped the artificial mass singularities from tearing the fleet apart, and for a moment, ten starships held forty singularities in a carefully maintained balance.

Then the singularities converged and the outside universe disintegrated into the gray shift of the Alcubierre-Stetson drive.

"We are en route," Voclain confirmed.

"Direct coms with all ships lost," Mac Cléirich reported. "Q-com links holding."

"I didn't expect Regalia's links to somehow fail," the Admiral said drily. "Get some rest, everybody. Eleven days, nine hours to Meridian."

Anthony knew that the battle wasn't going to come until after that, when they took the combined fleets into New Edmonton—but the *work* would begin in Meridian as he tried to forge two fleets' worth of fighter squadrons, a third of the personnel volunteers and new recruits into a unified force that could deliver the Admiral victory.

14

ANTHONY WAS able to leave the day-to-day operations of *Krakatoa's* flight group to Colonel Ó Cochláin, but that only made his own data-work come within the realm of *possible*. They weren't getting a lot of information from the rest of the Confederacy yet, but he was getting enough to create work.

His main task was reviewing the status reports of the squadrons aboard First Fleet. Forty-eight ten-ship squadrons, each fighter and bomber taking a crew of three, left a *lot* of personnel and maintenance records.

He didn't need to go over each individual officer's situation, thank-fully. He had status reports from the squadron commanders and the Chief Petty Officers responsible for their maintenance. Plus the commanders of the forty-or-as-many-as-the-ship-holds plane flight groups. Plus the full carrier strike-group commanders from the carriers and strike cruisers.

Forty-eight squadron commanders, all Majors. Twelve flight group commanders, all Lieutenant Colonels. Three strike-group commanders, senior Lieutenant Colonels on the strike cruisers, with the full Colonel Ó Cochláin aboard *Krakatoa*.

Sixty-three officers. And basically every officer came with an attached Chief or Senior Chief Petty Officer who had also submitted reports. Anthony had the high neural-interface bandwidth necessary to be a fighter pilot and could process entire pages of text in a moment— but *so did the people writing the reports*.

If someone without a fighter pilot's bandwidth had been handed the hundred and forty reports Anthony was reviewing, just *reading* them would have been the work of a few days. As it was, he'd spent an hour in his office and gone through the reports from all four cruisers.

He was looking at the list of twenty files in his implant for *Arctic*'s fighter group when the admittance chime sounded.

"Enter," he ordered. He had a mental bet with himself as to who the arrival was—and would have won, as Shannon Reynolds slipped through his door with catlike grace.

"Admiral," she greeted him. "It seems congratulations are in order."

"You knew that was coming before I did," he pointed out with a chuckle. "I'm surprised to see you letting Tecumseh out of your sight, though."

"I can only watch the Admiral so much, and he's *probably* safest here," she said, then sighed. "I hope. My coyote pups are mostly up to the job these days, though I had to leave too many of them behind on Dakota to watch Todacheeney and the President."

Anthony chuckled.

"And I see we prioritize the Old Man's girlfriend over the President of the Confederacy," he said. "And I haven't heard them called 'coyote pups' yet."

"Our Marines want to be the Confederacy's coyotes. Since I'm training them to be VIP protection, they're just pups to me." She grinned. "So, they're my coyote pups. I'm getting another platoon's worth tomorrow, but for now, I'm trusting the squad I hung on to to keep an eye on the Admiral."

"I see staying on Dakota while we refitted wasn't a vacation. Not that the refit was as busy for me as for others...but it wasn't quiet."

Eventually, Anthony would have q-coms with every fighter formation in the Confederacy, and *then* he would actually need a staff to help run the new Starfighter Corps. Until then, he was limited in how much he *could* do and was, mostly, able to keep on top of the Corps's needs on his own.

"So far, the biggest problem I've had is arms smugglers circumventing my carefully arranged schedules to get a meeting with the Admiral," she observed. "That and being far too busy to take advantage of Dakota's supply of *spectacularly* gorgeous young men and women."

She took a seat on his desk and grinned down at him. Anthony couldn't help but return the lascivious expression. Neither of them were wired for romance but both of them *were* wired for high sex drives, which was a problem in a military environment.

Before he could say anything else, she handed him a small scrap of distinctly recognizable fabric.

"Now, just *how* busy are you at this moment?" she purred.

———

They eventually relocated to Anthony's quarters, his pang of guilt over neglecting his work smothered first by Shannon Reynolds and then by the fact that they were in FTL. Nothing he was going through was immediately urgent.

He *needed* to know the status of his squadrons, but a few hours' delay wouldn't make any difference when they were still eleven days from their destination. Any arguments he made were excuses, but he also wasn't *actually* neglecting anything.

And the assassin-turned-bodyguard made some *very* compelling and acrobatic arguments, until the pair eventually found themselves naked on the couch in his quarters, splitting a pot of Scottish-style tea —black and brewed to death.

"This is starting to become a habit," Anthony finally noted. "I know we're both...wired one way, but I still wanted to check in and make sure *you* didn't think this was becoming something."

Reynolds chuckled and patted his thigh.

"You're convenient, fun in bed, sensible and *get* where I'm coming from," she told him. "And I, hopefully, fall into much the same categories for you. If this is a *relationship*, it's at best somewhere between friends with benefits and one so open, we forgot to install doors."

"We're on the same page, then," he said. "I was assuming 'friends with benefits,' but god knows rank and authority limit my ability to sleep around the way I'd prefer."

Despite the unfortunate circumstance with his last flight engineer and them making a pass at him, he knew better than to sleep with subordinates. He was *also* very clear with his partners about what was on the table.

It avoided complications in the future. It wasn't *perfect*—not everyone really understood what *aromantic* meant—but it had avoided problems through his career.

"Keeping Tecumseh alive is now my priority," Reynolds murmured. "We're on the same page there, too, I think. Without the Old Man...I don't know how long this Confederacy will survive."

"Give him time and he'll fix that, I think. Good leaders don't build organizations that need them to last."

"True enough, but these aren't ordinary times. My job is to make sure he lives long enough to build that organization." She pulled on a strand of her hair. "I need to stay sane in the process. Well, as sane as I am to begin with."

Anthony wasn't touching that with a stick. Shannon Reynolds was an attractive package and had become a friend, but she was *also* an assassin who'd been sworn to the service of the Commonwealth above all else—including such niceties as human life.

She'd chosen the ideals of the Commonwealth over its form, much as Anthony and Tecumseh had.

But she'd come to Anthony originally because she believed he would be loyal to the Commonwealth over Tecumseh—and, at least initially, she would have been right. Imperator Walkingstick had betrayed the Commonwealth Anthony Yamamoto had sworn to serve.

And now he couldn't go home. Not to the Scotland and highlands he loved. He'd made his choice, but he hadn't necessarily made his peace with it.

But *he* hadn't used the Commonwealth and its ideals as a substitute conscience—and he knew perfectly well that Shannon Reynolds had.

"How are you holding up?" he finally asked.

"The advantage of arguably being a sociopath is that I don't really suffer from guilt or second thoughts," she told him drily. "But...*fuck*, this was...big."

"Whatever happens, you know I am your friend, yes?" he said softly.

"Be careful what you commit to, Vice Admiral," she warned. "I've been called a lot of unpleasant things in my life, and many of them are true."

"You are an assassin, potentially a sociopath, broken in multiple key ways and loyal to the same cause I am," Anthony told her. "The Commonwealth we once served shaped you into a living weapon to enforce their will, but you chose another path.

"Shannon, *I know what you are.*" He let that sink in as he met her gaze. "And I am your friend. With benefits, yes, but your friend."

"Huh." She was silent for a few seconds, studying his face like she was looking for a trap. "Been a while since I had a friend I really trusted, you know. Allies, superiors, assets, informants...but not really *friends.*"

"Well, you've got me. And between me and the Old Man, we'll take care of you," he said. "You're not going to be alone again, Shannon."

She made an undignified sniffling noise, then shook herself.

"Okay, that is all very appreciated," she told him. "But I think I need more of those friendship benefits now."

15

By the time First Fleet reached Meridian, James Tecumseh was in live contact with over half of the Confederacy. Every system in the Dakota Sector had received a q-com. The Meridian Sector coms were aboard *Saint Bartholomew* and would be distributed from Meridian itself. They would take longer, but he already had far better coms than he'd had before.

Compared to the level of information flow and communication he'd been used to prior to the destruction of the Commonwealth's network, it was *nothing*. But it was enough for him to stay up to date and to know that the central government and the planetary governments were now talking to each other regularly.

He also knew that Arroyo's plebiscite had taken place while First Fleet was in Alcubierre drive—and an overwhelming supermajority of the population had voted for the Confederacy. That had been the only system anyone had truly worried about, but Governor Hoxha, Abiodun's boss, now had the clear will of the people behind her.

That meant that all twelve systems of the Confederacy were committed. A few referendums were still pending, but every result had been overwhelming. Unfortunately, James was grimly certain that even the *interim* memberships that hadn't been finalized yet would be enough to damn the systems in the eyes of the Commonwealth.

Or at least the Imperator. Walkingstick was not, in James's experience, one to suffer fools or defiance. The next few weeks and months were a danger zone, one where the Imperator's desires might well overwhelm his good sense and logistics, drawing the rump Commonwealth into an overextension that would hurt both the Confederacy *and* the Commonwealth.

"We have the Meridian Fleet on sensors," his operations officer, Wardell Carey, reported. The newly promoted Rear Admiral felt too young for his stars to James, but there was a lot of that going around.

"We're about four hours from Greenwich orbit," Carey continued, flagging the habitable planet on the displays. "Should we make preparations to head out again immediately?"

That was a good question. In theory, James should combine the fleets and head for New Edmonton *immediately*. He could even make an argument for not taking First Fleet into Greenwich orbit at all.

Of course, it would take at least two days to get the Meridian Fleet moving. Modesitt was a good officer, but the fleet would have been ready to defend the system, not deploy for a counteroffensive.

Plus, James was supposed to meet Trickster somewhere in Meridian, and he didn't know where. The arms dealer had control of this part of the deal, and that meant James had to make himself available.

"We'll keep the fleet ready to depart on minimum notice," he ordered. "But we'll hold off on plans until I've touched base with Modesitt in person."

He forced a smile, shoving aside the thousand and one issues currently in play.

"If nothing else, I have a new uniform for her with some extra stars."

Jessie Modesitt and James Tecumseh went back a long way, to the disastrous covert operation in the systems Rimward of the Alliance of Free Stars. She'd backed his play then—and, when given the choice in Persephone between believing him or her current commander, had mutinied against a Marshal of the Commonwealth.

There was little sign of any of that in the soft-faced dark-haired woman who looked at least twenty years younger than she actually was. She wore the uniform of a Commonwealth Rear Admiral, sans only the red sash, like she'd been born to it, and greeted James with a two-handed shake that took his hands in both of hers.

"It's damn good to see you, sir," she told him. "Though I'll admit I would have preferred *some* hint that I was following you into treason before you left for Dakota!"

"I didn't know then," he admitted. "But here we are."

"Here we are indeed. Alric is on the surface, babysitting the President as usual," she continued. "Not that President Downer actually *needs* watching or security, but it makes him happier to have a Lieutenant General around watching his back."

Arie Downer was the elderly Jewish politician who *had* been Meridian's Vice President, until Marshal Rutherford's plans had seen the planetary President murdered. Shannon Reynolds had rescued Downer from a cell, and apparently the man was relying on Confederacy Marines as a security blanket.

Given how thoroughly Downer had moved to reestablish order and then to support the new Confederacy, James wasn't going to begrudge him a Marine flag officer, even if that kept Modesitt and her partner, Lieutenant General Alric Barbados, mostly out of each other's beds.

"I'm sorry you two have to be apart so much," he murmured. "I know it's hard when you're in the same system."

"It's life in uniform and we knew the joke before we signed up," she admitted. "I'll admit I'm a bit surprised to see the entirety of First Fleet show up on my doorstep. *Relieved*, given some of the information I have, but I wasn't expecting you."

"There's a reason for that—and I'll want to see that information." If

Modesitt had information on what the League was doing, he'd trust that a *lot* more than information from criminals who wanted to sell him things.

"Of course."

She looked past him at the containers being off-loaded from the other shuttles—and at the garment bag that Rear Admiral Voclain was holding.

"You appear to come bearing gifts," Modesitt noted cautiously.

"New uniform for the Dakotan Confederacy Navy," James told her. "Madona, the Admiral's new jacket, please."

With Yamamoto, he'd been able to use Reynolds to half-ambush the man. But that had been aboard a ship where he had the full cooperation of the crew and flight deck staff. While *Saratoga* had been James's flagship once, she was Modesitt's flagship *now*, and he wasn't going to lean on her people to surprise her.

Still, Modesitt played along willingly enough, handing her jacket to her chief of staff as James's chief of staff opened the bag and removed the new jacket. Modesitt had turned her back to let Voclain put the new jacket on her, with its maroon lapels and shoulder boards...and the extra sleeve band and star of a Vice Admiral.

"This is the wrong unifo—"

"No, it's not," James said with a smile as recognition hit her. "The Cabinet made me a full Fleet Admiral. That means I need Vice Admirals to watch my back and run my subordinate commands. Since I was generally lacking in even *Rear* Admirals until I started throwing Confederacy stars around, that means I'm promoting the people doing the damn jobs.

"That's you and Admiral Yamamoto," he concluded. "He's going to run the entire Starfighter Corps—from *Krakatoa*'s flight deck, so far— and you're going to safeguard the Meridian Sector for me."

"I'm not sure..."

"Say *Thank you, sir, I'll do the damn job, sir*," James instructed.

She chuckled and threw him a crisp salute.

"Thank you, sir, I'll do the job, sir," she parroted back. "How does it go? *Until I die or you find someone better.*"

"Don't die. Your boyfriend will never forgive me."

"Fiancé," Modesitt corrected with a smile. "I proposed as soon as I realized just what you'd done in Dakota. The *upside* of serving a far-smaller nation is that I have a pretty good idea of where he's going to be.

"That'll help with the keeping-us-apart problem, at least."

James grinned approvingly.

"I'm glad for you both. Unfortunately, the uniform and the stars are only the beginning of our business. Shall we?"

———

Saratoga was an older ship but still newer than *King George V*, the *Monarch*-class ship that Modesitt had commanded in the Commonwealth Sector Fleet Meridian. The *Monarch* was now part of James's First Fleet, one of the three battleships he had in place to protect his carrier.

He'd traded *Saratoga* for a battleship and a battlecruiser. With *Saint Bartholomew* now in First Fleet, he could probably give *King George V* back, except that he wasn't sure if or when he'd be separating the two fleets again.

"So, what's the situation, sir?" Modesitt asked, gesturing for her office drink machine to dispense coffee for James and a glass of something black and fizzy for her. "You wouldn't have brought every ship in First Fleet here unless something was going on."

"From what you said on the flight deck, you may have some information on it from another angle," he admitted. "We have intelligence that Dictator Periklos has concentrated a significant chunk of the Stellar League Navy in the New Edmonton System, presumably as a precursor to an all-out invasion of what is now the Confederacy."

There was a long silence as Modesitt drank her soda, then she nodded.

"So, you left me a giant mess here," she pointed out. "Rutherford assassinated Admiral Washington; we *know* that now. With Marshal Amandine's death, Washington's death and then *Rutherford*'s death, you handed me the shattered wreckage of two fleets and a Sector that had been preparing for military dictatorship."

"And you handled it brilliantly, according to the reports I've seen from you, your subordinates and your political counterparts," James told her. "You calmed the political waters and reassured everyone that we definitely *weren't* following up on Rutherford's plan to make himself dictator.

"All the while calming officers and crews who were very nearly lured into treason by Rutherford—and helping Barbados prosecute the war-crimes trials."

He grimaced.

"I didn't want to leave that last entirely on you two, but I *had* to be in Dakota."

"You did," Modesitt agreed. "And if there's a reason I'm not completely freaking out over you handing me the second star you've given me in three months, it's because I know, damn well, that I did a job worthy of them here.

"No false modesty, sir; you handed me a giant mess and I cleaned it up for you. I am *proud* of the work Alric and I have done here."

"So am I," James said. "And you're now the second-ranking officer of the Dakota Commonwealth Navy, and the only reason you're the *third*-ranking officer of the entire armed forces is because I had access to Yamamoto to pin stars on him right away and I had to pick *some* basis for the order of the list I gave the Cabinet."

The theoretical date of seniority was identical for his two Vice Admirals, so Anthony Yamamoto was senior entirely due to being the first name on the list.

"But since you've been poking through that mess, it sounds like you found something?"

"I'm not entirely certain who was running Rutherford's intelligence net in the League," Modesitt said. "But we managed to find the contact information and *systems* in the surface base of the murderous bitch he left behind."

Given that a large chunk of said "murderous bitch"'s murderous desires had been aimed at then-Brigadier Alric Barbados, James wasn't surprised Modesitt took General Ana Cantrell's actions on the planet personally.

"Q-coms?" he asked.

"Q-coms," she confirmed. "Running through League systems, so I wouldn't trust them for anything *except* this, and I'm not entirely sure we're going to be able to pay Rutherford's contacts, but we linked back in and managed to get the information pipeline moving again."

"We'll find a way to pay them," James said firmly. "Somehow."

"Agreed. The immediate concern, though, is that we *also* have been warned that Periklos is moving against us," she said grimly. "A courier with our latest intel is about halfway to Dakota right now.

"He proclaimed Samantha Borgogni Proconsul of the League, then left her in New Athens with a newborn and half a dozen carriers to keep order. We're not sure what his strength is up to in New Edmonton, but he's *definitely* assembling a fleet there, and we are the only likely target."

That was the confirmation James had been both hoping for and dreading.

"That's the final mark, isn't it?" he murmured. "If we *know* he's got twenty-odd starships in New Edmonton prepping for war, we're the only possible target. Which means we have to judge ourselves as still being at war, which allows for much...uglier options."

"From the information I have, the odds are not in our favor," she warned.

"How much data do you have?" James asked. "All I know for certain is that there were sixteen ships in New Edmonton on the fifth."

Modesitt grimaced.

"I don't have hard data. I know what the Proconsul has in New Athens—four *Alberto da Giussano*–class carriers, four *Zara*-class cruisers and half a dozen condottieri ships."

"And there's few people in the League Periklos would trust with a dozen-plus starships," James noted. "Himself, Samantha Borgogni... Peppi Borgogni *was* on that list, but..."

Star Admiral Peppi Borgogni was hopefully under something of a cloud after being kicked out of Persephone by one James Tecumseh and what was now the Dakota Confederacy Navy. He was probably safe from most risks of that, given that his sister was Periklos's wife and apparently the Dictator's political and military deputy.

"There are a few others, but the League is still short on true Navy ships. According to Rutherford's intelligence network, there only *are* nine *Alberto da Giussano*s and five *Venices*, plus twenty last-gen ships.

"Even the Dictator's own navy is mostly made up of ex-condottieri ships."

Condottieri cruiser wasn't really a class of ships per se. Most of them were individually designed and built, but the mercenary companies that had replaced system-level militaries for most of the League had shared common tactics and operational needs.

Most condottieri ships were quite similar, fielding around a hundred starfighters combined with a decent lance and missile armament. Not many of them had been built since Periklos had taken over the League, but there'd been a *lot* of them around ten years earlier.

"So, he definitely doesn't have *more* than nine modern sixty-million-cubic-meter ships," James observed. "That's not as reassuring as I'd like it to be."

Seeing as how the DCN only had three sixty-million-cubic-meter starships *total*, that was.

"We *think* we're looking at four each of the *Giussano*s and *Venices*, backed up by condottieri cruisers in League commission," Modesitt said. "I'll have my analyst give your people our raw data, but we have confirmed that the younger Borgogni still has his flagship and has been sent to the far side of the League to stand guard against space dragons."

"But if he hasn't moved already, then he's expecting more than sixteen ships in the end," James murmured.

"One of our agents is in New Edmonton, and Periklos is *definitely* still there as of today," she confirmed. "So, he's waiting on more ships. He probably wants to make sure he has overwhelming force versus our entire order of battle."

"If he has eight modern ships, those can match off against the entire DCN," he admitted. "This could get real ugly, Jessie. And that's without taking into account the fact that the Commonwealth is going to receive our formal declaration of independence in a few days."

"Ouch." She sighed. "That's probably a good thing, but it does leave us in an awkward spot, doesn't it?"

"We stand defiant between a rock and a hard place," James

confirmed. "But I trust our people and I'm looking for answers. If nothing else...I've been promised q-coms and q-probes here in Meridian."

"That would be nice," she said. "From whom?"

"Therein lies the problem. I'm waiting to hear from an arms smuggler named Trickster—and I'm not certain how long I can justify waiting!"

16

Meridian System
18:00 February 20, 2738 ESMDT

"WE'RE SWITCHING SHUTTLES AND DESTINATIONS."

James was getting used to Reynolds' idea of *proper notice* for things like this and just threw his bodyguard a *look*.

"And why and to where?" he asked calmly.

"We're switching shuttles *because* we're switching destinations," she told him, gesturing for the Marines to fall in around them as they headed toward *Saratoga*'s flight deck. "Whatever toys Trickster has, they didn't get past me this time.

"*Someone*, presumably our new friend, attempted to covertly insert an appointment into your schedule. My filters caught it and I checked it out."

"And?" James asked. He trusted Reynolds' judgment, at least with regards to his safety, so if she was comfortable with making the meeting, he'd go along.

His main priority in Meridian at this point was to make contact with the arms dealer, after all.

"You're invited to dinner with someone who identified themselves by an icon of a sparkling box with a question mark on it," Reynolds told him. "The restaurant is in Jorvik, Greenwich's capital. It *exists*, which removes some of the risks, and General Barbados has already offered a Marine detail to secure your person on the surface if needed."

"So, you're sending them ahead to check the building?" James asked.

"Exactly," she confirmed. "We can make it to the city in just under an hour, and we *should* be able to make it to the restaurant in about thirty minutes from there.

"By taking one of *Saratoga*'s shuttles, we evade any clever schemes someone could have implemented in your shuttle from *Krakatoa*. Traffic in the city is still a concern, but General Barbados is providing the transport, and he seems trustworthy."

"If we can trust a shuttle from *Saratoga* and Vice Admiral Modesitt, we can trust a vehicle from General Barbados and the Marines," James said drily.

———

There was a problem with letting Alric Barbados and Shannon Reynolds pick a *secure* transport for a road trip through Greenwich's capital, but it didn't occur to James until he was walking out of the shuttle and Reynolds indicated the mobile block of starship-grade alloys waiting for them.

The only difference between a Horus armored personnel carrier and a Chariot main battle tank was that the former took all of the space required for the Chariot's main gun's power supply and ammunition storage and converted it into space for ten power-armored soldiers.

It had the same hull, engine and secondary weapons. Tank and APC alike both used Class Four mass manipulators to reduce their weight to something the tracks and backup wheels could handle, allowing them to haul a probably ridiculous amount of hyperdense ceramic armor.

"That has got to be overkill," James said flatly.

"I don't believe in overkill, Admiral," Reynolds replied. "Only *open fire* and *I need to reload*. Or, in this case, getting my charge safely to their destination...or not."

A pair of Marines in full power armor were standing next to the APC's open hatch, their sensors presumably sweeping the entire private spaceport to make certain no one had any clever ideas about nuking the vehicle or something similar.

"I would *prefer* to show some trust to the people of Greenwich and Jorvik, you know," he said mildly. "I suppose it's too late to change anything now?"

"Not if we want to be on time to meet Trickster—plus, the only way I can justify less armor than this is if no one knows where you are," Reynolds told him. "You are arch-traitor number one to any Commonwealth sympathizers in the Confederacy, Tecumseh. So far, no one has taken a shot at you, because it's been a very obvious waste of time.

"I'd like to keep my hundred percent record of convincing wannabe assassins not to bother."

James suspected there was a flaw somewhere in his bodyguard's logic, but, for the moment, it was easier to cooperate.

And this particular Horus, it turned out, had been rigged up for VIP transport. If he hadn't been heading to negotiations that might well decide the effectiveness of his fleet for the next two years, the wet bar would have been a welcome sight.

As it was, it gave him something to look forward to once the meeting was done.

———

Despite all of Reynolds' concerns, the trip to the restaurant was completely without incident. Stepping out of the armored transport, James took in the squad of fully armored Marines scattered around the area with a long-suffering sigh.

"I take it we scared off any other customers?" he asked Reynolds.

"The Marines haven't seen anyone except the restaurant staff," she replied. "Which, yes, is suspicious, but there is nothing in the building that has raised any flags on the sensors—they were expecting the sweep and cooperated entirely."

"Let's go meet our host, then."

The restaurant was named simply The Kettle. It was a square stand-alone structure in one of Jorvik's wealthier suburbs—but James realized the sign was brand-new. And once he was looking, he could see other signs of fresh repairs. The grass around the dark blue building was all brand-new sod. The parking lot had been resurfaced. Several chunks of wall had been rebuilt, let alone repainted.

"This place saw action during the fighting?" he asked.

"Yes, sir," one of the Marines replied. "One of Cantrell's battalion commanders dug into this district and refused to surrender. He used The Kettle as a command post and the building took a bit of damage as we dug him out.

"The General helped pay for the repairs, and the owners *like* us now," the Sergeant concluded, his grin audible in his voice.

"An interesting choice," James murmured as he entered the building. Another Marine was standing next to the door and jumped to open it for him—and he was almost surprised to find a civilian hostess waiting for him instead of more Marines.

"Admiral Tecumseh," the gray-haired woman greeted him with a carefully measured nod. "We are ready for you. Your table is this way."

Keeping half an eye on Reynolds for signs she'd detected trouble, James followed the hostess into the empty restaurant.

"We're alone here?" he asked softly.

"The Kettle doesn't reopen until the twentieth, Admiral," she told him. "You are our only guests tonight."

"I see. I appreciate the gesture, ma'am. Do you know anything about who we're meeting?"

"No. This was booked through your office, Admiral."

James nodded his acknowledgement of that as he bit down a sigh. Trickster, it seemed, was *showing off*.

From Reynolds' expression, she got the same impression.

"The bastard *let me* intercept that meeting setup," she hissed.

"Most likely, yes," James agreed. "Come now, Agent Reynolds. Show some respect for the tradecraft."

"All he needed to do was *ask* you to meet him somewhere," she replied. "*This* is just swagger."

And for all of said swagger, the table the Kettle staff led them to was empty. There were three seats, each with a glass of water, and no host.

"I see we will be waiting for our dinner companion. Have our people cleared the kitchen?" James asked.

"Ingredient by ingredient," the hostess told him drily. "Would you like me to bring some bread and appetizers?"

"Please. And a menu?"

James knew damn well when he was being played, and he had no intention of letting Trickster set the entire tone of the evening.

"Of course."

———

A younger waitress delivered a basket of warm fresh-baked bread and a variety of chicken wings, along with a single printed sheet of flimsy with a "menu" that was basically a list of what they would be served.

"Tasting menu, I see," James murmured. "Marines checked everything, right?"

"Three times, while I watched," a new voice told him. It was an odd voice, one that shifted modulations as the speaker appeared out of the same kind of holographic stealth screen Reynolds was fond of.

The stranger wore a clean-cut black suit with a tight collar, white gloves and a matching hood. Under the hood, they wore a mask with a checkerboard pattern of black and white squares. There was clearly an electronic voice modulator of some kind in the mask, and nothing in their build or movements would have allowed James to even guess at their gender, let alone identity.

"The Trickster, I presume?" James asked.

"Just *Trickster*," the arms smuggler replied. "Adding a definite article is just *pretentious*. And while I will freely engage in pretentiousness, that always felt like a step too far."

They hooked a foot around one of the chairs, spinning it a hundred and eighty degrees to sit on it backward.

"I, to be clear, have no idea what's on that tasting menu," they continued. "I'm looking forward to it."

"Can you eat through the mask?" Reynolds asked, her tone icy.

"It has a hinge, Agent Reynolds," Trickster replied. "It would be rude and all kinds of suspicious if I were to invite you to eat and not dine alongside you, wouldn't it?"

"I'm not sure which I'd find more reassuring, to be honest," James conceded. "But here we are. You have something for me."

Trickster chuckled.

"I have many things for you," they promised. "Though I discovered while looking into your background, Admiral, that we have a friend in common."

"I find that...unlikely," James said.

"You and I both owe Kyle Roberts our lives," Trickster told him. "I had the privilege of meeting him face-to-face before you did, in fact, and he's the only reason I'm here to make the offer I'm making."

Kyle Roberts was the Castle Federation fleet officer James had worked with after a pirate warlord had stolen a modern Terran battlecruiser and tried to set up a private empire out past the Alliance of Free Stars. James had been out there on a covert operation...and somehow, he doubted he really *wanted* to know where the Stellar Fox had been when Roberts met Trickster.

Especially given as "before James had met him face-to-face" lined up all too well with the raid by League fighters that had triggered a Commonwealth reprisal and started a two-front war Terra had proven unable to afford.

Another waiter appeared with a trio of soup bowls as James was digesting that timeline, and Trickster proved that the "hinge" in their mask opened barely large enough for a spoonful of soup, adding to the awkwardness of their reversed chair.

"I have the details of your offer from one Gamil Petersen," James noted. "Twenty-five thousand q-com blocks and a thousand probes, yes?"

"That's what I had when I sent GP to Dakota, yes," Trickster agreed. "But, of course, I have been digging since then. So, I have to ask, Admiral, how deep are thy pockets?"

James glared silently for a moment, then took a spoonful of his own soup without even looking. The heavily spiced lobster bisque wasn't quite what he was expecting, and he found himself coughing for a few seconds.

"I have ten billion Commonwealth dollars, in authorized drafts drawn against the Central Bank of Terra, ready right now," he told the arms smuggler. "Anything beyond that, I will need to take action to establish, but depending on what you have on offer, I may be able to make it happen.

"If, for example, you have Class One mass manipulators for sale, I will meet almost any price you can ask for."

"I *wish*," Trickster replied. "No, I just have roughly double the number of probes and entangled blocks GP originally offered. Not enough for you to get your fleet back to full standard for coms, but enough for you to equip squadron leaders or some such."

"I don't suppose you have *both* ends of the entangled pairs?" James asked. So far, no one in Regalia had raised so much as a peep over the fact that a bunch of their communicator blocks were being used for political communication by a Commonwealth successor state.

But he'd far rather control the switchboard end of his *military* coms —especially the tactical channels required for q-probe deployment.

"Pretty much everyone follows the standard of keeping one end of the entangled pair at the manufacturing plant," Trickster admitted. "Switchboard stations are such lovely, secure, multipurpose facilities, after all, until things go very wrong."

"I think a lot of people are going to be reconsidering that structure now. But fair." James shook his head. "I want the details, Trickster. *Whose* q-coms am I buying?"

The smuggler finished their soup and leaned back, one arm hooked around the back of their reversed chair to support themselves. A silent data handshake request appeared in James's implant, and he authorized it access to a quarantined part of his data storage.

A few seconds later, he sighed as he analyzed the data.

"So," he said conversationally, "how much is the *Castle Federation* paying you to help us fuck over the Commonwealth?"

Trickster laughed, making a vague handwavy gesture in the air as a pair of waiters appeared to replace the soup bowls with larger bowls filled with steaming rice and stew.

"I'm not sure if that's any of your business, Admiral," they noted.

"If I am being lured into being used as someone else's cat's-paw, I need to know," James replied. He wasn't, given his situation, entirely *opposed* to being used as the Federation's tool against Walkingstick's rump Commonwealth—not if it got him the support he needed—but he wasn't going to go into it blind.

He couldn't read much of Trickster's body language, and he wished he could see the stranger's eyes.

"The Federation and their allies certainly have an interest in seeing you continue to exist as a distraction to the Imperator and the Commonwealth," the smuggler noted. "And I imagine that your use of their communications may well result in some *conversations*.

"On the other hand, I'm not certain you're going to find any more *reliable* communications provided by anyone who doesn't have as strong an interest in your success, Admiral. The Castle Federation wants you to survive."

"Yes. And that means that *your* cost for the systems you are selling me is zero," James pointed out. "Possibly even negative, if Federation Intelligence is covering the costs *and* paying you to deliver them."

"You can't begrudge the middleman our profit," Trickster told him. "Without my organization, after all, you wouldn't have any chance at acquiring something like this at all."

"I recognize the value of your involvement here, Trickster, but we both *also* recognize that you're trying to get paid twice." James looked down at the stew in front of him and shook his head.

"I'll pay the ten billion, Trickster," he said firmly. "No more. You can decide, I suppose, how much of the extra you're willing to sell for that."

Trickster ate several bites of their own stew while they considered, then they finally nodded.

"Very well, Admiral. I had to try," they told him. "The cargo will be delivered from my ship in orbit tomorrow morning."

"Sooner would be better, if at all possible," James replied. "I would very much like to be on my way by *morning*."

"You're not paying enough for alacrity, Admiral," Trickster said. "But I suppose we could come to an agreement."

James sighed. Somehow, he wasn't surprised.

"What do you want? More money?"

"Always," the smuggler said with a chuckle. "But I am prepared to provide additional services. If you were to put up, say, another billion dollars, we could deliver the drones and com blocks by midnight ESMDT.

"Except for, say, ten drones…that we would connect to your network and then go let loose in New Edmonton to survey a certain fleet."

"That could be…useful," James conceded. Assuming, of course, that the smuggler's ship could get into New Edmonton without drawing attention. He had to assume that Trickster's vessel would appear to be a League transport to the League, which would let them deploy q-probes close to the enemy fleet.

He glanced at Reynolds. This was outside the woman's area of expertise, he supposed. On the other hand, it was well outside *his* area of expertise.

But he'd come ready for a number of possibilities. He withdrew a datastick from inside his uniform jacket—the storage device still marked with the symbol of the Terran Commonwealth Navy—and blinked at it as he fed it some new data.

"There." He passed the device over. "Eleven billion Commonwealth dollars. Authorized drafts on the Central Bank. Of course," he grinned coldly, "I'd suggest making sure you call those drafts before the Star Chamber does something outlandish to cut off funds."

The smuggler scooped the datastick off the table, holding it between two fingers as they presumably checked the details.

"A pleasure doing business with you, Admiral Tecumseh," they told him. "Though, on the topic of Class One mass manipulators…"

James sighed.

"If you can get your hands on any, we will pay market rate," he observed. Even that was a lot more money than he'd just handed over, but he knew he could make it happen. No matter what else happened over the next few years, Class One mass manipulators were always going to be a major restriction on the Confederacy's ability to build warships.

"I have to be cautious, however, in wondering just where you were planning to *source* said manipulators."

Every starship needed at least four Class One mass manipulators, after all, but building one was a slow and painstaking process that more resembled growing crystals than traditional manufacture.

"Salvage," Trickster said cheerfully.

In theory...that was doable. In practice...

"And where do you draw the line between salvage and *piracy*?" James asked grimly. He would *not* be party to buying mass manipulators cut from the ships of murdered civilians.

"Some salvage is active and some salvage is...*aggressive*," Trickster told him.

"We'll buy manipulators if you get them," James said with a sharp sigh, "but if I ever have reason to believe that you are murdering innocent spacers to *get* said manipulators, you'll find them mounted on warships hunting *you*.

"Understood?"

Trickster touched their chest and made an offended sound.

"Please, Admiral, business like this is built on relationships. That means I have to understand the limits of what I can sell you. Salvage from the unfortunate conflict between League and Commonwealth? That seems fair game."

It was grave-robbing, to James's mind, but Trickster was right. He'd refuse to take systems he knew innocents had been killed for—but he couldn't go so far as to refuse to buy systems taken from wrecked Commonwealth and League warships.

His understanding was that the exotic-matter coils in Class One mass manipulators weren't *likely* to survive the destruction of their starship—that was why salvage wasn't considered a major source of the manipulators for new ships—but even four coils out of, say, the forty ships destroyed when Star Admiral Samantha Borgogni had overrun the Commonwealth's Clockward Fleet would give him a sixty-million-cubic-meter warship.

And even *one* warship was a big deal now.

17

TRICKSTER WAS as good as their word. Exactly at midnight, one of the half dozen freighters in orbit had changed her beacon to start transmitting a pickup signal. Half an hour later, James watched from *Krakatoa's* flag deck as dozens of shuttles flitted around his starships.

"Allocation of the blocks is going relatively smoothly," Sumiko Mac Cléirich told him. His fleet coms officer had spent the trip out working through a plan for twenty-five thousand entangled blocks. She'd taken an extra twenty-five thousand in stride.

"*Krakatoa* is getting a full supply?" James confirmed aloud.

The standard load of entangled blocks for a Commonwealth capital ship was at least ten thousand. That was sufficient to run multiple holographic conferences with people in other star systems and link with dozens of q-probes.

"It was a toss-up," Mac Cléirich admitted. "My people went through the numbers a few times. We need to improve the civil communications net as well, and every fully equipped ship draws a *lot* of com blocks."

"Even with the extra blocks and going for half capacity, we can't equip the whole fleet," James noted.

"But we can't risk q-com blocks by putting them on starfighters," she replied. "That was the final deciding factor, sir—and you *did* sign off on the plan."

He chuckled.

"I did," he conceded. "But that was before we got double the number of blocks."

"It's still not enough," she warned. "With fifteen ships in the combined fleet and another two still in Persephone, we could use over *a hundred and seventy thousand* to equip the DCN. And that's before we started trying to include them in fighters, bombers, civilian ships or bases."

James grimaced. The average Commonwealth q-com switchboard station prior to the end of the war had held roughly a *billion* entangled blocks. A TCN ship had carried blocks from multiple switchboards, including several that didn't officially exist.

"We were putting five thousand into the civil network," he observed. "Then five thousand each on four command ships and at least *some* on the others."

Krakatoa, *Saint Bartholomew*, *Lexington* and *Adamant* had been the intended recipients of more complete arrays. The two established flagships and then the two most powerful battleships. The battleships had their flaws, but the *Resolutes* like *Adamant* were among the most survivable of his older ships.

"That was to give us a quarter of our ships able to control q-probes," the junior Admiral confirmed. "And without the need to maintain cross-Commonwealth communications and manage command fighters, we don't *need* more than five thousand per ship right now. So, I flagged a thousand to each star system for civilian communications, and then rounded out the numbers with eight thousand blocks flagged for military and military-industrial coms."

That was forty percent of their new blocks, two-fifths instead of the one-fifth he'd signed off on, and he raised an eyebrow at Mac Cléirich.

"Which is more important, sir? Eight command ships instead of six —or secure and stable long-term communications between our civil administrations and military shipyards?"

"The more ships we have with coms, the more dispersed we can make our forces and the more flexible our tactics can be." James sighed. "But you're right. We have transports lined up for the blocks?"

"I started organizing shipping the moment we hit orbit," she confirmed. "And, well, the difference between a few hundred and a few thousand q-com blocks doesn't really matter in the scale of an interstellar freighter."

"Okay. So, which are the extra command ships?" James knew which ones *he* would pick, but since Mac Cléirich seemed to have a solid handle, he was curious as to her plan.

"The battleships," she said with a shrug. "*Valiant* and *King George V.* I was considering the cruisers or even *Hollywood*, but…"

"None of our cruisers are modern and they were small when they were built."

The *Assassin*s and *Ocean*s—beam-focused battlecruisers and fighter-focused strike cruisers, respectively—that made up half the strength of the DCN were the products of an experiment with economizing on warships by the TCN's design bureaus.

So far as James could tell, the idea on the TCN's side had been a bluff. They'd sold the Star Chamber on the concept of the thirty-million-cubic-meter ships being cheaper and, via that supposed economy, they'd managed to get a hundred-ship construction program authorized.

Whatever he thought of the ships, that program had got the Commonwealth to the five-hundred-starship navy they'd maintained for his entire career. But he'd commanded *Monarch*s and *Ocean*s and *Assassin*s, and they simply couldn't match contemporary ships that *hadn't* been artificially shrunk.

"*King George* is a contemporary of the cruisers, but a battleship is just that much tougher," Mac Cléirich concluded. "So, that's six ships that can handle q-probes and maintain communications with each other and the civilians."

"It'll have to do," James agreed. "How long?"

There were two time constraints now before he could leave—but he'd already gone over the logistics plan with Voclain, Carey and Modesitt. First Fleet was actually going to require *more* logistics time than Meridian Fleet. Modesitt's fleet had been ready to move out and intercept an attack on any of the Meridian Sector's systems and had basically only needed to recall personnel from the surface.

The combined Dakotan fleet would be ready to move out by oh eight hundred hours, based on fuel, food, people and munitions. They'd even arranged to have *Lakewater* stocked up in the same time frame—though there wasn't that much spare space on the freighter at this point.

"Twenty-two hours," Mac Cléirich told him. "We can install and activate blocks under sublight thrust but not once we're in FTL. I *need* to be able to validate connections against someone I have a real-time radio connection with. I don't have half of the reports and metrics I'd get with blocks from TCN Logistics."

Which meant she needed to double-check things they'd have *known* before. James would have given a *lot* to be out of Meridian by oh eight hundred, but he simply nodded.

"Do it right," he ordered. "We're going to need those q-probes before this is over."

If nothing else, he knew the League had q-probes of their own. He had no interest in fighting *another* battle against them half-blind.

———

Rank had its privileges, offset by a thousand responsibilities—and many of what looked like privileges actually served those responsibilities. There was an obvious reason, after all, why a ship's captain had their own bathroom next to the bridge...

James certainly felt that being able to talk to Abey Todacheeney while over thirty light-years away was a privilege—but his *responsibility* was to update the interim President of the Dakotan Interstellar Confederacy and her right-hand woman.

"Trickster came through, but the source of the supplies is definitely a concern," he told the two women. "Every single entangled block and q-probe they're selling us is Castle Federation. The probes still have the Castle Federation Navy logo stamped on the side. Everything Trickster is providing us is directly out of the stockpiles of the unquestioned first nation of the Alliance of Free Stars."

"We're being used," Chapulin said quietly. "But I suppose the question is whether this is actually a *problem* for us."

"The Federation and her allies want the Commonwealth to be occupied," James said. "They're *ecstatic* if the Commonwealth disintegrates into successor states at each other's throats." He considered for a moment. "Based off some of the Federation officers I've met, I suspect they'd be just as happy without us being at each other's throats, but they want the Commonwealth broken."

"We're on the wrong side of the Commonwealth to be a threat to the Alliance," Todacheeney said quietly. "You know them better than I do, James. How is this likely to hurt us?"

"There are dangers," he warned. "We're encrypting all of our communications through our q-coms, but the downside of using someone else's switchboard station is that any eavesdropping they're doing, well..."

He shrugged.

"They have access to an entire planet's worth of computer infrastructure to decrypt our codes. Even this communication, which is on Regalia's network and Regalia has basically no irons in this fire, is vulnerable.

"But we *have* to communicate and that means we have to use the q-coms we have. Having Federation coms is to our advantage in many ways. As Abey says, we're almost on the opposite side of the Commonwealth from the Castle Federation and the rest of the Alliance of Free Stars. Any attention the Imperator turns our way is turned away from the Federation and the systems they are trying to protect."

"But they have their finger on a button that could kill our communications," Chapulin observed.

"Exactly. Not to mention the potential blackmail of claiming, in some circumstance or another, that we are their patsy," James agreed. "Or of simply *leaking* the information to allow someone else to claim such."

"Even if we never do business with them or even *talk* to them again, that we took their gear will always be something someone could hold against us," Abey said. "But we need it and they're probably one of the least dangerous sources to *get* this kind of bulk supply from."

"Agreed. For the stockpile Trickster was giving us to be of real use, it all had to be on one network," James noted. "I figured it had to be a state player, and I would have put decent money on it being Castle for all of the reasons I mentioned.

"I *do* expect them to call the favor in some day, but I don't expect them to use it against us. But you do need to be aware of how it *could* be."

"It's worth the risk," Chapulin agreed. "We'll watch the political consequences. You need to worry about the need and the use."

"Thanks to Rutherford, we know more than we did about what Periklos has mustered," James warned. "I'll send an info packet after the call." The bandwidth available right now couldn't handle *both* a video call and an unrelated data transmission, after all.

"We're estimating eight modern and eight older ships. Even the older ships probably outgun and outclass our own older vessels. The condottieri ships are more variable than I'd want in my own order of battle, but I doubt Periklos is bringing his *Ocean*-class equivalents. *He* has enough ships that he can use those for rear area security."

Which was what James Tecumseh would prefer to use his collection of thirty-million-cubic-meter ships for—except that of the seventeen active warships of the Dakota Confederacy Navy, *nine* were from that generation—and the three *Paramount*s were even older.

He'd relegate the smaller ships to secondary duties once he could, but for now, he was going to have to use them and use them hard. He worried about what that was going to cost his people along the way, but the situation didn't leave him any choice.

"The Cabinet has authorized you to do whatever you feel is necessary," Chapulin reminded him. "It seems that, for once, we have the intelligence advantage over our enemy."

"Unfortunately, that appears to be my only advantage," he said grimly. "The League has more ships and bigger ships. I would prefer *not* to fight them, but I don't see any choice but to start with a surprise attack and hammer them.

"We need to neutralize Periklos before it becomes necessary to deal with the Imperator."

"I wish I could hope for a peaceful resolution on all sides," the new President said.

"You are not that foolish, my old friend," Todacheeney replied. "We all know that Periklos will attempt to conquer and Walkingstick will attempt to control. It is in the nature of both men. Neither wishes to see us independent in the space between them."

"In most ways, Periklos is the lesser threat," James reminded them. "It is entirely possible that Walkingstick will retain control of the other ninety-odd Commonwealth systems, giving him an advantage in both ships and industry over Periklos."

"No, it isn't," Chapulin said. "We are starting to fill in some of the gaps in our information, James. The Brillig Sector hasn't broken away from the Commonwealth as a group...but at least four of the seven systems that make up the Sector have seized all Commonwealth resources and facilities in their systems.

"The peace treaty that the Star Chamber accepted also required the Commonwealth to allow plebiscites for independence in ten systems on the Rimward frontier by the Alliance of Free Stars. And the two systems already in Alliance control were *never* going back.

"We may be the first to deliver formal notice to Earth and have a decent chance of being the single largest secessionary state, but we are not alone in our defiance. The Commonwealth is fracturing, James. It was, I am afraid, inevitable."

"I didn't expect us to be the only ones," he conceded with a grimace. "But despite everything...I'd hoped the Commonwealth would survive."

"You know as well as we do what the price of that would have been," Todacheeney reminded him. "Walkingstick would keep the Commonwealth together, at any cost. But when we were presented with the sacrifice his plan required of Dakota and Meridian..."

"I know." He stared blankly into space for a moment. "I fear what I set in motion, but I recognize the inevitability. It just..."

"You and I both swore to preserve the Commonwealth and its ideals," Chapulin reminded him, the ex-Marine looking tired. "And in the end, we had to choose between three ideals and one."

"I know." He shook himself. "It's just late and we've been working for a while here. We expect to move out around sixteen hundred hours. We will arrive in New Edmonton on the twenty-seventh. And then… we will see."

"You will fight," his President told him. "You will secure peace for the Confederacy."

"I can't promise peace," he warned. "I can only promise defiance. I do not expect to find peace with the Stellar League in a field of broken ships and dying spacers. Only time."

"Then we will stand defiant," Chapulin said. "You may have shown us the path, Admiral, but this is *our* path—as a nation, as a people. We are behind you."

She stretched and smiled sadly.

"That said, it's late here as well. *I* am going to close out this meeting and go to sleep. But I do believe Ms. Todacheeney has some news for you."

The interim President of the Dakotan Interstellar Confederacy gave them both a grin that wouldn't have looked out of place on a mischievous schoolboy, and then bowed her way off the video conference.

For his part, James turned both a pleased smile and a questioning eyebrow at his lover.

"News?" he asked. "I take it the Assembly of Nations made it official?"

Abey stopped with her mouth open and stared at him for a second.

"Yes," she admitted. "The vote was this morning. I am now formally and officially First Chief of Dakota. How did you *know*?"

"It was either you'd accepted that job permanently or you were pregnant," James said with a chuckle. "And since *both* of us have contraceptive implants, I figured the latter was unlikely without prior discussion."

She made a jokingly rude gesture at him.

"I have *no* interest in surprise babies," she said drily. "*Planned* babies, we can talk about in a year or two. Though accidents *do* happen."

That was why most militaries insisted on reproductive-control implants for all service personnel, regardless of their equipment. Uterine controllers were the second-most-common personal implant after standard neural interfaces, and while testes control systems were rarer, all serving TCN personnel had one or the other.

And all serving *Dakota* Navy personnel now.

"'Planned babies,' huh?" he echoed back at her. That was an... intimidating thought, even for a man who'd talked twelve star systems into secession from history's most powerful interstellar nation.

"In a year or two," she repeated. "Once things are calmer and we have a chance to make longer-term plans."

"That makes sense." He smiled sadly. "A conversation to look forward to, I guess. Once we manage to get my grandmama off of Earth. She's safe enough there, I hope, but if we're talking about children..."

"Of course we'll want her to meet them," Abey agreed. "You need to meet my parents, for that matter. We've just had no time."

"That's going to be our story for a while; you know that."

"I know. Right now, I'm scheduled to be talking to the headdress makers in six hours." She shook her head. "Mine is going to be a *lot* less impressive than Quetzalli's. She was a Marine, an officer. I...I'm an economist turned bureaucrat turned politician, James. I don't even know what achievements I have that are worth including on a formal headdress."

"It's not your call," he told her. "That's a decision for the makers— and for your colleagues, your friends and your tribe. You don't get to decide what honorifics you wear, Abey. Your *community* decides the honorifics you've earned.

"And if the Assembly has decided you are First Chief, I guarantee you they have a few in mind."

"How do you think they're going to commemorate *seduced the admiral into not becoming a warlord*?" she asked innocently.

"I was never going to be a warlord, regardless of whether you seduced me," James countered. "I knew my duty. And I fell in love with Dakota, I think, before I ever fell in love with you."

She smiled and blew him a kiss.

"I know. I love you. Go rest, my Admiral. There's a lot in front of us both."

18

Sol System
16:00 February 24, 2738 ESMDT

JAMES CALVIN WALKINGSTICK, Imperator of the Terran Commonwealth, made a specific point of two things with regards to the Star Chamber of the Interstellar Congress.

The first was that there were *always* Marines in the Chamber. Walkingstick had co-opted or removed all of the Lictors of the Congress. The security people of the Star Chamber were now loyal to *him*—but he still made a point of having at least two dozen of his Marines in the massive space that served as a buoyancy chamber of the floating base of Earth's first space elevator.

He and Congress maintained the illusion that the august body of politicians had *voluntarily* appointed him Imperator of the Commonwealth. But it was only an illusion, and Walkingstick, at least, would allow neither himself nor the elected representatives to forget the reality.

The Lictors reported to him, but the Marines were a constant reminder of the reality of the current Commonwealth.

The second of his two specific points was that while there had been a specific desk and station installed for him, he did not, generally, join Congress for their deliberations. He showed up to random discussions to remind them that he existed, but he did so without announcement, as his schedule allowed.

If nothing else, being in the Star Chamber depressed him. It reminded him of the extremes he'd gone to and the utter failure of his dreams and goals. It had been three months since he had seized control of Earth, and while he was grimly determined that his Imperatorship would *end*, even he couldn't see when or how.

But, like the Imperatorship itself, some things were required. So, today he once again entered the massive space that Congress called home, striding down the sloping ramp to the central stage amidst the auditorium-style seating.

Light normally streamed into the Chamber from floor-to-ceiling windows that opened out onto the Atlantic Ocean, only needing the modern artificial lights to fill in the shadows. Today, though, those lights were at full strength, bringing a brilliant light to the Star Chamber that only barely beat back the overwhelming storms outside.

The lights highlighted the banners of the Commonwealth's hundred-plus worlds—and even now, the Star Chamber didn't know how many of those systems still honored their authority. The Alliance had demanded the severance of two worlds—worlds even Walking-stick would admit had legitimate grievances—and independence plebiscites on ten more as part of the peace deal.

Those votes would be held in the next few days, but it would be weeks before they knew the results. Many other worlds and systems had simply gone silent, potentially lacking ships to carry their messages even now.

But it had been almost five months since the Alliance's "Operation Medusa" had crippled the Commonwealth's communications. *Some* communication should have arrived. Messages had flowed back and forth between Terra and Dakota, after all, and Dakota was twenty days' flight away.

It was an unexpected silence in even that chain that had brought Walkingstick to the Star Chamber, though, and the storms outside were a match for his mood as he took his seat. His desk took up the spot to the left of the central stage, empty for two hundred years to intentionally unbalance the room toward the Speaker's desk on the right side.

A ship had arrived from Dakota. But instead of bearing messages from Marshal Tecumseh, advising Walkingstick of the man's acceptance of his command and progress toward accelerating the warships under his care, the crew had only communicated with the Congress delegations for the worlds of the Dakota and Meridian Sector—who had then scheduled a presentation to the Star Chamber.

"Speaker."

The frail-looking woman at the other desk rose at his single-word command, walking to the lectern at the center of the dais and surveying the other seven hundred politicians in the room.

Walkingstick could *feel* that something was wrong in the chamber. The gathered representatives and senators knew it as well as he did. For the delegates of two entire sectors to all request the same thing… It had put the presentation at the top of the Chamber's priorities.

"Members of the Interstellar Congress, we have received a formal request from the senators and representatives of Dakota, Shogun, Gothic, Desdemona, Krete, Arroyo, Meridian, Cancer, Delta Zulu, Hachette, Lulu and Persephone to permit a special presentation by a delegation from the Dakota System government."

Frail and pale as Janet Lane may appear, there was a core of iron to the wispy Speaker or she'd never have risen to her position. She'd adapted to the new order surprisingly quickly, too—probably because she realized that Walkingstick had *planned* to replace her with Michael Burns, the head of the Committee on Unification and Walkingstick's closest ally in the Chamber.

"We took a recess after the vote to allow the delegation to arrive from orbit," Lane continued. The recess had *also* allowed Walkingstick to arrive, but the Congress could maintain their illusions for the moment.

"The Interstellar Congress of the Terran Commonwealth is now prepared to hear the presenter."

Walkingstick supposed he could have silenced the woman Dakota had sent, or even forced her to tell *him* what she was there to say in advance. But if his suspicions were correct...well.

If his suspicions were correct, he was going to have work to do— and mourning of a valued protégé.

The tall woman from Dakota walked down the same ramp he'd taken a few minutes earlier, but Inmaculada Haines didn't have nearly the presence Walkingstick had spent years cultivating. She was a tall woman with clear Spanish features, but she carried herself like the mousy bureaucrat her file said she'd been.

Haines was the Director of Infrastructure and Maintenance for the Dakota Sector. Her job had dramatically expanded in importance with the collapse of the communications network. What was she doing on Earth?

Outwardly withdrawn and cautiously eyeing Lictors and Marines alike, she still stepped up onto the center stage of the Star Chamber without a moment's hesitation. She nodded calmly to Janet Lane and then replaced the Speaker behind the lectern, looking up at the Congress.

She also, Walkingstick noticed, was completely ignoring him. An interesting choice. A dangerous one.

A crack of thunder and lightning overwhelmed Haines's first words, forcing her to pause and wait a moment for the storm to calm.

"My name," she finally repeated, "is Inmaculada Haines. I have been designated to speak as the representative of twelve star systems. I have served in the Commonwealth's public service for thirty-eight years.

"I am not, unlike the members of this Chamber, an elected voice. I am a bureaucrat and a public servant, as much bound in my way by oath and honor as the soldiers and spacers of our military. Like our soldiers, I am sworn to uphold the ideals of the Commonwealth.

"Unlike our soldiers... Democracy. Justice. Equality. Freedom. These are things that impact my work every day. Every day of every week of every year, there are untold billions of public servants in the Commonwealth who work to uphold our ideals and missions."

It was funny, Walkingstick reflected. Haines was still physically withdrawn, still...*mousy*. But she was also ignoring him—and there was no way she didn't understand the true balance of power in the Star Chamber.

Her apparent passivity was a lie, and *that*, in its own way, was as dangerous as flashing eyes and angry proclamations.

"When the communications network for the Commonwealth fell, public servants like me placed our resources and knowledge at the disposal of the planetary governors. In Dakota, this resulted in the Sector Governance Conference."

Haines looked up and surveyed her audience, then returned her gaze to the lectern in front of her.

"In the pursuit of maintaining services and protection for the people under our command, we asked this Chamber for a special status, a formal delegation of authority to allow us to maintain the services and so forth that our sector required."

Walkingstick clenched his hands into fists. This was *definitely* heading in the direction of his worst fears, and he sent the Marines *outside* the Star Chamber a message from his neural implant. He might only have a platoon in the Chamber itself, but an entire *brigade* had taken up residence on the Atlantic Elevator Platform.

"The worlds of the Dakota Sector have their grievances with this Congress," Haines continued. "They have raised them before, and, yes, many hoped to use that delegated authority to solve some of those grievances.

"But the objective was to preserve the Commonwealth and her people. Treason in the Meridian Sector brought their worlds into our fold as well when their military commander sought to make himself a warlord and cut a deal with the Stellar League."

Which explained why Walkingstick wasn't getting much news from *that* quarter. The same Lictor he'd sent to deliver Tecumseh's Marshal's mace had been supposed to *deal with* Hans Rutherford if the man had taken that path.

It seemed Tecumseh had beaten him to it.

"In all that we did, including sending our fleet to defend Meridian, liberating Persephone from League invasion, even attempting to assemble a provincial sector-level government, it was always our intent and desire to remain loyal citizens of the Commonwealth.

"And then Imperator Walkingstick sent a Marshal's mace to James Tecumseh. This Chamber didn't send a mace. The *Imperator* did. One man gave an order to turn our entire sector into a feudal fiefdom, bound to the will of a single soldier."

That wasn't how Walkingstick would have characterized it, but he knew this wasn't a discussion.

"Prudence dictates that long-established government should not be thrown aside for light and transient causes," Haines told them all, her tone still calm, her gaze still downcast. "But to draw from an ancient document with meaning here: *We hold these truths to be self-evident, that all are created equal, that they are endowed with certain unalienable rights, that among these are life, liberty and the pursuit of happiness.*

"Imperator James Calvin Walkingstick chose to order our Admiral to deny us liberty. To impose upon our worlds and our people a forced-labor-and-tribute program in the pursuit of the massed construction of new warships—warships with which, I assume, he intended to subjugate the entire former Commonwealth."

Walkingstick figured that none of this was *actually* a surprise to most members of the Interstellar Congress. But Haines was laying the groundwork for her point.

"You may as well make your point, Director," he called out. "This dancing around the point serves no one, I think."

Haines finally raised her eyes and met his gaze, and her next words echoed with the tombstones of history.

"When in the course of human events, it becomes necessary for one people to dissolve the political bands which have connected them with another, and to assume among the powers of the earth, the separate and equal station to which the laws of nature entitle them, a decent respect to the opinions of mankind requires that they should declare the causes which impel them to the separation."

The preamble to the American Declaration of Independence. Fancy words, and ones soaked with blood to a child of the Cherokee.

"Is that, then, your position?" he asked softly.

Haines removed a parchment envelope from inside her jacket and laid it on the lectern.

"This is the formal note from the governments of Dakota, Shogun, Gothic, Desdemona, Krete, Arroyo, Meridian, Cancer, Delta Zulu, Hachette, Lulu and Persephone," she listed off.

"We will serve no tyrants, no masters. We must, therefore, acquiesce to necessity, which requires this separation, and hold the Commonwealth as we hold the rest of humanity: enemies in war, friends in peace.

"These twelve systems and the secondary dependencies that make up our Sectors solemnly publish and declare that we are and rightfully should be free and independent systems. We absolve ourselves of all allegiance to Terra and dissolve all political connection between ourselves and the State of the Terran Commonwealth.

"As free systems, we have full power to levy war, conclude peace, contract alliances, establish commerce and engage in all other acts of independent systems. As such, we declare with one voice the formation of the Dakotan Interstellar Confederacy, to stand unified against the universe.

"To stand defiant against all tyrants. On this day, before this chamber, we declare our independence."

————

Director Haines might *appear* mousy and withdrawn—and, Walkingstick reflected, likely *was* to some degree—but she had dropped the single largest bomb that had ever been detonated in the Star Chamber. He'd been afraid of it, half-expected it when he hadn't heard from Tecumseh, but it was still a shock to hear the words said out loud in the Star Chamber.

Before anyone could say a word, Haines was walking back toward the exits—and the Senators and Representatives of twelve star systems were rising to go with her.

"Marines."

That was the only word he said, but it was enough. The doors swung open and a second platoon of Marines marched into the room, filling the exit with a line of black-armored bodies holding stunners.

"The Commonwealth has never acknowledged the legitimacy of any system to withdraw from our sacred unity," he told the traitors, his voice soft—but the acoustics of the Star Chamber were intentionally amazing. "It is, has and always will be the position of this Chamber that all humanity is destined to unify under our banner and hold membership in this very body.

"Defeat in war may force some flexibility, but the independence granted by the terms of our treaty with the Alliance is, at most, temporary and all involved know it," he continued. "Your words today, Director Haines, are treason."

"I am no longer a citizen of this Commonwealth," she replied. "I am, in fact, the accredited ambassador of the Dakotan Confederacy to this body. And as the former representatives and senators of our worlds leave, I will remain—with a small staff—to negotiate the terms of our future relations.

"As such, I claim diplomatic immunity for myself and my staff," she concluded.

"You are a traitor, Ms. Haines," Walkingstick told her bluntly. "And if the esteemed Senators and Representatives join you in this, they will join you in a cell."

"We are elected to serve, not to command." The speaker was probably the youngest member of the twelve delegations glaring at the Marines blocking their way, a redheaded woman who was one of the representatives for the Cancer System. "If the people of Cancer have voted to withdraw, we will withdraw."

"You will withdraw *to a cell*."

"Then so be it," she told him, turning to face him and stand next to Haines. "*No tyrants, no masters.*"

He was going to hear that phrase a *lot*, he suspected.

"And what happens, I wonder, to the Commonwealth personnel and factories and ships and stations in your precious Confederacy?" he sneered.

"All have been nationalized to serve the new government," Haines told him levelly. "I am more willing to discuss terms under which the

Confederacy will compensate the Commonwealth for the resources in question. We do not wish this to be a violent separation."

"Then *what*, pray tell, happened to Marshal James Tecumseh?" Walkingstick snapped. He'd asked one of the few people he trusted outside his immediate staff to take over the Dakota Sector. He *knew* that Tecumseh would find the balance he needed, between protecting the people of the sector on one hand and providing the fleet the Commonwealth needed on the other.

And it seemed those orders had damned the man…except that Haines straightened and met his gaze firmly after that question. It wasn't guilt that drove her defiance now.

"*Fleet Admiral* James Tecumseh now commands the Navy of the Dakotan Confederacy, always and forever the first and most trusted defender of our rights and nation!"

With one sentence, Haines tore the ground out from underneath Walkingstick's feet. *Tecumseh* had betrayed him? *Tecumseh*?

"Arrest them all," he ordered the Marines. "Traitors will get their day, I suppose," he told Haines. "But the Star Chamber will not be your court. Your illegitimate Confederacy will not be saved in this room.

"It will be damned where false rebellions have always failed: on the field of battle."

19

Sol System
21:00 February 24, 2738 ESMDT

"THE EXPEDITIONARY FLEET is standing by to deploy."

Admiral Lindsay Tasker had been Walkingstick's senior task force commander when he'd fought the Alliance of Free Stars. Now she was his senior admiral—and the woman he'd tasked to have a strike force ready to deal with the first clear rebellion.

"Thank you," Walkingstick told her, his words surprisingly calm even to him. The storm around the Atlantic Elevator suited his mood, but he'd left that behind to return to his flagship.

Saint Michael was one of the handful of *Saint*-class battleships remaining to the Terran Commonwealth Navy. He'd *had* five, but he'd sent *Saint Bartholomew* to deliver his will to both the Dakota and Meridian Sectors.

One way or another, *Saint Bartholomew* was no longer available to him.

"The traitors?" he asked the other person in his neural network as he stalked into his flag conference room.

General Pearle Krizman grunted, her voice audible in both his implants and his ears as the conference door slammed shut behind Walkingstick, and he turned his attention to the physical gathering of his senior officers.

It was a very sparse crowd, even for the small meeting room, including exactly one civilian—and Senator Michael Burns had barely made it through the door behind Walkingstick before it slammed shut.

Admirals Lindsay Tasker and Mihai Gabor were the matched set of officers who'd served as his right and left hands in the Rimward Marches. Now Tasker commanded the Expeditionary Fleet and Gabor led Home Fleet.

Between them, they commanded one hundred and ten starships, the vast majority of the warships available to the Terran Commonwealth—and the only ones available for Walkingstick's immediate orders.

Krizman, for her part, was now the General Commanding of the Commonwealth Marine Corps and the unquestioned stick to any carrot Walkingstick used to command the Star Chamber. Despite the desk he'd stuck her behind, she remained one of the largest and most heavily muscled humans he'd ever seen.

"We've secured the delegations for the so-called Confederacy systems," she confirmed. "Along with Director Haines and her people. My Marines have also taken control of *Paradise by Twilight*, the transport she arrived on."

"Any resistance?" Walkingstick asked. He didn't sit, even as he gestured for Senator Burns to take a seat at the table. He had too much anger running through him as he stalked to the head of the table.

He'd *made* Tecumseh. He'd certainly kept the man's career from ending when Tecumseh had allowed Kyle Roberts to gun down a Commonwealth war criminal in front of him.

And now Tecumseh had betrayed him.

"There was a team of traitor Marines on board," Krizman said grimly. "They resisted as non-lethally as they could. One of my

Marines is dead, so are five of theirs. I have two dozen wounded and seven prisoners.

"They couldn't stop us taking the ship, but they *did* manage to hold on long enough to physically destroy her main data cores and purge her entire computer network."

"So, *Paradise* is a useless hulk. And we have no data on what Tecumseh is getting up to."

"Unfortunately, sir. My apologies."

"None required," Walkingstick told her, though he knew his anger was audible in his tone. It wasn't anyone *there* he was furious at, after all.

He turned to Tasker, eyeing the blonde woman carefully.

"The Expeditionary Fleet?" he asked. "You say they're ready?"

"We've been cycling which ships are at full readiness and which ships have crew on the planets very carefully," she confirmed. "I have two *Saints*, four *Volcanoes*, six *Hercules* and twenty-two older ships fully crewed and ready to go. We can sortie inside six hours."

"If you're willing to swap ships, I have fifteen *Resolutes* and *Lexingtons* I can cut free to send with you to replace the ones with crew on shore leave," Gabor suggested. "It will leave Home Fleet in a bit of a lurch but only for about two days as we rearrange *our* shore leave schedules."

"Do it," Walkingstick snapped. "But we'll have *three Saints*."

"Imperator?" Tasker took a moment, then nodded.

"I will be taking personal command of the Expeditionary Fleet," he told his close council. "We *do* have q-coms available for the *Saints*. Not enough for standard q-probe operations, but enough to coordinate fleet groups and for me to maintain contact with Earth."

He turned a heavy gaze on Burns.

"I will need you to act as my deputy with the Chamber, Michael," he informed the Senator. "I cannot afford to have Earth fragment behind me."

"It won't," the white-haired Black man assured him. "But... James...I feel I have to be the voice of dissent here."

Walkingstick ground down his initial retort. There was a reason Burns felt he could use the Imperator's first name, after all—he *trusted* the Senator, as much or possibly more than the military officers in the room. The officers in this room had talked Walkingstick into treason, yes, but it had been Senator Michael Burns and his wife Hope who had warned him about the Star Chamber's plan to scapegoat and execute him.

"If anyone has earned that right, it is you," he conceded. "But this may not be the time, old friend."

"If not now, then there will never be a time," Burns replied. "We need to consider whether this is the type of defection we want to take our planned path against.

"The Expeditionary Fleet exists to bring rebels back into line, yes, but this Confederacy doesn't feel like what we were expecting. We expected warlords and glorified pirates—and I *still* expect to see those. Too many areas are still quiet, still unresponsive. Entire sectors have likely disintegrated, and restoring *them* to the fold is a service to everyone.

"But the Confederacy is not what we expected. They are at least taking the *form* of a democratic state forged on the same ideals as the Commonwealth. They are secessionists, yes, but potentially also an *ally* against the forces tearing us apart, not an enemy.

"Or, at the very least, an enemy who can be *ignored* and left as a buffer against the League."

That last definitely sounded more like the man who'd masterminded the Unification campaign for the last fifteen years to James Walkingstick, but the Imperator slowly shook his head.

"That almost makes it *more* important that we bring them to heel," he noted. "This Confederacy *may* be honest in their ideals. They may be aping them to fool us—but if we let their secession stand, others *will* ape those ideals to cover their crimes.

"More, the Dakota System contains one of the Project Hustle yards," he warned grimly. "With the destruction of the vast majority of our building yards, those six shipbuilding slips are a critical portion of our ability to replenish the fleet.

"We *must* retake those shipyards *before* those six ships are deployed against us. Both to have access to those ships but also to avoid the losses of having to *fight* them."

Walkingstick now knew *exactly* how many yards he still controlled. One of the Project Hustle complexes had been in Dakota. A second had been in Procyon, long the "poor sibling" of the Core Systems. The third was in the Serenity System, a hundred and sixty light-years from Sol in the opposite direction of Dakota and, so far at least, seeming cooperative.

He could rely on the nine slips in the shipyard complex at Proxima Centauri. There were two "prototyping yards" still in Sol, hidden out at Charon and far from anywhere the Alliance had attacked. There were two other major shipyards, nine more slips in total, in the Core Systems—and all of the Core Systems had fallen into line.

But that meant that the Commonwealth had only thirty-eight warship slips in total...*including* the six at Dakota and the six at Serenity.

"We need those yards," he concluded softly. "And we need to demonstrate that we will not tolerate secession. It has always been the legal opinion of the Commonwealth that, once brought into unity, a system cannot leave it.

"If we do not maintain that position, we face the ultimate destruction of our state. The best way to avoid having to spill an ocean of blood is to prove our willingness to spill a lake of it at a moment's notice."

The small room was silent and Walkingstick swept his gaze across his people.

"I admit that my emotions are in play," he warned. "I regarded James Tecumseh as a protégé, and he has betrayed my trust and my faith. I *will* take personal command of the Expeditionary Fleet and bring him to heel.

"But the *mission* is necessary and logical. We decided before that we needed to step on the first rebellion *hard* to maintain unity."

He shook his head.

"Everything we have all done for the years and decades leading us to this room has been in pursuit of the unification of all humanity," he reminded them. "If we falter now—if we show weakness now—all of that has been for nothing.

"We owe it to our children and to the people we serve to maintain that unity." He touched the golden eagle he wore in place of his old admiral's insignia.

"The day will come when I lay aside this eagle and return the authority I have taken," he told them. "But until then, we must stand as one. We are the guardians of humanity's unity. We can neither falter nor fail, or we will allow more blood to be spilled than any 'mercy' of ours could spare.

"This Confederacy of James Tecumseh's must fall. Our unity *must* stand."

No one argued. Burns' gaze looked shadowed and he glanced away from Walkingstick, but he finally nodded.

"It is my task, my friend, to be the slave in the conqueror's chariot, whispering *You too are mortal*," the Senator told him. "If we are wrong, we may doom millions. We cannot fail."

"We will not," Walkingstick assured them all. "Lindsay, Mihai— sort out the details of the transfer. We'll have *Saint Anthony*, *Saint Michael* and *Saint Brigid* as task force flagships with q-coms.

"I want a complete order of battle for the EF inside an hour. We leave orbit at oh four hundred hours."

"Understood, sir!"

————

Commonwealth flagships were built with virtual-reality chambers for the Admiral's private use. The *theory* was that they were used for conferencing and meditation, though Walkingstick knew perfectly well that every admiral had used them for porn at least once.

Walkingstick mostly used it for meditation. Especially now, with the weight of a hundred worlds and half a trillion lives on his shoulders. He'd made his choices and he was...content. He hated himself, and yet he was content.

"Stars know the truths here," he murmured. His preferred meditation was just...sitting in the void, looking at a visualization of what his surroundings would look like with no ships. No space stations and orbital foundries and battle platforms and all the other paraphernalia of the orbit of mankind's homeworld.

Just stars.

Stellar Spiritualism was closer to an organized and formalized pattern of agnosticism than an actual religion, a recognition that the stars themselves represented a greater and more energetic power than any divinity humanity had ever imagined up.

The Universe itself was the guiding light of Stellar Spiritualists, and Walkingstick could...respect that. He wasn't truly a member of their numbers, but he came closest to following that path.

So, he sat amidst a swirling array of unblemished stars and considered the road before him.

He would bring fifty interstellar warships to the Dakota System. He would, he was certain, do so well before anyone in the Confederacy would expect him to arrive—just *logistics* for the deployment should have taken him several days to sort out.

Except that Tasker's Expeditionary Fleet had been assembled for exactly this purpose and been kept ready to go. *Saint Michael* had been kept ready as a matter of course, a long-standing habit of Walkingstick's.

They'd swap out some warships with the vessels from Home Fleet who had full crews aboard, but the main strength of the Expeditionary Fleet was the logistics train, and all of those vessels were ready to go.

Speed and aggression were key. He'd hit the central system of this new Confederacy before they expected him and with far more force than they could possibly counter. *Hopefully*, Tecumseh and their fleet would be in Dakota, following the same logic of centralization Walkingstick was following.

He'd force their surrender, hopefully recapture some of Tecumseh's ships intact, and be back in Sol before two months had elapsed. Then the Dakota Sector and Meridian Sectors would fall into line and the example would be made—if he hit them hard enough and fast enough, potentially made without an excessive amount of bloodshed.

No secession from the Commonwealth would be tolerated. The Imperator would attempt to bring his wayward protégé to heel with shock more than violence, but if the Confederacy chose to fight...

Well, he was bringing fifty warships, and his worst-case estimates said Tecumseh had *maybe* forty—and more likely half that.

20

Deep Space
19:00 February 28, 2738 ESMDT

"OFFICERS AND SPACERS, I give you the Confederacy and the future!"

"The Confederacy and the future!"

James made a mental note to find out which of his staff had come up with the toast Voclain had just given. The Commonwealth Navy's traditional toast was *"Terra, Unity, Freedom!"* which definitely wasn't going to work for the Confederate fleet.

But the toast that everyone had just chorused back in *Krakatoa's* flag mess was *perfect*. The future was what the Confederacy had to be about, after all.

"Thank you, Madona," he told his chief of staff, rising and holding his own wineglass up. "In a different time and a different place, we'd have more people here tonight. We *are* joined by Commodore Volkov and *Commodore* Jack."

Using the courtesy title for Volkov's XO got the chuckle he was aiming for.

"We're also joined by Vice Admiral Yamamoto and Colonel Ó Cochláin," James continued, indicating the two Starfighter Corps officers, "and, thanks to the abundance of fresh-faced Rear Admirals from my own staff, I think we're at risk of imploding from too many stars in one room!"

Safely wrapped in the warp bubble of the Alcubierre-Stetson drive, it was doable to pull together the senior officers of the ship and the four junior admirals that made up James's staff. James had written the promotion list to keep the seniority between the four the same as it had been before—hence Voclain giving the toast as the most senior of them.

"If our communications were more up to it, we might have linked in Vice Admiral Modesitt and her staff, but here we are," he concluded. "We're a bit less than twenty-four hours from our destination, and it seemed a good time to pull us all together for a theoretically social dinner."

The chuckles faded as his collection of senior officers leaned in for his next words. No one in the room mistook the meaning when the Admiral said a dinner was "theoretically social."

"We've spent the last seven days running our people through virtual exercises, facing the realities of our plans and studying the intelligence we have on the Stellar League Navy. I won't pretend I'm not going to miss *Goldwyn* and *Champion*, but that's life. We *needed* them at Persephone."

"Have we made contact with them?" Ove Bevan asked, James's intelligence officer steepling his hands in thought.

"About four hours ago," Mac Cléirich confirmed after glancing at James. "Commodore Gold sends her regards to everyone."

"And has been ordered to stay put," James added. "Which took some convincing—not that two *Paramount*s would have made that much difference here, but she's also a *week* away.

"Whatever happens in New Edmonton, I don't think two carriers showing up in a week is going to change it."

Not only did the *Paramount*s lack any real weapons *other* than their starfighters, the two hundred starfighters the two ships carried were *League* fighters, the pilots Star Admiral Borgogni had left behind when he'd abandoned the system.

"Right now, we remain blind to what is going on in our destination," James continued. "I've been promised a fix for that, but we'll see. Our source for our new coms systems and drones has proven reliable so far, but I'm concerned about relying on them for tactical intelligence.

"As of the last information Admiral Modesitt had, the League formation is in a trailing orbit of Notley, New Edmonton's main inhabited planet. I remind everyone that, thanks to the Commonwealth's operations in this system, Notley is fortified to hell and back again."

"What about the base at Red Deer?" Bevan asked. "I know Amandine had anchorages there."

Red Deer was the New Edmonton System's second gas giant—and where the Commonwealth had anchored their fleet for the extended failed siege of the system.

"And we blew them up when we pulled out. The only thing around Red Deer now is debris, so far as I know," James replied. "Thankfully, Periklos wants to keep his strike force mobile and has kept them out of Notley's gravity well—and away from the fortifications.

"A tactical error on his part, if he's kept it up, but he has reason to believe our intelligence is limited."

"But if our criminal friend gets us live intel..." Bevan murmured.

"Then it is an opportunity, yes," James confirmed. "Certainly, there is no way we can engage the fortifications at Notley. Any battle in New Edmonton needs to be over *before* the forts' starfighters can get involved."

"I wonder..." Voclain trailed off.

"Madona?" James asked. Everyone in the room was almost certainly reviewing their information on the New Edmonton System now.

"It might be more than just keeping his fleet mobile," she murmured.

"My understanding," Yamamoto burred from his own chair, looking at his glass of wine carefully, "is that the League's internal politics are a cesspit. Periklos's control hangs by a thread, and he has many enemies who would rather see him disappear.

"Putting himself in range of, what is it, five thousand missile launchers? He might consider that unwise."

"Perhaps," James conceded. "But that *won't* be the case while there's a hostile fleet in the system. That has always been the League's saving grace—and what has allowed Periklos to survive the war with the Commonwealth, too.

"Against an external threat, the Stellar League fights as one. Once we're in the system, any petty—or even not-so-petty—differences will be put aside to fight us."

"Especially here," Bevan reminded them all. "For almost two *years*, the League and the Commonwealth fought over this system. And while the Confederacy may have seceded, all the League citizens are going to see when they look at us is Commonwealth warships."

"Invading their space again," James finished. He sighed. "I wish there was another way, but we can't wait for Periklos to attack *us*. This has to end."

"Those politics are a complicating factor," the intelligence officer warned. "There are a lot of people who won't cry if Kaleb Periklos runs into the wrong end of a missile, even if he *does* take the cream of the League's war fleet with him."

"Politics are always complicated," Yamamoto observed. "Politics are what got us into this entire mess in the first place—both the war and Walkingstick's coup. Even the Confederacy's politics are going to get complicated faster than we'd like."

James considered the meetings he'd been in—and, among other things, Patience Abiodun's willingness to use her system's relative poverty to subtly influence the actions and decisions of the entire Confederacy.

"They're already complicated," he told his admirals. "But the leadership of the Confederacy, by and large, is trying to do the right thing. That's important."

"I wish we knew more about League politics," Voclain said. "It's possible we could use them against Periklos and head off this entire invasion."

"I've spent twenty years on the League side of the Commonwealth," Bevan told her. "I was on the team that did the analysis that led to the Navy recommending that we let Periklos get away with seizing power.

"There was an argument then that if the TCN *didn't* intervene when someone violently seized control of a theoretically democratic country, we were betraying a lot of the ideals we upheld," the intelligence officer reminded them. "And twelve years ago, we were far enough along in rebuilding from the *first* war with the Alliance that we probably had the ships to intervene.

"But we knew damn well that the moment a Commonwealth ship entered one of the system-states, their civil war was going to end within hours and we'd see every one of those condottieri companies pointed right at us.

"Plus, well..." Bevan shrugged. "The folks in that analysis department in Centauri had all been on the League beat for at least half a decade. We *knew* how much shit and blood was concealed behind their illusion of gentlemanly warfare.

"Just because they'd *formalized* the inter-system-state fights and would put them aside against an external threat didn't make those little wars any less real. A lot of people were dying, losing livelihoods and being displaced while the condottieri and the League's wealthy argued over territory, power and money."

The intelligence officer drained his wine glass in a single swallow.

"In the end, *we* funded Periklos," he admitted. "And that's still classified as all hell, but I'm not sure how bound up I am by Commonwealth secrecy laws anymore."

James had guessed that years before, but it was clearly a surprise to several of his officers.

"We were, I suspect, trying to put an end to the chaos of those 'little wars,'" James told the others. "Periklos has stabilized the League in a way those sixty-odd systems haven't seen in a century. He's using internal peace to bankrupt the condottieri, forcing them to accept SLN contracts and, eventually, buyouts.

"But right now, so far as I can tell, all of that hangs on *him*."

"That's part of why he married Samantha Borgogni," Bevan pointed out. "She was one of the top Condottieri admirals before she joined the SLN and became a Star Admiral for him. About two years ago, she was the name who was starting to float around intelligence circles as the most likely threat to him.

"There are a lot of commanders and planetary leaders who would pull their fleets and systems away from the League's central control if Periklos died—but none of them have the strength to actually break away while the current centralized structure *exists*.

"Borgogni was the first admiral we saw who had the potential to seize *control* of that centralized structure. And Periklos co-opted her quite neatly, so far as I can tell."

"Which means she's sitting in that centralized structure with a powerful support fleet," James noted. "So, what happens if Periklos dies *now*? She's clearly his designated heir."

"All of those commanders and planetary leaders who don't have to face down the League's main battle line are going to make a very different calculation if Periklos is dead and his main battle line with him, aren't they?" Yamamoto asked. "So, what, the League turns back into a dysfunctional disaster?"

"One that still regards themselves as at war with us. It's not a great situation," James warned. "But again, I don't see an alternative. The League's politics aren't going to undercut Periklos any time soon—and if he adds another dozen system-states at the point of his battle fleet, that will help soothe the mood of the oligarchs who dislike him."

"Under giant piles of stolen money," Voclain said grimly. "We know how *that* works."

"Yeah. Because we all helped do it for *our* oligarchs," Carey growled.

Every eye snapped to the most junior member of the flag staff. The fair-haired Alpha Centauri–born officer looked back at them all defiantly.

"We all know we did it," he told them flatly. "I'm from *Centauri*, people. I've watched my own system get rich on 'services' provided to the new systems brought into the Commonwealth. We mostly made things better, but by the eternal stars, we sucked a lot of money out of their economies doing it."

The dining room was silent for a long time before James sighed.

"We all know he's right," he told his people. "If we can't admit that *now*, when we've already walked away from the Commonwealth, we never will. The Commonwealth was supposed to make the galaxy a better place by unifying it. But even where we *did*, we sure as hell didn't do it as *charity*."

"And we all knew the Pacification Corps existed," Mac Cléirich reminded them. "If the Commonwealth was as good a thing as we all tried to convince ourselves it was, why did we have a specialty force dedicated to breaking the will of planetary populations and bringing them in line?"

"We don't have to beat our people up over what they did for Terra," Voclain said firmly. "But...*we*, the *command staff*, need to recognize and face it."

"We're not going to be conquering any star systems for the Confederacy," James said. "The DCN has a purely defensive mandate. That's part of why this whole preemptive counterattack makes me worry. I'd rather begin as we mean to continue.

"This whole discussion of the League's politics, though..." He considered. "I have the shape of something rattling around my head. I'm not solid on it, though. It'll depend on what we see when we arrive."

"Sixteen hundred twenty-five tomorrow we drop out of FTL a light-day short of New Edmonton—Notley, specifically," Carey told them. "Shortly before that, our 'intelligence source' is supposed to start feeding us data."

"Surprisingly, I think our source is reliable," James admitted. "I'm not certain what kind of risks they're willing to take or how detailed the information we receive is going to be, but I am confident that we *will* get something.

"Enough to assess Periklos's strength, anyway."

And while they were waiting for *that*, he was realizing he needed to have a conversation with Modesitt—and whoever back on Meridian had access to the intelligence network Rutherford had built in the League.

21

"WE HAVE A LINK," Mac Cléirich reported. "Forwarding information to all consoles. Looks like just one probe so far... No, we just connected to another."

James didn't wait for his analysts to get to work. He pulled the feed from the q-probes directly into his implants and threw the information up on the main flag bridge display. A third and fourth q-probe feed joined the datastream as his flag staff all linked in.

Two more drones completed the base cardinal directions, the six robotic spacecraft drifting away from Trickster's ship on cold gas thrusters. Mass manipulators allowed those thrusters to be more efficient than the usual laws of physics would suggest, but they still paled compared to the matter-antimatter reaction that fueled the probes' main drives.

"Flight patterns were preprogrammed before launch," Carey reported, the operations officer sounding vaguely irritated. "Two more drones on the line toward the main fleet concentration, but I have no control."

"We weren't expecting control," James replied. "We were promised *data*—which we are getting."

The initial six-drone spread would give them visibility in an expanding sphere around the freighter. It wasn't perfect—it never was —but it was a live datafeed from the heart of a system a light-day and change away.

Part of the problem, James realized, was that they weren't getting any data from the freighter at the heart of the sphere. He was getting live data from all of the q-probes, but that bubble would rapidly leave Trickster's ship behind.

Which was, he presumed, the point. Their criminal acquaintance was covering their own safety first.

"We have ten q-probes in play," Carey finally concluded. "Main-drive activations have been staggered to conceal their origin point if the stealth protocols fail, but..."

"But?" James prompted.

"These are Castle Federation Navy drones," the ops officer reminded him. "From the reports I've read, *we* were never able to localize all of them, even when we knew the things were there."

"Theirs were always better than ours," James agreed. Now that Carey had pointed it out, he took a moment to study the drones' sensor data on each other. "And now that I can see it more clearly, I'm guessing there were a *lot* more of the sneaky bastards out around us than we ever thought."

"Stealth" on q-probes was more a matter of *can't be reliably hit* than *can't be seen*. Right now, though, the q-probes Trickster had sent out into the New Edmonton System were trying not to be seen, and they were doing a significantly better job of it than their Commonwealth cousins would have managed.

"What have we got on Periklos?" he asked. Part of the reason for poking at the drones themselves had been to give Carey and Voclain's team time to analyze the League strike force.

"The fleet is still in a trailing orbit of Notley," Voclain reported.

"They're in extreme missile range of the forts around Notley, roughly two light-minutes away."

Capital-ship missiles—like the Stormwinds in James's own magazines—had the same acceleration as torpedoes or fighter missiles but a full hour of flight time. The fortifications around the inhabited planet could put a missile into any target within four *light-minutes* of Notley.

It would just take those missiles a long time to get there, long enough that James didn't truly consider forts two light-minutes away a factor in the battle. Not when Periklos had conveniently positioned his fleet outside the gravity well of the planet, anyway.

"He is making it easy for us, isn't he?" James murmured. "I wonder…"

"If it's a trap?" Bevan asked, the intelligence officer glaring at the display. "It *has* to be. Why else would he be that far out from the planet?"

"A few reasons," James noted. "And the most likely? He's concerned about whoever has the big red button on the thousands of missile launchers in Notley orbit. If he doesn't trust the local defense command, he doesn't want to hand them a knife at his throat."

"He's also trying to make his logistics easier, and without *knowing* he's got the fleet on their own, we could easily assume he's in Notley orbit and under the umbrella of her guns," Voclain pointed out. "He's not quite far enough out for easy jump in or out, after all. It can be done, but it's risky. All he's really doing is cutting about eight hours off his loop when the rest of his fleet arrives."

"I'm not sure how much 'rest of his fleet' the League can come up with," Carey warned. "We're collating data on the individual ships, but we're looking at twenty-six hulls."

James exhaled a shocked breath.

"That's more than we were expecting," he said mildly. He'd known about *sixteen*. The only good news he could think of was that there only *were* ten each of the SLN's two modern sixty-million-cubic-meter ship classes.

And the other twelve ships were supposed to be tied down. Mostly in the fleet that Periklos had left his wife and Proconsul to keep order in his absence.

"We're still working on the breakdown, but there are only eight sixties," Carey reported. "We've got ten thirty-fives, four fifties, and the rest are forty million cubic meters."

"Some of those have to be logistics ships," Voclain suggested.

"Assault transports," James told her. "It's an invasion fleet, after all. Borgogni had pulled them back after they attacked Persephone. Do we know how many were in that fleet?"

The flag bridge was silent as his staff worked through the information.

"Four," Bevan finally told him. "All were forty-million-cubic-meter ships that had been refitted from freighters bought from the Commonwealth."

"That IDs our four forties then, doesn't it?" James said. "Go through the rest, people. We need to *know* what we're up against."

And maybe, as the q-probes got closer, he'd be able to match the data file he'd received from Meridian to one of those ships.

―――――

"The core of the fleet remains aligned to our prior intelligence," Voclain reported a few minutes later. "Q-probes are close enough for us to get class identifications, at least.

"We're looking at four *Alberto da Giussano*–class carriers, four *Venice*-class battlecruisers, four modern-ish condottieri or ex-condottieri fifty-million-cubic-meter ships, and eight older Condottieri ships around the thirty-five mark.

"Then two logistics ships and four assault transports," she concluded.

James considered the numbers and the math. It did not look good.

"Last intelligence on the bomber-versus-starfighter loadout for SLN cruisers?" he asked.

Somebody had stolen the Commonwealth's bomber and torpedo designs before they had entered mass production—and it had been New Athens Armaments that had produced the first version outside the Commonwealth. While James now figured he knew who had actually stolen the technology, letting NAA produce the first derivatives had been a clever plan on the Alliance's part.

"Last intel was that the only bombers were being carried on the SLN carriers," Bevan told him. "Five eight-ship squadrons for each *da Giussano*. The cruisers are all fighters, but if they're actual League Navy ships, they're carrying Xenophon-type fighters. Comparable to our Katanas."

"So, a hundred and sixty bombers and over two thousand modern starfighters," James concluded. "Plus over two hundred missile launchers, even ignoring the Notley forts."

"Yes, sir."

That left the Dakotan force one small advantage: he had more bombers than the League fleet and almost as many missile launchers. Unfortunately, he was outnumbered three to one in starfighters, and only his battleships could match even the *older* League cruisers for the strength of their positron lances.

And since the effective range of a positron lance was a function of the beam power and the strength of the electromagnetic deflectors on the target, that meant that James's older ships were outranged by everything in the enemy fleet.

"Threading the needle is our only option, isn't it, sir?" Voclain suggested softly. "We are badly outgunned."

"He's made it easier on us, but that's what it feels like," James agreed. "Threading the needle" meant riding the line between being torn apart by gravity flux and dropping out of FTL to arrive closer in to a gravity well than was safe.

They could, if their navigators managed to ride that line, drop the entire fleet inside the range of his oldest ships' energy weapons. Or even closer—inside the range of the seventy-kiloton-per-second secondary guns meant to shoot down starfighters.

It would be risky as hell. They'd drop out right in Periklos's face and hammer his newest capital ships with everything they had.

"If we can take down the *da Giussanos* before they can launch their bombers, then bring in our own carriers farther out..." He let the soft words hang in the air, then shook his head.

"We have to send the battleships in ahead," he decided. "Maybe the battlecruisers, but the *Ocean*s have to stick with the carriers. Put all the bombers together."

It would be a suicide run. Surprise would let the Dakotan battle-ships get in the first hits, but warships were eggshells armed with nuclear hammers. At ranges too close for electromagnetic fields to deflect streams of positrons, they'd be hammering the League fleet with pure antimatter—but the battleships simply didn't have enough guns to take down the entire fleet before they returned fire.

And the Dakotan ships were just as much eggshells as the League's. If they took out the SLN formation's eight modern ships—probably doable—it would reduce the odds and maybe even shatter the enemy morale enough that the survivors would retreat.

But none of James's four battleships would survive the run. Adding the battlecruisers would increase the likelihood of shattering Periklos's armada, but would also add to the death toll. A *Saint*-class battleship like *Saint Bartholomew* had eight thousand people aboard. The older ships were around five thousand.

And James Tecumseh couldn't see a way to get those ships out. They'd *win*—he'd likely trade seven ships for at least fourteen, gutting the invasion fleet and leaving only their oldest ships to face his carriers and strike cruisers—but he'd sacrifice almost half of the entire Dakotan Navy to pull it off.

"Once we drop out of Alcubierre, we'll divide the fleet into two task forces," he said steadily, not letting any sign of his internal turmoil show in his voice. "Task Force Eleven will consist of all seven battle-ships and battlecruisers. Task Force Twelve will consist of all carriers and strike cruisers.

"Vice Admiral Modesitt will take command of Task Force Twelve from *Saratoga*," he continued. "I will transfer to *Saint Bartholomew* and take command of Task Force Eleven."

The flag bridge was silent for at least thirty seconds before Voclain finally spoke up.

"Sir, we can't lose you."

"We can't lose half the *fucking* Navy," James snarled, then took a long, shuddering, breath. "Apologies.

"The possibilities in front of us are ugly," he continued. "We have to consider options we do not like, but the greatest flexibility and options will be left if I command Task Force Eleven.

"I need you all to go through the sensor data on the League ships. I need to know *everything* about them. Everything, people.

"You have about an hour."

"Less. We'll be transferring with you," Carey pointed out.

"No," James said gently. "Dakota needs its crop of new Admirals. Either we will pull through or we will not, but I am not taking my entire flag staff into a mission with this kind of odds."

———

Reynolds intercepted him halfway to the flight deck, the assassin waving James's Marine bodyguards to step back as she fell in beside him.

"Do you have a *plan?*" she asked acidly. "Or are you just going to charge to your death and create a glorious bloody legend? Because believe me, Admiral, the Confederacy needs a living James Tecumseh more than it needs a martyr and a legend."

"I have an idea," he conceded, keeping his tone mild. "I'm *trying* to leave critical people behind to make sure things hold together no matter what happens."

Reynolds clearly didn't get the hint, keeping pace with him as the ship shivered through the exit from warped space.

"You'd serve the Confederacy best by making sure they stay alive," he finally told her.

"If there is a ship in this fleet that I am most worried about letting you spend time on, it's *Saint Bartholomew*," she replied. "I wouldn't put it past Hardison to have left some traps in the computers that are just...*waiting*. So, if you're boarding her, I'm going with you."

James snorted softly.

"I think I may have laid the biggest trap for myself," he admitted. "But that's called *duty* and I walked into it a long time ago."

"You're promising me a plan, Admiral. Better follow through," she told him. "Because I *don't* want to die today, but I'm sticking to you like glue.

"I am *not* going to be the one who tells Abey Todacheeney you got yourself killed in a damn fool stunt because you weren't prepared to order someone else into the breach."

He sighed.

"*The man who gives the order should swing the sword,*" he quoted at her. "But it's more than that. If my idea works out, it *has* to be me."

"Someone else would get it wrong?" she asked.

"No. Someone else wouldn't be heard."

22

"WE WEREN'T EXPECTING to see you back for this, sir," Commodore Arjun Ferreiro told James as the Admiral stepped off the shuttle ramp.

"I have a crazy plan, Captain Ferreiro," James admitted. "And I can't leave it to anyone else to execute."

"Is it the kind of plan that takes down a fleet half again our size without a suicide sacrifice play?" Ferreiro asked drily.

"If it works. If it doesn't work, we could be in major trouble. It's *that* kind of plan."

Arjun Ferreiro had been James's chief of staff when he'd commanded one part of Sector Fleet Dakota. Now he commanded the second-most-powerful warship in the Dakotan Navy and, after Jessie Modesitt, probably knew the fleet commander better than anyone.

"*Saint Bartholomew* is fully up to speed and ready to do her duty, sir," the battleship's commander said. "Flag bridge is online, but I don't have any staff."

"That's fine. Do you have links to the rest of TF Eleven?"

"Yes, sir. Sublight for the battlecruisers, of course, but we do have q-coms with the other battleships."

"Good, we'll need that."

James was already considering his options. A zero-zero course to Periklos's fleet at their full Alcubierre-Stetson-drive acceleration would take two and a half hours—a light-year per day squared translated to a "mere" hundred and thirty thousand gravities, after all.

"Do you have orders for us, sir?"

"Give me...ten minutes on the flag bridge," James said. "I need to go over the data from the tactical teams. Then, if everything is right, well."

He smiled thinly.

"Are you willing to fly into hell at my side, Arjun?" he asked softly. "I have no guarantees this will work, only that we're all going to *die* if I've misread the situation."

"Sir, every officer and spacer in the Dakotan Confederacy Navy followed you into treason," Ferreiro pointed out. "I've been under your command since you arrived here, questions of your honor, integrity and competence hanging over your head.

"I've seen nothing in the last year to justify those questions. Nothing to make me hesitate. Lead on, Admiral, and we will follow."

"Be careful, Captain, I haven't even told you the plan yet," James said with a chuckle.

"Does it have a chance of getting through this without wiping out half of our fleet? I can do the math on what will happen if we take four battleships and three battlecruisers into the heart of Periklos's fleet, sir. We'll gut them, we'll save the Confederacy...but none of us will be coming back, either."

"It has a chance," he told his subordinate. "But I don't know how big of one."

"Sounds better that no chance at all. Let's make it happen."

———

Identity match: eighty-five percent probability.

James was alone in the flag bridge, which meant no one was there to hear him curse.

Eighty-five percent.

It was a hell of a probability to bet an entire war on. And eighty-five percent was just the chance that they'd correctly identified the ship. There were a dozen other places his intelligence could be wrong.

"It's more like fifty-fifty," he said aloud, staring at the two silhouettes and their associated emission spectrums. One was from the intelligence he'd had forwarded from Rutherford's network. One was extracted from the q-probe data even now flowing in from Notley.

"Sir?"

He looked up to see Reynolds slipping in the door.

"Reynolds."

"I heard…swearing?"

"I am known to do that, Agent," James pointed out.

"Usually one word at a time, sir."

"Right." James swallowed down another round of expletives and turned back to the display.

"Agent, what's the worst odds you've ever launched an operation on?" he asked softly.

"In what sense? Of pulling the mission off? Usually pretty solid. CISS always gave us the resources we needed."

"How about in the sense of the mission achieving the actual goal?" he countered.

"Despite what CISS would have everyone think, the folks planning the operations are far from omniscient," Reynolds said slowly, stepping up to look over his shoulder. James doubted she could make sense of the two diagrams—not even all naval officers were sufficiently read up on this kind of analysis to make a guess.

"Political assassination is never an exact science. Things…*happen*," she continued. "Officially, we only launched ops where we were certain we'd have the result we were after. But even killing the only person involved in something sometimes isn't enough to stop it.

"People become symbols. Martyrs for their cause—and then the political movement you were trying to cut off before it exploded turns into an active rebellion."

She shook her head.

"Most of the time, true odds were fifty-fifty. In hindsight, I'm not sure I trust *any* of the assessments. But I wasn't the one making the calls. Just the one taking the shots."

James chuckled.

"Amazing how much fleet operations have in common with assassinations," he said grimly. He gestured at the display. "Eighty-five percent chance that I've identified the right ship. Maybe seventy-five percent chance that my intelligence is correct as to what *is* the right ship.

"And then the last little bit...of which way does a human jump."

"Individual humans are a *bitch* to predict," Reynolds told him. "CISS liked to claim that their psych profiles and intelligence analysis gave them a sixty-three percent success rate in predicting well-researched targets response to specific actions."

"Sixty-three percent, huh? With a profile I don't even have."

"Exactly. Sometimes...well, sometimes, you just have to throw the dice."

James mimed throwing a set of craps dice onto the holoprojector's base and looked at the display.

"Eighty-five percent that our Bogey Battlecruiser Three is *Genoa*," he told her. "Which is *supposed* to be Periklos's flagship."

"Sounds like assassination might be closer to fleet operations than I think," Reynolds said drily.

"Perhaps. But today..." He sighed.

"Today it's time to roll the dice."

Silent commands opened a channel to Commodore Ferreiro and his flag staff.

"It's time, everyone," he told them. "*Saint Bartholomew* will enter warped space as soon as you're ready, Captain Ferreiro.

"The rest of Task Force Eleven will maintain a live q-com with *Bartholomew* and warp space fifteen minutes after we do. Task Force Twelve will warp ten minutes after that."

23

New Edmonton System
02:30 March 2, 2738 ESMDT

A SHIP under Alcubierre-Stetson drive was invulnerable, inviolate. Locked in its own private universe, the regular world was merely a strange bow of light visible for those brave enough to look outside an ordinary window.

A ship in warped space wasn't *quite* invisible—but it was untouchable. Even for the last few minutes, where their velocity dipped below that of light, they were difficult to see—and blind.

But for the first time since the Alliance of Free Stars had shattered the Commonwealth's communications, James Tecumseh had q-coms and q-probes. The robotic spacecraft circled Periklos's fleet at a million kilometers, giving *Saint Bartholomew*'s crew a view of their target only a few seconds out of date.

They knew where their enemy was and their enemy didn't even know they were coming.

"We have *Genoa* dialed in," Ferreiro told James. "Are you sure about this, sir?"

"If I were sure about this, the rest of the fleet wouldn't be coming in on the sequence needed for the backup plan," he pointed out. "One way or another, *this* invasion is going to stop."

The Commodore chuckled grimly.

"That's for sure. Sixty seconds. Hold on to your hat."

The air was already keening around James. Threading the needle was always a *fascinating* experience, though at least they weren't going deep this time. Periklos had wanted to cut his deployment time down and had believed he'd know if Dakota moved.

He'd been *wrong*, but the sound tearing at James's eardrums was a reminder that the universe wasn't *happy* to have humans twisting space-time into pretzels so they could violate its fundamental laws— and inside the gravity wells of large objects, that discontent became even more evident than usual.

There was enough time for one final check. *Saint Bartholomew's* systems were all green. The rest of the battleships were fifteen minutes behind them. The carriers and cruisers were ten minutes behind that.

The command ships were dialed into the same sensors he was. The rest of the fleet had enough q-coms to get a go-no-go signal, which was all they were going to need today.

"Thirty seconds. All hands stand by. All lances fully online."

James was still linked to the battleship's bridge, listening to the calm reports. The keening was growing even sharper, and he pushed past it, taking a final few moments to make sure his uniform was as presentable as possible.

It was silly...but it might well matter.

"Five seconds," Ferreiro said sharply. "We're almost there."

"Execute Counting Coup, Commodore," James ordered softly.

The battleship crashed back into reality like a breaching whale, her emergence locus nailed down with every bit of precision that her crew could manage. Across a single light-day, they'd nailed it within five hundred kilometers—and emerged barely five *thousand* kilometers from the Stellar League Navy battlecruiser *Genoa*.

Dictator Kaleb Periklos's personal flagship.

Twenty-four positron lances flared in space, their targeting updated in the quarter-second between emergence and activation. Enough anti-matter to obliterate even the most powerful warships blazed out into space…and missed *Genoa* by less than a kilometer on all sides.

"Dictator Periklos, this is Admiral James Tecumseh," James said into the video pickup on the bridge grimly. "I do believe I have just demonstrated that you are *dead* if I choose it. You cannot destroy this ship before we fire again, and *Genoa* will not survive that strike.

"We both know your vision for the League will not last without you. If you value the mission you swore to preserve, let's talk.

"I won't demand your surrender," James told the other man. "But I *will* demand an end to this pointless fucking war."

———

For five seconds, the frozen tableau of *Saint Bartholomew* and *Genoa* dominated James's displays. Ten seconds. The fleet around them was equally frozen, presumably having seen James's message and decided to wait and see what their Dictator did.

The two ships were basically in each other's back pockets by space-combat standards. There would be *just* enough warning if *Genoa* acti-vated her lances for *Bartholomew*'s crew to fire. If Periklos wanted a fight, it would be a mutual suicide pact between the two flagships.

Then, of course, the rest of the Dakotan battleships would arrive and take out the other modern League ships. The confusion of Perik-los's death might buy them the edge they needed to punch though and escape intact. It might not.

But whether James Tecumseh lived depended on the Dictator of the Stellar League.

Fifteen seconds. Twenty.

"What is he *thinking*?" Reynolds muttered at the back of the flag bridge.

"Hopefully, about his mortality, his wife and his weeks-old daugh-ter," James replied.

"Radio link!" Ferreiro's com officer reported, the man half-shouting in shocked surprise.

"Connect it to the flag bridge," James ordered.

A moment later, a hologram of a heavyset man in a stark white uniform appeared in front of James. Kaleb Periklos had more muscle than fat to his bulk, but he was still an absolutely immense man. His white uniform lacked insignia, announcing that the color was enough for everyone to know who the wearer was.

Or that everyone should *know* who the wearer was, regardless of insignia, medals or anything else. This was, after all, the Dictator of sixty-plus star systems and some two hundred billion people.

"Admiral James Tecumseh," Periklos greeted him. "You appear to have a strong sense of the dramatic—and you most *definitely* have my attention. Before I agree to anything, before we *speak* of anything, I must ask:

"Who do you speak for?"

James smiled thinly. Whatever else had happened over the last few years, Kaleb Periklos almost certainly held a grudge against the Terran Commonwealth.

"I am now the Fleet Admiral, commanding, of the Navy of the Dakotan Interstellar Confederacy," he told the other man. "I speak for the interim government of the worlds that *were* the Dakota and Meridian Sectors—worlds that are no longer part of the Terran Commonwealth and have no desire to be involved in any continuation of the Commonwealth's war with the League.

"But since you gathered an invasion fleet within striking distance of our systems, a point needed to be made."

"A point." A wry smile crossed Periklos's face, hardly the reaction James had expected in the circumstances. "I do believe I'm going to have to issue clean shipsuits for a large portion of *Genoa*'s crew, Admiral Tecumseh, so let us consider your 'point' made.

"Let us speak. Given that *your* ship is currently surrounded by my ships, I feel the best measure to make this actually work is if I come aboard *your* vessel." The wry smile turned into a clear smirk. "I will be coming neither alone nor unarmed. I presume that is acceptable."

"So long as you are prepared to make peace with the Confederacy, we are prepared to speak," James told the other man carefully. "Bring whatever you must."

The channel closed and James released a long sigh.

"Sir?" Ferreiro asked after a moment.

"There will be a shuttle coming from *Genoa*," James told him. "Send the no-go signal to the fleet. Battleships will adjust to emerge at the carrier emergence point, and the fleet will stand by for further orders."

"And what if this is an attempt to remove our advantage, sir?"

"I give it about one chance in three at this point," James admitted. "But for two chances in three of peace with the League...I have to take the risk.

"Make certain we have a space near the shuttlebay ready for diplomatic negotiations."

24

"No-go. We have a no-go signal from the Admiral."

That was *not* what Anthony had been expecting. The pilot was wrapped up in the acceleration couch on his starfighter, like every other starfighter pilot, gunner, and flight engineer aboard Dakota's fleet.

"What is he *doing*?" he demanded on a private channel to Mac Cléirich. It probably wasn't fair to expect the communications officer to know what the Admiral was thinking, but when basically the entire Navy of their fledgling nation was halfway into a do-or-die charge...

"Being clever," Mac Cléirich said grimly. "The no-go signal was fleet-wide, but that's all the cruisers *could* receive. Battleships are diverting to our emergence point. Suicide charge appears to have been diverted."

"Any more detailed orders?" Anthony asked. "Other than *Don't fight the battle we came here for*?"

She chuckled grimly.

"Not yet. You and Modesitt are the Vice Admirals. I think that makes it all your call."

Anthony swallowed several *very* Scottish expletives, eventually settling on a phrasing that made no sense to anyone. Including him.

"*Haggis.*"

"Sir?"

If he had to make a call, he needed more data.

"Get me a q-com link to Modesitt," he ordered. "And see if the rest of the flag staff can get Admiral Modesitt and me any information on what the Old Man is doing."

The last thing Anthony Yamamoto wanted to do was accidentally undermine Tecumseh's plan—but the Admiral had given them so little explanation beyond that he was taking *Saint Bartholomew* in first that even *Anthony* wasn't sure what Tecumseh was doing.

Except that it was crazy...and based on the no-go order, it was *working*.

Krakatoa was still in warped space. So was *Saratoga*—but, thanks to their Trickster-provided coms, Anthony could speak with the other Admiral.

"It *looks* like the Admiral has convinced Periklos to at least *talk* peace," Mac Cléirich told him. "*Saint Bartholomew* has taken up position a thousand kilometers away from *Genoa* and...a shuttle is due to bring the Dictator aboard *Saint Bart* shortly."

"So, the Admiral has gone insane," Modesitt observed as she joined the link. "Someone spent too much time with Kyle Roberts."

"That's not a name that should be associated with any Commonwealth officer," Anthony replied. He was *aware* that James Tecumseh had spent time working with the Alliance against pirates, but the details were vague.

"Yes, well, our mission went all kinds of sideways, and the Stellar Fox was in the area to help us pick up the pieces," the other Vice Admiral told him bluntly. "Not happening this time, but it seems that Tecumseh picked up some of the Fox's tricks."

"So, what do *we* do?"

"Concentrate the fleet at the emergence point and back the Admiral's play. Unless you have another idea? You *are* senior."

That sent a chill down Anthony's spine. Somehow, *command of the entire Starfighter Corps* was sufficiently abstract not to sink in the same way *You are arguably in command of this battle fleet* did.

"I think both of us know any seniority between us is a matter of paperwork, not reality," he told her. "And I don't see another plan. We'll put...a third of the fighters and bombers into space and hold the rest at the ready.

"That will give us a decent immediate strike if needed but with the rest of the fighters on standby. We're emerging *in* missile range for the capital ships, so we're presenting a threat no matter what we do.

"Our job now is...to look intimidating," he concluded. "We all drop out of FTL at twenty million kilometers, and it gets very clear to the Dictator that we are present and prepared to play. He'll also probably realize just what the original plan *was*—and hopefully catch on that the Admiral made a *choice* not to kill him and shatter his fleet."

"Our losses would have been brutal," Modesitt told him. "But... that *was* the plan."

"Periklos doesn't care what our losses would have been," Anthony pointed out. "*He* cares that the only reason he's still alive is because the Old Man decided he'd rather preserve our fleet than wreck the League for the next decade."

———

The downside of accepting that they *weren't* about to launch the full fleet strike was that Vice Admiral Anthony Yamamoto had no business in a starfighter in anything *less* than a full-deck strike—and the carrier task force was still twenty minutes from emergence when they received the no-go order.

There was *plenty* of time for Anthony to extract himself from his starfighter and return to the carrier's fleet CAG station on the flag bridge. And despite his residual fighter-jock instincts, he knew what his job was.

He was still grumpier than he should have been when he took his seat on the flag bridge with an acknowledging nod to the rest of the flag staff.

"All fighters are standing by. Every third squadron is prepped for launch," Brahms said in his head.

At some point, Anthony would concede he needed a staff. For now, the DCSC's Command Master Chief was *managing* the Vice Admiral—and Anthony was allowing himself to be managed.

"Thank you, Chief," he murmured.

"Task Force Eleven reports emerged and in position," Mac Cléirich announced.

"Updating tactical feeds to layer in their sensors," Carey added.

Anthony picked up those feeds in his implant, orienting himself to view the main tactical display. If the Old Man wasn't around, he supposed *he* should be using the flag bridge to its full potential.

Task Force Eleven's six ships formed a phalanx of green icons on his display, a shield that the carriers and strike cruisers would emerge behind. Beyond them was the hailstorm of red icons representing the League Fleet—with the single solitary green icon representing *Saint Bartholomew* in the center.

"Q-probes have picked up one shuttle launching from *Genoa*," Carey said. "Course is toward *Saint Bartholomew*."

"So, either it's a giant bomb and all of this was a ploy to disable *Saint Bartholomew* without losing their fleet...or the Dictator is actually going to talk," Anthony noted. "At least the *quiet* part of the Admiral's threat will be present, yes?"

"Shuttle has a five-minute flight time," Carey confirmed. "We are emerging...now."

Eight ships burst out of FTL, the keening Anthony had been forcing himself to ignore vanishing with a tactile popping sensation.

"Ready squadrons launching."

Twenty-two squadrons of Katana starfighters and six of Longbow bombers. Anthony didn't even need to look to confirm the numbers; he *knew* what the orders he'd given would result in.

"Get everyone formed up, defensive perimeter," he ordered. "Link us in with *Saratoga*."

As much as possible, he was planning on letting Modesitt take the lead with the actual *fleet*, but he had his own part to play. Even as he gave audible orders to the flag-deck staff, he was reviewing the fighter positions in his implant and ordering squadrons to new positions.

They'd given up their best advantage with the goal of avoiding a fight. If things went wrong now, it was up to Jessie Modesitt and Anthony Yamamoto to pull the DCN out of this mess—preferably while doing enough damage to leave Periklos unwilling to continue his war against the Confederacy.

Tecumseh's plan was clear now, but Anthony Yamamoto wasn't sure how far *he'd* trust a man who'd imposed a military dictatorship on over sixty star systems. There were lines, after all, that soldiers weren't supposed to cross.

He knew James Tecumseh wouldn't cross them—*knew* to his bones. He lacked anything close to that certainty when it came to Kaleb Periklos.

25

THE FIRST PEOPLE off the League shuttle were a trio of young men in matching dark blue suits. They said nothing, spreading out in a clearly practiced movement that let them get eyes on the entire shuttlebay.

James didn't need Reynolds' almost-invisible snap into ready stance to know what kind of people the Dictator of the Stellar League had sent out ahead of himself. He could see it in how they moved, how their gazes swept the entire space.

None of the three was armed with more than a small pistol—but James had very carefully never looked too closely into what kind of "pistol" Reynolds carried on duty. He suspected it had a price tag to rival a small spaceship and could probably *kill* a small spaceship.

Periklos's three escorts might not officially be assassins, but they definitely had a skillset and a bearing that reminded James of Reynolds —and clearly set all of *his* assassin-turned-bodyguard's alarm bells ringing.

Nothing about the visible squad of Confederacy Marines seemed to bother the guardians, though, and Periklos emerged from the shuttle a minute or so after they did.

There had very clearly been some genetic engineering in the League man's family history. Periklos had seemed immense on a holographic call, but James had assumed, however unconsciously, that the pickups had been set up to exaggerate the Dictator's size.

The opposite had very clearly been the case. Kaleb Periklos towered well over two meters tall, with shoulders and muscles to scale with his height. James had met enough strange and unusual people and varieties of humanity over the years to take just about anything in stride—he'd worked with the pirate Antonio Coati, for example, who'd had glittering scales for skin!

So, despite Periklos's unusual scale, James stepped forward calmly to greet the leader of the Stellar League.

There was a tilt to the man's smile that suggested he'd *expected* James to be taken aback. He paused for a moment at the top of the shuttle ramp to adjust a weapon belt holding a pistol and a rapier with a complex golden guard.

"Admiral James Tecumseh," he greeted James, ignoring Reynolds and the Marines as he stepped forward and offered James his hand.

"Dictator Kaleb Periklos," James replied, taking the proffered handshake.

Periklos tightened his grip once he had James's hand, raising the pressure to see what James could take. James smoothly met him pressure for pressure—since *his* hand was entirely artificial, it was a question of when the Leaguer would let go.

For half a second, James suspected that the Dictator might push it hard enough to actually *break* something. He was certainly willing to meet the man's dominance display grip for grip, locking gazes with Periklos as he slowly increased his grip pressure.

Finally, Periklos released the handshake, his gaze surprised as he glanced down at James's hand.

"I lost both arms and a leg in the service of the Commonwealth, Dictator Periklos," James told the man brightly. "I hope *not* to lose the last limb in the service of the Confederacy. *Saint Bartholomew's* crew have set up a meeting space for us.

"Shall we?"

"Lead on, Admiral Tecumseh."

———

In James's educated and experienced opinion, the Commonwealth had been far too willing to conduct its diplomacy from the decks of a warship. They had, at least, built their ships to allow their diplomats and local commanders to meet the people they were intimidating with style.

The space Commodore Ferreiro's people had set up for James was designed for just this kind of purpose. The battleship had a series of spaces that could be divided up into highly secure meeting rooms or combined into several intimate dining spaces or larger meeting rooms —or *all* combined into a massive banquet or event hall.

At that moment, the entire space had been combined into one. The security systems were slightly more visible this way, but the *true* point of it was that there was one table in the middle of all of that space.

In Commonwealth service, the walls would have been hung with the Commonwealth and TCN flags. The Confederacy hadn't quite managed to *decide* on things like flags yet, so *Saint Bart's* crew had taken the banners for the twelve systems and lined the walls with those in a repeating pattern.

Twelve system flags and the red-knife insignia of *Saint Bartholomew* herself repeated around the room, a massive space that *echoed* with their footsteps as James led the way to the midsized conference table at the center of the space.

James gestured Periklos to one of the two seats at the table and took his own chair opposite the man. Reynolds dropped into parade rest behind his right shoulder, and he waited as the massive Leaguer poked carefully at the chair.

The seat was an actively adjusting ergonomic masterpiece, something the Commonwealth Navy literally ordered by the *million* to get the price down to something reasonable, and it readily expanded and adjusted to provide space for Kaleb Periklos.

The Dictator made a relieved sound and settled into the seat, waving his own bodyguards back as he studied James across the table.

"Rutherford, I expected to fuck the Commonwealth," he finally said. "You, though. You never seemed the type."

"We all find ourselves called to duty in different ways," James told him. "The worlds that were the Dakota and Meridian Sectors are now the Dakotan Interstellar Confederacy. But you knew that. And you were going to invade us anyway."

"I did know that," Periklos conceded. "I see we're not playing diplomatic footsy today."

"We're not here to find pretty words and share baby pictures. We're here to avoid a war my country doesn't want and yours doesn't need," James snapped.

"I mean, if you want baby pictures, Sam has sent me about three thousand in the last couple of weeks," the Dictator of the League replied, his body language nearly completely changing as he shifted into *excited new father* mode. He restrained himself after a moment, though, returning to *ruthless warlord*.

James couldn't help himself. He laughed.

"I see that even at our most ruthless and pragmatic, humanity is still vulnerable to their own babies."

"Everything I have done, Admiral, was for the future of the League," Periklos told him. "To know that *my daughter* will see that future... It makes a lot of things more immediate in a way I hadn't anticipated. And I haven't even had a chance to hold Bastilla yet."

"That sounds like it's more productive than invading the Confederacy to me," James said drily.

"That depends on the politics. Peppi Borgogni fucked up. More by trying to force a Condottieri company into a losing battle than in yielding Persephone, if I'm being honest," Periklos said. "But somehow, despite *never* having punished an Admiral for failures that weren't their fault before, people seem to expect me to punish my brother-in-law and say I am weak for not doing so.

"Say that I have *lost face* because of Peppi's withdrawal. So, here we are, with a strong feeling in my supporters and enemies alike that I need to wipe away that failure by retaking Persephone."

"We both know that this negotiation is effectively taking place with our guns in each other's mouths," James replied. "You're not getting Persephone back. If you're unwilling to concede that, we're both going to end up dead—and I suspect the Confederacy will survive losing me far better than the League will survive losing you."

"The League would survive losing me," Periklos told him. "But the *modern* League, the real central authority, the pause on the internal strife, the *end* to the pointless dying…that will fade. I have not yet built those changes into our foundations."

"Whereas I am but one soldier. The Confederacy needs the leaders and voices gathered on Dakota to survive. I am just their shield. I will not permit you to attack our systems, whatever the price."

"I am prepared to extend the same offer my wife made Rutherford," Periklos told him. "Transfer sovereignty of the Persephone System, and we will leave your little nation alone as we move against the rest of the former Commonwealth."

"Did I fucking stutter?" James barked. "We will yield nothing. The only concession I am prepared or authorized to make is that I *didn't* blow your flagship apart the moment we came out of warped space. The *plan* would have wiped out your entire fleet.

"You assumed we didn't have FTL probes or FTL coms and that you were safe. You were wrong. The only reason you aren't *dead* is because I chose to try to talk.

"We did not invade your systems. We did not *execute* half the fucking members of one of your planetary legislatures. Your brother-in-law is guilty of *war crimes*." James glared at Periklos. "I am prepared to let all of that go in pursuit of peace, but do not play games with me, Kaleb Periklos.

"Neither of us would survive this becoming a battle—but I suspect I am far more prepared to die than you are."

"Peppi was perhaps…overzealous, but his actions were within the scope of securing an occupied world," Periklos told him. "And the Commonwealth *did* invade us, Admiral. We had *nothing* to do with the

Tau Ceti raid, but rather than accept our offers of assistance in investigating the attack, you invaded *this* system."

Which had begun the back-and-forth seizure, loss, siege and re-seizure of New Edmonton that had defined the war between Commonwealth and League.

"And we are not the Commonwealth," James said softly. "I believe you, Admiral, that you were not involved in the Tau Ceti incident. I'm...confident, at this point, that the Tau Ceti incident was a covert test of the same methods and intelligence that would eventually deliver the destruction of the Commonwealth's entire communication infrastructure.

"The Confederacy has seceded from the Commonwealth. We will not be dragged in the muck with a nation whose choices we did not agree with. Yes, Confederacy systems were used as bases for the Commonwealth Navy in those operations, but they will not be so used now. I can promise that.

"The question I find I must face is whether I can trust the promises of the man who *murdered* Marshal Amandine when she came to negotiate peace," James concluded.

Periklos held his gaze for a long moment, anger flashing in his eyes to match James's own wrath, then exhaled it all in a long sigh.

"It's all bullshit, isn't it?" he asked conversationally. "The worst part to *that* particular mess, Admiral Tecumseh, is that even the *truth* sounds like the kind of propaganda excuse dictators and war criminals use to cover their own actions.

"That truly *was* an overzealous subordinate exceeding their orders and authority. Star Commander Kleio Whalen *should* have escorted *Saint Raymond*, *Mare Frigoris* and *Essex* to meet Peppi Borgogni. He had two of our old *Athens*-class battleships and that was the *plan*.

"And then somebody on *Essex* managed to push every button a man who'd lost two older brothers and a father to Commonwealth punitive expeditions could have. And Kleio Whalen blew three Commonwealth warships to hell."

"Speaking of war crimes, I suppose," James said drily. "What, sixteen thousand people killed because you can't control your battleship captains?"

"Whalen was delivered to Athens in chains and, frankly, Sam almost killed him when she arrived in-system. My wife did *not* take breaking our oath of safety lightly, Admiral."

"That means very little to the dead. So do your protestations of *normal operations* on Persephone," James told him. "But the Confederacy is not at war with the League. Not yet."

"The difference between a Confederacy that contains systems, officers and ships that were all too recently involved in the attack on our territory and the Commonwealth that ordered those attacks seems... semantic to me," Periklos told him. "So, tell me, Admiral Tecumseh, how do *you* see this resolving?"

"I'd settle for an agreement that the Confederacy isn't the Commonwealth and therefore isn't at war with the League," James replied. "I'd *love* a formal mutual nonaggression pact. We're not going to attack you, and I am...prepared to trust your word if you commit to the same in return."

"And if I tell you, Admiral, that I will not deal with *any* Commonwealth successor state that does not acknowledge the Commonwealth's war guilt and pay reparations for the attack on our systems?"

James smiled thinly.

"The Dakotan Confederacy is entirely willing to acknowledge the *Commonwealth's* war guilt for the attack on the Stellar League, recognizing that the so-called 'punitive expedition' was launched without sufficient investigation of the attack on Tau Ceti," he told Periklos.

That, after all, was basically free as far as he was concerned.

"War reparations, however, are something you should discuss with the Star Chamber delegation the Commonwealth sent to negotiate with you. The Confederacy did not launch that war and is not responsible for the actions of the Commonwealth Navy during it."

"I *did* discuss it with them," Periklos told him. "It was part of the package of demands I sent them back to Earth with—I'll note that *they* got in and out safely."

He sighed.

"Which is not something I enjoy having to specify. Would you like me to shoot Whalen as part of the peace deal?"

That was the first time Periklos had spoken in such a way as to imply the deal was a matter of *details* rather an insurmountable problem, and James barely managed to conceal a sigh of relief.

"I think I'll leave him in your custody for the Commonwealth to ask for his head," he told the League Dictator. "For ourselves, I will make the acknowledgement of the Commonwealth's war guilt on behalf of the Confederacy, and I will commit the Confederacy not to attack the League."

James didn't *like* Periklos. The man was surprisingly charming in person, but he was also a ruthless dictator with the blood of tens of thousands—probably *hundreds* of thousands—on his hands. But with a tyrant to the left of him and a tyrant to the right, he didn't have much choice.

He needed peace on at least one front. By preference, *both*, but despite his assurances to the Cabinet, he *knew* Walkingstick. He knew the Imperator would not rest until the Commonwealth was reunified or James Calvin Walkingstick was dead.

Periklos was silent for a full minute, eyeing him levelly.

"Are you aware of the traditions around Condottieri swords, Admiral Tecumseh?" he finally asked.

"I am not," James admitted, surprised by the apparent tangent.

"The Condottieri companies of the Stellar League are born out of a romanticization of a particularly messy period of Italian history on Earth," Periklos told him. "Just as the entire structure of a league of system-states is born out of a romanticization of particular periods of *Greek* history."

"As I recall, the various Greek city-state leagues were thinly concealed empires," James pointed out.

"And the Italian Condottieri were often only one step removed from bandits on a *good* day," the modern League's leader told him. "Humanity's ability to romanticize history is surprisingly useful, especially when we're building new structures and new ideals.

"Out of the *particular* fascination with the Italian Condottieri that birthed our mercenary fleets came an obsession with the swords of that era, and the tradition rose of senior Condottieri officers having Renaissance-style dueling swords upon getting their own ships."

That, at least, explained *why* Periklos was carrying the sword.

"The tradition is that the sword should be *usable*, even recognizing that a starship captain is never going to use it," the Dictator noted drily. "We've also had almost four hundred years since the founding of the League to build new and messy traditions around the blades, too.

"One of those is a recognition of the fact that the Condottieri companies had relationships, oaths, surrenders and conflicts entirely separate from those of their employers. The contracts were ironclad, and the companies went to war and agreed to peace with their employers, but the Condottieri also wanted war to be a survivable business."

"For them, at least," James murmured. Part of Periklos's official justification for seizing power and imposing central rule onto the League had been to stop the inevitable casualties when two fleets had even a "polite" war in a star system.

"Agreed," Periklos conceded. "But to achieve that, they needed a way to *know* that, contract or no contract, a defeated mercenary company *was* going to remove themselves from the conflict at hand. Mercenary companies couldn't sign treaties, and while our contracts were solid, something *more* was needed."

Periklos removed his sword, scabbard and all, from his weapon belt and laid it on the table—hilt toward James.

"So, upon surrendering, a Condottieri Admiral gave up their sword to the victor," he murmured. "It was both a recognition of defeat and a necessity—and a solemn commitment to withdraw from the conflict they had clashed in.

"The tradition *now* is that a company will do everything within its power to avoid further conflict with the person holding the sword for at least two years," Periklos conceded. "I have yielded my sword once in my entire career, Admiral Tecumseh—to Samantha Borgogni, ironically, almost twenty years ago."

"And now?" James asked, looking at the archaic weapon on the table.

"And now I am giving my sword to you. You will provide me with a formal statement of your assessment of the Commonwealth's war against the League. We will take each other's word, for now, on a cease-fire—and over the next couple of days, our staffs will hash out a mutually acceptable commitment of mutual nonaggression.

"But understand that to *me*, the sword is a sacred promise," Periklos told him. "Break faith with me at your peril, Admiral Tecumseh, but you have your peace."

Slowly and a bit hesitantly, James reached out and picked up the sword. It was sized to Periklos, which made it an unwieldy hunk of metal to his hand, but that only made the weight of the commitment involved in the gesture more obvious.

"The Confederacy will keep faith with the League for as long as faith is kept with us," he promised. "You have my word—and that, to *me*, is a sacred promise."

26

THE SWORD LOOKED SURPRISINGLY at home in James's office aboard *Krakatoa*, surrounded by the decorative fingerweaving of his tribe's ancient style and propped up on the two lucite-encased pieces of his Marshal's mace.

Abey Todacheeney's touch was clear throughout his working space —somewhat ironically, since she'd taken on the task of recruiting local Shawnee artisans on Dakota to create the hangings well before they'd entered any kind of personal relationship.

Even James's *desk* was a masterpiece of blending the old and new, a hand-shaped behemoth with distinctive wave patterns from Shawnee art burned into it that contained the latest in modern technology.

The intent, as he understood it, had been to both remind him that Dakota was home to the largest number of his tribespeople outside Sol —and, between that reminder and the gift itself, to help bind him to a world that depended on him for security.

He supposed it had worked, though he didn't think he'd changed his plans for the desk any more than he'd changed them for the girlfriend.

The girlfriend who was currently late for their scheduled call. Fortunately, the usual laws of Murphy applied, and the seal of the *original* Dakotan Confederacy—the coalition of tribal leaders that served as Dakota's planetary government—finally vanished from above his desk.

The holoprojectors around his office flickered for a moment, then created the illusion that the First Chief of Dakota was sitting across the desk from him. She'd have the opposite setup on her side, he knew, with him appearing on the supplicant side of her formal desk.

"Abey," he greeted her. "Good to see you."

"A bit late in the whole *prepared to die for my country* process to be talking to me, isn't it?" she asked acidly.

James winced.

"Did you think, for *one* moment, that maybe you should have talked to me before you charged off to die gloriously?"

"I had to do it," he told her. "I'm not sure Periklos would have listened to anyone else, even with the stunt we pulled."

"I'm not arguing that, James," she told him. "I'm *telling* you that you damn well should know better than to launch a suicide mission without *talking to me.*"

James looked down at his desk, but he could feel her eyes burning into him.

"There was very little time and I didn't think," he admitted. "And what thinking I *did* do was that if I looked you in the eye and told you my plan, I wouldn't be able to do it. It's hard to commit to a suicide mission when you have too much to live for."

The silence hung in the air for far too long.

"I'd like to say I wouldn't have tried to talk you out it," she told him. "I'm not sure that would be honest or fair of me, but I want to say it. As a politician and a leader, I can see what you did and why. Your plan would have made sense...but I'll admit I'm selfish enough to tell you to send someone else."

"I couldn't have," he told her. *"The man who gives the order should swing the sword.* I won't send people to their deaths without riding with them.

"And Periklos would only have listened to me."

"I suspect twenty-four positron lances might have convinced him to listen to someone else," Abey said drily.

"Who else would he have believed had the authority to negotiate on behalf of the Cabinet? The man is a military dictator—he wasn't going to negotiate with a starship captain. He might not have even thought the *Cabinet* had the real power to negotiate."

"So, it had to be you, did it?"

"Yes."

He looked up and met her gaze. She looked...less angry. Not calm but *less* angry.

"And I should have talked to you," he admitted. "But I didn't think of it, because I was so focused on preventing a war—or winning the battle if I couldn't."

Abey sighed.

"I'm an economist, a bureaucrat and a politician," she told him. "But even *I* recognize that you cannot always ride into fire with your people. Part of your job, James, is going to involve sending people to their deaths and not being able to go with them."

"I know. But it's the hardest damn part," he conceded. "I owe it to my people to make their sacrifices worthwhile—and *yes*, sometimes that means I have to live when I send people to die. In this case, my hatred of that concept lined up neatly with the need to have someone there that Kaleb Periklos would see as a worthy counterpart."

"Or so you convinced yourself."

James swallowed his immediate retort and focused on the sword sitting in front of him for a few seconds.

"It is almost certainly a good thing," he finally observed, "for both myself and the nation I serve...that the woman I love is eminently capable of seeing through layers of self-deception even I don't realize are there."

"We also serve who pop commanders' overinflated egos?" she asked sweetly. "But seriously, James, do *not* go off on another suicide charge without at least talking to me. Can you even *begin* to imagine how I would be feeling today if Periklos had taken the shot?"

"No," he admitted. He really had no idea how that would have felt —he was dating a politician. *He* didn't need to worry about her doing something suicidal.

"I can," she said. "Because I've spent the last few hours looking at the fact that my boyfriend decided he was prepared to sacrifice himself for his ideals and his nation and didn't bother to even *tell me himself* before charging off."

"My only defense is that I didn't die and I managed to make peace with the League," James said quietly. "But yes, I should have talked to you first. Even if only to say goodbye."

"If you'd said goodbye, I would have told you that you were being a melodramatic prick. At least you can learn, I think."

He chuckled.

"I will try," he promised. "For now, we have work to do."

"You mean the head of government for the Confederacy's capital planet *shouldn't* set up a meeting with the Confederacy's senior military commander just to tell her boyfriend off?" Abey asked.

The amusement in her voice was a good sign that he was at least *being* forgiven, though he wasn't necessarily forgiven *yet*.

"I'm scheduled to brief the Cabinet on this situation at twenty hundred hours," James told her. "I think you're actually supposed to be briefing *me* on what's going on back home in my absence."

"That sounds vaguely correct," she agreed. "So."

The astrographic map of the Confederacy appeared between them.

"We now have official q-coms with every system," she told him. "All of the Meridian systems and Shogun are online with the full q-com array you sent out. We're still a few days away from that arriving here in Dakota, so this particular call is locking down our *entire* planetary communication capacity."

"I forgot," James admitted after a moment. "Amazing how quickly habits return."

"Less than a year without instant coms, and now we're starting to get them back," she agreed. "It won't take long for this to just be a minor blip for most of us."

"How long until we have our *own* network?"

He had very specific rules and plans in place with regards to the Castle and Regalia networks, and he had faith, if nothing else, in the encryption protocols they were using.

"It took us longer than I like to think about to get the initial manufacturing systems online," Abey told him. "Our first entangled blocks should be entering testing in the next week or so, but it'll take time to get production up to anything useful—and we still need to *build* a new switchboard station."

"The engineers are telling me that there's a degradation issue with having both sides of the block in gravity wells."

"Technically, there's a degradation issue with having *either* side in a major gravity well," James told her. "My understanding is that the array for a normal communication system on a planetary surface has to be replaced about thirty percent faster than the same array on a starship."

"Having that extra decay on *all* of our q-com blocks..."

"Given that we're currently up to a production of *one* block every twelve days, I can see the problem," she agreed. "But they're working on it. We've also laid the first keels for your guardships in the civilian in-system shipping yards."

The personally painful part of the meeting appeared to be over, and James leaned forward, focusing on the work. He needed to be fully up to date on the civil side of the Confederacy before he spoke to the Cabinet.

Even if his girlfriend *had* taken advantage of that need to give him a well-deserved lecture.

———

"Interesting times you have brought us, Admiral."

Sanada Chō sounded somewhere between amused and *fascinated* with the situation as the Cabinet digested the initial summary James had laid out.

"What is the current status, then?" Papadimitriou asked. "We are at peace?"

"We are at peace," James confirmed for the Persephone Minister. "Rear Admiral Voclain has spent the last six hours in a virtual conference with a gentleman from New Athens who apparently acts as Periklos's portable diplomat."

"Do we have any real concerns about the terms?" Abiodun asked. "It seems rather straightforward—we won't attack them if they don't attack us."

"In theory, yes," James agreed. "But what happens, Minister, if the Brillig Sector applies for membership in the Confederacy? Are those systems covered under our agreement with the League? What happens if a single system in the Cossack Sector, which borders the League and is likely to be their next target for annexation, becomes aware of our agreement and petitions for membership in the Confederacy even as League fleets enter their system?"

"In a perfect world, we would defend them and Periklos would honor that," Chapulin said quietly. "But this is not a perfect world. So, an agreement on, well, how early a system has to apply for membership for this pact to protect them makes sense."

"There are few details that are likely to raise concerns," James continued. "But there are details that need to be *agreed* on. Our major concession, of course, is our formal statement that the *Confederacy* acknowledges the Commonwealth's war guilt for the conflict with the League.

"That puts us on the League's side in a future peace conference—and that the statement comes from me, a former Commonwealth admiral, gives it weight that Periklos will beat the Star Chamber over the head with."

"Is there still a risk that Periklos will change his mind and attack your fleet?" Leon, the Minister for Desdemona, asked softly. "Practically our entire Navy is in New Edmonton right now. We are vulnerable."

"We are. But we have positioned our fleets approximately ten million kilometers apart," James reminded them. "I no longer hold a blade to Periklos's throat—but if we can't trust him to honor the ceasefire *here*, we can't trust him to honor the main peace treaty."

"Can we?" Leon asked bluntly. "We're talking about a man who seized direct control of a group of star systems that arguably weren't even an actual *nation* prior to him. He has slaughtered millions to establish and maintain his power base.

"Can we truly expect this man—this *monster*—to keep his word?"

James didn't answer immediately, rolling Leon's words around in his head. He then adjusted the camera pickup sending his image to Dakota to include the sword sitting on his desk.

"I don't know," he told them. "I do know this: I researched what he told me about his sword. Every word was true. The Condottieri companies actually keep *records* of Admirals' swords.

"This one is his. Only once before in his life has Kaleb Periklos yielded his sword. He kept that promise, avoiding conflict with Samantha Borgogni's company until his seizure of the League Conclave made him Dictator and she was contracted by a resisting star system."

"You think the sword alone makes his word mean something?" Abiodun asked.

"No," James conceded. "I think the sword means something to *him*. And I think that he wants the Stellar League to survive as an integrated and centralized nation that he can pass down to his daughter's generation, if not to his daughter herself.

"For that to happen, the League must be respected on the interstellar stage. And that can only happen if the League is known to honor their word and their treaties. If he breaches this treaty with us, Periklos will become an interstellar pariah, wiping away the last chances of *anyone* expecting the League to keep their commitments.

"He knows that. He can't afford that. So, yes, I believe that we can trust Periklos to honor the treaty."

The call was silent and James waited for one of the Cabinet members to say anything.

"We told you to do whatever it took to end the war with the League," Quetzalli Chapulin reminded her cabinet. "You did. More successfully than we dared to hope for. An *end* to this conflict, before it even truly begins, is worth some risk.

"It certainly doesn't harm us—at all—to concede Terra's war guilt over the attack on the League. I have always wondered just what was going through the Star Chamber's minds when they authorized that!"

"The belief that they were the true and ultimate arbiters of all humanity's fate," Sanada Chō warned grimly. "A belief that may yet doom *us*. How quickly, Admiral, will you be able to return to Dakota?

"We have no way of knowing Walkingstick's reaction to our declaration of independence, but the only people who could exert any restraint on the Imperator are the same people who sent a punitive expedition into the League in response to what their analysts *have* to have known was an Alliance covert op."

"A direct flight from here to Dakota will be fourteen days," James replied. "We need to sort out this treaty first, and I have the distinct feeling that will go better if the fleet is here. If necessary, I will leave a team behind to negotiate the details, but I *think* we should have those details sorted by tomorrow."

"We are already into the window where Walkingstick might reach Confederacy space before you do, depending on his reaction to our note," Abiodun said. "Arroyo is vulnerable already."

"Walkingstick won't attack Arroyo," he told the Cabinet. "That's not how he thinks; it's not how he operates.

"The only reason he didn't move against the major capitals in the Rimward Marches was because he never received enough ships to match the Alliance hull for hull. If he'd taken his full hundred-odd ships to, say, the Star Kingdom of Phoenix, he'd have taken the system —and then been descended on by *two* hundred Alliance capital ships.

"That war was a series of actions between small numbers of capital ships because he needed to reduce the Alliance's overall hull numbers to a point where the forces he'd been allocated could take on a majority of their fleet at once—because that's what he was going to face the moment he went for any of the capitals."

James paused, looking at the map of the Confederacy hanging in the air in front of him. He *knew* the way Walkingstick thought, the way the Imperator would choose to fight. It wasn't a reassuring knowledge, because he could put together the pieces on how Walkingstick would react and move.

He *hoped* that the delegation they'd sent would be allowed to negotiate and establish a peaceful relationship, even if he knew Walking-stick would only regard that as a temporary measure while he stabilized the rest of the Commonwealth.

But he suspected that Walkingstick was completely incapable of accepting a large, organized secession from the Commonwealth.

"So, what do you expect him to do here?" Chapulin asked. "You served with him."

"He's going to come for Dakota," James concluded frankly. "He's going to assemble a fleet powerful enough that he believes he can overawe our defenders, including our fleet, and head straight for what he'll see as the center of the rebellion.

"Our main hope is that the Imperator remains sufficiently constrained by the Star Chamber to be forced to negotiate," he admit-ted. "Regardless, logistical requirements of a fleet of that scale mean we're looking at a minimum of three days, more likely four, before he could leave Sol.

"Assuming that Walkingstick immediately rejected any concept of peace and began organizing a fleet from his central forces within hours of our courier's arrival, he still could not have left Sol before February twenty-seventh at the earliest."

He shook his head gently as he ran the math through his implant.

"That makes the nineteenth the real beginning of our threat window," he said. "I plan on spending two more days here in New Edmonton to attempt to get the main articles of the nonaggression treaty established.

"That will see the fleet back in Dakota for the eighteenth, before we expect Walkingstick to arrive," he promised.

"Which still leaves the question, Admiral, of how do you plan to defend even this system against the Imperator?" Leon asked. "You said that he will bring enough of a fleet to overawe us."

"Yes. And we have two key advantages against the Commonwealth now, advantages I think will be enough to turn the tide," James told the Desdemonan Minister.

"First, we will be fighting for our new home and our new nation. There will be no retreat, no hesitation. We *must* hold. Walkingstick, however, has the same limitations on his new-ship supply as we do.

He has more ships and more yards to replace them, but it will be months before he has *any* new ships—and he has both a larger area of responsibility and a lot more questions about it.

"*We* are not wondering if the Gondola Sector is going to stay loyal to the Commonwealth or not, after all." The Gondola Sector was as far away from both the League and the Alliance as possible, five inhabited systems far to counter-clockward. That same location put it a long way away from Dakota and irrelevant to the new Confederacy.

"I expect Earth to retain control of about half of the Commonwealth at least," James estimated. "Walkingstick will need to provide security and a measure of *threat* to those systems to keep them in line. He *cannot* afford significant warship losses at this point."

James spread his hands.

"Secondly, *we* now have tactical q-coms and working q-probes," he told them. "I expect that the rump Commonwealth has begun limited production of entangled blocks, but I cannot see any way they have produced *enough* to allow Walkingstick's fleet to have tactical FTL communications."

"You think you can defeat him?" Chapulin asked.

"I think I can make him *hesitate*," James conceded. "After that, it will depend on how determined the man is. It is possible that Walking-stick will push an assault on Dakota with sufficient fervor that we will lose the system and most or all of the DCN."

That hung on the virtual conference for a long few moments as the admission really sank in.

"Perhaps we should have left him in the dark after all," Hjalmar Rakes, the Minister for Krete, said softly. "Does he truly have enough ships to do this?"

"We don't know." James would let the Cabinet draw their own conclusions and hopefully be more optimistic than he was, but he wasn't going to lie to them or provide them with false hope.

"We *know* that Home Fleet was destroyed," he told them. "We *know* that the Rimward Fleet took heavy losses in the final days of the war, with the Alliance doing everything in their power to keep the Commonwealth's attention focused on the front.

"But...the Core Worlds sent their defense fleets to Sol, and Walking-stick brought the Rimward Fleet home. He has all of those ships."

Including at least one battleship that James Tecumseh had commanded in the past, the Admiral knew. Unless, he supposed, *Saint Anthony* had fallen in the final actions of the war.

"He can deploy more ships than we can," James concluded. "What he *cannot* do is *lose* those ships. Every hull he loses is an active blow to his ability to maintain the Commonwealth."

"But what we do not know is the calculus in his brain," Abey Todacheeney reminded the Cabinet. "Because our *existence* is also a blow to the Commonwealth. So, somewhere in James Calvin Walking-stick's mind, the math is being done on how many ships he can lose to bring us to heel."

27

New Edmonton System
10:00 March 3, 2738 ESMDT

"I AM BEGINNING TO UNDERSTAND, sir, why Condottieri are trusted to keep their contracts."

James raised a questioning eyebrow at Madona Voclain as the stewards delivered coffee around his breakout room. All of his senior staff were present for the update meeting, with Modesitt linked in virtually from *Saratoga*.

"Is this your first encounter with a League lawyer?" the Vice Admiral asked with a chuckle. "They are a...fascinating breed, aren't they?"

"I think I might prefer them to the Terran breed, but the process is certainly *exhausting*," Voclain replied.

"I'll admit I've never looked over Condottieri contracts, but I'm told they're written in relatively plain language?" James asked.

"And they won't use one word when twelve are more understandable," his chief of staff told him. "Understandable, yes. Also long. Very,

very long. And I don't think Chifuniro Malewezi has any intention of letting this treaty be any less specific and clear than the contracts they're used to negotiating."

"Are we going to have any problems?" James asked.

"We've had a few minor sticking points where they and I have gone back and forth a few times before settling on a compromise, but nothing major enough that either of us needed to go up the chain," she said. "It's been an educational process, sir, but so far, we seem to be on much the same page.

"It's taking time, more than I might like, but they seem determined to get the treaty done and *right*."

"And it helps *my* paranoia that the Dictator sent half of his ships away," Modesitt added. "I wasn't expecting that."

Periklos hadn't even *said* anything to James, but his invasion transports and all of the old thirty-five-million-cubic-meter Condottieri cruisers had moved out earlier that morning—and their vectors had clearly been toward New Athens.

"I suspect, given that he sent them back to New Athens, that someone was giving his wife grief," James said. "Which would be a terrible idea *without* Periklos sending reinforcements, from what I can tell, but he'd send them anyway now he doesn't need them here."

"That gives us some safety margin," Yamamoto agreed. "While at the same time, it's not like we can threaten New Edmonton. The Notley forts have us well-matched, even *without* twelve modern warships hanging around, watching us."

The DCN now had a slim *numerical* edge over the remaining League ships, but the League ships were significantly bigger on average. Periklos had sent away his smallest ships, leaving him with his solid core of fifty- and sixty-million-cubic-meter ships.

He still had James's fleet outmassed and outgunned...but the gesture was still real. And appreciated.

"Do you think you'll have the negotiations wrapped by tomorrow?" James asked Voclain. "I've promised the Cabinet we'll be home by the eighteenth. We'll need to move out tomorrow afternoon."

"If either of us had a decent template for this, we'd be done already," Voclain admitted. "As it is...I'm not sure tomorrow is going to happen. I'll be back on the conference with Malewezi at eleven hundred hours, and we'll do our best."

"We may end up needing to leave you behind," James warned. "Our best option may to be leave you with one of the *Assassin*s for a base of operations as the rest of the fleet returns to Dakota."

"I can work with that if I have to, sir," she promised. "Or, potentially, depending on how the Dictator is feeling about Notley, we can rent an office on the planet and Malewezi and I can go sort it out there."

"I'll leave the details with you," he told her. "But recognize that if you *aren't* going to be done by twelve hundred hours tomorrow, you're going to have to stay.

"So, plan for that."

"I'm your chief of staff, sir," the Rear Admiral said wryly. "*Planning* is what I do."

"I know. That's why I'm giving you enough information *to* plan," James noted.

A chuckle went around the room and James took a long sip of his coffee.

"Carey, is there any reason the fleet won't be able to move out tomorrow?" he asked the ops officer.

"None," the junior Admiral said instantly. "We fully refueled and restocked in Meridian, and we were expecting to fight a battle here in New Edmonton. Getting out of the gravity well will take longer than our actual preparations."

"Good. We'll plan to move out at thirteen hundred hours tomorrow," James ordered. "We'll clear the gravity well at sixteen hundred hours and be in Dakota before anyone starts worrying."

As if the Cabinet wasn't *already* worrying. But that was their job.

"What about the Meridian Fleet, Admiral?" Modesitt asked. "Even with a peace deal with the League, we need to keep some force in the sector—but I haven't heard any planning about a separate deployment."

James nodded and leaned forward, meeting the gaze of his holographic subordinate.

"There was a conversation that Anthony Yamamoto and I had

when we were first dealing with this mess," he told her. "Talking about his ancestor and the Second World War. There is a train of thought that the Japanese lost the Battle of Midway and began the decline to their defeat because they didn't have the number of carriers necessary to absorb tactical setbacks.

"Marshal Admiral Yamamoto made the error of dividing his fleet—repeatedly, both allowing three carriers to be destroyed or disabled prior to Midway and then *again* by sending two carriers to the Aleutian Islands campaign. Given the politics of Imperial Japan, it is likely he had no choice, but those five flight decks would have given the Kidō Butai a level of resiliency that could have turned the tide."

He grimaced.

"We find ourselves in a similar position," he concluded. "There are two types of potential missions ahead of us, Jessie: those that require the full force of the Dakotan Navy and those that do not justify the full force of the Navy.

"For the moment, until we have at least some clarity on the plans and reactions of the Commonwealth, we need to keep the fleet concentrated." He sighed. "I'm aware that's pulling you away from your fiancé and the system you've been making a home for some time now."

"Duty calls, sir," she told him. "I'll be *happier* if my long-term posting ends up being Meridian—or if Barbados and I end up on postings close to each other, at least—but I put on the new uniform when you handed it to me. I took the job, and if I couldn't take the joke, I should have said no."

"It's a shitty joke, but we all knew what it was when we put on the uniform," James said with a sad smile. "If it helps, the Meridian Sector *will* be a Vice Admiral post with a fleet, going forward. But we need your fleet at Dakota for now.

"We'll move everybody out tomorrow and get our overpriced hunks of metal and guns back to Dakota. *Before* Walkingstick tries to take it away from us."

28

New Edmonton System
18:00 March 3, 2738 ESMDT

THE UNIVERSE HAS VERY little sympathy for assumptions made by anyone, however well-thought-out, well-intentioned or justified. Somehow, when Mac Cléirich used an emergency protocol to access James's office coms, he knew he'd missed something.

The rock-hard weight that settled into his stomach suggested that it was something big.

"Admiral, what is it?" he asked.

"We have an unknown access protocol on the q-com network," she told him. "Our security protocols managed to isolate it, but it appears to be harmless."

"And yet you just overrode my communications to tell me about it," James pointed out. "So, 'harmless' doesn't sound quite right."

"It's a repeating signal, a request for an open communication channel with you."

"Any identifiers?"

"It's signed *Your mutual friend with Trickster*."

"So, the Federation," James concluded grimly. He'd expected something like this sooner or later. "Can we sanitize and secure the channel?"

"We can. I… Despite what Bevan thinks, I'm pretty sure they *let* us intercept it. Remember that the Federation owns our entangled blocks," she warned. "I'm with Bevan on thinking our encryptions are holding for the moment, but…"

"But they have full access to our coms and all it will really take is time," James concluded. "Sanitize it, isolate it, secure it…but put our benefactor through to my office."

He swept the digital files he'd been working on away with a thought and a gesture. He still had Periklos's sword sitting on the two paperweights that had been a Marshal's mace, but he figured that couldn't hurt. Thanks to Abey and Dakota, his office was impressive enough that he wasn't going to worry about making a show.

It took Mac Cléirich three minutes to set up the call, and for a moment after connecting, all that James saw was a picture of a decorative stained-glass window—showing what his implant identified as a copy of the Bayeux Tapestry showing the invasion of England.

An odd choice—and one he only managed to identify before the image vanished because of his implants.

The stained-glass window was replaced by a man in a plain office. The virtual-conferencing software replaced half of James's office with the stranger's and presumably did the same on their end.

James silently observed the stranger while he waited for them to speak. The presumed Castle Federation Intelligence agent was an elderly man, with a wispy white goatee and a bald head marked with faint liver spots. His office was a clearly intentional blank, with no decorations or active screens—or if there *were* anything, it was being removed before the transmission was sent.

"Admiral James Tecumseh," the man finally greeted him.

"You have the advantage of me," James replied. "I know that you are an intelligence agent of the Castle Federation and, I'm guessing, one that's worked with Trickster in the past. That *suggests*, to me, that I am speaking to the mastermind behind the Tau Ceti incident and the cause of the war between the League and the Commonwealth."

The stranger smiled and gave James a small golf clap.

"I'm...actually impressed, Admiral, though I'll admit not many people have all of the pieces that you do," he said. "I will neither confirm nor deny *any* of your analysis. Take that as you wish."

"If you are not prepared to tell me who you are, sir, I'm not sure there is a point to this conversation," James noted.

"You can call me Mr. Glass," the old man told him. "I will be transparent enough to confess that, yes, I work for the Castle Federation, and I am the source of the entangled-particle blocks we are using to speak right now."

"The necessity of knowing what switchboard network we're using does render any attempt at disguising the source of the q-coms pointless. What do you want, Mr. Glass?"

"Well, I *was* going to ask if you had resolved the situation with the League to your satisfaction, but I believe I see Kaleb Periklos's sword sitting on your desk," Glass said wryly. "Which, according to my understanding of Condottieri traditions, means you've found some level of peace with the man."

"I'm not certain there is any satisfaction in the resolution for anyone—or if it's your business at all."

"We both know what my business here is," Glass pointed out.

"You want the Confederacy to be a thorn in the Commonwealth's side," James replied. "Much as I dislike being the proxy in a proxy war, it will be some time before we don't need an external source of q-coms and q-probes."

"Indeed." The Federation officer leaned forward, studying something on James's desk. "Is that...a Marshal's mace cut in two and turned into paperweights, Admiral?"

"Wasn't my idea, but I certainly enjoy the symbolism," James replied. He shook his head. "You did not insert yourself into my communication channels to ask about the contents of my desk, Mister Glass."

Glass chuckled. "You came highly recommended; do you know that?" he asked. "We have more mutual friends than you think. I don't think Admiral Roberts quite *realized* what I was digging for when I asked him about you, but he was quite complimentary.

"Not many people would have the integrity or the spine to make common cause with their enemy against a pirate who'd stolen one of their ships."

James sighed. "What do you *want*?" he demanded.

"Firstly? To confirm, as I said, that you had resolved your business in the New Edmonton System. Despite my best efforts, my direct resources have so far failed to produce any useful information. So, I figured I would go to the horse's mouth, so to speak."

James glared.

"We haven't broken your encryptions, if that's what you're thinking," Glass told him. "As I'm sure your intelligence people have told you, we probably *could* have—if I were able to dedicate more resources to this project than I honestly have access to.

"And if I had *that* many resources, I'd be sending you *warships*."

That was *not* a tone he'd expected.

"And why would you do that?" he asked.

"Because the Confederacy represents the best of what the Commonwealth was *supposed* to be—and Imperator Walkingstick represents the worst of what the Commonwealth *is*. We need you to survive, Admiral Tecumseh—not just as a thorn in Walkingstick's side but as a beacon to show the *good* that can come out of the fall of the Commonwealth.

"The Commonwealth itself may not be salvageable, Admiral—but you and the Confederacy are showing that parts of it are worth preserving. Worth fighting for. The Federation won't fight *for* you, Admiral—but we have a *lot* of reasons to help you fight for yourself."

"That's a heartwarming line of bullshit to keep us in the fight against your enemy," James pointed out. It *sounded* reasonable enough and true enough, but it didn't change the reality.

The Castle Federation wanted to use the Dakotan Confederacy to keep the war against the Commonwealth going. He had no choice but to accept their help, but he *knew* what they were doing.

"Your cynicism is entirely justified. I don't need you to believe that we have more motives than the pragmatic, but I'd like you to at least consider the possibility." Glass shook his head. "If nothing else, if our relationship is built on more than pragmatics and politics, it's easier for us to maintain an active connection.

"And if we'd been in more-active communication, we could have had this conversation as soon as you'd resolved matters with Periklos."

Something in Glass's tone sharpened that weight in James's stomach.

"And what exactly is 'this conversation,' Mister Glass?" he asked.

"Imperator Walkingstick had prepared an entire battle fleet to deploy against the first major rebellion he received news of," Glass told him, each word a brick through the glass house of James's carefully laid plans. "He arrested Inmaculada Haines and the Star Chamber delegations of the Confederacy systems as soon as she delivered your declaration of independence. He then seized *Paradise by Twilight* with his Marines and deployed almost immediately toward the Dakota System."

James was silent, staring at the stranger as Glass calmly laid out the doom of his nation.

"An expeditionary fleet of fifty warships and ten assault transports left the Sol System oh four hundred hours ESMDT on February twenty-fifth," the Federation agent told him. "Assuming no detours or preparatory stops, Imperator Walkingstick will enter the Dakota System at approximately oh four hundred hours on March seventeenth.

"Two weeks from today."

"And you're telling me this *now*," James snarled. "Not yesterday. Not last week. Not *on the fucking twenty-fifth when the bastard moved.*"

"I didn't *know* until almost a full day after he'd moved," Glass replied. "If you'd asked me a week earlier, I would have figured he would have at least *talked* to Haines before launching an all-out assault. I'd have been wrong.

"By the time I knew, you were already halfway to New Edmonton, Admiral, and there was no point in telling you until you'd dealt with Periklos. And I couldn't confirm what the hell had gone down in New Edmonton.

"Hence my violating at least half a dozen standing policies of Federation Intelligence to reach out to you," he concluded. "Now I know you're done in New Edmonton and *you* know that Walkingstick is moving on Dakota."

"We're already out of time," James snapped. "I needed you to tell me this *yesterday*. Or this morning. Or...far enough in advance that *I* was making the decision on when to use it!"

"I told you as soon as I could be certain it would be *useful*," Glass told him. "What you do with this information is up to you, I suppose."

"What do you think I'm going to do with it?" James replied.

"I'm assuming you'll be steering for the sound of the guns. In which case, good luck. I have irons in the fire to back you up, Admiral Tecumseh, but...the Confederacy has to survive Walkingstick's attack first."

"Your concern is noted. Now, if you'll excuse me, I have work to do."

————

It was always James's preference to get buy-in for major decisions by discussing them with his staff in person. In the absence of true face-to-face meetings, holographic or videoconferencing would work—but there needed to be live discussions, preferably where he could see people's faces.

At that moment, there was no *time,* and he sent an emergency signal into *Krakatoa*'s networks. The ubiquitous neural implants of the twenty-eighth century meant that his people could conference in from anywhere while doing anything.

Mental icons flickered live as his staff joined the call, followed by Modesitt. Yamamoto was missing, but he'd find out why later.

"Sir, what's going on?" Carey asked.

"Our tentative allies in Castle finally made contact and dropped a bombshell," James told them all. "Walkingstick left Sol on the twenty-fifth of February with a sixty-ship invasion force, heading for Dakota."

On this kind of connection, he could *feel* his people's emotions. It wasn't a reliable or coherent thing, but it was present—and when everyone on the channel was feeling the same shock and fear, it was easy to pick *that* out.

"Voclain, I need you to transfer to *Lakewater*," James ordered. "We don't have time for you to book an office on Notley and we can't spare a warship."

He raised a mental hand before she could argue.

"We *also* can't afford to let this treaty fall by the wayside. I will talk to Periklos myself, but you will need to remain in the system and continue the negotiations. Pick a staff to take with you, pack your things—but you need to be on *Lakewater* in thirty minutes.

"Everyone else"—his mental attention took in his staff and Modesitt—"go through every ship as fast as you can. Any potential shortages need to be made up from *Lakewater* or the other ships inside that same thirty minutes.

"We are three hours from being able to warp space, people, and I want to be under Alcubierre-Stetson drive before midnight," he concluded.

Yamamoto's presence finally joined the call, an odd mental fuzz to it that James wasn't sure he'd ever felt on an implant conference. An icon popped up, marking that the fighter pilot was basically speed-loading the conversation to date—something not even all naval officers could do.

"I'm on it," Carey replied crisply, vanishing from the channel a moment later. Voclain didn't even bother to announce her departure.

"How bad is the timing?" Modesitt asked softly.

"Bad," Yamamoto told her before James could reply, a new chill of fear wiping away whatever odd energy the pilot had carried into the call. "Do we know *what time* they left Sol?"

"Oh four hundred hours," he told the two Vice Admirals. "He will arrive at Dakota in the early morning on the seventeenth of March.

"*We* cannot be in Dakota prior to the late afternoon on the same day. If we made *no* logistical changes and could somehow warp space from here, we'd still arrive eight hours after he did."

That was the cold equation of space and time, even with faster-than-light travel in play. Walkingstick had farther to go—a hundred light-years versus forty-eight—but he'd left that much earlier, and both fleets had functionally the same acceleration.

One light-year per day per day, to a maximum of ten light-years per day that didn't come up on journeys of a hundred light-years or less. Every hour that James and his people waited was an hour that Walkingstick and his battle fleet had in Dakota without being challenged.

"Should I make contact with Commodore Gold?" Modesitt asked. "We can have *Champion* and *Goldwyn* meet us at Dakota?"

"Do it," James ordered. "I'm not under the illusion that two hundred ex-League fighters are going to make a difference against Walkingstick, but every little bit will help."

"Can we stop him?" Yamamoto asked.

"I don't know," James admitted. "But I *do* know that we have to try. That was our promise. We will have to be clever. We will have to be careful.

"But we *have* to fight."

"What about the League?" Modesitt asked.

"Whatever peace we have forged with Periklos, we are not allies," James said grimly. "I would not trust that man with a fleet in Dakota."

"I don't mean Periklos," she replied. "I meant the Condottieri."

"Where else in the galaxy can you hire mercenaries with A-S warships?" Yamamoto asked after a half-second pause. "I hadn't thought of it."

"Neither had I," James admitted as he considered the possibility. "I have to talk to Periklos, but...I don't think the timing is going to work, but perhaps we should send out the call anyway."

There were no Condottieri in New Edmonton, only ships of the League navy itself. That meant that any Condottieri they *hired* would be coming from other star systems and would take even longer to reach Dakota than First Fleet would.

And James was grimly aware that First Fleet was already going to be too late.

29

New Edmonton System
18:30 March 3, 2738 ESMDT

ANTHONY DROPPED out of the mental conference with a groan, falling back onto his bed in a vague semblance of relief. The *reason* for the meeting had certainly made for all the effects of a cold shower, but he'd been off duty and Reynolds had ambushed him in his shower.

With that thought, he realized he wasn't sure where the assassin had *gone*—and then he remembered that he'd turned his shower *off* earlier and it was running now.

He crossed his quarters to check through the door and saw that she'd left both the door to the head and the one to the shower itself open as she abused his flag-rank hot-water ration.

"Well?" she asked, turning to face him and intentionally giving him a complete view. "Bad news, I'm guessing, but I figured I'd leave you to it."

She chuckled. "I'll admit having *that* interrupted by an emergency call is a new one."

Anthony flushed.

"Emergencies aren't known for their consideration," he told her. "I need to check in with my people. We're on the move."

The amusement vanished from the woman's body, and suddenly Anthony's friendly lover was gone—and the assassin who'd killed people to maintain the political stability of the Commonwealth stood naked in his shower.

"Walkingstick moved too fast."

"Two full days faster than our worst-case," Anthony confirmed. "He'll be in Dakota before we possibly can be."

"Federation Intelligence?" she asked, seemingly oblivious to her nudity as she turned off the water and stepped out into the bathroom.

"Admiral didn't give details, but he confirmed that."

"I need to parse that," Reynolds said thoughtfully. "Probably sit down with Bevan, go over what we know about whoever contacted Tecumseh and what we think Castle likely wants from us—and is prepared to put up to *help* us."

"So far, the q-coms are a pretty big deal," Yamamoto reminded her. "And any warning at all about the Imperator…we wouldn't have been leaving for at least another *day* without the information."

"I know," she agreed. "Which also makes everything that much more…fluid. I need to go check in with Lieutenant Revie and the rest of my pups. Then Bevan."

"And I need to go over the readiness of our entire fighter force and check in with my subordinates in Dakota," he said. "'Fluid' is a good word."

She flicked a droplet of water off her breast and chuckled.

"Even if we were both enjoying *other* activities involving fluid a bit more," she admitted. "Duty calls."

"It does," he agreed. "But please do put on *some* clothes before you leave my quarters?"

––––––––

The changes in the uniform barely registered to Anthony now. In some ways, the eagle embroidered onto the indigo blue lapels still surprised him more than the shoulder boards or the three stars of a Vice Admiral. He didn't miss the sash, though he kept having moments where he expected things to be purple that were a much darker hue.

Entire expanses of *Krakatoa*'s flight deck had been repainted—not because anyone had said it was required but because the Chiefs had decided they wanted to mark the change. Nose markings on the fighters were now indigo instead of purple; deck markings that had been purple were now indigo.

And every symbol of the Commonwealth Starfighter Corps had been removed, replaced with a new emblem—the same eagle insignia as the lapels, on a silver laurel crown.

By the time Anthony was halfway across the deck, even without his having said a word or given an order, Colonel Ó Cochláin, Chief Brahms and half a dozen Lieutenant Colonels had emerged from nowhere by apparently Brownian motion, falling in around him as he reached Primary Flight Control and turned to face them.

"Linking to the other CAGs," he warned them aloud. That was why he'd gone to PriFly, where a briefing lectern included a holographic pickup.

He waited a moment for the senior officers of the other two carriers and the cruisers to pick up the transmission.

"The shit has well and truly hit the fan, people," he told them all harshly. "Current estimate is that Walkingstick will be in Dakota twenty-four hours before we can make it."

He was only addressing the officers, but the flight deck was as silent as it was physically possible to be. *Everyone* was listening.

"All squadrons are to review their logistics supplies," he continued. "First Fleet is moving out immediately. We have a limited time window to pull supplies from *Lakewater*—she's being left behind to serve as at least a temporary base for Rear Admiral Voclain's diplomatic mission.

"Anything that you are short—anything you might *need*—flag it *now*," he told them. "We'll make it work somehow.

"Then we're throwing every pilot, gunner and engineer into the best training scenarios we have. Best guess is that we'll be outnumbered at least four to one in starfighters and bombers. They have the same ships we do. The same tactics we do. The same training, too.

"So, we have fourteen days, people, to find enough weaknesses in our own ships, our own tactics and our own training to level a four-to-one disadvantage."

The *good* news was that there were hundreds more starfighters in Dakota, and if they could get the timing right, they might be able to bring that disparity down to two-to-one.

Assuming there was anybody *left* in Dakota by the time they got there.

"We're going to need every clever idea, every dirty trick, every deception you've ever thought about, planned or seen someone else throw at you."

He shook his head grimly.

"We knew this was coming, people. We might have hoped that the Commonwealth would let us go, might have considered the option that they'd send less than overwhelming force...but we all knew, from the moment we followed the Old Man into treason, that we were going to have to face our old friends and comrades at horrific odds.

"But I will remind you all—and I know damn well every one of our people is going to see this," he observed. "I will remind you all what we are fighting for: the ideals and the people of the Dakotan Confederacy.

"We *chose* this. We *chose* to honor the ideals of the Commonwealth over the nation. And we followed Admiral Tecumseh down this path, *knowing* where it would lead.

"So, while we fight for what the Commonwealth should have been, we *know* our old friends, our old comrades...they all know why we fight.

"*The moral is to the physical as three is to one,*" he told them. "And not only are we certain in our beliefs and our morals...but the people we have to fight? They *can't* be—because they know why we walked away. They know why we fight.

"And they know that we are right."

30

New Edmonton System
19:00 March 3, 2738 ESMDT

"My dear Admiral Tecumseh, you appear to be leaving us at quite a pace."

James wasn't sure when he'd graduated to "my dear Admiral" with Periklos. Mostly, he suspected that the Dictator was messing with him.

"We have unfortunate news, and First Fleet and I need to move." He paused and glanced down at the sword on his desk. "I trust to your honor, Dictator Periklos."

"Walkingstick has moved," the League's leader concluded. "I'm sorry, Admiral. My intelligence sources in Sol are still fragmented after the collapse of the Commonwealth q-com network. I did not know."

"You knew he was going to."

"Yes," Periklos conceded. "Prior to our 'meeting,' I intended to take advantage of him moving against you to seize the Meridian Sector while he took Dakota. I suspect that many of your worlds, Admiral, would rather be part of the League than the Commonwealth."

"And we chose *neither*," James told him. "We chose defiance."

"Yes, you did," the Dictator said with a chuckle. "And I have to respect that, Admiral Tecumseh, I really do. You do not need to worry about the League. We may not yet have a treaty bound in ink and electrons, but you have my word and my sword.

"If you will allow it, I will have a transport shuttle rendezvous with your flagship and deliver a communications system hooked into our q-com network," he continued. "That way, we can remain in contact as you leave this system and we can avoid future misunderstandings or concerns."

"That seems…wise to me," James conceded. "I suppose we could also use a link to your network to contact the Condottieri companies."

"You could," Periklos agreed genially. Despite his attempt to appeared surprised, it was clear that had also been in his mind.

"I am afraid that the timing is poor from your perspective," he continued. "While you have my word that we will not attack your systems—and I *won't* permit the Condottieri to break my word for me —so long as you remain our potential enemy, the Condottieri will not contract with you.

"Once the treaty is signed, some will. Others will wait and see. It will be some weeks at least—more likely months—before you will be able to hire a significant number of our Condottieri warships."

"I expected nothing different," James told him. "None of them could reach Dakota in time, regardless."

"And even if you would trust *my* ships, I doubt I am able to send enough to make a difference in Dakota's fate," Periklos noted. "I could see perhaps some of my remaining cruisers, but I suspect you would need the entire fleet I have in New Edmonton.

"And then, well, even I might be tempted by possibilities."

"We are no longer enemies, Dictator Periklos, but we are not allies," James said grimly. "We will not fight you, but we will not trust you to fight for us. Condottieri contracts are one thing, and we may lean on them in the future, but for now…this war is our war."

"When you do plan to hire to Condottieri, talk to me," Periklos told him. "I *may* be prepared to subsidize contracts—quietly, of course—if you hire certain companies. Those companies will serve you well...and it will serve *me* well to have them outside the League!"

"I will consider it."

It was a surprisingly useful offer, James knew. It wouldn't matter to *Dakota* if the companies they hired were Periklos's problem children. None of the Condottieri were likely to breach any contract, which meant they would serve well—and the Confederacy hiring them would get them out of Periklos's hair.

But that was the next campaign. For this one...he had First Fleet.

"Good luck, Tecumseh," Periklos told him. "Give Walkingstick my regards when you send him to hell."

———

"What do we *do*?"

"That, I'm afraid, is going to be entirely up to you," James told Chapulin grimly. "We'll be in warped space in just under three hours, but we're almost fourteen days from Dakota."

"We cannot surrender," the new President replied. "That would be the easy option, I suppose, but then we're right back where we started."

"I honestly did not expect the Imperator to deploy this quickly or in this much force," he admitted. This was just him and the President of the Confederacy, a private call in which he could be honest.

"I also expected him to at least *consider* talking!"

"I didn't," Chapulin admitted with a tired expression. "But I knew the logistics that were in play, and I hoped that the Star Chamber could still exert some restraint on him."

"I think we can safely say that the Star Chamber is either completely cowed or completely behind Walkingstick now," James noted. "He managed to put *half* of the warships I think he has access to into a deployed fleet inside twenty-four hours.

"I didn't necessarily think he could *spare* fifty starships. I was expecting more on the order of thirty, which would have been bad enough."

"How exactly were you planning on dealing with *thirty*, Admiral?"

"Deceit, feint and a lot of mines," James said wryly. "The last, at least, you have. Dakota has no dedicated battle platforms yet, but you always had simple fighter bases. You have five hundred starfighters and the mines."

"I vaguely recall signing off on those," Chapulin replied. "Care to explain how they're going to save us?"

"They won't," he told her. "But what they *will* do is make Walkingstick hesitate once he realizes they're there. There are ten thousand capital-ship missiles and twenty thousand torpedoes in single-shot launchers ready to deploy.

"They were *supposed* to be controlled from that battle station division we never quite around got around to finishing, but a couple of the q-probes we've sent you will allow *Ajax* to act as a central gunnery suite.

"Commander Abram's ship might not have her own launchers or beams online right now, but she has targeting computers and control systems. Get Abram to get enough of their people back aboard to use *Ajax* as a command center.

"If you set it up correctly, Walkingstick will never know where the missiles are being controlled from—and that's *important*. *Ajax* has minimal defenses. If the Terrans take a shot at her, we lose a modern battlecruiser before we can get her back in commission."

"I will talk to Abram and the rest of the uniforms you've left us," the President said gratefully. "We won't surrender, James. We have to spin out time until you get back."

"It should be less than twenty-four hours after they arrive," he told her. "And I don't think he'll expect us that quickly. That's our big advantage here. We have one last shot at surprise."

"What about Base Łá'ts'áadah?"

"Commodore Krejči has four *Zion* battle platforms, and we've expanded his fighter wings, too," James replied. "I'd *love* to say you should pull those battle stations and his four hundred fighters to Dakotan orbit, but…"

"We can't afford to let Walkingstick wreck those yards. We need to defend them, too."

"I hate saying it, but in some ways, it's almost more important to hold Base Łá'ts'áadah than it is to hold Dakota herself," James said quietly. "Walkingstick is a Unification fanatic and now the unquestioned leader of the Commonwealth, but he *isn't* a murderer or a *direct* war criminal."

There were definitely questions about responsibility for the war crimes carried out by the Rimward Fleet. They hadn't been *common*, but some of them had certainly been *dramatic*—and while Walkingstick had ordered the arrest and execution of the officer behind the devastation of an entire planet, it had been the Alliance who'd caught him in the end.

For all that, though, James didn't expect atrocities or war crimes if Walkingstick took Dakota.

"If we knew you could liberate the system, perhaps," Chapulin told him. "But, truthfully, what are our odds here, James?"

"Once those mines are up and rigged with targeting via the q-probes, you should have enough firepower to hurt their fleet," he told her. "*Badly*. Badly enough that I think there's a chance you'll make him blink, make him hesitate long enough for us to arrive.

"Then we can either pin his fleet against the minefields or lure him into their range. Either way, the mines are going to be the key—and he knows it."

That was the problem, he supposed. Both he and Walkingstick were working from the same playbook. Walkingstick had *written* large chunks of said playbook, too.

What he *wasn't* going to tell Quetzalli Chapulin was that he was pretty sure Walkingstick was a better tactician and strategist than he was. The edge, he hoped, was thinner than the Imperator thought— but it only added to the need to be sneaky.

"We'll have full q-coms by the time he gets here," she told him. "Litter the system with q-probes in passive mode so we know his every move. When you get here, you'll know where he is and what he's doing; I can promise you that much.

"And I can promise you that he's going to *pay* for Dakota. I suspect I'm high on his list of people to shoot, but I'm hoping he won't bombard the planet. We will find every trick we can over the next two weeks.

"When the dust settles, win or lose, Walkingstick is going to regret he decided to pick this fight."

"He will," James confirmed grimly. "We did not come this far to lay down our arms at the first hurdle. Is the Cabinet with you?"

"The Cabinet, the Governors, everyone," she confirmed. "We will fight, James. We will be here when you get here.

"You have my word—Dakota *will* stand."

————

A half dozen similar conversations later, exhaustion left James leaning back in his chair, staring at a display of the space surrounding *Krakatoa*.

Fourteen other starships flanked the big carrier, all of them hurtling through space on pillars of flame at two hundred gravities. The smallest and lightest of them was twenty-five million cubic meters and ten million tons of mass.

Wars had been fought and won with smaller forces than First Fleet. Even the Commonwealth preferred deploying in groups of eight to ten at most. Larger fleets were *administrative* units, with few capital-ship actions except for the largest involving more than a dozen ships total.

His fleet, after all, represented the *entire* annual industrial and economic output of a wealthy star system. The construction programs being discussed for the Confederacy going forward were going to consume something around ten percent of the entire economy of twelve star systems, much of it in the support infrastructure to build the complex and precious exotic-matter coils that underlay the Class One manipulators.

The cost of maintaining the DCN was going to be extravagant, even in *his* opinion, but Walkingstick was busy demonstrating exactly why it was needed. Without the modern warships to match the Commonwealth in hulls and tonnage, they were always going to be vulnerable to Terra concentrating their forces and flinging them at the Confederacy.

He couldn't see it happening more than once. Walkingstick had an amazing percentage of the ships of the TCN still under his command, even after losses, defections, secessions and just lost communication, but he was going to be responsible for most of the Commonwealth. Even James's worst-case estimates figured the rump would retain control of about forty star systems—and that would include the Core, the twelve wealthiest star systems in human space.

But while that industrial might would underwrite Walkingstick's *ambitions*, it also came with responsibility. Not every secessionist state would be a democracy looking to be left alone like Dakota. Rutherford had tried to found an expansionist empire in the Meridian Sector, and if he'd succeeded, he would have been eyeing the surrounding Commonwealth systems as prey.

For Walkingstick's Imperator title to be anything but a power grab, the man had to secure the systems that wanted to stay in the Commonwealth before he could try to forcefully retake systems that had left.

The communications lag had required the concentration that had enabled this attack, but as the communications networks were reestablished by couriers and limited q-coms, the TCN would be faced once again with the responsibilities to match its weight.

If the Confederacy won this fight, they'd buy time—and if enough time elapsed, Walkingstick wouldn't be *able* to muster a major fleet for a long, long time.

But first…the Dakotan Confederacy had to take nineteen starships, a handful of battle platforms, a few hundred planet-based fighters and thirty thousand quick-and-dirty one-shot missile mines against the full flower of the Commonwealth Navy, the hard-edged veterans of the Rimward Fleet.

James wasn't sure how he could win.

All he knew was that he couldn't *lose*.

31

Deep Space
10:00 March 10, 2738 ESMDT

"Imperator on deck!"

"At ease."

The exchange was ritual at this point. Walkingstick had used *Saint Michael* as his flagship for almost five years, since well before the war with the Alliance of Free Stars. The flag-deck crew on the battleship knew exactly how much credence and ritual to give the arrival of the Imperator in their space.

His people had built the habits when he'd been their Admiral, and he'd never seen a reason to change his desire for both a strict minimum and a strict maximum of ceremony and respect, either as Marshal or Imperator.

Everyone in the massive circular space acknowledged his arrival and then returned to their work. The flag bridge was a circular space almost a hundred meters across, a specialty installation on *Saint*

Michael introduced early in her construction to make her even more of a command ship than the rest of the *Saints*.

Without access to FTL communications, the flag-deck crew had a lot less to do in FTL than usual. Less than a third of the usual crew were on duty, a change that Walkingstick had approved. The rest were engaging in training or working in other departments to cross-build experience and skills.

The thirty or so people who were left in the room—a third of a normal shift and a tenth of the battle-stations crew—were handling the limited communications with *Saint Brigid* and *Pelée* that they did have, as well as the link back to Earth.

Their communications weren't as pervasive or as high-bandwidth as they were used to, and Walkingstick expected to badly miss his q-probes—but at least the rebels of the Confederacy would have the same limitation.

"Imperator." The officer he'd come to see greeted him with a small bow. Rear Admiral Pich Misra was a newcomer to the Imperator's staff—and even their uniform was so new it squeaked. Like many of the Lictors that Walkingstick had sent out into the Commonwealth, Misra had been a member of the Commonwealth Internal Security Service.

Misra had transferred into the TCN and the Imperator's personal service when Walkingstick had realized that his near-future operations were almost all going to be inside Commonwealth territory.

They were a Cambodian Khmer, with sharply flattened features with a visible tracery of silver circuitry around their face and running up under thick black hair. As a member of the self-described Transhumanist movement, they were openly artificially intersex along with their more visible cybernetics.

Walkingstick found the whole concept laughable—the average human brain was roughly eleven percent silicon by adulthood. Transhumanism had very much taken over humanity, though claiming further journeys were necessary seemed strange to him.

But Misra was a *very* good analyst.

"You said you wanted to see me?" Walkingstick asked.

"We've been running through the information we have, and I've completed the assessment you asked for," Misra told him. "Would you like to hear my thoughts?"

"Please."

Walkingstick settled into parade rest behind the intelligence officer as Misra gestured a presentation into the air.

"There are a lot of unknowns at play in assessing the strength of the Confederacy's navy," they warned. "We know, for example, that the Clockward Fleet under Marshal Amandine was shattered by the League—but we don't know the exact losses entailed in that scenario.

"Sector Fleet Meridian had four capital ships, and Sector Fleet Dakota had seven. Combined with the Clockward Fleet, there were sixty-five Terran capital ships in the area of concern."

"And there's no way Tecumseh has them all," Walkingstick replied. "The League killed Amandine and wrecked her fleet—and we know that Rutherford had his own schemes in Meridian."

"Psych profiles suggest less than a five percent likelihood that Rutherford and Tecumseh are cooperating," Misra noted. "But in that scenario, the rebels will have access to *all* of the survivors of those three fleets."

"I know Tecumseh," the Imperator pointed out. That was why he was there, after all. He'd *trusted* the Shawnee Admiral—only to have that trust thrown back in his face. "Your psych analysis is likely overestimating the chance that he'd go along with Rutherford's plan to make himself emperor."

"Potentially. Certainly, an *alliance* between Dakota and Meridian, with Rutherford in charge in Meridian, is a low-order probability—but it is a *higher* likelihood than Rutherford accepting a position in this Confederacy where he is not in charge."

"And we *know* the Meridian Sector joined this rebellion as a body," Walkingstick said.

"Indeed. It seems a reasonable conclusion, then, that Rutherford met Tecumseh and is either dead or otherwise neutralized," the analyst concluded. "In that scenario, also, we are looking at the Confederacy possessing all of the survivors of the three fleets in question.

"Losses against the League and in the conflict between Tecumseh and Rutherford are difficult to project. We don't have enough data,"

Misra said. "Erring on the conservative side, we believe the Confederacy likely has somewhere between twenty-five and thirty-five warships."

That lined up with Walkingstick's rough estimates. He'd figured twenty to forty, if he was being honest, but the number of unknowns was a problem.

"Even knowing the number of hulls is only so useful," he reminded Misra. "There is a vast gap in capability between the rebels having thirty-five *Assassins*, *Oceans*, and *Paramounts*—and them having 'merely' twenty newer ships."

"We have the full table of organization and equipment for all three forces that Tecumseh is likely to have been able to acquire ships from," the spy told him. "There weren't twenty modern sixty-million-cubic-meter ships in those formations. Amandine had twelve and Sector Fleet Dakota had one. Even assuming they took *Saint Bartholomew* intact, that would be a maximum of fourteen truly modern warships.

"And we *know* that Amandine lost all three of her *Saints* in the ambushes that killed her and took out her fleet."

Walkingstick grimaced. Those details had finally made their way back to Terra. They'd known Amandine was dead for a while, but the Star Chamber delegation sent to the League had been sent back with, among other things, a list of known dead and prisoners that confirmed the results of the ambush on the Marshal and the loss of three precious modern battleships.

They'd also been sent back to Terra with demands for admissions of war guilt and massive reparations. He was due for a meeting with Michael Burns on that in a few hours.

"So, most likely, we're looking at maybe five modern ships backed by twenty to thirty older units," Misra concluded. "Given that the Clockward Fleet, for example, included the only two *Monarch*-class battleships still in commission, it is likely that most of the older ships are from the thirty-million program."

Walkingstick wasn't entirely enthused with the fact that his Expeditionary Fleet had twelve ships from that building program, but he, too, was limited by what he had to hand.

"Regardless of the hull numbers, what do you think he's *doing* with them?" he asked.

"Tecumseh's record suggests that he is a competent but not spectacular commander with an unusual amount of moral courage," Misra laid out crisply. "Most of the *issues* seen in his career have come either out of factors beyond his control or the simple fact that moral courage, in this case, is defined as doing what *he* judges to be right as opposed to what his superiors would want."

"Which leads us to where we are," Walkingstick noted.

"Indeed. So, we need to understand the admiral's limitations and needs. He needs to secure against both the Commonwealth and League. Without a potential diplomatic solution on either side, his new nation is trapped between two enemies that can swallow them whole.

"He cannot concentrate his forces against us or the League without leaving systems he is supposed to defend vulnerable. He will need to keep his largest concentration at Dakota, but I do not judge it likely that the Confederacy will have more than fifteen ships to defend their capital."

"He understands the concept of concentration of force," Walkingstick pointed out. "Tecumseh will know that he cannot defend against us with fifteen ships."

"And he may recognize that and be prepared to take the necessary risks—but with a twenty-day command-and-control loop, I do not believe he will be able to convince his civilian government of that. All evidence we have suggests that he lacks the independence to exercise the moral courage necessary for a full concentration in the absence of proper communications."

"We brought the ships to deal with him having *forty* capital ships," Walkingstick noted. "We're refining the analysis, which is good. The more detail and better estimates you can give me, the better. I want to know what we might have missed."

"The question is not the ships," the intelligence officer told him. "The unknown factor is the industrial might of the Dakota System in particular. None of the systems in this so-called Confederacy are poor, but Dakota has found a particularly interesting niche of being a sanctuary for traditional underdog cultures, providing them with an enduring flow of high-quality immigrants dismissed elsewhere, and a willingness to carve up anywhere they aren't living on for raw materials.

"Dakota itself has very limited planetary industry, but the orbital industry around the main world and the exploitation of the asteroid belts are almost at core-world levels. It is...physically impossible for them to have commissioned new warships, yes, but the mass production of starfighters and munitions of all kinds almost certainly commenced last year."

"Without launch platforms, I'm not concerned about missiles," Walkingstick said drily. "Starfighters I'll watch for, but a bunch of boxed missiles are a resource to be seized, not a threat to be feared."

Misra coughed.

"What?" Walkingstick asked.

"Tecumseh fought in the Rimward Marches, Imperator. He saw the Fox in action—and even *I* know of times the Fox used missiles without launchers as a defensive asset."

"Missiles don't have the protection to spend significant amounts of time in orbit," he countered. "That trick only worked with q-probes to give you timing."

"I remind you of Dakota's industry," the spy said simply. "It is entirely within their capacity to manufacture a single-use launcher—or missile mine, I suppose—that will protect the missiles for some time."

Walkingstick had to pause and process that concept. He was primarily an *offensive* tactician, after all.

"Damn, that makes sense, doesn't it?"

"It is certainly a possibility that occurred to *me* upon reviewing records of the Rimward Wars and the potential assets available to the Dakota System," Misra demurred. "I must warn against it, as it seems...obvious, after all."

There was a potential reprimand in that, but it was one Walkingstick would let go. Misra had, after all, done exactly what the Imperator had asked for—and pointed out something he hadn't considered.

———

Saint Michael might not have a full suite of entangled blocks—and the blocks she had were linked to a network with very few other nodes—but she had enough to enable a proper holographic conference between the Imperator's office and Earth.

Walkingstick was familiar with both members of the dark-skinned couple on the other side of the call. Senator Michael Burns and his wife, Hope Burns, were long-standing allies of his. Michael Burns was two decades older than his wife, but both were accomplished politicians.

Michael Burns had headed up the Star Chamber's Committee on Unification, the body tasked with coordinating the inevitable process of bringing all humanity under the Commonwealth, for over a decade. Hope Burns had served Alpha Centauri as first a representative and then a senator for over a decade before accepting a posting to the diplomatic corps and serving as a high-level ambassador.

It had fallen to her to negotiate the peace terms with the Alliance of Free Stars—and on the way to those negotiations, she had warned one James Calvin Walkingstick of the Star Chamber's intention to scape-goat him for the loss of the war—and likely to *execute* him for its consequences.

"Michael, Hope," he greeted them. For all of the political back-and-forth and his own efforts to create and maintain a cult of personality in the TCN and the Star Chamber alike, the Burns were friends as well as allies.

"James," Senator Burns replied. "It's an awkward position you've left me in here, you know."

"I know," Walkingstick agreed genially. "But you could always have stopped the Chamber deciding to execute me for losing a war they never gave me the resources to win."

"Now is not the time for that argument, boys," Hope Burns said sharply. "The Imperatorship is where we are and what we have to work with. So, we will work with it—and we will save our damn country.

"Right now, that means Michael and I get stuck as the visible face of the Imperatorship while you fight the wars we need you to fight."

"Exactly," Walkingstick agreed. "I am the hammer. You two need to be the softer touch. I will bring people back into the Commonwealth, and you will make them happy to stay."

"We'll try," Michael Burns promised. "But this is a giant mess. The Star Chamber has spent the last day and a half debating the League demands."

"We basically gave the Alliance everything they wanted," Walkingstick noted. "I'd like to avoid rolling over for *everyone*, but I recognize that our situation is...complicated."

"The Alliance of Free Stars was always the greater threat, compared to the League," his old friend reminded him. "While their Operation Medusa likely exhausted the majority of their resources, an *exhausted* Alliance still likely had as many ships under arms as the League did.

"And demonstrably knew where to hit us. We agreed to a situation we knew perfectly well they could *force*, at least in terms of the plebiscites and yielding the Presley and Starkhaven Systems."

"I still think the Star Chamber underestimates just how badly Operation Medusa had to have cost the Alliance," Walkingstick said mildly. "But..." He shrugged. "It wasn't like I could fight a war without q-coms against an enemy with them. A battle, maybe, but not a war."

"The other part is that the Alliance is just that," Hope Burns reminded him. "An *Alliance*. The Federation values the Commonwealth as an ideal, at least, in that we are the largest democracy in human space. The Coraline Imperium, on the other hand, sees that same structure as a threat to their constitutional monarchy—and has a leadership that is determinedly of the opinion that there are only two kinds of enemy."

"The one you're still fighting and the one that's dead," Michael Burns finished for her. "But that balance let us sneak through with a treaty that, by and large, recognizes that their main concern is protecting themselves from us, and we're basically kneecapped from offensive operations for a generation."

"The League, on the other hand, still has an active fleet but never had the strength for real counterstrikes against us," Walkingstick guessed. "So, what's the sticking point?"

"Basically? Plebiscites are cheap. The democracy-over-all types in the Chamber are prepared to accept the results of a legitimate referendum, and the Unificationists figure we can retake any system that slips away over the course of a generation. So, the Star Chamber can be sold on holding the votes that were the Alliance's largest demand.

"But the League wants actual reparations. Periklos basically wants money to rebuild New Edmonton, with enough loose cash left over to bribe his oligarchs and businesspeople into supporting his centralized regime long enough to pass it on to a new generation."

"And an admission that we started the war, formally acknowledging that the League didn't attack Tau Ceti," Michael added to his wife's explanation. "Which…well, despite what a plurality of the Star Chamber seems to think, was obvious to many of us at the time."

"And became *blatant* when Periklos refused to work with the Alliance after we attacked him," Walkingstick observed. "If the League had *actually* been involved in the attack, their offer of cooperation would have been a gold-plated win for him. Instead, he went his own way."

"We have a copy of his formal note to the Castle Federation," Hope Burns noted. "He explicitly accused them of sourcing League fighters from the black market and carrying out a covert operation specifically to get us to attack him.

"The words *go fuck yourselves* are actually in the note."

Walkingstick chuckled in surprised amusement.

"That's probably not an absolute first, given human history, but it must have had an impact."

"So far as we know, the Alliance never reached out again. They do have open diplomatic relations with the League, though, so Periklos knows *exactly* what we conceded for peace with the Alliance."

"And he likely thinks that money means less to us than worlds," Walkingstick said, his humor fading. "Which it *should.*"

"Except we're going to be losing worlds and systems left and right, and the monetary resources of the Commonwealth government and the Central Bank of Terra are a key part of bringing them back into the fold. The amount of money that the League is asking for could seriously undermine our ability to operate in the next few years."

"Money can be created, if necessary," he pointed out. "The CBT is entirely capable of printing dollars from thin air if needed—and if the price of paying off the League is inflation, we can absorb that and use it to our advantage."

Inflating it away was, after all, a very traditional way of handling government debt.

"I agree," Michael Burns conceded. "But the Star Chamber is balking at the cost, especially as the only place we *know* the League has attacked is, well, now in open rebellion. Allowing the League and Confederacy to bash their fleets against each other is potentially to our advantage."

"Remember that a significant portion of the Stellar League's firepower is available for hire," Walkingstick said. "If the Confederacy makes peace with them first, those mercenary warships may help hold us off."

"Is that a concern, Imperator?" Hope Burns asked. "My understanding was that the Expeditionary Fleet should be more than sufficient to secure the rebel sectors."

"Even in my worst-case assessments of the strength available to the rebels, we have them badly outnumbered and outgunned," Walkingstick confirmed. "But capturing and securing twelve inhabited star systems takes time. Even if we force the surrender of their leadership on Dakota, the member worlds may continue to defy us.

"Our primary objective is the shipyards in Dakota and the partially built eighty-million-cubic-meter warships there," he reminded them. "Once we have secured those yards and Dakota itself, the only remaining objective is Tecumseh's fleet.

"Once the fleet is neutralized and Dakota is secured, it is only a question of time—but they could extend both the timeline and the cost of securing these sectors by bringing in League mercenaries.

"A reasonable counteroffer to Periklos, I suspect, is that we pay him off in exchange for him preventing the Condottieri from fighting for our secessionists."

"Agreed," Michael Burns. "But...may I make a recommendation, James?"

"Michael, you and Hope are potentially the only people left I trust to speak their minds to me fully," Walkingstick admitted. "That is the cost of what it takes to be here. Even my officers... I trust them to do their jobs and be honest with me about our missions, but I worry that they may hesitate to tell me what they do not think I want to hear."

He knew *damn* well what he'd created around himself to shape his rise to power and the risks involved. Even encouraging his people to be forthright with him wasn't guaranteed to stop an echo chamber forming.

"Let the Star Chamber hash it out," his friend told him. "They'll feel more useful, and I'm quite certain I can move things in the right direction. If necessary, you can step in as the hammer and impose what the three of us know is the best option, but if we let the Star Chamber get to that point on their own..."

"They won't feel *quite* as much like you've run roughshod over their power and prerogatives," Hope Burns concluded for her husband. "The role we have created for you has no limits on its power. But the more we allow the Star Chamber to *pretend* they are independent, the happier they will be."

"And the better off they will be when the time comes for me to lay down the mace," Walkingstick replied. "I do not wish to be Imperator forever and I have *no* desire to create a dynasty. Sooner or later, I will step aside, and the Star Chamber *must* remember how to govern."

"Then I think we are on the same page," the Senator told him. "I will manage the Star Chamber for now, but unless they badly misstep, I think I can get them to recommend the right course of action."

"Keep me informed," Walkingstick ordered. "But for now, yes, let's give them the rope to run. I have a war to fight.

"Unity *must* be preserved—and I will demonstrate that to these rebels with fire and steel."

32

Deep Space
08:00 March 12, 2738 ESMDT

"THAT'S GOING to be one hell of a risk, sir," Commodore Krejči told Anthony. "Has the Admiral signed off on this?"

Despite Anthony's own stars, he understood entirely who the muscular officer who ran Base Łá'ts'áadah's defenses meant. The Dakotan Confederacy Navy would have dozens of Admirals of one tier or another by the time they were done growing—but so long as James Tecumseh lived, there was only going to be one "the Admiral" in the DCN.

"I have full authority to redeploy the fighter wings as I see fit," Anthony pointed out mildly, only the thickening of his Highland brogue suggesting his irritation.

That wasn't really directed at Krejči. There were two Commodores and four Wing Colonels on the holographic conference with him—and every single one of them was in Dakota. Technically, Commodore Krejči and Commodore Biro were DCN officers, but Biro was in the same situation as Krejči—they commanded the launch platforms for Anthony's starfighters and bombers.

"But yes, I have discussed the plan with Admiral Tecumseh," he continued, surveying the six officers who were responsible for the six hundred starfighters still in the Dakota System. "And the basic problem is this: the hangar platforms in Dakota orbit are too damn vulnerable and too close to necessary civilian infrastructure.

"There is no question that those platforms constitute legitimate military targets, but the potential collateral damage of their destruction is unacceptable."

"We don't have space for another three hundred fighters at Łá't-s'áadah," Krejči warned. "We can rig up gantries to let the crews *leave*, but we'll have to cycle birds carefully to keep them armed and fueled. I *think* we can put up the flight crews without having to hot-bunk them, but it'll be tight."

"The key is to arrange things so that our defenses are *not* laid out the way Walkingstick expects," Anthony told them. "Łá'ts'áadah is going to be high on Walkingstick's priority list, but you're not going to get the lion's share of his attention. Backing up the *Zions* with a lot more fighters than he's expecting *should* let you sucker-punch whatever detachment he sends after the Hustle yards.

"Every ship, every *starfighter*, you can take down before First Fleet arrives helps reduce the odds. We've got surprises waiting for them in Dakota orbit, and transferring the starfighters will do more to help defend Łá'ts'áadah than it will hurt the ability to protect Dakota."

"And as you said, the hangar complexes would draw fire toward the civilian infrastructure," Commodore Biro conceded. "But...sir...we can't transfer three hundred starfighters without the civilians seeing. We're going to need to get approval from the Cabinet."

"Then ask for it," Anthony ordered. "The President understands the situation—she used to be a Marine. She gets it."

"We're putting a lot on the q-probes and the missile mines," Krejči noted. "Even with surprise on our side...the odds are long."

"The odds are horrific," Anthony said. "But we will fight regardless. Talk to President Chapulin, Commodore. She understands the risks that must be taken if we are to have a chance of winning this."

Not even a good chance. *Any* chance.

———

Virtual reality flickered around Anthony as the representation of *Krakatoa*'s flag bridge vanished in a ball of fire, yet another clever plan for allowing a thousand starfighters and bombers to fight four thousand ending in ignominious failure.

Anthony wasn't pulling his people into his test sessions yet. His Colonels and Lieutenant Colonels were taking part in daily planning sessions that included war-games scenarios—and those were depressing enough.

His own simulations were run with even-uglier assumptions than he was having his team use. He suspected Tecumseh was doing something similar, because the fleet staff scenarios resembled the ones he was running his subordinates through.

Fifty starships versus seventeen was a hard set of odds to overcome. The assumption they were using in the main scenarios was that even Walkingstick was going to have ten *Assassins* or *Oceans* in his order of battle.

That brought the weight and number of starfighters down—but not enough. Not really. Not when they *also* had to figure that the Commonwealth had sent at least fifteen modern sixty-million-plus-cubic-meter ships—and the DCN only *had* two of those.

The DCN had twelve thirty-or-less capital ships. Anthony figured the Commonwealth had *at most* ten, and his own scenario was based around *zero*.

Even in the default scenario of ten thirties in the Imperator's order of battle, he couldn't see a way to take on the invasion fleet. They'd have two more ships at Dakota than they had right now—but the two *Paramounts* that had been guarding Persephone were carrying ex-League Xenophon-type fighters.

Comparable to the Katanas, yes, but using different missiles and electronics. Coordination was going to suck, but he couldn't give up those two hundred starfighters.

The only chance Anthony could see was to somehow divide Walkingstick's fleet and arrange a defeat in detail—but the Imperator understood the principle of concentration of force as well as they did.

They had to lure the Imperator into a mistake—except that the unquestioned master of that kind of deception, at least on a strategic and operational level, *was* Walkingstick himself.

Or maybe the Federation's Stellar Fox, Anthony reflected. Rumor did put that man behind the entire scheme that had crippled the Commonwealth, after all. That body blow to Commonwealth communications and shipbuilding had been a superb piece of strategic misdirection.

But Anthony Yamamoto couldn't see a way to pull that off on the scale of a single system.

He barely noticed Shannon Reynolds slipping into his office as he kept staring at the replay of the latest *clever idea*. He was looking for any mistakes he'd made in executing the plan, but...

"I'm guessing that one simply didn't work?" she asked.

"Yeah. I was hoping I'd screwed up a part of it, but no," he admitted, still watching the display. "Which makes that the...twenty-sixth way I've discovered to get all of my people killed."

"Tecumseh's only at seventeen," the assassin told him. "But I suppose the moving parts in his scenarios move slower?"

"And Tecumseh has more actual work to do in FTL than I do," Anthony noted. "Not least the political hand-holding required to keep our civilian leaders from panicking."

"I sit in on a lot of those meetings, you know." Her tone pulled his attention away from the simulation at last. "Our civilian leaders aren't panicking, Anthony. They don't see any answers to this mess, but they're not panicking and they're not giving up."

"Fair," he conceded. "I haven't really been paying *that* much attention to our new government. I probably should be, but I've been busy."

"All work and no play makes Anthony a dull boy," she told him. "Not that I'm one to talk. Bodyguarding a man who has *no concept* of how much of a symbol he is to this new nation is...*breathtaking*."

Anthony chuckled. He knew, through a rumor mill that had been *very concerned*, that Reynolds had managed to find time to sleep her way through assorted shipboard personnel well separated from the Admiral's immediate surroundings.

She had a solid sense of boundaries. So did he, which was part of why he *wasn't* cutting a swathe through the ship. Theoretically, the Marines and Navy personnel were still "fair game," but the stars added a level of weight to any proposition that he didn't want to deal with.

"So long as you keep him alive. I need him to somehow find a way out of this mess," he told her. "Because I'm not seeing it. We need to stop the Commonwealth at Dakota, but the only ways I see to do so involve convincing one of the best tacticians of our generation to divide his forces in the face of insufficient information."

Reynolds was quiet for a moment, then hopped up onto his desk and settled down cross-legged where his hologram had been a moment before. She rested her chin on her hand and studied.

"You know, I looked into your big famous ancestor while I was deciding if you were the right officer to use to watch Tecumseh," she told him. "Dug a bit deeper when things got personal."

"And?" he asked. Things hadn't grown *personal*, he suspected, until well after they'd become *intimate*. They were friends now, but their friendship was almost incidental to their sexual interactions.

"Just thinking about that description," she told him. "One of the best tacticians of the time dividing his forces in the face of insufficient information. Sounds like Isoroku Yamamoto planning the Battle of Midway."

"The Marshal Admiral thought he had the upper hand, in numbers, tech and tactics, *and* that he knew what was going on," Anthony murmured. "But the US Navy had broken his ciphers and had more information than he thought they did."

"But arrogance and the certain knowledge that he *was* one of the best tacticians of his age that helped get him there," Reynolds murmured. "I haven't met Walkingstick...but somehow, I don't think the man who convinced the Star Chamber to give him a fleet to conquer seventy star systems and then turned around and made himself dictator is *humble*."

"We can't build a battle plan around the Imperator getting full of himself and making mistakes," Anthony told her.

"No, but you need to allow for the possibility and have *options* for it," she said. "Because we know he's coming and you should be able to see everything he does. And I wonder..."

"What?" Despite the professional nature of their conversation, normally a control mechanism for him, he was suddenly *very* aware of how far into his personal space Reynolds had moved. His inability to get laid was making him more distractable, he realized.

At least Reynolds was a *safe* distraction.

"Two things," she told him, and something in her voice told him he wasn't the only one distracted. "The first is professional, and I want you to make a note of it for later."

"Which is?"

"Does *Walkingstick* know we have q-coms?" she asked softly. "Or is he going to be assuming we have the same lightspeed limitations he has? Because I can't think of any way that he *would* know that Castle and Trickster supplied us with those, which means we have an ace up our sleeve."

Anthony considered that.

"Information and intelligence and communications," he realized. "He might figure we have something like the first batch we bought, limited interplanetary coms, but he's not expecting us to be able to get full telemetry from sensors in Dakota."

"You know the details better than I do," she agreed. "Like I said, note that for later."

"Why? What was the second thing you were wondering?"

Rather than answering aloud, Reynolds slid bodily off his desk and into his lap.

33

Deep Space
16:00 March 15, 2738 ESMDT

"WE ARE OUT OF TIME."

James nodded silently at Abey's words. They had just finished an extended, multi-hour briefing on the plans to defend Dakota against the Commonwealth Fleet, and a small timer hung in the corner of his vision as he looked at his girlfriend.

Thirty-six hours remained before the expected arrival of Imperator Walkingstick. Everything that could be put in place had been.

"I'm guessing you haven't announced anything?" he asked.

"No, though we've stepped up enough emergency-preparedness drills and so forth that everyone with a brain knows we're expecting *something*." She shook her head. "Táálá'í'tsin wasn't designed for security bunkers. If nothing else, we can't protect the tree itself, and I don't know how well my people would take it getting damaged."

The titular *one tree* of Táálá'í'tsin was over a kilometer high and a hundred and fifty–plus meters wide at the base. It was the largest of

Dakota's greatwood trees by a significant margin, some unique conflu-ence of soil and climate and luck letting it grow to a third again the height of its next-tallest relative.

The original Navajo colonists had taken it as a sign—and one of the first acts of Dakota's planetary government had been to lock in an iron-clad set of protections around Táátła'í'tsin's tree in particular and the greatwoods in general.

"Walkingstick is smart enough to realize that damaging Táátła'í'tsin is a good way to turn Dakota into the kind of bleeding sore of an occu-pation that *breaks* empires," James said wryly. "I have to hope he recog-nizes that a soft touch is his best plan."

"Not least because you plan on kicking his ass all the way into next year?" she asked.

"Hopefully." He shook his head. "A lot of it depends on what he does when he arrives, love. If he plays it smart and takes the right steps, I have some surprises that can even the playing field, but…"

She studied his face in the hologram.

"He's going to win, isn't he?" she asked softly.

"We need him to make a mistake," James told her. "Otherwise…we have q-probes, FTL communications, we'll know where he is…" He shook his head. "I can make seventeen ships fight like thirty with that advantage, but he's bringing *fifty*."

"We're going to fight, James."

"I know. I just…have to wonder if maybe that isn't the best plan."

"We have to fight. We owe it to our people; we owe it to *ourselves*," she told him fiercely.

"I just remember Persephone," he admitted. "Where the League *shot* a tenth of the planetary parliament in their conference hall. My bodyguard is a woman who used to be tasked to assassinate leaders of organizations before they even *became* rebellions.

"I can't help but feel that you and the rest of the Cabinet are in direct and immediate danger."

"We are," Abey agreed. "At a minimum, we are going to pay for daring to rebel with our freedom—and quite possibly with our lives. But we will fight on. We have to."

"I never expected to face this overwhelming a force," he told her. "I feel like I led you all into a trap without even realizing it."

"We walked this path in full knowledge of the risks, James." She shook her head. "The alternative was unacceptable. What was demanded of us was too much. So, we fight. We stand."

"And now we might fall."

"We will not." Abey spoke fiercely enough to yank his attention back to the moment, and he met her gaze. "You made this possible, but *we* chose it. Someone has to take a stand. Someone has to prove to Walkingstick that his dream of unity is a nightmare."

Looking at the fire in her eyes, James realized that he might have fallen in love with the Phoenix. Not just in the woman he loved but in the nation he had chosen.

"We will rise from the ashes," he whispered. "I'm coming."

"I know," she told him. "And I believe that Walkingstick will fail and that we will be victorious. But whether we win or fall, someone has to stand up and say enough is enough.

"You put the words in the declaration we sent Terra yourself, James," she reminded him.

"Someone has to stand defiant."

34

EVEN IN THE LITTLE THINGS, the Expeditionary Fleet showed the lack of instant communications. Before Operation Medusa, Walkingstick would have taken his fleet right up to the gravity-well line around Dakota, roughly five light-minutes from the planet, and expected his ships to emerge in perfect formation.

Now...he'd brought his fleet out of FTL six light-hours from the planet to make certain they were organized and ready. He'd thought he was being overcautious when he'd made that plan in Sol.

"What *happened*?" he asked his flag-deck staff, keeping his tone calm.

"Minor variations in timing and energy levels across a hundred light-years," his chief of staff said quietly. "What would normally be corrected for almost automatically now results in...this."

Rear Admiral Clarette MacGinnis had picked up a new star with her new job. His former operations officer now ran his staff—and his staff was now responsible for far more than a single fleet.

The delicately built raven-haired woman had risen to the challenge with aplomb, and Walkingstick was planning on giving her a *second* star to make certain people respected her authority beyond simply acting as an avatar of *his* power.

"How bad is it?" he asked, looking at the scattered green icons on his display.

"*Vesuvius* is the farthest forward, having overshot by just over a light-minute," MacGinnis told him. "*Saint Anthony* is the farthest back, having *under*shot by about the same. We'll get everyone sorted out, but it'll take a few minutes."

"Do we need to get everyone physically together *here*, like lost children, or can our navigators manage to coordinate a six-light-hour jump to Dakota's gravity well without losing ourselves?"

"Well, truthfully sir, a one-in-five-hundred-million error radius won't be a problem when we're making a six-light-hour jump," she pointed out. "We're just used to our error radius being orders of magnitude less than that because we were able to update everyone's final courses as we went."

Two-minute round-trip communications were going to be enough of a pain, but Walkingstick nodded his acknowledgement of the logic. One light-minute over one hundred light-years was *incredible*...by any standard except what he felt his fleets *should* have been able to do.

"Get updated data from anyone's navigation departments," he ordered. "Thirty minutes should be enough to get everyone sorted and ready to make the final jump?"

"More than, sir," MacGinnis promised. "We can probably do it in ten."

"Take thirty," he told her. "Because if one of our carriers overshoots by a full light-minute as we're heading into Dakota, we're going to *lose* her. Do not assume, for one moment, that the people James Tecumseh trained won't leap on that."

"Fair enough, sir. We'll triple-check everything."

"And while we're at it, run me scan data on both Virginia and

Dakota," Walkingstick instructed. "The plan was to spend five minutes getting the lay of the land and reorganizing.

"Since we're taking thirty to reorganize, let's make sure we know what our friends have been up to for the last few months!"

The first and most obvious conclusion was disappointing.

"Tecumseh isn't here," Walkingstick concluded swiftly. There were, in fact, *no* active warships in the Dakota System. There were the ones under construction he was expecting at the Hustle shipyards at Virginia-11 and…

"MacGinnis, do we have an ID on the ship at the trailing Lagrange point?" he asked, flashing a highlight over to the chief of staff's implants even as he zoomed in the main holographic display.

His flag deck had the full crew on duty now, almost three hundred people working to make sure one James Calvin Walkingstick was fully informed on what was going on. Most of them were *currently* running navigation support to make certain that the Expeditionary Fleet arrived at Dakota in formation instead of scattered across two light-minutes.

"Her IFF is offline and we're too far out for detailed breakdown," his chief of staff reported after a couple of moments. "She's definitely a sixty-million-cubic-meter ship and she's definitely offline. Minimal power signatures. Profile suggests a *Hercules*, sir."

"Keep a team watching her," Walkingstick ordered. "I want to know if she so much as *twitches*. A single *Hercules* won't change anything today, but she could cause some real trouble if she moves at the right moment."

"It looks like her primary zero-point generators are offline," one of the techs reported. "It's hard to say, but she may be on station power. She's under repairs for *something*, after all."

"And the mostly likely culprit is the League," Walkingstick agreed. "Just keep an eye on her, son. Better to watch a threat that doesn't materialize than write her off and be wrong."

Leaving the battlecruiser to the designated team, he turned his attention back to the second prize of this whole affair. Base Łá'ts'áadah was the third of the Project Hustle yards and held keels for a good chunk of the Commonwealth Navy's next generation of warships.

There was no way in void or stars that Walkingstick was leaving those ships in anyone else's hands, not after the Alliance had destroyed every eighty-million-cubic-meter warship in the TCN *and* half of the hulls under construction across the Commonwealth.

He needed those ships and he needed to make an example of a large secessionist movement—and since the Dakota System had those ships, their volunteering for the latter need had been *highly* useful.

But Base Łá'ts'áadah was also the only place in the system that the Commonwealth had fortified, and he ran a professional eye over the details. Most of them lined up with his expectations. Four *Zion*-class battle platforms. A few starfighter squadrons visible.

And...

"I need eyes on the *Zions* at Base Łá'ts'áadah," he murmured, his flag staff almost automatically assigning a set of analysts in response to his soft-spoken request. "There are additional constructs on all four stations. What are we looking at?"

They were spindly things, barely visible at this range—the system's geometry meant they were farther from the shipyard than their target planet—but he could only think of a few things that would be worth attaching extra structure to a space station for.

"Looks like support gantries of some kind," the blonde Lieutenant Commander who stepped into the analysis role told him. "Can't tell at this range if they're running fuel pipes along them, but it would make sense if they're using them to hold additional starfighters."

"Are they blocking the stations' line of fire?" Walkingstick asked.

"It looks like they're blocking the lances but not the missile launchers," she replied instantly. "We're resolving, but I make it eighty-plus percent likely that there are starfighters on those gantries. They're using them to support holding additional squadrons for the defense of the shipyards.

"It would be awkward and potentially require the crew to enter their fighters via vacuum, but they could cycle the arming and crew-rest periods, double their number of fighters. Maybe even triple it."

"Clever," he observed. "With no major energy signature change until the fighters come online. Flag that for tactical and for Admiral Tasker."

His overall plan for the system was still amorphous and taking shape in his head, but he hadn't brought his most-capable fleet commander along to *not* use her for an independent command.

"MacGinnis, I'm flipping you a TOE," he told the chief of staff. "Twenty-ship task force, designated E-Two, under Admiral Tasker. They'll stay with the main fleet for now, but if Tecumseh is elsewhere, that gives us a window of opportunity."

"Yes, sir."

TF E-2 would be anchored on the carriers *Pelée* and *Tambora*, with Tasker's flagship *Saint Brigid* to provide heavy hitting power. He was giving her all twelve of the *Assassins* and *Oceans*, with five *Lexington* carriers to round out the numbers.

That would give her forty percent of his hulls but leave two-thirds of the firepower with Walkingstick. He'd keep them together unless he saw an opportunity...but the absence of the rebel fleet definitely limited the risks of dividing his force.

With that sorted—he trusted MacGinnis and Tasker to handle the reorganization before they jumped to Dakota—he turned his attention to their next stop.

Dakota was a gorgeous planet, he reflected. Her people had spent a vast amount of effort protecting her original ecosystem while integrating Terran crops and modern technology. Part of that had been keeping basically *all* industrial development off the planetary surface.

That resulted in the planet having an orbital ring and space-station cloud to rival most core worlds. The core worlds, though, were old enough, rich enough and cynical enough to maintain fortifications in their skies.

Dakota had been colonized as the Commonwealth was taking form. The world had never *been* independent and had never faced an outside threat. At no point in the system's history had it come under attack. There were no fortresses in the orbital infrastructure.

There were high guard corvettes, he noted in passing. The space-going equivalent of the old coast guard, they'd almost certainly *try* to fight, but the hundred-thousand-ton sublight ships weren't even a match for an equivalent tonnage of starfighters.

There were enough of them to register as a factor but not enough of them to be a concern. At least one battle station appeared to be under construction, but without access to the prefabricated components that made up *Zions*, it was clearly taking time.

Other than the incomplete fortress, he didn't see *any* signs of new defenses around Dakota. Had they thought that the Commonwealth would blithely let their rebellion stand? Or had they simply not had the resources?

And where was their fleet?

"The lack of pre-deployment intelligence is definitely uncomfortable," he murmured to MacGinnis. "I wish we knew where Tecumseh and his ships were."

"Unless he's already on his way here, he's a minimum of twelve days away," she pointed out. "And that's assuming they get a message out."

"Tecumseh's fleet appears to be the *only* real threat these rebels have to offer," Walkingstick replied. "We will ignore any and all attempts to send courier ships out."

He smiled coldly as his chief of staff processed that order.

"We *want* them to come to us," he concluded. "We'll take our time and we'll secure Dakota carefully, but until we have neutralized Tecumseh's fleet, this campaign cannot end."

And even if he successfully forced the rebel government into a full surrender, as he hoped, he wouldn't trust that Tecumseh was going to honor that surrender until he had the man under lock and key and every one of his ships in Terran hands.

35

Dakota System
05:45 March 17, 2738 ESMDT

THE SEVENTY-FIVE-MINUTE JUMP from the outer reaches of the system to the edge of Dakota's gravity well was enough time for Walkingstick to set up his office for proper presentation. Two Commonwealth flags hung from crossed spears on the wall behind him—and the wall itself was a screen showing Earth from orbit.

Walkingstick himself had rechecked his uniform and the long braid of his hair. He knew the image he presented, and every aspect of it was critical for the task in front of him.

An almost-subliminal drumbeat echoed through the space as he considered that task. His sixty ships would present an almost unassailable argument. It fell to his words and his presence to close the deal, to drive the so-called Confederacy to surrender without a shot fired.

He put his chances at about two in five, but shock and aggression were as much weapons of war as any missile or positron lance.

"Emergence in sixty seconds," MacGinnis's voice said in his

implant. "All fighters standing by to launch. Any adjustments to the plan, sir?"

"Would be a tad late, wouldn't it?" he asked drily. "You know the drill. Fleet will advance in formation at two hundred gravities. We do not give them time to think."

All things were relative. The approach from five light-minutes would take four hours, but that was normal. That he was bringing his ships in at full Tier Two acceleration would help. He might even need to send the fighters ahead, but that was a call he'd make when the time came.

His drumbeat echoed in his veins as the mass of *Saint Michael* shivered around him and his fleet arrived in realspace in full array. The sensor data was feeding directly into his implant, and he smiled thinly to see the Expeditionary Fleet formation was *perfect* this time.

The core of his fleet were veterans of the Rimward Marches Fleet, forged and hardened in the fires of the only near-peer conflict the Commonwealth had ever fought. Only the sheer distance and the lack of expected coordination had led to their disarray when they'd arrived in the outer system—but if they'd made their leap all the way to Dakota the first time, that disarray would have undermined the presence they needed to finish this without bloodshed.

But now he would speak to the leaders of Dakota with an immense battle fleet at his back. No single star system could support the armada he'd brought. No single *sector*, even, could support a fleet of fifty warships, let alone the ten invasion transports that may as well have *been* warships.

Walkingstick rose from his seat, a gesture sending the chair into a concealed cupboard on one side of the room. He stood square to the pickups, letting them scan the space and his posture, and then commenced recording.

"People of the world of Dakota," he greeted them all. "I am James Calvin Walkingstick, charged by the Star Chamber of the Terran Commonwealth as Imperator. Tasked to maintain the integrity and *unity* of the Commonwealth in these trying times."

He smiled, letting his expression ride the line between threatening and reassuring.

"A delegation was sent from Dakota to declare you and eleven other systems in rebellion against Terra. By the authority of the Star Chamber, it is my duty to inform you that this rebellion must end and you must return to the fold.

"I understand that these are dark and trying times," he echoed with a sad shake of his head. "But that is no reason to betray the sacred trusts the worlds of the Commonwealth have placed in each other. I understand that you were afraid, but you have committed a grand mistake, one that I must rectify.

"I require the surrender of your planetary government and orbital defenses immediately. If we have not received that surrender by the time my fleet enters orbit, we will take whatever measures are necessary to secure the Commonwealth's authority here.

"I do not lightly or by choice take this path," he concluded. "I ask that you show wisdom and recognize the folly of the choices and declarations that led us here. Lay down your arms, children of Terra. We need not shed blood today.

"But we *will* be reunified."

———

There had been a time when such a demand would have been responded to within minutes. Possibly even seconds, if the recipient had access to Commonwealth q-coms—and most planets had at least *some* entangled blocks on the Commonwealth network.

Even outside the Commonwealth, their q-com network had been the glue holding together the thousand disparate switchboards into a network. The Alliance had destroyed *that* as well, and Walkingstick doubted they'd even considered that consequence.

But with that loss, it was a ten-minute round trip just for light to pass back and forth between his fleet and the planet. And then they'd have to *find* the people with the authority to surrender. Walkingstick figured it would be at least twenty minutes before he heard back—though he wasn't sure what time it was in the Dakotan capital.

It was a surprise when his communications staff pinged him at *exactly* ten minutes, letting him know that a transmission had come in for him.

Wordlessly, he played it. There was no point in a live channel yet, but he would be there until a final decision was made.

The recording showed a long conference table, carved from what he guessed was the local wood, with thirteen people gathered around it.

Then his brain caught up with what the table was made from. It wasn't just *the local wood*. The conference table was made from *Dakotan greatwood*, a tree the local government did not allow harvesting of. To find a single piece of greatwood deadfall large enough to make a table from must have been a sending from the stars.

And they'd made it into a table for *these* people. It was a small thing —but James Calvin Walkingstick understood subtle theater, and he knew the message that Dakota was sending.

He recognized only one of the people around the table, one of the two women at the end in complex feather headdresses. The one he recognized was Quetzalli Chapulin, the dark-skinned elected First Chief of Dakota.

The one with the green sash of a Commonwealth Marine Colonel woven through her headdress. The presence of the *second* woman with a First Chief's headdress, though, told him that Chapulin had been promoted even before she spoke.

"Imperator Walkingstick," she greeted him. "You are late."

Her casual tone, her dismissive words, even the *body language* that Chapulin used as she spoke, hit him like a body blow. He'd been expecting…something. Fear. Trepidation. *Surprise*, at least.

"We expected you earlier this morning, given your departure time from Terra," she continued, and a chill ran down his spine.

They'd known he was coming? That suggested unpleasant things in terms of Confederate assets on Earth—or, at least, allies with such assets who were prepared to sell that information to Dakota.

"Your presence here suggests that you did not listen to Inmaculada Haines's presentation," she continued. "I assume you at least read our formal note, but it seems I must repeat it anyway.

"We will serve no tyrants, no masters. We must, therefore, acquiesce to

necessity, which requires this separation, and hold the Commonwealth as we hold the rest of humanity: enemies in war, friends in peace."

At least she wasn't going to repeat the *entirety* of their self-righteous parroting of the American Declaration of Independence. If nothing else, the Navajo woman had to be as aware of the blood-soaked hypocrisy of the American founders as she was.

Both of their ancestors had suffered at the hands of the men who'd written those words, after all.

"We recognize, as you seem to not, that the Terran Commonwealth was founded on four principles: Democracy. Freedom. Justice. Unity. They were intended from the beginning to be equal, the pillars on which to build a better future and a better universe for all mankind.

"And yet, over the years, the Commonwealth has failed all of these, one way or another," she told him. "But our greatest crimes, Imperator Walkingstick, have always been committed in the pursuit of *unity*.

"And so, when your demands arrived here, we made a choice. To honor the best of what the Commonwealth was *supposed* to be rather than kneel to the worst of what it had become.

"We sent Inmaculada Haines to you, to serve as an ambassador and to lay the groundwork for a peaceful separation. We wished to greet the Commonwealth as friends, to work together in peace for that better universe.

"But you are here."

The other twelve people Walkingstick could see in the video were silent, but he could tell that Chapulin spoke for all of them. If they'd been live, he'd have cut the woman's prattle off by now.

"*Enemies in war, friends in peace,*" she echoed. "You have chosen war. We will serve no tyrants, no masters."

She smiled, a surprisingly gentle expression.

"We do not wish to be the enemy of Terra, Imperator, but you have laid our homeworld's feet upon a path that is not easily turned from. Those sacred bonds you mention require one last attempt, though.

"Dakota will not kneel. We choose defiance, Imperator Walkingstick, and we choose the path of fire. Approach this world and the blood shed will be your own. We are not defenseless, and we will not surrender.

"Leave, James Calvin Walkingstick, or become everything our shared ancestors would have known was evil."

The message ended and Walkingstick stared at the wall for a long moment. The drumbeat in the background of the room echoed in his ears, and he swallowed a stream of curses in a slew of languages.

Who did she think she was? Faced with an armada like the galaxy had rarely seen, she had chosen to waste her time on pointless moralizing. Dakota had betrayed the greatest sacred trust in the history of mankind, and she wanted to tell *him* he was failing the ideals of the Commonwealth?

Exhaling a long breath, he leaned into his war drums and brought up the recorders again.

"Quetzalli Chapulin," he greeted her. "You are far too willing to condemn your people. Do you truly think that everyone who follows you has so blithely thrown aside the sacred trust of our shared history, the sacred bond to our ancient home, to Terra and the nation we built together?"

He shook his head.

"You moralize at me," he told her. "But your self-righteous prattle is a shield over the greater sin. The Commonwealth *must* hold together. The future of *all* humanity depends on it. Your prattle will not shield you from missiles and Marines.

"You have until my ships enter orbit to surrender," he concluded. "After that, my Marines will secure Dakota however is necessary."

He ended the recording and gave the shutdown order to his office systems. He was done talking now—the only message he was going to reply to now was Dakota's surrender.

The drumbeat faded into silence as he walked onto *Saint Michael*'s flag deck. The only reason his office didn't open *directly* onto the flag bridge was an intentional separation to stop *ask the Admiral* being the default response to questions that came up while he wasn't there.

"Are we ready?" he asked MacGinnis.

"Entirely," she confirmed. "All fighters and bombers are deployed, and we continue to advance in basically parade formation."

The massive holographic display at the center of the flag deck confirmed her words. Sixty large green icons held the center of the display, but the speckled green dots of over five hundred bombers and twenty-five hundred starfighters swarmed around them.

The entire Rimward Marches Fleet, tasked to conquer seventy-plus star systems, had only been about twice the size of the Expeditionary Fleet at any given time. Between losses, repairs and generally tour-of-duty rotation, Walkingstick had gone through almost two hundred and fifty ships in that fleet over the years, but it had peaked around a hundred and thirty at its largest.

"I wonder if an actual parade formation would have made the point better," he murmured. There were a few in the handbook, after all. He could have his ships and fighters form up into the shape of a swan or a dragon or something similarly silly.

It would make the point of how little Dakota could do to threaten him. But then...

"I want CIC and our analysis teams to go over the sensor data from Dakota orbit again, especially as we are closer and have better data now," he ordered softly. "I am reasonably sure Chapulin is posturing, but she seems to think she has the ability to threaten this fleet.

"If there is a danger, I want to know."

"Yes, sir." She paused. "Four civilian ships have broken orbit since we arrived sir. Destinations appear to be Arroyo, Shogun, Gothic and Meridian."

"Send one of the strike cruisers to attempt to intercept each of them," Walkingstick ordered thoughtfully. "They need to *fail*, of course, but I don't necessarily want the rebels to think we *want* them to get word out."

"Tecumseh will know it's a trap regardless," MacGinnis warned. "He's not stupid and he can probably match thirty ships against sixty in his head."

"He has to either fight or surrender," the Imperator replied. "He *has* to. Or he's failing whatever oaths and promises he has made to these people.

"No, Rear Admiral MacGinnis, he will come once he knows we're here. He will find every trick that he and his staff and captains can come up with to throw at us. He might even find something that turns the odds a bit in his favor, but he can't overcome two-to-one."

"Why would he even try?"

"Because James Tecumseh does not have it in him to do what he thinks is the wrong thing," Walkingstick said with a sigh. "It's why I thought I could rely on him as a strong right hand here in Dakota... and it's also why he betrayed me.

"And it's why I know he's going to come. But those ships line up with my estimates of where his fleet might be—and they give us a timeline. As of right now, he doesn't know we're here. He *can't*. Even if Dakota knew we were coming somehow, *he isn't here*.

"And if *he* knew we were coming, he would be here. So, assume he's in Arroyo. Eleven and a half days for the round trip—five days and fifteen hours for the transport to get there, once they're in FTL. Same for him to get back, once he's in FTL."

Walkingstick considered the situation and shook his head.

"We'll assume Tecumseh will be here in *five* days," he concluded. "But until then, we have the whip hand in this system, and I plan on using it to present the good Admiral with a fait accompli when he arrives."

36

"WE ARE NOW in missile range of Dakota orbit," MacGinnis reported. "We have not detected any attempt by the locals to target us with scanners.

"We have picked up two more of what we believe are orbital forts under construction, but they are even less complete than the first one we located. So far as we can tell, sir, Dakota is utterly defenseless."

Walkingstick mentally held his breath for a moment after that. He knew as well as anyone not to taunt Murphy—even if it did look true.

"Wait, sir, we have something," one of the analysts declared—allowing Walkingstick to release the momentary tension.

"What have you found?" he asked.

"A number of the civilian facilities have what appear to be identical modules attached to them," the young woman reported. "Closer analysis suggests fighter bays, sir. We estimate they could hold two squadrons apiece, and we've picked up twelve of the modules so far."

"So. *Not* defenseless," Walkingstick noted. "Well done, Lieutenant."

He turned back to MacGinnis and his main display, gesturing a highlight onto the hangar modules.

"Of course, if they have two hundred and forty starfighters, why aren't they in space?" he asked.

"Planning on surprising us at close range?" she suggested.

"Maybe. Those hangars would need to be capable of a far faster launch than I'd expect of a module designed and built in less than six months," he replied. "But that might be it. Especially if they already *have* deployed the fighters and they're just better at hiding than we suspect."

"It is extraordinarily unlikely they could hide two hundred–plus Katanas or Longbows from us at this range, sir," she said. "Even with their drives off and hidden behind civilian structures, their zero-point cores would show concentrations of radiation we'd be picking up."

Walkingstick was silent. He could think of a few ways to avoid that, but most of them would require long-term planning and prework—and he wasn't convinced the Dakotans had received *that* much warning.

"What are you thinking?" he murmured.

"Sir?"

"Chapulin clearly believes that they can hurt us, if not drive us off," he reminded her. "I'm guessing we didn't receive any surrender messages as we entered range?"

"Negative."

He looked at the main display and gestured a new highlight into existence. The three forts under construction were about where he'd expected—in a higher orbit than the civilian infrastructure and reasonably distant. No one wanted to risk collateral damage, after all.

"Let's make a point, shall we? Target the forts," he ordered. "One missile each. Fire when ready."

That took a few seconds to get underway, then *Saint Michael* shivered as three of her launchers spoke.

A tension that Walkingstick hadn't even realized had been present on the bridge suddenly broke, a ripple of...not relief, but something close to it, sweeping through his staff.

They'd fired the first shots. Whatever happened now, they were committed.

"Missiles are running true," MacGinnis told him. "Flight time fifty-nine minutes."

"Let's see what they do."

That was the real question. Walkingstick was certain, now, that the rebels had some trick up their sleeve. Misra's missile mines, perhaps. At this range, though, he wasn't expecting reliable targeting—if those forts had any defenses online, the missiles he'd fired were going to fail dramatically.

It would also be over four and a half minutes before the Dakotans saw his missiles. The same before he saw their response. Lightspeed lag *sucked*. He'd far rather have a dozen q-probes in orbit of the planet by now, telling him all of their secrets in real time.

Instead, he was fumbling in the dark, limited by the same laws enumerated by scientists eight hundred years earlier.

His own ships were accelerating toward the planet, chasing after their own missiles even as the far-speedier weapons left them behind.

"Nine minutes since launch," someone announced. "We should be seeing their reaction just about…"

There was a long silence, broken by at least a dozen different voices shouting the same alert.

"*VAMPIRE! VAMPIRE! VAMPIRE!*"

"Details, MacGinnis," Walkingstick ordered calmly. He could see the cascade of new red icons on the display, now hurtling out toward his own ships. In the back of his mind, he absently ran the numbers. With his own ships' velocity and acceleration, those missiles were going to reach him far faster than he liked.

Before, in fact, his missiles reached the forts.

"Numbers, unclear. Source, unclear." MacGinnis shook her head. "Estimate five thousand plus missiles, all capital-ship-grade, launched from Dakota orbit."

"Threat?" Walkingstick asked.

"Moderate," she told him. "Between the fighters and the fleet's missile defenses, we should be able to take out most of them. And at this range, they'll almost certainly lose some of them just by the command-and-control loop.

"But that kind of mass launch… Yeah, some might get through."

"The saying *eggshells with antimatter hammers* exists for a reason, Rear Admiral," Walkingstick noted mildly. "It only takes one of those missiles to kill several thousand of our people."

That was war…and yet.

"Any change to our orders, sir?" she asked.

Walkingstick hesitated. He didn't *like* it, but he did it. A year earlier, he'd have ordered the fleet to damn the missiles and go in at full speed. He'd a lose ship, maybe two, but the aggression and shock would carry them through and deliver victory.

He *knew* that if they landed their assault, they'd win. There was no real question of that. But…if he went in as aggressively as he wanted to, they'd lose ships. Not just starfighters—*capital ships*.

One, maybe two to this salvo—and he would bet money that there were more.

"All ships reverse acceleration," he ordered calmly. "Let's get out of range and see what they do next. Find me the launchers," he continued. "Whatever they are, I bet money they can't dodge.

"Let's not lose anyone we don't have to when a little bit of caution will deliver victory without us losing a single ship."

37

IT RANKLED. Not just for Walkingstick, he could tell. His entire flag-deck crew found the concept of retreating uncomfortable, even when it was *clearly* the best choice.

It took them most of an hour to shed the velocity they'd acquired since entering normal space, but from the moment they started decelerating, Walkingstick knew his fleet was safe from the missiles. They had vastly greater acceleration than his ships, but not *enough* greater to overcome his course reversal.

So, while the range dropped precipitously for most of that hour and the Dakotan missiles' velocity toward his people kept rising, the math was clear. The incoming weapons would run out of fuel eight million kilometers short of the fleet's zero-velocity point.

"Zero velocity in the next three minutes," MacGinnis told him. "Do we have a next step, sir?"

274 | TO STAND DEFIANT

"Have we located the launchers yet?" he asked.

"We've backtracked to where some of these missiles came from, and we think we've identified the signature of their launchers. Single-shot boxes, as you anticipated, sir. Glorified mines."

"Misra was the one to make the guess," Walkingstick replied. "It was a good guess. Something like this is the weapon of a trapped animal, Rear Admiral. Take that signature and locate the rest of their launchers."

"I'm not sure I see the point, sir?"

"Mines don't dodge, MacGinnis," he reminded her. "We can send missiles in with the final portion of their flight being ballistic and detonate them in the middle of minefields.

"If they've got another five or ten thousand capital-ship missiles floating in orbit, we can locate them and pick them off from well outside their powered range," he explained. "It will take some time—and a great deal of care to avoid collateral damage—but we can pluck Dakota's fangs in under a day with just the battleships."

Even the older battleships, the fifteen *Resolutes* that made up easily half of the Expeditionary Fleet's missile power, had deeper magazines than the cruisers or carriers. Walkingstick would preserve the cruisers' magazines for the battle to come against Tecumseh.

But he could easily spare ten, fifteen thousand missiles to clear his path to Dakota.

"And we have that time," MacGinnis assessed with a nod. "Minimum five days until their fleet arrives, after all."

Walkingstick nodded. He was glad to note that she'd taken the five-day estimate—which was assuming that either a ship had been sent before they arrived or that Tecumseh, like Walkingstick, had q-coms with his home base—to heart and was basing her thought processes on it.

"Exactly. So, we'll pull back, out of range of their missiles, and bombard their minefields from four light-minutes away." He smiled thinly. "We will be *scrupulously* careful to prevent any kind of collateral damage, of course. There will be no intentional atrocities under my direct command, and I'll be *damned* to the void if I'll let there be accidental ones!"

"Of course, sir."

"Dakotan missiles have lost thrust," an analyst reported. "Range approximately ten million kilometers."

That...wasn't right.

"Confirm that time window," Walkingstick snapped. "Total flight time."

"Thirty-four hundred seconds, sir."

Thirty-four hundred seconds. That was short. Too short. The rebels had the same Stormwind Vs as filled his own magazines—one thousand fifty gravities of acceleration for thirty-six hundred seconds.

"What was the estimated flight time when they launched, assuming we cut acceleration to zero?" he asked.

"Thirty-four-fifty seconds, sir."

Walkingstick glared at the holographic display. The missile icons were diffusing now. Not *much*—there wasn't *that* much uncertainty to where a ballistic missile was, but his people no longer had them nailed in as closely as when the missiles were accelerating.

"They have at least fifty seconds left on their drives," he said aloud. "That's a risky play with an eight-minute command-and-control loop...but they knew they weren't going to hit us if they didn't do *something*."

"Sir?"

"Send the fighters out," he ordered MacGinnis. "The missiles are programmed to travel ballistically and then reactivate for a terminal mode, probably around two million kilometers.

"The starfighters can get closer while they're ballistic and use their missiles and lances to clear them away."

He shook his head.

"Find me the rest of those mines," he ordered. "These people are *way* too clever for my peace of mind!"

The starfighters had been *waiting* for the order to do something. *Anything.* Fighter crews didn't like being stuck in fleet patrol, but Walkingstick hadn't had a target worthy of them.

Now he had a threat that needed them, and he could *feel* their glee as he unleashed them.

Two hundred and fifty-two squadrons of Katanas, one of the most advanced and powerful starfighters ever built, flashed away from his fleet at five hundred gravities. The capital ships would keep opening the distance from Dakota, but now the fighters got to play.

"They won't be able to stop them all," he murmured. "What was the final number?"

"Six thousand exactly, sir," MacGinnis told him.

"Fleet will stand by all missile defenses," he ordered calmly. "Standard defensive formations. The fighters will whittle them down and we'll clear the leftovers."

On the main display, the hostile missile icons sharpened as the fighters closed and their sensors dialed in the currently silent weapons. Then the fighter salvoed their own missiles, the shorter-legged Javelins blazing toward their larger cousins with suicidal determination.

The ballistic state the missiles were in was harder to target in some ways and easier in others. They weren't evading and they weren't running electronic warfare. They were easy targets—once they were located.

Antimatter explosions sparkled across the display, and Walkingstick watched calmly as the estimated count of weapons began to drop faster and faster.

"Fighters have penetrated the missile cloud and are reversing course," MacGinnis noted.

"And the missiles are now back online," he said softly, watching as the icons lit up again. Now the Stormwinds unleashed the full power of their ECM and artificial intelligences, disappearing into clouds of jamming and artificial radiation.

"Fighters cleared at least four thousand. Defensive perimeter engaging."

It had been a long time since this part of a battle had involved anything except waiting for Walkingstick. Lasers and positron lances glittered in space around his fleet, while jammers and decoys sang their deceptive songs.

He couldn't focus on even *Saint Michael*'s fate. He needed to watch the whole situation, looking for the patterns, the flaws...the accuracy that the missiles *shouldn't have had*.

Against two thousand missiles fired an hour earlier, with an eight-minute command-and-control loop working from sensors sixty million kilometers away, the jammers and decoys should have been devastating. They were effective, yes…but they should have been even *more* effective.

And because they weren't, missiles got through. Not many. But… enough to hurt.

"*Saint Brigid* reports two hits," MacGinnis said softly. "Eleven across the *Resolutes*. No critical damage; all ships remain functional."

Walkingstick exhaled a breath he hadn't realized he was holding.

"Get everyone out of range," he ordered. "Get the fighters back aboard and rearmed, then nail down those missile locations.

"Once that's organized, I need a full active sweep of the space around, maximum intensity."

"Sir?" she asked, surprised.

"Those missiles weren't being guided by sensors in Dakota orbit," he told her. "Those missiles were being guided by q-probes in our immediate vicinity.

"Somebody sold the rebels probes and q-com blocks on an alternate network. *Find me those probes.* I would really prefer these people *not* be looking up my kilt, Rear Admiral MacGinnis!"

His comfortable assumption that James Tecumseh had been twelve days away was gone as well. His once-paranoid five days was now the *main* estimate.

On the other hand, if Tecumseh had known the Expeditionary Fleet was coming the moment they'd left Terra, he'd have been waiting for them. At some point between Walkingstick leaving Sol and arriving in Dakota, the rebels had learned he was coming.

They had q-probes and q-coms. Probably not enough to equip an entire fleet, but enough that he had to assume Tecumseh knew he was there.

"When did you know?" he whispered, too quietly for anyone else to hear.

That was everything. But unless the timing had been *completely* wrong, Tecumseh should have either been *there* or would have had to be somewhere else.

Assume the Dakotans had warned Tecumseh of his arrival by q-com...but if Tecumseh wasn't *there*, then the rebel fleet was presumably in Meridian. Eleven days away.

So, when had the Dakotans known?

38

It took them another thirty minutes to fall back to four light-minutes, hopefully well outside the range of the missile launchers in Dakota orbit. There was still no point in taking risks. In some ways, Walking-stick knew, he was better off if Tecumseh arrived while he was carrying out a long-distance siege of Dakota.

"We have some good news and a few bits of bad news," MacGinnis told him.

The Imperator hadn't moved from in front of the main holographic display. There were a thousand possibilities of how the next few days could go, and he needed to decide what his best options were.

"Bad news first," he said calmly.

"We haven't nailed any of them down, but there are *definitely* q-probes out there," she told him. "Their drives are offline, which makes them..."

"Effectively invisible, if they're at all modern," Walkingstick concluded for her. "As expected."

He hadn't expected that when he'd arrived—a strategic miscalculation that worried him—but from the moment the locals had shut their missile drives down for a ballistic component, he'd known the probes had to be there.

"Continue," he ordered.

"We don't believe we've identified all of the launchers in orbit," she warned. "But we backtracked the missile launches we *did* see, and we believed we've nailed down the signatures. However, we can't tell at this range whether a particular launcher has already fired.

"We will need to destroy *all* of the mines, including the six thousand that already fired, because we can't tell the difference."

"We have the munitions to expend."

His battleships carried fifty missiles per launcher. His modern battlecruisers had *seventy*, even if the older ones carried the same thirty as the strike cruisers and carriers.

"We...may not have *enough* munitions to spend, sir," MacGinnis told him. "We have identified at least twenty-five *thousand* mines."

"I expect about twice that," Walkingstick noted. "I presume they're clustered to some degree, which will allow us to neutralize multiple mines with a single missile. We have the time to wait until we see the results of each salvo."

"We hope, sir."

He smiled.

"A good point, Admiral MacGinnis. What was that good news you mentioned?"

"We successfully destroyed the forts that were under construction," she told him. "It's likely that they were using them for fire control of the mines."

He shook his head, though his smile hadn't faded.

"No, they were too easily destroyed," he concluded aloud. "They probably evacuated them as soon as they saw our Cherenkov arrival flares, if not sooner. They knew the forts were dead the moment we were in active missile range."

"They need a fire-control center *somewhere.*"

"Yes, but they have q-coms. So, there are relay satellites in orbit, linked to their q-com network, and their command center is under a bloody mountain somewhere."

He shook his head.

"I want a firing plan worked up for taking down the mines, Rear Admiral," he ordered. "Use the *Hercules*es and all of the battleships except *Saint Brigid.*"

"Yes, sir. Ops is working on it—I'll update their constraints."

"Then get me a link to *Saint Brigid.* Admiral Tasker and I need to have a chat."

————

The chair that Walkingstick took a seat in as Lindsay Tasker joined him was entirely virtual. He was in the main command seat on his flag bridge, allowing himself to sink into a virtual-reality conference space.

The two chairs were the only things in the VR space that appeared artificial. They were on a small plateau near the top of a mountain, a blizzard raging around an invisible bubble that "protected" them from the storm.

Walkingstick had a taste for dramatic backdrops for this kind of meeting, and Tasker just shook her head as she took her own seat.

"Well, so far, this has been interesting," she told him. "We didn't anticipate the rebels having q-coms, let alone q-*probes.*"

"I was expecting the mines," Walkingstick said mildly. "But the q-coms throw a wrench in a lot of things, Admiral Tasker."

"I'm guessing you want me to take E-Two and do something with them?" she asked.

"That's why I set it up in the first place. *Timing* is everything now, Admiral. We know that Dakota knew we were coming. I'm not sure how, but it's not like the Expeditionary Fleet's exit from the Sol System was hard to miss.

"So, anyone with agents in Sol would have had that information to sell them."

"Which leaves the question of *when* they learned," she said, echoing his own thoughts.

"They did not learn immediately after we left Sol. If they had, Tecumseh would be here, with everything he's got. So, at some point in the last twenty days, they were sold that intelligence."

"Which means our comfortable estimate of when their fleet will arrive is now utter garbage," Tasker murmured, looking past him at the blizzard storming around them. "And we now have *no* idea when the rebel fleet will arrive."

"I think we still have some time. And I want to use that time as effectively as possible."

An image of the Dakota star system appeared in the middle of the plateau.

"Which means *this*." The map zoomed in on the inner of the two gas giants—and its eleventh moon.

"The shipyards."

"The shipyards," he confirmed. "Base Łá'ts'áadah. Four *Zion* platforms, two hundred starfighters. Except we know they're using temporary structures to increase their fighter strength, and it's a safe assumption they've laid minefields out there, too.

"I *think* that we're looking at most of their capacity for producing those in Dakota orbit. But I need to *know*. I also need to know that those Project Hustle hulls are in Commonwealth custody before the rebels accept that they have lost."

"You're worried they'll destroy them."

"Yes. Until Tecumseh gets here, they will hang on to hope," he said. "Even they'll know it isn't much of a hope, but they will have hope. So long as they have hope, they will not destroy those ships. Since those ships are the main reason we're here…"

"How many assault transports are you giving me?" she asked. "As we set it up, E-Two doesn't have any of them."

"Take four. It's overkill, but we won't need them for Dakota for another day at least. Reducing those mines is going to take time—a resource we no longer have in abundance, but one I will spend rather than risk this fleet."

"Should we take the entire fleet to Base Łá'ts'áadah?" Tasker suggested. "If we're basically leaving Dakota until after Tecumseh arrives…"

"Our best chance to end this without a fight is to present Tecumseh with a situation he cannot salvage," Walkingstick told her. "Shock and awe. When the rebel fleet returns to this system, I want both Dakota and Base Łá'ts'áadah in Commonwealth hands.

"If we can make Quetzalli Chapulin sign a surrender agreement, the same stubborn honor that led him to rebellion should compel Tecumseh to honor it," he concluded. "We will take control of the q-probes, we will secure the shipyard and we will secure the planet.

"But to make this work, we need to do all of that in about thirty-six hours."

Tasker grimaced. Both of them were doing the same math, and the navigational course took shape on the holographic map.

"A hundred minutes to reach space we can warp," she noted. "Hour and a half after that to reach the gravity well of Virginia. But unless we want to push *hard*, we want to come out of FTL eight light-minutes out."

"Another five hours to reach the base, but they'll come out to fight you," Walkingstick observed. "Probably send the fighters forward and engage you at extreme missile range."

"Unless they have a lot more fighters than I'm expecting, seven carriers will *more* than handle them," Tasker replied. "With the cruisers in support, they'd be better off surrendering."

"The whole bloody system would be better off surrendering," the Imperator of Terra observed flatly. "But they are determined to fight. So, Base Łá'ts'áadah will fight. You will summon them to surrender, but you will not wait for their response."

"I will need time to pull E-Two out of the main fleet and coordinate the troopships," she warned. "Eight hours to get there, yes, but I need time to organize and talk to the captains."

Walkingstick conjured a second display into existence, of the current position of the Expeditionary Fleet. As he did so, the first missile salvo launched, hundreds of weapons blazing out toward Dakota.

"Thirty-six hours," he repeated. "In twenty-four hours, I expect to have reduced the minefields and launchers sufficiently to advance on Dakota. I'll need the assault transports back by then."

Again, they ran the numbers as both of them looked at the maps and displays.

"I need four hours," she noted. "Six would be better. We had no opportunity to coordinate E-Two while we were underway, and I hadn't done more than notify the captains that this was a possibility since we arrived."

Walkingstick didn't let his wince reach his physical or virtual form. He'd assumed that the reorganization of the Expeditionary Fleet into two task forces could take place while they were in FTL...and since only three of his fifty ships had q-coms, that had been impossible.

"Four hours, then," he conceded. That was longer than he'd like, but to organize a force of twenty warships and four assault transports out of a larger fleet, it was probably *fast*.

"That will let us get a sense of the effectiveness of our bombardment as well. It will be slow, since I want to see the results before we launch our second salvo."

"Better slow than running the fleet into fifty thousand missiles," Tasker observed drily.

"And that, Vice Admiral, is why we're being careful," he replied. "I doubt they have the fire control to manage that, but a Stormwind is a smart weapon. They're *better* with live control and q-probe targeting, but left to their own devices, fifty thousand of them will still hurt us."

"How solid are we on those thirty-six hours?" she asked.

"That is how long it will take us to secure the system," Walkingstick told her. "Ground fighting may take a bit longer, depending on how foolish the rebels decide to be, but splitting our fleet into two task forces and securing Base Łá'ts'áadah while we reduce the minefields speeds up the process.

"My guess is that Tecumseh was in Meridian, due to some stunt of the League's. Splitting the difference says they learned about our movement ten days ago. If that's the case, he'll arrive in thirty-six hours."

He smiled thinly.

"It's our most likely scenario. If he was in any of the Dakota Sector systems or if they'd heard sooner, he'd be here already."

But even if he had the timing wrong, even the task force he was giving Tasker should be able to fight clear of anything Tecumseh did. And that was assuming his *worst*-case strength for the rebel fleet—he definitely had scenarios where Tasker's TF E-2 outgunned the entire rebel fleet on their own!

39

THE DOWNSIDE to having interstellar coms again was the ability to watch the world James had sworn to defend be attacked and be unable to do anything about it.

"They've reduced the minefields by about thirty percent so far," Carey reported.

Krakatoa's flag deck holographic display was focused on Dakota, with green icons marking the fields of single-shot missile and torpedo launchers, red icons marking the distant Commonwealth fleet, and silver icons marking the civilian orbital infrastructure.

"For four salvos of five hundred missiles apiece, that's close to impressive," James murmured. "Two thousand missiles in trade for fifteen thousand."

"Dakota Command has no way to disguise or hide the launchers," Carey said grimly. "Not without risking the civilian stations."

The minefields had been carefully positioned away from the primary infrastructure ring—like most planets, an informal zone at geostationary orbit above the equator. The defenders had maintained a minimum distance of ten thousand kilometers between the defensive satellites and any civilian space stations.

Walkingstick was now demonstrating *why* that was needed, as anti-matter explosions gutted the fields again and again. Whoever was doing the Imperator's targeting knew what they were doing—and had a *damn* good understanding of the strengths and weaknesses of the one-shot launchers.

"They can't save them and they can't use them," James noted. "But...they're doing what they were put there to do."

"Buy time," Voclain finished for him, the chief of staff standing beside his operations officer. "It's an expensive delay."

"The part that I'm pleased by is that they clearly haven/t recognized that there are two *types* of mines there," he told his staff. "Only fifteen thousand of those mines are full capital-ship missiles. The other thirty thousand are just torpedoes. Hell, I think some of them might even be Javelins."

The torpedoes, at least, were just as deadly as the capital-ship missiles within their range—but if Walkingstick had recognized that only part of the minefields could match his range, he'd have tried to eliminate them first.

"What about our detached friends?" he asked. "Any idea what they're up to yet?"

Forty-five minutes earlier, over a third of the Terran fleet had started accelerating back out-system.

"They're going *somewhere*," Voclain told him. "Which tells us at least one thing, I think."

"Oh?"

"Walkingstick has at least q-com-equipped command ships," she concluded. "Or he wouldn't split his forces. He never struck me as the type to give up control of his fleet."

"He has commanders he trusts," James pointed out. "He rarely commanded forces in the war himself. But...he was always in instant contact with them all."

"He knows we're out here and he's probably guessed that we're closer than he expected. He's dividing his forces, but he'll make sure they can communicate," she said. "But even if he has q-coms..."

"He's not sending that task force outside quick-reinforcement range," Carey finished for her. "They're going to Base Łá'ts'áadah."

James nodded slowly. He'd been coming to the same conclusion himself, but it hadn't been solid enough for him to tell his people.

"We have q-coms with Base Łá'ts'áadah, yes?" he asked.

"We do," Mac Cléirich confirmed. "And they also have deployed thirteen q-probes to provide live data on their surroundings. It's not as dense a field as we put up around Dakota itself, but it'll improve their targeting and we'll get all of their information."

"Well. Isn't that convenient?" James murmured.

"I feel it necessary to note, for the record, that we absolutely *cannot* transfer you to the battleships this time," Voclain told him drily. "Whatever clever idea is in your head, you're doing it from here."

"I know," he conceded. "And yes...I'm thinking along those lines. But there's a lot of things in play here."

"Of course, sir. Shall we have the fleet adjust course to arrive at Base Łá'ts'áadah instead of Dakota?"

Even the detached task force had almost double First Fleet's volume and starfighters. They had enough information that James knew Walkingstick had sent *all* of his thirties with the detached fleet, which brought the number of missile launchers down to roughly parity...

But it laid bare the fundamental problem they faced. Walkingstick could afford to detach a secondary force that outgunned the entire Dakotan Navy.

If they were going to even those odds, they needed to do something risky. Something that could well cost James ships and people he didn't want to lose.

But if he didn't take any risks at all, they were going to lose *everything*.

"Yes," he finally answered Voclain. "Fleet will adjust course for Base Łá'ts'áadah. If the Imperator is going to give us the opportunity to defeat part of his fleet in detail, we'd be fools not to take it."

And if they were going to lose against the detached task force, well...they were doomed from the start.

40

Deep Space
15:30 March 17, 2738 ESMDT

FIRST FLEET WAS STILL trillions of kilometers away, hurtling into a starbow of smeared blue light as they warped space toward the Dakota System, when the detached Commonwealth force emerged from their own bubble of warped space.

"Base Łá'ts'áadah reports contact on the q-probes," Mac Cléirich reported briskly. "Range is...eight light-minutes, one hundred forty-four million kilometers."

James let out a breath. Hopefully, none of his people had realized just how much tension he was holding. He hadn't made it to his rank and authority *without* being able to conceal his emotions—but up until that moment, he hadn't been certain his plan would give them any chance at all.

First Fleet was still two hours away from Virginia themselves, but the Commonwealth task force was now back in real space and subject to the normal equations of mass and thrust.

The concern that had lingered in the back of his mind was that Walkingstick's subcommander might have decided to cut the time and distance as close as possible. It was far easier to enter a gravity well than exit it, after all, and while James doubted *any* navigator could thread the needle all the way in to a gas giant, they could have cut five or six light-minutes off the range.

At eight light-minutes, though, it would take them almost five hours to reach Base Łá'ts'áadah—and James was only *two* hours away.

"Somebody guessed wrong," he said aloud. "Let's not rush to correct them, shall we? Get me Commodore Krejči."

Their q-coms were focused on telemetry data right now, and Base Łá'ts'áadah didn't have that many entangled blocks in the first place. But *some* planning needed to be made, and a voice call was more than enough.

"Admiral, it's damn good to hear from you," Krejči greeted him. "I'd like to hope this call means you're planning on doing something about that fleet heading my way."

"We're two hours out, Commodore," James told him. "I need you to keep them coming in and I need you *not* to engage until we arrive."

"They may not give me a choice, sir. It depends on when they launch their fighters. If they launch immediately, the birds may get here before you do."

"Whoever is over there is playing it safely," James noted. "They think they have time, so they're going to focus on achieving their objectives while preserving their ships. *Time* is a secondary consideration...and that, Commodore, is going to save you."

"I damn well hope so, sir."

"Hold your fighters until they launch," he ordered. "And make it look like you responded to their launch after lightspeed lag. Do *everything* you can to convince them you don't have q-probes."

"Easy enough at this range, sir. But what happens when you get here?"

James smiled.

"Then the people who value unity over justice are going to have a very bad day."

———

"That *has* to be Tasker."

"Sir?" Voclain asked, turning at James's words.

"They launched at *exactly* sixteen hundred thirty," he told her, gesturing at the display showing the Terran Commonwealth fighters departing their carriers and cruisers. "They could have launched at sixteen twenty-eight, that would have been an hour after they arrived. But they waited those extra two minutes to allow someone to put neat numbers in their after-action report.

"It's by no means enough of a delay to cause *any* real tactical or operational issues, but it speaks to a certain kind of mind. And while there are at least four officers I could see Walkingstick giving that kind of subordinate-but-independent command to…Admiral Lindsay Tasker is the one with that kind of brain."

"Does that change our approach, sir?" his chief of staff asked.

James considered his memories of his former commanding officer. His term serving in the logistics section of the Rimward Marches Fleet had mostly been reporting to Tasker, and she had always been a very *particular* woman.

"She is very specific, very by-the-book," he noted. "Not unwilling to throw the book out the window, but sticks to the cautious and practiced approach unless given a reason.

"She'll hold one squadron in ten of the fighters back for CAP and send the rest forward with the bombers."

"Exactly by the book," Voclain murmured. "Even though she doesn't know how many fighters Łá'ts'áadah has."

"She's assuming—correctly, let's be honest—that she can keep a hundred and forty fighters with her ships, and that thirteen hundred fighters and two hundred and fifty bombers are more than enough to handle the Base."

The analysts were still trying to break down the exact numbers of fighters that had launched from the Commonwealth fleet, but they knew *exactly* which classes the detached task force was made up of now.

Three modern ships: one *Saint*, two *Volcano*es. Five older carriers,

Lexingtons. Twelve of the old thirty-million-cubic-meter ships, half battlecruisers and half strike cruisers.

"She has some real vulnerabilities in that fleet mix," he noted aloud. "But then, she's not expecting anyone to be hunting her with battleships. Outside of that *Saint*, every battleship *she* knows about is currently blowing up our minefields."

A process that was forming a steady metronome of fire in the back of everyone's minds. After seven hours and six salvos, almost half of the defensive missiles were gone. Even anticipating this exact counter, James had expected them to survive for at least twenty-four hours in enough strength to deter the main fleet.

Instead, it looked like they'd be *completely* cleared after sixteen hours. Walkingstick's people might have lacked q-probes, but they were impressively capable at both sensor analysis and shooting.

None of that was a great sign for the next few hours and days. James knew his people were good, but he was grimly aware that Walkingstick's Rimward Marches Fleet had been the most veteran and elite formation the Commonwealth Navy had possessed.

"Base Łá'ts'áadah reports all fighters are standing by for mass deployment at sixteen forty hours," Mac Cléirich told him. "They'll help keep the good Admiral's after-action report neat for her."

Unlike Admiral Tasker, James knew *exactly* what Base Łá'ts'áadah had for starfighters: five hundred Katanas. No bombers. No surprises. Just five hundred of the best starfighters the Terran Commonwealth had ever built...who were going to have to go up against *fifteen* hundred of the best starfighters the Terran Commonwealth had ever built.

James had a lot of clever ideas for how to win this battle, but as he watched those two numbers take shape on the display in front of him, he was grimly aware of one very distinct problem:

There was no way Commodore Krejči's starfighters could stop the fighter strike heading toward the shipyards. So long as the task force was behind those fighters, they were dangerous.

But what he was afraid of now was what they'd do if he succeeded in taking out Tasker's fleet. Would those flight crews surrender—or would they decide to, if nothing else, deny the Confederacy the six all-too-vulnerable hulls sitting in the yards?

Even a single squadron of starfighters could obliterate those ships, setting Dakota's construction program back years. The Commonwealth wouldn't get what they were after—but the Confederacy would be in serious trouble.

So, not only did James Tecumseh have to defeat a fleet of warships with twice his cubage and starfighters...he also had to do so in a way that prevented the enemy starfighters from destroying the construction yards themselves.

And regardless of whether he succeeded at that, he'd *then* have to deal with the *other* enemy fleet in his system.

He'd had easier days.

41

THE LAST MINUTES TICKED AWAY, and Anthony Yamamoto checked over every aspect of his starfighter again. Without q-coms on the starfighters themselves, he *needed* to fly into action with the fighter force. Commanding the formation would leave Navarro and Gunther handling more than the engineer and gunner were *supposed* to handle normally, but he hadn't had a chance to put his thoughts around a command starfighter into action.

But so long as he was still aboard *Krakatoa*, he was still receiving full information from the q-probes arrayed around Base Łá'ts'áadah. He had effectively live information on the enemy starfighters and bombers and slightly delayed information on the capital ships two light-minutes farther out from the base.

It might have been his own biases, his professional focus and tunnel vision, but he couldn't help but feel that the *starfighters* were the problem.

The Commonwealth fleet was trapped in Virginia's gravity well. First Fleet could *enter* that area, but the Terran ships couldn't leave it. With only a hundred and forty starfighters shielding the Commonwealth ships, Anthony was confident in his ability to take out—or, at a minimum, cripple—the enemy fleet with his fighter strike.

That left the fighters as the wildcard. There was no way the fighters from Base Łá'ts'áadah could successfully stop four times their numbers. Anthony didn't know what the Admiral was thinking, but he *did* have the emergence locus for the fleet.

The carriers and cruisers were marked for roughly thirteen million kilometers ahead of the Commonwealth fleet. Matched with a full-deck strike, that would let him put his torpedoes on target less than twenty minutes after they arrived—followed shortly afterward by his fighters' main missile strike and supported throughout by the capital-ship missiles.

The battleships, all *three* of them, were going to drop right in front of the Commonwealth ships, unleashing their heavy beams at point-blank range. There might only be one battleship in the Commonwealth formation, but the other nineteen warships weren't lacking in positron lances.

Heck, even the *troop transports* had positron lances. Picking a fight at that range and those odds was suicide, even for battleships. It would gut the attacking fleet, clearing the way for the fighter strike...but it wasn't *necessary*.

The plan would work, Anthony knew that. It would also cost too much—he knew *that*, too. They hadn't had time to fully workshop it in detail, and he hadn't had a chance to talk to Tecumseh.

But there were four minutes left and they had neural implants. It was enough time. Maybe.

And when a *Vice* Admiral wanted to talk to the Admiral, connections closed surprisingly quickly.

"Admiral, I think we're making a mistake," he told James swiftly, intentionally compressing his sense of time to allow for the conversation.

"I can think of two I know I'm making; I just can't see alternatives,"

Tecumseh replied bluntly. "We need to take out that fleet. Everything else is secondary."

"We also need to be able to engage the main fleet and need to stop those fighters reaching the yards."

"I know," the Admiral agreed. "And what we've set up is the best way. I think."

"You're thinking like a battleship captain," Anthony told his superior and friend. It wasn't even an accusation or a complaint. It was a statement of fact that both of them could accept.

"I'm listening," Tecumseh said softly. "We don't have much time and I don't know what we can change...but I'm listening."

"Don't need to change much, but I think we need to..."

———

In the Commonwealth Navy, Anthony had known only a few Admirals who would—or even *could*—have adjusted their entire battle plan on the fly in the last few minutes. He'd known a similar number who would have adjusted their battle plan based on suggestions made by a Starfighter Corps officer—and while the overlap was significant, it wasn't perfect.

James Tecumseh fell into that overlap—and since James Tecumseh was going to set the standard for the Dakotan Confederacy Navy going forward, that gave Anthony hope for the future.

And the adjustments that Tecumseh had made to Anthony's suggestions gave him hope for today. There wasn't much they could change in the final minutes before emergence into realspace...but they could change *enough*.

The timer ticked to the last few seconds, and the starfighter commander took a deep breath, linking in to his starfighter and his command networks. Right now, he had direct links with every fighter on *Krakatoa* and a relayed link through the q-coms with the fighters on *Saratoga*.

The rest of the ships didn't have the bandwidth for telemetry and tactical networks. Just enough to receive the updated general orders.

Orders that took every ship in the fleet past their original planned emergence points as the keening wail of threading the needle echoed in Anthony's ears—and into normal space ahead of the Commonwealth fighter wing as a single mass.

Fifteen warships belly-flopped into reality in perfect formation, a wall of metal and fire blockading the starfighter strike charging toward Base Łá'ts'áadah.

"Scramble, scramble, scramble!"

Anthony's order crossed the networks of the fleet, even as he was trying to locate the *missing* pair of warships.

"*Champion* and *Goldwyn* missed the mark," Navarro reported. "Looks like Commodore Gold realized they weren't going to stick the landing and aborted on her own authority—q-coms say they're still *alive*, but they had to break away."

Their Katanas slammed into space as the engineer's words echoed through the starfighter's internal network. Every member of every fighter's flight crew was riding their implants, holding on to seconds like misers grasping gold.

The tactical crews of the starships were doing the same, and the positron lances of an entire fleet woke around the starfighters as they blazed into space. Both carriers had broadside launch tubes, capable of launching a quarter of their wings every fifteen seconds—and Anthony had led the first flight group out of *Krakatoa*'s tubes.

The fleet's main guns, the six-hundred-kiloton-per-second guns of the older ships, and the megaton and megaton-and-a-half of the battleships and *Krakatoa*, were terrible at targeting maneuvering starfighters. But they had the range against starfighters' limited deflectors, and the Terran spaceships hadn't expected the intervention.

Targeting data had been fed to the heavy lances from the q-probes, and dozens of bombers died in the first moments. By the time Anthony's fighter was in space, the Commonwealth fighter formation's existing velocity had brought them into range of the secondary lances, the ones *intended* to kill starfighters.

And even the ancient and almost obsolete *Paramount*-class *Hollywood* had fifty of those.

"All fighters," he barked. "Hold your missiles; engage with lances only. Break and attack!"

The Terran ships were starting to react, but it was still entirely defensive. No starfighter pilot ever planned for unexpectedly ending up in range of an entire enemy battlefleet. Ambushes were deadly for a *reason*, and Anthony led his own starfighters in a brutal exploitation of the Commonwealth's moment of weakness.

It took just over twenty seconds for the starfighter formation to pass through First Fleet. A few missiles were launched at the Confederacy ships, but none connected—and not one of the Terran starfighters made it past.

In twenty seconds, the entire tone of the battle around Base Łá'ts'áadah had changed. The Commonwealth Task Force was still hurtling toward the Base at five percent of lightspeed—and Anthony's starfighters and bombers were now accelerating out to meet them.

"Base Łá'ts'áadah fighter wings, adjust your acceleration," he ordered. "Rendezvous with First Fleet and cover them against missiles. You are our Carrier Space Patrol now."

He'd rather leave a CAP behind out of his own ships, but that wasn't an option. Not now that he was lacking the two hundred Xenophons from the Persephone carriers.

"Twelve minutes to torpedo range," Gunther told him. "Enemy fleet has not adjusted course."

"They think they can bull through our starfighters," Anthony murmured, looking at the Commonwealth formation. He had live data —for now—and they didn't, but that still seemed a bit foolhardy on the Terrans' part.

"Or they think they don't have a choice," the gunner noted. "Fifteen thousand KPS toward the moon and we have a three-hundred-gee acceleration advantage. They can't retreat, they won't surrender and they still have an edge in hulls and volume over the main fleet."

"She's moving the cruisers forward to provide cover for the carriers," Anthony observed. "Let's let her play that game. Target all torpedoes on the cruisers."

Over seven hundred torpedoes on twelve ships wasn't a guaranteed kill, but it was going to make a hell of a mess of the Commonwealth ships. Plus, they weren't the only toys in play. The first salvo of capital-ship missiles struck home before the Commonwealth task force had sorted out their missile defenses.

Lightspeed delays had stolen the enemy's warning, and two hundred–plus missiles were basically *in* the TCN's defensive perimeters before they even knew First Fleet had arrived—and whoever had set up the salvo had taken advantage of the fact that they had live targeting and full details.

Two hundred capital-ship missiles against twenty-two warships was a threat but one that could be handled. With only a minute's warning, it came down to individual ships' crews—and two hundred missiles against even a *Saint*-class battleship taken by surprise was a losing hand for her crew.

Without even a single missile of her own launched, the *Saint* at the heart of the Commonwealth task force vanished in a ball of antimatter fire. More missiles came in on the tail of the first salvo, a steady beat every thirty seconds—though Commonwealth counterfire commenced swiftly enough.

But it was late. Disorganized. Individual ships firing their own salvos to get the missiles into space—the missiles that the veteran crews *knew* needed to be launched.

"They got the flagship," Anthony observed, then switched to a wide network channel. "All gunners and pilots: missiles aren't the priority but they're going to fly through us. Lances and lasers are free to deploy. Every one of those birds we shoot down is one the fleet doesn't have to handle."

He was starting to realize he should have just ordered the Łá't-s'áadah fighters back to base. They weren't going to rendezvous with First Fleet until all of this was over. But if *his* strike went wrong, Krejčí's fighters might be all that saved the capital ships.

"Ten minutes to torpedo range," Gunther warned him.

Anthony's own focus was on the missiles in front of him. He wasn't even getting a missile out of each salvo. He hit maybe one missile in every three salvos—but even his torpedo bombers had antimissile lasers.

Eighty-four squadrons were trying to shoot down a hundred and eighty missiles each time. They weren't getting them all—Anthony was rusty, but he was still better than a lot of his pilots.

But while the fleet might be challenged by a hundred and eighty missiles, they could easily handle the thirty or forty that were making it past the fighter wings—and the Commonwealth force *didn't* have an eight-hundred-fighter screen.

They had fourteen squadrons, and those planes were doing everything they could. But each time the missiles got close, the radiation storm covering the next salvo was worse.

The first salvo had killed the most survivable unit in the enemy fleet. It took six more salvos to take down one of the *Ocean*s, the *least* survivable unit in the fleet.

But the loss of the strike cruiser weakened the defenses further. Four more salvos took down one of the *Assassins*—and one of the *Volcano*es blew apart just as the bombers blazed into their own range.

"Hold torps to the cruisers," Anthony reiterated in the final seconds. "The Navy has kindly upped our torp-to-target ratio, so let's take them down."

Now he had seventy-two torpedoes for each of the ten remaining cruisers. If they'd been modern ships, he'd have concentrated his fire, but against the obsolete thirties...it would do.

The starfighters were in front of the bombers, providing a shield against any attempt by the enemy to send fighters or missiles at the bombers themselves. Now, as the range hit a *mere* fourteen million kilometers, the squadrons of Katanas split apart like a deadly origami fold.

The maneuver was well practiced, smooth and beautiful—and it exposed eighteen squadrons of bombers. All of them fired as one, a perfectly coordinated launch that unleashed seven hundred–plus five-hundred-ton torpedoes.

"Reform formations; stand by for mass missile launch," Anthony ordered. "Gunther, run me my target likelihoods."

They had to launch the first missile salvo before the torpedoes hit. Without q-probes and q-coms, he needed to pick his targets then. The command-and-control loop was too long to adjust after he saw the results of the torpedo strike—and the odds were too long for him to *wait*.

He had three salvos of missiles. After that, it was down to either positron lances or the Fleet—and the Confederacy couldn't *afford* to leave it to First Fleet.

"Pentagonal allocation," he said aloud, letting the system and his people interpret that into the battle strategy. "First quintile, target the fighters. Second quintile, *Volcano*-One. Third quintile, *Volcano*-Two. Fourth quintile, *Lexington*-One. Fifth quintile, *Lexington*-Two.

"Two salvos on fighters and *Volcanoes*. Fourth and fifth quintiles, switch to *Lexington*-Three and *Lexington*-Four.

"Final salvo, targets by opportunity."

And if he tried very, *very* hard, Anthony Yamamoto could almost ignore the fact that he was targeting the same types of carriers he'd spent his career flying from.

Now the enemy starfighters were moving, lunging forward from their own ships to try to intercept the incoming torpedoes. There were no *good* options for the Commonwealth CAP at this point, but that was the best of their bad options.

He'd allocated himself to the "first quintile." Seventeen squadrons of fighters and three of bombers would combine their launchers against the starfighters, and he narrowed his focus as the battle closed.

The Commonwealth ships kept up their missile fire, and the chaos of their first salvos was gone now, replaced by the deadly competence of veteran crews and squadrons. They'd lost over a third of their launchers now, though, and his fighters were still winnowing the salvos down before they reached First Fleet.

Not one missile had hit the Dakotan ships. The elimination of basically the entire Commonwealth fighter strength and their flagship in the ambush had tilted the tide, and Anthony Yamamoto rode that tide into the teeth of the enemy.

The automated network flickering back and forth between the fighters included hundreds of human minds and literally thousands of specialized artificial ones. The allocation of enemy targets was almost automatic, and Anthony barely skimmed it before releasing missile launch authority to Gunther.

Thousands of missile icons erupted into space around him as the fighters finally reached their deadliest range. To an untrained eye, it would have been a chaotic disaster of radiation and engines and fire— but Anthony's eye was far from untrained.

He watched the chaos take shape and understood the patterns. He saw the first positron lances reaching out from the Commonwealth fleet, main beams trying for the one-in-a-thousand chance that might save a ship.

His people weren't the hardened veterans of the Rimward Marches, but they'd earned their own spurs well enough. A single starfighter died before the torpedoes struck home...and the wall of fire that hundreds of antimatter warheads conjured was brighter than suns.

None of the cruisers survived, and his fighters and their missiles charged into the space left by their absence. Fighter missiles struck home, the Commonwealth's three salvos far less carefully timed or aimed than his but no less dangerous for that.

Dozens of his people died in the fire of their enemies' missiles, but their own weapons struck home as well. Despite Anthony's allowance, neither *Volcano* survived the first salvo.

And not one Commonwealth ship survived long enough for the fighters to bring their own positron lances into action.

42

IN THIRTY MINUTES, every part of James Calvin Walkingstick's plan had disintegrated into bloody fire.

With the loss of *Saint Brigid* and *Pelée*, he no longer had visibility to the end result of the battle at Łá'ts'áadah. But given that by the time *Pelée* had been taken out by rebel fighter missiles, only a handful of *Lexington*-class carriers had been left...the only real question was whether they'd surrendered before the incoming fighter strike had finished them off.

A deathly silence had fallen across *Saint Michael*'s flag bridge.

"Do we have an assessment on the strength of Tecumseh's fleet?" he finally asked aloud.

The shocked silence continued for a moment, and he rose, looking around at his staff.

"Well? We have lost before," he reminded them harshly. "We have lost ships, friends, battles. But *we are the Commonwealth*. We endure. We survive. Our victory is inevitable because *unity* is inevitable."

That seemed to stiffen some spines and nerves, and analysts got back to work.

"Any change to the fleet orders?" MacGinnis asked.

"Accelerate the mine-clearing bombardment," Walkingstick said softly. "We'll have a bit less than five hours before Tecumseh gets to us. Otherwise, stand the fleet down to status two for the next three hours."

"Sir?"

He smiled thinly.

"The laws of physics play no favorites, Rear Admiral. The same journey that Admiral Tasker took to reach Łá'ts'áadah is the one that Tecumseh must take to reach us. And I doubt he brought anything less than his full strength against Tasker, either.

"So, we have four and a half hours. Maybe five, depending on how much time he takes to sort out his forces."

That wasn't going to be as much as Walkingstick would have hoped. TF E-2 was just...*gone*. Twenty capital ships of the Terran Commonwealth Navy, wiped out in thirty minutes. Over a hundred thousand human beings and the entire annual economy of a wealthy system just...gone.

And unless he misjudged the data he'd already seen, Tecumseh hadn't lost a single ship pulling that off.

"We might need to reassess that 'competent but not spectacular' assessment of the good Admiral," he murmured. "*Posthumously*, I hope."

That got him a dry and humorless chuckle from his chief of staff—and an even-drier cough from Rear Admiral Misra as the intelligence officer joined them.

"It appears we have some work to do," the ex-CISS spy said grimly.

"Or we underestimated quite badly. What does Tecumseh have?" Walkingstick repeated.

"Analysis makes it fifteen ships," MacGinnis reported. "Two modern sixties, two fifties, a forty and ten thirties. Hard to establish the breakdown—but we're ninety percent one of the thirties is a *Monarch*."

"Every *Monarch* in commission was in one of the fleets his ships have to be from," Misra observed. "Fifteen ships is quite a bit fewer than we expected."

"Sadly, that shortage doesn't seem to have saved *a hundred fucking thousand* of our people," Walkingstick snarled.

"No," Misra conceded. "I think we need to continue this discussion in private, Imperator."

He had no idea what the spy wanted, but Misra was probably right on *that* point. It had been a long time since Walkingstick had lost that many of his people at one stroke—and the last person to do it to him had been the architect of Operation Medusa.

The plan that had destroyed the Commonwealth's communication network...and, if James Walkingstick failed, might still destroy the *Commonwealth*.

————

"We still have the fucker outnumbered two-to-one, and we're between him and the government he's hitched his star to," Walkingstick noted as the door to his office closed behind Misra. "He's hurt us, but he can't win."

"He doesn't need to win, Imperator," they said bluntly. "That's why I wanted to talk to you in private. *Think*, sir."

"You're on dangerous ground," Walkingstick growled.

"We just lost more ships in half an hour than we're going to build in the next two years," the spy told him. "Most of them were older ships, yes, but frankly? For the next decade or so, our total *number* of hulls is going to matter more the capability of those ships."

The Imperator inhaled heavily, trying to control his anger.

"We will still win this."

"I'm not arguing that. What I'm asking is how much will it cost... and whether the Commonwealth can afford to pay that price."

Walkingstick knew what the spy meant and snarled wordlessly.

Seventy ships in Home Fleet at Sol. Another thirty scattered through the Commonwealth that he was *reasonably* sure would follow his orders. And then the Expeditionary Fleet, now a mere thirty ships itself.

That morning, the TCN had mustered one hundred and fifty starships, a pale shadow of its former self. Now it commanded one hundred and thirty. Over ten percent of his total strength, gone. Two assault transports, each carrying ten thousand Marines, gone.

"We also need to consider the price of withdrawing," he told the spy. "We owe it to Tasker and her people to finish the job. If we retreat now, from the first great challenge to the Commonwealth's unity, how many systems will it cost us?"

"Six," Misra said flatly. "Maybe five, maybe seven, but most likely six. Added to everything else, if we back down here, we'll be down fifty systems out of the Commonwealth's hundred and six. Maybe fifty-five left."

Walkingstick stared at the intelligence officer.

"This Confederacy is the only revolt we know of," he noted.

"You have the damn reports, James," they snapped. "If we had let the Confederacy go on their own, we'd have lost about forty-five systems including them. Now, if we manage to retake them, we'll hold those twelve systems. Six more that are wavering *might* see our victory as reason to stay in. But we'll still lose thirty systems.

"So, we have to maintain security over seventy-five star systems if we win here. Fifty-five if we withdraw. And it's not like we're going to get Tecumseh's fleet intact out of this, is it?"

"He won't surrender," Walkingstick agreed grimly. "If he was going to surrender, he'd have done that before he took on Tasker. Now... Now he has to fight, but he still can't win."

"But he knows the math we have to do," Misra said. "How many ships can we afford to lose, Imperator? We can *win*, yes. But in taking Dakota, do we risk the Commonwealth?"

"Against fifteen ships, ten of them ancient? No," the Imperator said aloud, running through the scenarios in his head. "He'll have reinforced his fighters, replaced any losses he took against Tasker with ships from Łá'ts'áadah. But he can't replenish his munitions, and he fired off *half* of his older ships' magazines.

"He has two modern and three useful ships. The rest are obsolete, and he won't have a chance to replenish their magazines. We *still* have more starfighters, bombers and missile launchers than he does. We'll lose fighters, but I think we can take the rebels down without losing capital ships."

Walkingstick met Misra's gaze and managed, barely, not to glare at the spy. The officer was doing *exactly* what Walkingstick needed him to do. Whatever else happened, someone had to sit in the general's metaphorical chariot and whisper *You too are mortal.*

"If we secure this so-called Confederacy, we stem the bleeding," he told the spy. "We save eighteen systems, by your math. Tecumseh has to have every ship he has here. Sweeping up the rest of the rebel systems here will be straightforward.

The *Hercules* under repair at Dakota's Lagrange point and the warships under construction at Łá'ts'áadah would help make up for the loss of Tasker's fleet in time. Nothing was going to bring back the dead, but James Walkingstick would honor their memories by achieving the goal they'd died for.

He was going to save the Commonwealth.

"I have *one* suggestion, then," Misra told him. "Let's move the fleet out of Dakota's gravity well. If you defeat Tecumseh, it won't matter if it takes an extra day or two to eliminate the remaining mines—but if they've got another trick up their sleeve, we have more flexibility if we have the *option* to bolt into FTL.

"And he's already demonstrated his willingness to push gravity wells on the attack. We gain nothing by being only a couple of light-minutes inside the gravity well—and we gain quite a bit by having the option to retreat."

"I have no intention of retreating," Walkingstick said grimly. "I came here to bring this Confederacy back into the Commonwealth. I do not plan to *fail*."

"You should not be prepared to sacrifice the Commonwealth to secure the Confederacy, Imperator. If we fail to plan for all options..."

"Then we are planning to fail," he conceded. He sighed and *did* glare at the spy. "Thank you for bringing this conversation into private.

"*Not* doing this in front of the crew is definitely wiser." He shook his head, aware that he was still scowling. "And, Pich?"

"Imperator?" the spy said carefully.

"This *is* your fucking job," the ruler of the Commonwealth told his intelligence officer flatly. "Keep doing it, even if it seems like I don't want to listen."

"Like you, Imperator, I am tasked to preserve the Commonwealth above all else."

43

Dakota System
18:30 March 17, 2738 ESMDT

"THEY HAVE BEGUN MANEUVERING out from Dakota," Carey reported.

"Somehow, I doubt the Imperator is running," Voclain added drily.

James grimaced. They'd just killed roughly a hundred and twenty-five *thousand* people wearing their old uniforms. That should be enough death for one day...but it wasn't going to be. He and Walkingstick still had business.

"Walkingstick is opening his options," James told his staff. "He'll zero-zero just outside the gravity well, keep a bit of a base velocity as he waits to see what we do."

"We could try and jump them," Voclain suggested.

"He'll have his ships' main guns set to auto-target any unexpected arrivals," the Admiral replied. "Risky as hell to do that normally, but he *knows* we're coming and are going to be spending at least part of our time in A-S."

"Depending on their computers... Ugh." Carey looked vaguely ill. "Even with q-probe targeting data, they might well fire before we do."

"Most likely, we'd *both* fire," James agreed. "And he has seventeen battleships to our three, even ignoring the battlecruisers or the fact that the *Volcano*es have decent lance armament."

He shook his head.

"We'd take out maybe ten of their ships in exchange for our own complete annihilation. Without surprise, there's no real advantage to the jump."

"We're not exactly going to win a missile or a starfighter duel," Carey said grimly. "Ten of his ships might be more than we'll take out in a straight fight."

"The key here is the math in Walkingstick's head," James murmured. "How many ships can he afford to lose...and how many does he think he's *going* to?"

"In his place, I'd have put that first number at a lot less than twenty," Voclain pointed out. "He's already lost twenty ships. But they're deploying fighters, too. Sweeping for probes."

"It's a good thing they're preplaced and cold," Carey replied, the operations officer checking his displays as he spoke. "Even their fighters will need to be basically on top of them to pick them up."

The fighters weren't *quite* more likely to collide with the q-probes' radiator cables than detect the robotic spacecraft, but in passive mode, the drones were spectacularly hard to see.

Significantly more so, James knew, than the Commonwealth's version. They were probably going to have to dismantle some of the Federation drones to see if they could pick up the tricks involved.

After the battle was over. Right now, he needed every set of eyes he could get.

"Assuming they go for zero vee outside the gravity well, they'll settle on their main position in about an hour and forty-five minutes," James said. "We'll still be an hour from clearing *Virginia*'s gravity well at that point.

"We'll know everything about their position, and we'll be able to pick our range."

He was leaning toward *well outside missile range* and sending his starfighters in to even the odds. It looked like most of Walkingstick's carriers had been at Łá'ts'áadah, which meant that he was better positioned in a fighter duel than anything else.

Better didn't mean *good*. Walkingstick still had over thirteen hundred fighters and bombers to his less than nine hundred.

Though if he managed to find his lost sheep before then…

"Any word from Commodore Gold?" he asked.

Champion and *Goldwyn* had supposed to be coming in on their own but synchronized with the rest of the fleet. They'd missed the emergence locus and, thankfully, their two hundred fighters had been unnecessary at Base Łá'ts'áadah.

Though the League Xenophons' more-powerful positron lances might have been useful.

"We just got an update," Mac Cléirich told him. "The Commodore sends her apologies, but it appears they miscalculated their vector when leaving Persephone. Both of the carriers missed Virginia by over three light-days."

James winced, unable to prevent himself from visibly reacting. The *Paramount*s were the oldest ships still in Commonwealth service, usually reserved for *very*-rear-area commands and shuttling starfighters around behind the main battle fleets.

That meant they rarely moved independently and didn't get the highest quality of crews—or navigators. He suspected that *Goldwyn*'s navigator had graduated at the bottom of their Academy class *and* then had allowed themselves to get rusty.

"I'm not sure I even need to *order* remedial training for her navigators," he observed mildly. "What does that make their ETA to rejoin us?"

"If we send them target coordinates *now*, they'll arrive twenty-five minutes after us," Mac Cléirich told him. "The longer we hold off, the later they'll be. Our coms with them are *very* low-bandwidth, remember."

He nodded and stepped over to the main display to study the layout.

"Give me Walkingstick's vector," he ordered. "And highlight Dakota's gravity well."

A red line projected out from the cluster of icons marking the Commonwealth fleet. A gray sphere appeared around the planet, stretching out five light-minutes from the planet. It intersected with a sphere of the same color reaching out eight light-minutes from the central star, but the Terran ships were heading away from that.

"So, he's going to stop around here." James highlighted a zone on the display with his implants. "I *don't* want to fight a missile duel, not to start, so we'll want to be at least seventy million kilometers from him."

That zone picked up a pale green tone as he considered the map. Seventy million kilometers was a *long* damn way, but it was also roughly the range of a Stormwind V capital-ship missile from rest.

"A long-range missile duel might actually be to our advantage, sir," Voclain pointed out. "We have q-probe targeting and he doesn't."

"Which makes our missiles about twice as effective at long range, yes," he agreed. "Except that they have almost *three* times as many launchers as we do. We'll use the fighters to level the odds first."

New lines and colors appeared on the display as he worked through the numbers and then nodded to himself.

"We'll emerge *here*, one hundred million kilometers from the Commonwealth fleet," he told them. "That will give the fighters lots of opportunity to lure their Commonwealth friends out to play."

"And the *Paramounts*, sir? I suspect Admiral Yamamoto would love to have those Xenophons backing up his fighter wings."

"Bring them in at the exact same spot," James ordered. "They'll be behind us by the time they arrive, but that's to our advantage…"

He stared at the display in silence. Commodore Gold's carriers had lost their fighters in the battle at Persephone, to a combination of direct losses and Yamamoto stealing their survivors to fill out other squadrons.

They'd filled the two carriers with defectors from the League, pilots *and starfighters* left behind when Star Admiral Peppi Borgogni had chosen to preserve his ships rather than risk retrieving his own fighters.

The two *Paramounts* were Commonwealth-built carriers, but they carried full decks of League starfighters.

"Sir?" Voclain asked.

"Just a thought," James murmured. "A possibility I'm going to examine as we close with the enemy."

Because he knew he couldn't actually *beat* Walkingstick. What he *needed* to do was convince the Imperator that the price to retake the Confederacy was more than the Commonwealth could afford to pay.

44

A TIMER in the back of Walkingstick's mind was ticking toward zero. They didn't *know* when Tecumseh would make his move—Virginia was nine light-hours away, after all, and he'd lost his only q-com-linked sensors with the ships that carried them.

But Walkingstick knew the performance envelopes of every ship in Tecumseh's command. He knew the vector they'd been on when *Pelée* had been destroyed. He knew what Tecumseh could or couldn't do—and he *knew*, in his bones, that the only thing Tecumseh was going to do at that moment was steer to the sound of the guns.

Which meant he'd be arriving *somewhere* near Dakota in the next fifteen minutes.

"Take the fleet to full battle stations," he ordered. He'd kept them at minimum readiness for three hours, relying on the laws of physics to protect them while he rested his crews, and only brought them to alert status two after that.

Now the time had come.

Silent alerts flickered out across the remaining thirty warships and eight assault transports of the Expeditionary Fleet. Lights in the corridors changed tone,—not enough to cause issues with vision but enough that every officer and spacer *knew* what was going on, in case they somehow missed the messages sent to their implants.

"Crews are falling in," MacGinnis told him. "I suspect most of our people were halfway to battle stations already."

The Book called for a standard scramble from alert status two to battle stations of five minutes—half the flight time of a modern torpedo. Walkingstick had required *four* minutes of the Rimward Marches Fleet, and he doubted Tasker had let that standard slip for the Expeditionary Fleet's warships.

His people completed the scramble in one hundred and fourteen seconds.

"Screens remain clear," an analyst reported crisply. "No contacts within lightspeed-lag limits."

"All main guns are on auto-target and auto-fire," MacGinnis murmured, barely loud enough for Walkingstick to hear. "Which makes my skin *crawl*, sir. We don't make our AIs stupid, but they are..."

"Focused," he finished for her. "They are coded with a level of tunnel vision no human could match, and auto-fire removes much of the contextual control they *do* have."

"But if they try to jump us like they did Tasker's fighters, they're going to have a real bad day."

"Exactly. Starfighters?"

"First wave is deploying now," she confirmed, following his change in topic. "CAP is expanding their zone out to half a million kilometers. All fighters will be up within the next sixty seconds."

"Still no contacts inside lightspeed-data zone."

Walkingstick nodded his acknowledgement of both reports and checked the time. They were now inside the window he was expecting Tecumseh to arrive—but he also wasn't expecting the Confederacy Admiral to emerge on top of them.

"Seventy or a hundred, do you think?" he asked MacGinnis conversationally.

"Sir?"

"What range do you think Tecumseh chose? If he comes out at seventy million kilometers, he's courting a missile duel using his q-probes to reduce the odds against him. Hundred million, he's aiming to lure our fighters out and take them down before attempting a torpedo strike."

"He's still pushing against the numbers on the fighters," his chief of staff noted. "But...I'm guessing a hundred million."

"He could hot-deck the five hundred from Base Łá'ts'áadah," Walkingstick observed. "They'd need to launch pretty much immediately, and he'd have difficulty rearming them, but that would even up the numbers of Katanas. Plus, my money says the Katanas at Base Łá't-s'áadah are the ones from those hangars we spotted in orbit of Dakota. They'd be going home *through* us rather than returning to his carriers."

"That would only get him up to about parity with our starfighters, and we'd still have more bombers," she said. "But that would make sense. A dangerous game to play, but he'd manage his risks, I guess."

"The whole game is dangerous. The question is how does Tecumseh think he can win this?" The Imperator shook his head. "And the answer is that he knows he can't."

"Then why is he still fighting?"

"Because he knows there is a level of losses we *cannot* take in exchange for reclaiming Dakota," Walkingstick told her. Their conversation was *very* quiet, and the acoustics of the flag bridge were designed with extreme care. A loud voice, attempting to project, would travel from the command bubble to the entire cavernous space.

A quiet conversation like this wouldn't leave the bubble at all.

"So, he needs to convince us he can inflict those losses—so we withdraw without fighting," MacGinnis realized.

"And one of the best ways he can do that is to eliminate our fighters. I *will* withdraw if we lose the majority of our fighter strength—but I *also* won't send our fighters out into a duel I don't think they're going to win."

Walkingstick smiled grimly as he watched the displays

"We can't lose many more capital ships after losing Tasker's fleet, but we *can* afford to lose starfighters. A Pyrrhic victory in the starfighter duel may still serve my purposes."

"Contact!"

The shouted report interrupted their conversation, snapping the attention of every person on *Saint Michael*'s flag bridge to the main display.

"Fifteen contacts at one hundred million kilometers," the analyst continued after a moment. "Emergence was at twenty-two forty-seven."

Five and a half minutes earlier. Lightspeed delay.

"Thank you, Lieutenant Commander," Walkingstick told the woman. "Get a team on breaking down what we're looking at.

"Fleet will maintain defensive formation and maneuvers. Let's see what Admiral Tecumseh does now."

The Confederacy fleet had begun a smooth acceleration toward Dakota. Their course *also* happened to be toward the Commonwealth Expeditionary Fleet, but Walkingstick suspected the course for Dakota was intentional as well.

Tecumseh had secured one of the two things worth fighting for in this star system. Now he was coming for the other one, and Walkingstick was in his way. The Commonwealth fleet still had *plenty* of time to recall their fighters and make the flight to lightspeed, but the Imperator wasn't seeing any reason why he should.

"Do we respond to their course, sir?" MacGinnis asked. "Send the fighters out to meet them?"

"Not yet," Walkingstick told her. "Watch for their fighters; get me numbers and course."

"It's looking like standard complements for all of their ships," an analyst told him. "Eight hundred–plus ships. We can't identify fighters versus bombers at this range yet. We'll nail that down in a few minutes."

"And Tecumseh already knows everything about us," the chief of staff muttered bitterly. "When do *we* get q-probes again, sir?"

"Our production is far from sufficient to risk entangled blocks in sensor probes," Walkingstick admitted. "Years, I'm afraid, Rear Admiral. Because no one is going to sell *us* the things, even though they'll happily trade them to our rebels."

"Feels like there's a message in that."

Walkingstick turned a sharp eye on his chief of staff.

"The only 'message' is that humanity is a stubborn, fractious, impossible lot," he told her. "And yes, we fucked up the wars that got us here. Mostly by letting ourselves get lured into a fight with the League.

"We made enemies and they're using our weakness against us. But the Commonwealth remains the best game going and the brightest light for humanity's future. We defend that light, Rear Admiral MacGinnis. Whatever it costs.

"The rest of humanity will follow in the end. They're just going to kick and scratch a bit along the way."

She nodded her understanding and her acceptance of the mild rebuke.

Walkingstick knew there were moments, faced with the overwhelming opposition from the rest of the human race, that unity seemed not only less than inevitable but even *wrong*. But he only had to look at the world behind him to understand what he was fighting for.

Dakota had been *completely unfortified*. A sector capital, capable of building eight starships simultaneously even without the Hustle Yards and possessing wealth beyond any pirate's dream of avarice, had been practically undefended.

That was what the Commonwealth had given her worlds. That was what James Calvin Walkingstick was fighting to defend—what he would sacrifice anything or anybody to preserve.

"Sir," a very junior officer interrupted his thoughts hesitantly. "We're receiving a transmission from empty space, about ten thousand kilometers off *Saint Michael*'s starboard bow?

"It's addressed to you. Full official com codes, but..."

Walkingstick swallowed a curse.

"Active-pulse that section of space and locate the q-probe transmitting," he ordered, then took a breath. "Hold fire on it for now. Once we've located it, set up a live channel. I'll take it in my office."

He had time, after all, before the final battle would be joined. He would see if he could end this with words.

After all, the Commonwealth definitely held all of the *swords*.

"Imperator Walkingstick. Your promotion suits you poorly."

Walkingstick glared at the younger man in the hologram above his desk, noting the additional stars on the slightly modified uniform.

"And yours appears to speak to the errors of those giving it," he replied. "I would have thought they would have learned from my mistake."

"They did. I am, as I have always been, merely a military officer," Tecumseh told him. "I am no governor, no warlord. Merely the Admiral tasked to defend these worlds."

"And yet you have brought chaos to them. All you had to do was follow orders and the Commonwealth would have stood." He snorted. "Hell, all you had to do was *argue with me*. We could have found a middle ground!"

"No, *Imperator*."

The title hung in the air and the two men glared at each other.

"Your title alone speaks to the failure of all that the Commonwealth is supposed to be," Tecumseh continued. "You are the dictator of Earth and whatever Commonwealth worlds you hang on to, whatever illusions and webs you weave on Earth to make the Star Chamber feel better."

"They were going to kill me and break the Commonwealth themselves," Walkingstick countered. "My people told me we had to fight, and they were *right*. The Commonwealth was going to fall, James Tecumseh, and I am fighting to save it.

"I have no intention to hold this power forever. I will be the Commonwealth's Cincinnatus, not our Caesar."

Tecumseh shared Walkingstick's coloring, though *now* the Imperator focused on the differences. Walkingstick's braid went halfway down his back, where Tecumseh's was cut short at the nape of his neck. Tecumseh was a smaller man in general, half a dozen centimeters shorter than the Imperator, with sharper, almost Caucasian, features.

"You could never be either of those for the Commonwealth," Tecumseh told him. "The Commonwealth was never meant to have an office of supreme power. We had evolved past the need for it. The Star Chamber may have misstepped, but they were the elected government of a hundred and six worlds.

"And now they are a rubber stamp you use to make yourself feel better. The Commonwealth had *four* principles, Walkingstick. Four. Not just unity."

"Without unity, democracy, freedom and justice cannot be protected," Walkingstick argued.

"Without freedom, unity is just oppression. You cannot sacrifice all the Commonwealth is supposed to be to preserve its *borders*. The Commonwealth is not supposed to be an empire built on blood and steel. We made a *mistake* letting it become that."

"The worlds we conquered prospered," the Imperator argued. "I've seen them, before and after being brought into the unity, Tecumseh. You underestimate how much good we have done."

"Maybe. But force cannot liberate anyone from *themselves*." Walkingstick shook his head.

"It was an error, I see, to think you had the spine and stomach for the work needed. You are naïve, Tecumseh, and you have always seen a refusal to compromise as a substitute for true willpower."

"And you have always been blind to the damage you cause," Tecumseh said softly. "To the chaos your fleets and invasions left in their wake, and now to the destruction you have wrought on the very thing you try to protect."

Walkingstick *tried* for *sadly disappointed*, but he suspected all he was managing was an angry glare.

"Everything I have done, I have done for unity and the betterment of all mankind."

"I know. That's the problem, isn't it?" the younger man asked, his sad calm undermining Walkingstick's certainty.

"You aren't the Commonwealth's Cincinnatus or her Caesar, Imperator Walkingstick. You are her *Sulla*—and any legacy you build will be destroyed by the precedent you have set.

"The Commonwealth may have been sick. But you are the man who killed her and set out to wear her corpse as a party outfit."

For a moment, Walkingstick literally saw red as his anger overcame him. Years of practice calmed his words as he glared at the younger Admiral.

"You can throw all the words you want," he finally ground out. "But you cannot win this battle."

If Tecumseh had brought the fighters from Base Łá'ts'áadah, he might have had a chance. Walkingstick wasn't going to point out *that* particular error for his former protégé, though.

"I need your ships," he said bluntly. "I need these systems. Surrender, and I can even use *you*."

That would go against the grain for a lot of his people after the destruction of Tasker's fleet, but he'd just lost his top Admiral. He needed a replacement, much as he would want to keep Tecumseh carefully under his own eye for a while.

"You came to these worlds with a battle fleet and an invasion force to reconquer us for nothing more than your wounded pride and illusions," Tecumseh told him. "I will not kneel. I swore to stand defiant, Imperator Walkingstick, and I will not break faith with these people as you broke faith with me."

From where Walkingstick sat, the breaking of oaths and faiths had gone the other way around—but it was clear that they were well past words now.

"So be it," he growled. "You cannot save your rebel sectors, Tecumseh. I will crush you. I will crush their defenses. I will bring these worlds back into the Commonwealth, and they will be *better* for it. You have my word."

"I have not yet begun to fight, Walkingstick. You have *my* word on that."

Walkingstick cut the channel with a sharp slash of his hand and opened a link back to MacGinnis.

"Admiral MacGinnis?"

"Sir?"

"We're done talking. Destroy that probe, then get the fleet moving."

45

BETWEEN LIGHTSPEED LAG and his conversation with Tecumseh, it had taken fifteen minutes for Walkingstick to get his fleet moving after the Dakotans had arrived.

Not that it made that much difference. The Dakotan starfighters were moving ahead of their starships, but not with any great aggression. The rebel ships were accelerating at two hundred gravities, and the starfighters were only up to three hundred.

They were slowly opening the distance between themselves and their motherships, but Walkingstick wasn't taking the bait. His own starfighters were temporarily burning at four hundred gravities, but their goal was only to open a small distance between themselves and his main fleet. They would accelerate for ten minutes and then cut thrust, allowing the fleet to match velocity roughly a light-second behind them.

Without q-probes to warn them of incoming fire, that extra few hundred thousand kilometers could save the capital ships from missiles—but he wasn't going to risk sending his starfighters forward.

Walkingstick figured his fighters would win that duel, but he didn't need to risk it or take the losses even victory would entail. Very few tactical problems were nails, but sometimes, the best solution was to form up a giant hammer and beat the enemy senseless.

"Any surprises?" he asked, projecting his voice across the flag bridge. He figured one of the dozens of analysts and junior officers would have said *something* if things were going amiss, but it never hurt to check in.

"Nothing so far," MacGinnis told him. "I'm not sure what Tecumseh thinks is going to happen. Fifteen ships, half of them obsolete trash, against the prime of the TCN..."

"He's..." Walkingstick searched for the right words. "*Bluffing* isn't the right word. He *is* committed and he *will* fight, but he's hoping that once we accept that he's going to fight, we'll assess the losses and decide we can't afford them."

"We've run the numbers," his chief of staff said. "We will take losses. Heavy ones, if he's really willing to press all the way to lance range. Most or all of our fighters and probably five or six of the older ships."

He nodded grimly.

"We can afford that better than we can afford to lose twelve star systems," he told her. *Or eighteen*, he reflected, glancing over at where Misra stood. The spy was a silently ominous presence, quietly inserting themselves into the tactical feeds and drawing their own conclusions.

Walkingstick trusted Misra to interject if there was a real problem. They were running an entirely independent review of the analysis and intelligence—presumably through their staff elsewhere on the battleship rather than *entirely* in their own head—and the double check could make a difference.

"Status change," one of the analysts reported. "Rebel fleet has activated a suite of jammers and decoys. We're losing long-range data integrity."

"They're a long way out," MacGinnis said. "What are they hiding?"

"Potentially, they're making sure we aren't sending ballistic-mode missiles their way. Without q-probes, they just turned any extreme-range targeting solution to crap."

Except that the Expeditionary Fleet didn't have enough spare missiles for him to launch that kind of attack, and Tecumseh knew it. Walkingstick's former protégé had been watching the entire battle for this system in real time, after all.

Tecumseh *knew* that the Expeditionary Fleet had burned down their missile stocks neutralizing the orbital mines. Walkingstick suspected the Commonwealth still had more missiles left than the rebels did after the battle at Łá'ts'áadah, but he definitely didn't have the missiles to waste trying for a golden BB.

"Spread our sensor drones wider," Walkingstick ordered. "Let's get a better view and see what's *behind* their little shield."

"To get that far out, we'll have to accept some lightspeed delays on the transmission from the drones, sir," MacGinnis warned.

"We're still ninety-seven million kilometers away from the rebels. We can afford five seconds' extra delay on the sensor data. Spread the drones. Admiral Tecumseh wants us focused on his ships and not on what's behind them.

"I want to know why."

Even sensor probes with a thousand gravities of acceleration took time to travel a million-plus kilometers, but Walkingstick could see the sensor data updating and expanding as they did. His probes might not have the quantum-entangled blocks that would give him instant data anymore, but they still had all of their sensors, engines and stealth systems.

"It doesn't look like there's *anything* behind them," MacGinnis finally told him. "They've run up a number of decoys, and we can't distinguish between real and false targets in their main fleet at this point, But since we *know* there are fifteen warships there, not forty-five, that's not going to do them any good."

"And we'd have spotted anyone new arriving," Walkingstick agreed. "Cherenkov flares aren't particularly subt—"

"*Cherenkov flares!*" Three analysts had shouted at once but only one continued the report. "Multiple Cherenkov flares at the original emergence point—estimate twenty-plus starships."

"Well, that's...unexpected," the chief of staff said slowly.

Walkingstick strongly suspected her calm was shock, but she'd snap out of it quickly enough.

"Please, Admiral," he observed. "We just noted that Admiral Tecumseh is making solid use of his drones and his jammers. The likelihood that he has another twenty-odd ex-Commonwealth ships floating around is low."

"If it was five more ships, I'd buy it," Misra noted, the cyborg intelligence officer appearing without a noise before they spoke. "I could see them having another five that had been positioned somewhere else, at Persephone, say, that got the warning at the same time Tecumseh got it in Meridian."

"They would have needed to get moving even faster than his main fleet," Walkingstick said. "There's nothing in either sector that's *only* six hours farther away than Meridian."

"Or perhaps Tecumseh was not at Meridian and we are only guessing," the spy said calmly. "But given the losses we have been *told* that Amandine suffered at the hands of the League, there is no way there are another twenty ships out there for Tecumseh to have gathered."

"We have initial identifiers on the ships. Emissions suggest a mix of thirty- and fifty-million-cubic-meter Condottieri cruisers..."

Walkingstick barely even registered the analyst as the words sank in.

"Condottieri mercenaries. Surely...he was at war with the League, same as us. Surely, they wouldn't have..."

"Periklos hates us," Misra noted. "He might be willing to compromise with our rebels, but...there are only about forty-five true Condottieri mercenary ships *left*."

"Except there are sixty fifty-million-cubic-meter *ex-Condottieri* ships in the SLN. And the fact that there are over forty true Condottieri warships left gives Periklos cover for a lot of things. Including poking his thumb in the Commonwealth's eye."

Walkingstick could feel the tension in the entire bridge. Thirty on fifteen was a fight they would win, handily. The price might be higher than he feared, especially given that Tecumseh had q-probes and he didn't, but the CEF would win.

Thirty against thirty-five, though... That wasn't nearly as clear.

"Tecumseh's fleet has adjusted acceleration to rendezvous with the newcomers. The newcomers are now maneuvering forward at two hundred gravities."

Walkingstick stood on a mental precipice, staring at the third fleet in the star system.

"I don't believe you," he whispered to his distant enemy. "I won't be fooled."

But if he was *wrong*...

"Have we detected any starfighters yet?" he asked.

"There's enough jamming in both forces to make it hard to tell," MacGinnis replied. "If they're going to try and rendezvous their fighter forces, though, we'll see them soon enough."

"The range is too long for certainty," Misra murmured through Walkingstick's implants. "How close are you prepared to get? It might only be a handful of ships, pretending to be more. It might be *more* ships, pretending to offer a relatively even battle to lure you in."

"If they *are* Condottieri, it's more likely ten than twenty. But if it's the League Navy...Periklos is unlikely to have joined someone else's war with only Condottieri cruisers. He would not risk challenging us without sending enough ships to be certain of victory."

"And if it's just a deception, we could throw away our best chance to reclaim these two sectors," Walkingstick told the spy silently. Their conversation flashed between their implants, but he saw the man nod.

"Fighters detected around the new force!"

"Confirm that," Walkingstick ordered as he turned to look at the analyst who'd spoken.

"Numbers are unclear, but we're looking at a minimum of five hundred more starfighters," the analyst said, their tone admirably level. "Classes are still resolving... Wait, no."

"Commander?"

"We have confirmed Xenophon-type starfighters, sir. Exact distribution of classes and whether there are bombers present is still uncertain, but we have resolved the lead element of one hundred Xenophon starfighters."

Walkingstick looked at the display. That removed the most comfortable possibilities—both the chance that there were *no* ships out there and the chance that what he was seeing was just a handful of Dakotan ships.

"Assuming half of those starfighters are drones," he said mildly, "that's a minimum of, what, three modern Condottieri cruisers? The fifties?"

"Yes, sir," MacGinnis confirmed, then swallowed. "We just picked up a second wave of five hundred fighters, sir."

Walkingstick balanced on the mental fence for ten long more seconds, then sighed and closed his eyes.

"A thousand starfighters calls for at least ten modern League warships," he observed aloud. "We might be able to win this battle… but it could cost us the Commonwealth."

It could still be a bluff. There were definitely ships out there and definitely *League* starfighters out there, but that didn't mean it was a fleet of twenty capital ships with a thousand starfighters.

But there was definitely *someone* out there. And the line of whether Walkingstick could afford the losses had been thin enough against the fifteen ships he'd known Tecumseh had.

"You know the right answer," Misra's voice said in his head. "Do you have the moral courage to walk away? Can you do what you know James Tecumseh would do?"

"That's a low blow," he replied on the implant coms, but it drove the point home and he straightened his shoulders.

"Orders to all ships," the Imperator of the Commonwealth said firmly. "Adjust course for optimal recovery of the starfighters and prepare for A-S entrance.

"Our course is for Sol. The Commonwealth requires this fleet to survive…at any cost. Even this one."

46

"I THINK we can shut them down now," James ordered softly, watching the bright blue Cherenkov radiation of the Commonwealth fleet's exit.

"It won't save them," Carey warned, the ops officer looking at the same fading glow. "We ran those decoys to hell and back again—and the mass manipulators on those shuttles are completely dead."

"I'll hold off on writing the shuttle flotilla off *completely* until the engineering chiefs have been over them," James said. Faking a Cherenkov flare was *doable*, but it was far from *easy*. They'd left most of First Fleet's shuttlecraft behind them and rigged up a heterodyned reaction to use their Class Two mass manipulators to trigger warp bubbles.

The manipulators didn't have the ability to *sustain* those bubbles. The phenomena had promptly collapsed, creating Cherenkov flares almost identical to the arrival of a starship.

"Six are just...*gone*, sir," Voclain told him. "There was a reason the engineers insisted that nobody was allowed on them."

His fifteen ships carried ninety shuttles in total, and they'd left eighty of them behind, rigged to create twenty Cherenkov flares. And six of them appeared to have been either vaporized or torn apart in the process.

"The decoy drones are done; they'll require major refitting before we can use them again," Carey repeated. "But they're retrievable."

Two ships. Two ships, two hundred starfighters, eighty shuttles to fake the Cherenkov flares, and twenty decoy drones programmed to match Periklos's fleet at New Edmonton.

"If we hadn't spent as much time as close to his fleet as we did, we never could have done this," Voclain murmured. "We had everything we needed to fake it, but...damn. I'm surprised they bought it."

James shook his head, studying the screens as *Champion* and *Goldwyn* retrieved their starfighters—the two hundred Xenophons that had been *absolutely* critical to selling the illusion that a League fleet had arrived.

"We didn't need to make Walkingstick think he was going to lose," he reminded them. "We needed to make Walkingstick think victory was going to cost more than he could afford. A giant question mark in the equation was always going to be enough.

"*If* the decoys held together."

The thirty decoys in the main fleet body had accompanied the fleet and been able to draw power from their motherships. Their main use had been to act as jammer relays—and, James had hoped, to make Walkingstick think he was hiding something.

The twenty that had been key to everything had been running on their own power plants, and they weren't designed to have to imitate a ship that thoroughly for that long.

"I was afraid that one of the drones was going to run out of fuel or blow an emitter," Carey admitted. "I'm not sure that would have been enough to give up the game, but...it would have raised a lot of questions we didn't want them asking."

"Honestly, all I wanted was to get them asking questions," James told his people. "They knew we were committed, that we were going to run all the way in and smash them as hard as we could. So long as Walkingstick thought they could do that without losing too many ships, he'd take our best punch.

"But the more questions got asked…"

"Well, congratulations, sir," Voclain told him. "You just convinced the most powerful man in the galaxy to back down with a bluff and a busted flush."

"Time will tell how much it bought us," James replied. "Let's get the fleet into orbit and in a defensive array. We've got a lot of work ahead of us…but thanks to Trickster, the Federation and our little game here…we've got a chance to *do* that work."

———

Unfortunately, the Abey Todacheeney in James's office was neither physically present nor alone. All he wanted to do was wrap his girl-friend in his arms, to hold and be held as a reminder that they'd somehow made it through the impossible.

Instead, he was facing the entire Cabinet of the Dakotan Confederacy.

"Initial scans strongly suggest that the entire Commonwealth force is headed back to Sol," he told them. "There are some oddities in the signatures, but not enough for us to be concerned that Walkingstick is playing games.

"The Commonwealth is withdrawing back to Sol."

"I'm guessing that doesn't exactly mean *peace* with the rump Commonwealth?" Patience Abiodun asked. "The Arroyo government will be…worried until such time as we have some kind of agreement with them."

"I am not certain that Imperator Walkingstick will *ever* allow the Star Chamber to officially acknowledge any secessions," James warned. "We will use our q-coms, q-probes and ships as possible to provide security across the Confederacy, but we will continue to risk Commonwealth aggression."

"How do we stop that?" Sanada Chō asked. The Minister for Shogun looked surprisingly fresh for someone still up in the middle of the night—and who, like the rest of the Cabinet, had been up for almost twenty-four hours now. "Can we even?"

"Short of somehow removing Walkingstick peacefully, I don't know if we can stop it," James admitted. "The rump Commonwealth is going to be a continuing danger to the successor states around her. Even if Walkingstick eventually concedes and steps down, well..."

He shook his head.

"He's the Commonwealth's Sulla, not her Cincinnatus," he told the Cabinet, echoing his words to Walkingstick himself. "Like Sulla with the Roman Republic, he's *trying* to save the Commonwealth. But like Sulla with the Republic, he has created the precedent of military officers seizing power.

"All of Sulla's attempts to reform the Republic came to nothing because of the men who came after him and followed his example." James shrugged. "Whatever Walkingstick does, I fear we will see the same thing in the Commonwealth.

"He cannot save the nation we once served. He has killed it. The only question is what will rise from the ashes—and we can't affect that. We can only look to how we build our own nation."

"So, we watch our borders, make peace where we can, build our navy as rapidly as we can and hope that Walkingstick doesn't poke the wasps' nest twice," Chapulin said grimly.

"It's not a great situation, but it's the one we have," Chō agreed. "And we only have that thanks to Admiral Tecumseh."

"It's late and we're all swamped, so all I can say now is that you have the thanks of every member of this Cabinet and, likely, of every citizen of this Confederacy," Chapulin told him. "We will find some way to better acknowledge your people's triumph soon, but triumph they did.

"Our priority now is to calm the nerves of our people. Once that is done, we can prepare for the challenges ahead."

"I don't know about anyone else, but *my* priority is to either get aboard *Krakatoa* or get the Admiral down here," Abey said, earning her a flush from James and chuckles from the rest of the Cabinet. "Professional comes before personal, yes, but I believe the professional might just be handled for the night!"

James was about to agree fervently—and then an alert triggered in his implant and he swallowed a curse as he reviewed the information.

"Admiral?" Chapulin asked after several moments of silence on his part.

"Cherenkov flares," he reported grimly. "Multiple ships appear to have short-jumped and turned around."

There was a long moment of frozen fear.

"How many?"

"Still resolving," James admitted. "My apologies, Ministers. It appears I still have some work to do!"

––––––––

As James strode back into *Krakatoa*'s flag deck, he swiftly realized that nobody *else* had left yet.

"Didn't we stand the fleet down to status two?" he asked drily.

"We did," Voclain confirmed. "And…well, your entire staff appears to have decided to stay up just that *bit* longer. As long as you do, I suspect."

He gave her a level look, then shook his head and turned back to the display.

"What do we have?" he asked.

"They dropped out at a hundred and twenty million kilometers," she told him. "They can't have gone very far, given that they turned around and were back inside two hours."

"They're definitely Commonwealth, then?"

"A *Saint*, a *Volcano*, a *Lexington* and a *Resolute*," Carey confirmed. "We're hoping to have them IDed momentarily. There is a q-probe nearby that we're vectoring toward them, but we won't receive any lightspeed transmissions for a few more minutes."

"Any maneuvers?"

"Negative, they are holding position at their emergence point. The carriers haven't even launched fighters."

James nodded silently and replayed the few minutes of footage they had from the probe on fast-forward.

"They emerged together, definitely coordinated," he noted. "But they might have done that when they dropped out of the FTL in the outer system. They don't *look* like an attack group. I'm curious about who they are..."

"The *Saint* is *Saint Anthony*, sir," Voclain told him. "That's...your old command, isn't it?"

"A couple back, but yes," James agreed. Given the demands of the war against the Alliance, it was likely that somewhere around seventy-five percent of his old crew would be aboard her, too. They'd been ready to fight him; he didn't doubt that.

He found himself wondering, though, if Captain Kenojuak Ohaituk, his old executive officer, was still aboard. Ohaituk had been a Dakotan native, now that he thought about it.

"The other ships are *Vesuvius*, *Essex* and *Reliant*," Carey added a few moments later. "Files are incomplete but, I make the commanding officer of *Vesuvius* Commodore Kenojuak Ohaituk."

James chuckled quietly.

"Think of the devil, if not speak of him," he noted. "Kenojuak Ohaituk was my XO on *Saint Anthony,* and I was wondering if he was still aboard. It seems that he had a different path to walk."

"What do you want us to do, sir?" Carey asked.

James looked over at Sumiko Mac Cléirich.

"Care to use a q-probe as a relay again, Admiral Mac Cléirich?" he asked her.

"I can do that. You want to talk to them?"

"I suspect, my friends, that they want to talk to us."

———

It took about five minutes to get everything set up, and then James found himself facing the holographic images of four starship commanders.

He knew Commodore Kenojuak Ohaituk, of course. He and the heavy-faced Inuit officer had bonded over being Old Nations officers in a Navy that was very much built on European mores and structures. *Vesuvius*'s Captain looked like the last few years had treated him well —he'd clearly put on weight, but it looked good on him.

Commodore Sakshi Gupta, however, he didn't know. *Saint Anthony's* new commanding officer was a complete unknown to him.

The other two officers, Paquito Bowman and Wilhelmina Pietri, were both natives of Confederacy worlds, at least. Gupta...he wasn't sure about.

"Admiral Tecumseh," Ohaituk greeted him as the conference call connected. "I imagine you've guessed, but we're all here to defect. You appear to be in charge of protecting our homeworlds and...well, doing a better job than a certain other Admiral I could name."

"You are more than welcome," James told them. "You understand, of course, that we'll need to keep you well away from Dakota for the moment while we establish your bona fides. I know you, Kenojuak, but I don't know your crew. And I can't put sending Trojan horses past Walkingstick."

"I did not want to fight Dakota," Bowman said softly. "Arroyo is my home. I did not believe my crew would follow me into defecting, not until after you had broken Walkingstick's will. Then I asked...and the answers surprised me."

"Oh, defecting was *your* idea, was it?" Gupta asked, her tone acidic enough to etch metal. "That must have been nice."

James eyed the woman.

"Commodore?"

"This was your ship once, Admiral Tecumseh, and I have commanded her for less than six months," Gupta replied. "You appear to have made a great impression on *Saint Anthony's* crew, because I was presented with a very binary set of choices: lead *Anthony* in defecting to the Confederacy or be imprisoned."

The channel was silent for several seconds.

"I will not force you to serve the Confederacy, Commodore Gupta," James finally told her. "If you wish to be repatriated to the Commonwealth, I should be able to arrange that."

"I am, unfortunately, entirely certain on the fate that awaits a captain who permitted her ship to mutiny and defect to a secessionist state," Gupta said slowly. "And I realized, in that certainty, that the Commonwealth I swore to serve is dead.

"Her ideals appear to live on here. I will give you a chance to prove that you are worthy of them. Until then, whether I agree or not, *Saint Anthony* is yours."

Which meant that the attack on Dakota was well and truly over.

"That's it, then, isn't it?" Voclain asked as James passed the ship captains over to a junior officer to provide instructions. "The beginning of the end for the Commonwealth?"

"Maybe," he conceded. "Or the end of the beginning of the end?" He stared at the display with the four starships whose crews, some twenty-three thousand strong between them, had *chosen* the Confederacy over the Commonwealth.

"We cannot bear the Commonwealth's burden for them," he finally told her. "We can only look to the beginning of the Confederacy...and we can only keep faith with ourselves."

JOIN THE MAILING LIST

Love Glynn Stewart's books? Join the mailing list at

GLYNNSTEWART.COM/MAILING-LIST/

to know as soon as new books are released and for special announcements.

ABOUT THE AUTHOR

Glynn Stewart is the author of *Starship's Mage*, a bestselling science fiction and fantasy series where faster-than-light travel is possible–but only because of magic. His other works include science fiction series *Duchy of Terra, Castle Federation* and *Exile*, as well as the urban fantasy series *ONSET* and *Changeling Blood*.

Writing managed to liberate Glynn from a bleak future as an accountant. With his personality and hope for a high-tech future intact, he lives in Southern Ontario with his partner, their cats, and an unstoppable writing habit.

VISIT GLYNNSTEWART.COM FOR NEW RELEASE UPDATES

CREDITS

The following people were involved in making this book:
Copyeditor: Richard Shealy
Proofreader: M Parker Editing
Cover art: Viko Menezes
Typo Hunter Team
Faolan's Pen Publishing team: Jack, Kate, and Robin.

facebook.com/glynnstewartauthor

OTHER BOOKS BY GLYNN STEWART

For release announcements join the mailing list or visit **GlynnStewart.com**

STARSHIP'S MAGE
Starship's Mage
Hand of Mars
Voice of Mars
Alien Arcana
Judgment of Mars
UnArcana Stars
Sword of Mars
Mountain of Mars
The Service of Mars
A Darker Magic
Mage-Commander
Beyond the Eyes of Mars
Nemesis of Mars
Chimera's Star *(upcoming)*

Starship's Mage: Red Falcon
Interstellar Mage
Mage-Provocateur
Agents of Mars

Starship's Mage Novellas
Pulsar Race
Mage-Queen's Thief *(upcoming)*

DUCHY OF TERRA
The Terran Privateer
Duchess of Terra
Terra and Imperium
Darkness Beyond
Shield of Terra
Imperium Defiant
Relics of Eternity
Shadows of the Fall
Eyes of Tomorrow

SCATTERED STARS

Scattered Stars: Conviction
Conviction
Deception
Equilibrium
Fortitude
Huntress
Prodigal

Scattered Stars: Evasion
Evasion
Discretion
Absolution *(upcoming)*

PEACEKEEPERS OF SOL

Raven's Peace
The Peacekeeper Initiative
Raven's Course
Drifter's Folly
Remnant Faction
Raven's Flag *(upcoming)*

EXILE

Exile
Refuge
Crusade
Ashen Stars: An Exile Novella

CASTLE FEDERATION

Space Carrier Avalon
Stellar Fox
Battle Group Avalon
Q-Ship Chameleon
Rimward Stars
Operation Medusa
A Question of Faith: A Castle Federation Novella

Dakotan Confederacy
Admiral's Oath
To Stand Defiant
Unbroken Faith *(upcoming)*

AETHER SPHERES

Nine Sailed Star
Void Spheres *(upcoming)*

VIGILANTE
(WITH TERRY MIXON)

Heart of Vengeance
Oath of Vengeance

**Bound By Stars: A Vigilante Series
(With Terry Mixon)**
Bound By Law
Bound by Honor
Bound by Blood

TEER AND KARD

Wardtown
Blood Ward
Blood Adept

CHANGELING BLOOD

Changeling's Fealty
Hunter's Oath
Noble's Honor
Fae, Flames & Fedoras: A Changeling Blood Novella

ONSET

ONSET: To Serve and Protect
ONSET: My Enemy's Enemy
ONSET: Blood of the Innocent
ONSET: Stay of Execution
Murder by Magic: An ONSET Novella

STAND ALONE NOVELS & NOVELLAS

Children of Prophecy
City in the Sky
Excalibur Lost: A Space Opera Novella
Balefire: A Dark Fantasy Novella
Icebreaker: A Fantasy Naval Thriller

Made in United States
North Haven, CT
05 January 2025

63974244R00212